COLD IN
THE SHADOWS

COLD IN
THE SHADOWS

Toni Anderson

ALSO BY TONI ANDERSON

For my brother, Ian.
Who tried to teach me physics.
And failed.
Hopefully he has better luck with the RAF.

CHAPTER ONE

T HE OLD TRUCK Audrey Lockhart had borrowed from the research station pinged noisily as she turned off the ignition and stared at the tropical surroundings of the Colombian rainforest. It was only five PM, but this close to the equator the sun set early, and it was already getting dark. She jumped out and dragged her heavy rolling suitcase from the bed of the truck before hefting two large bags of groceries, her laptop case, and a light rain jacket into her arms.

The Amazon Research Institute where she did her field-work was associated with local universities, who ran field courses and rented space to visiting scientists. Audrey had been coming out here on and off for the last five years and loved Colombia—the lush green forests, abundant wildlife, the salsa dancing, even the crazy road system and general lack of amenities. Life was simpler. The pressures of her academic life fell away like broken fetters. The only downside was that the little cabin provided by the institute squatted at the top of a steep hill, with no road access. She started slogging upward.

After a series of early morning flights from Miami to Bogota to Leticia, she'd driven straight to the research station to check on her frogs. She'd rushed home to Kentucky a few weeks earlier when her sister's life had hung in the balance. Thankfully her sister had recovered. In Audrey's absence, her grad student Mario had looked after her animals and had done such a good job she'd given him a few days off in reward.

Plastic from the heavy shopping bags cut into her fingers, and they doubled in their pain-in-the-assedness by hitting her shins with every step. Orff's distinctive "*Carmina Burana*" chime sounded on her phone. She huffed out a frustrated breath and set down the shopping bags to dig her cell out of her pocket. If she didn't answer her mother would panic.

"You didn't call to say you arrived safely," Sandra Lockhart said in a querulous voice.

"I was gonna call as soon as I got to my cabin." She looked longingly up the hill.

"Considering all the other things I have to worry about I'd have thought you'd at least have the courtesy to call as soon as you landed."

"Sorry, Mom." Audrey rubbed her forehead. Back home in Kentucky, Audrey could go weeks without seeing her parents, but as soon as she headed south of the equator her mom freaked, and needed daily reports. It got old fast. "Everything's okay with you guys, right?" She deflected. "No emergencies?"

"Your dad is putting Redford to bed." Redford was her two-year-old nephew, father unknown. "Sienna went out on another date with Devon."

And wasn't *that* awkward—her drug addicted sister dating Audrey's ex-boyfriend.

"I think he's smitten." Her mom sounded thrilled. Probably because Devon was heir to a billion dollar pharmaceutical fortune. She'd certainly been pissed when Audrey had stopped seeing him.

Audrey didn't want to deal with the drama anymore. Except she was stuck with this new reality for the foreseeable future.

"Let's just hope she can stay clean, huh?" Audrey winced at the cynicism of the words, but past experience had taught her to expect the worst. Sienna's accidental OD in December had been the third in five years. Audrey had resigned herself long ago to it only being a matter of time before they buried her sweet, beautiful sister. But until her sister was ready to kick her drug habit nothing was gonna change, and Audrey only made it worse by pushing too hard.

Although, really, what was worse than dying and leaving your precious child an orphan?

It wasn't Audrey's problem—not right now. Her problem was catching up with her research after a month-long absence. "I gotta go, Mom. I need to unpack my groceries."

"Be careful down there."

Audrey refrained from telling her she'd experienced more violent crime in the States than she'd ever experienced here. It wouldn't help. She said goodbye and hung up. Then picked up her heavy bags and struggled up the hill.

The noise of insects grew increasingly loud as if they were working their way up to a rousing crescendo. The sweat and grime of the day clung to her skin even as the cool breeze stirred the hairs on her nape. She couldn't wait to have a shower, crawl into bed, and sleep for eight hours straight.

A wave of unease stole over her as she became aware of how dark it was. In the five minutes since she'd parked, dusk had eased into the velvet blackness of night. The porch light on the cabin hadn't come on the way it was supposed to—the bulb must have burned out.

The snap of a twig made her startle and glance around.

Oh, no, you don't. No running from shadows.

She pushed aside the fear that wanted to rear up and forced herself to keep moving, one awkward step at a time. One tragedy was not going to define her life. *She* was the lucky one.

Living through violent crime made her sister's choices all the more frustrating, but that was the beauty and burden of freedom and personal choice. Not everyone got it right. Audrey dragged her load the final few steps to her front door and searched her pockets for the key. It was so dark she could barely see her hand in front of her face. Behind her, the scream of a howler monkey filled the air.

Her heart virtually stopped. Then she laughed and the tension eased. She loved the wildlife here—except for the cockroaches. She could definitely live without the cockroaches.

Using touch alone, her fingers scraped over the smooth wood and found the cool metal of the lock. She inserted her key and stepped inside, flipping the light switch. Nothing happened. Dammit. She was going to have to head back down the hill and talk to the caretaker.

An arm snaked around her middle, pulling her roughly against an unyielding body. Terror flooded her mind as a gloved hand clamped over her mouth.

No, no, no!

Her assailant hauled her off her feet, and she dropped the groceries. Eggs smashed against the tile floor. The scent of sweat, the power in his arms, the rigid muscles of his chest told her the attacker was large, physically fit, and male. She drove her heel backward, connecting with his shin, but her sandals made little impact. Adrenaline flooded her body, reminding her of another time, another pulse-pounding moment of terror when she'd thought she was going to die. Reaching behind her, she dug her nails into the flesh of his waist. He hissed as she scratched him, then shook off her grip like she was an annoying fly. He carried her to the kitchen and maneuvered her until she lay face-first on the unforgiving floor.

He grabbed one of her arms, wrenching it behind her back. Pain shot to her shoulder blade and she yelped as he looped something thin and stiff over her wrist, roughly jerking her other hand to meet the first. He tightened the plastic zip ties and her arms were securely bound.

Oh, God!

He was going to rape her. She was going to die.

Panic detonated like a nuclear device inside her brain. She scrambled like a mad thing, twisting and squirming, then found her voice and screamed. His weight crashed full-force onto her chest and stole the air from her lungs. Her cry was smothered and she could barely move. This couldn't be happening.

"*No te voy a hacer daño.*" The voice was a hoarse whisper of Spanish. A local? *I'm not going to hurt you.* Sure. That's what murderers and rapists said so people didn't give them any trouble while they destroyed your life. "I have a message for you." English this time.

She wheezed. "Most people use email, asshole—"

The pressure on her back increased as he gave her his full weight. God, why hadn't she kept her stupid mouth shut? Tears pricked her eyes. Her wrists strained against the tight plastic as he straddled her back then swiveled toward her feet. She kicked at his face, but he captured her legs one at a time, and wrapped another tie around her ankles, cinching it tight. Less than twenty-seconds and she was trussed up like a Sunday frickin' roast. He rested on top of her for a moment, breathing heavily. She grabbed his testicles and squeezed.

He swore and shifted quickly out of reach, turning to face forward again, putting even more of his weight on her back as he lay down on top of her. Her skin crawled.

Then he chuckled. "*Luchadora.*"

Feisty? She wasn't feisty, she was furious.

Nausea threatened. "Please, I-I can't breathe." Terror made her voice thin, and she tried to force herself to calm down even as her heart raced. It was impossible. She wasn't too proud to beg. She didn't want to die.

Her vision wavered. The walls pressed in on her. The sound of her heartbeat thrashed in her ears. The floor was unrelentingly hard against her cheek, the tile digging painfully into her hipbones and breasts. She went inside herself, concentrated on trying to expand her ribs. After five long seconds of silence, the man eased up the pressure on her back, enough that she could suck in a little oxygen. He moved warily, even though it was hideously obvious she wasn't the threat. She twisted her head to look at him, but it was too dark to make out any distinguishing features. He wore black clothes and possibly even a mask.

Maybe he wouldn't kill her if she couldn't identify him?

She tried to swallow, but there was no saliva left in her mouth. The last time she'd been this scared her best friend had died in her arms.

"*Tengo un mensaje para ti,*" the man repeated in deep rough Spanish.

"I don't understand what you're saying!"

He leaned closer. His warm breath brushed her ear. "*Yo se cuando estas mintiendo, chica. Para que sepas.*" *I can tell when you're lying, chica. Good to know.*

She was obviously an American, so how did he know she spoke Spanish?

"I will say this only once. You need to pay attention." He spoke English now with a thick guttural accent.

Pain shot along her arms whenever she tried to move. Escalating, paralyzing fear held her immobile.

"It is over."

What! What did that even mean? Was he going to kill her? She drew in a breath to scream, but a gloved hand clamped over her mouth, the supple leather cool against her skin.

"The Gateway Project is finished." The voice turned menacing. "Whoever is giving you orders is acting on his own. We will find this person, and we will shut them down. You do not want to be around when we do."

He released her mouth.

"I don't understand." She twisted around to try and look up at him. "Is this some kind of joke?"

He ran a gloved finger over her cheek. "No joke. This is your only warning, *chica*. Do not make me regret not killing you."

She had no idea what he was talking about, but anger replaced fear, and she glared at him in the darkness.

"Eyes on the floor," he ordered.

She did as he said. The pressure eased on her chest as he climbed to his feet and she inhaled a much-needed full breath. She braced herself. For a couple of seconds there was nothing but silence. She looked around, but the man had disappeared as silently as he'd come.

Relief hit her like a two-by-four.

What the hell just happened?

More importantly, had he gone for good, or was he coming back?

Alarm propelled her into action. She used her elbow to push herself into a sitting position. She shuffled over to the unit next to the kitchen sink and put her back to the cupboard, leveraging herself up against the smooth wood until she was on her feet. Awkwardly she jerked open the cutlery drawer, holding onto the edge, almost falling over. Her fingers scrambled through the silverware until she found a serrated blade. Trying to keep her balance, she leaned over the countertop and sawed at the stiff plastic that bound her hands behind her back. It took time because of the crappy angle. She sucked in a hiss of pain when she scratched herself on the arm. Finally, the tie came loose with a jerk and she set to work on her ankles.

If he came back… *Oh, God.*

She sawed faster and her legs sprang apart. She kept hold of the knife as she skirted her scattered belongings and smashed groceries, pausing when she reached the wide-open doorway. She peered out into the night, but could see no one. A howler monkey shrieked in the jungle, but her assailant had disappeared. She hoped the bastard was bitten by a snake, or broke his leg tripping over a tree root.

Asshole.

She eased gingerly down the first set of steps, uncertain of her footing in the dark. As soon as she found the paved path she ran, heart pounding from rage and relief, chest tight from being scared out of her mind. Her wobbly legs carried her toward the caretaker's cabin.

Please be here.

The sound of insects pierced her eardrums like tiny

screams. The shadows teemed with a million unseen eyes. Sweat ran down her sides, and the scent of her own slick fear rose up to choke her. She reached the caretaker's home and hammered on his door. "Open up! Let me in."

It seemed to take forever, but finally she heard footsteps. The man pulled open the door, and she dipped under his arm.

"Help. Help me. Someone attacked me in my cabin. They threatened to kill me. Call the police."

He followed her inside, dark eyes wide with alarm. "*¿Estás herida? ¿Viste quién era?*" *Are you hurt? Did you see who it was?*

Her throat was raw from the effort of holding down emotions that now threatened to choke her. "I didn't see his face. He was talking about some Gateway thing. I have no idea what he wanted from me."

The man's eyes flared as they ran over her and rested on her bloody wrists, and on the knife. "Did he rape you?" He switched to English.

She shook her head, grateful to have come away from this encounter without any real physical harm—although she knew from experience how damaging the psychological aspect could be. "He tied me up and threatened me, but he didn't actually touch me."

The man's eyes narrowed as he spoke to her. "There are some bad people around here. Some very bad men. Are you sure you want to talk to the police?"

Because sometimes the local cops cared more about the bad men than the victims—that's what the caretaker was trying to tell her. Audrey was an American. She knew the difference between right and wrong, and just because the asshole hadn't raped or beaten her didn't mean he hadn't done

9

those things to someone else. If reporting this saved one person, it was worth it.

"Call the cops." She shivered as she remembered his strange warning. "I want this bastard locked up."

THE CALL CAME at two AM.

His hand groped on the side table before he found the receiver. "What is it?"

At first the words didn't make sense, the accent thick and hurried, making it difficult to understand. Audrey Lockhart. Attack. Masked man. He stared groggily at the ceiling of his bedroom.

"Tell me exactly what she said in the report," he mumbled.

Two words had him wide-awake in an instant. He swung his legs out of bed and padded across the room.

"Read it again," he demanded. He could almost hear Audrey snapping irritably at the local cops. Someone had attacked her and warned her that The Gateway Project was finished, but she had no idea what that was.

He went to the window, his pale reflection staring back at him. He reached out to touch the cold glass and connected with his fingertip.

This was what he'd wanted, he reminded himself. This was the culmination of a game he'd been playing for so many years he'd almost forgotten it had to end. He was hit by an unexpected pang of grief and regret. However, he couldn't risk anyone finding out the truth behind his carefully constructed lies.

"What should I do, *amigo*?" asked the Colombian on the

other end of the phone.

A network of frost crept between the windowpanes and a shiver worked its way over his naked skin. Time to finish this. Time for the endgame.

"Get rid of the report. Kill the woman."

CHAPTER TWO

A CCORDING TO PATRICK Killion's favorite data analyst at the Agency, he was a half-inch short of being the perfect romance hero. As long as the inch she was talking about was his height and not his dick, he didn't give a rat's ass.

Today, at a measly five foot eleven and a half inches, he towered above the locals. His height, combined with his sun-bleached blond hair, meant he definitely did not blend in with the Colombian population. He didn't bother to try.

The CIA dealt in threat assessment and probability levels, manipulation and human intel. Lockhart's appearance, expertise, hidden Cayman Island bank account, and the fact she was in the right place at the right time for Vice President Ted Burger's murder, made her his number one suspect. So, despite FBI ASAC Lincoln Frazer telling him to back off yesterday, he was still following her. He couldn't walk away.

Last night he'd shaken the tree to see what fell out.

He ignored the twinge to his conscience. He'd been a little rough. He hadn't wanted to risk her getting the drop on him. He had given her a get-out-of-jail-free pass and probably saved her life—that should count for something.

Except she hadn't behaved as she should have. She hadn't called her employer. She hadn't grabbed a bag and run. Instead she'd reported the assault to the local cops and had gone in to work today. Maybe she'd been busy destroying evidence or delaying until the last possible moment before she made a mad dash for some small private airfield. Maybe she was overconfident about her abilities. Or maybe she was innocent.

It was the last "maybe" that bothered him.

As he stood in line for a ticket to the ecological park, a pretty redhead in a strappy top and high-heels eyed his neon orange T-shirt and red plaid shorts with a distasteful grimace. He'd committed a class-A felony and the fashion police were about to convict.

"Airline lost my luggage." Killion raised his palms in a pitiful shrug, putting enough misery into his travel-worn appearance that the woman's expression immediately shifted from disgust to empathy.

"That blows. How long ago?"

"Two days now. They swear they'll get it to me sometime today—"

She gave a disbelieving snort. "Yeah, they once lost my luggage on a trip to Mexico and by the time it arrived I was getting on the plane home. Worse, they refused to reimburse all the clothes I needed to buy..."

Off she went, and he was in. Phase one of this mission accomplished. He walked into the conservatory as part of a group of American tourists, rather than as a single white guy traveling alone. They milled loosely about, looking at Lepidoptera specimens that fluttered about like giant-sized pieces of confetti.

A family of seven—five women who all looked like they'd rather be at the mall, an older man, and a teen who read every piece of information like he was cramming for a test. Killion stayed close to the stacked redhead because he looked like the kind of guy who'd stay close to a stacked redhead, but he also chatted to the others in the group, gleaning information. They were down from Florida, visiting family over Christmas. The Americans had arrived in a large minivan with an armed driver, but the driver stayed with the vehicle so they weren't too worried about security. In this country, staying in one spot for any length of time meant you attracted attention—and not the, "Oh my, don't you have pretty eyes" kind of attention.

It wasn't a good thing.

Hot sun bore down on the forest canopy that shaded the ecological park. The small interpretive center affiliated with the Amazon Research Institute attracted local schools as well as the occasional tourist, but it was Monday, January 5 and schools were closed until after Epiphany. The place was deserted except for this little band of intrepid explorers. The ground steamed and sweat beaded on his skin as his adopted people wandered slowly from enclosure to enclosure. A rivulet of perspiration soaked into his shirt.

A huge yellow butterfly drifted over his head and landed on a piece of cut fruit on the feeder tray. The redhead barely contained her squeal of excitement and took twenty pictures with her little point-and-shoot. Killion's point-and-shoot dug into his spine and held fourteen rounds. Their group finally headed into the amphibian enclosure where decaying damp earth mixed with traces of ammonia, and the musk of rotten leaves.

Welcome to the jungle.

His new friend grabbed his arm, pointed. "Aren't they cute!" A minuscule, neon-yellow frog was stuck on the side of a glass tank.

"They may look cute"—said a familiar voice with just the

barest hint of a Kentucky twang—"but one golden poison dart frog contains enough toxin to kill ten-to-twenty grown men." Dr. Lockhart wore spectacles on a string around her neck and reminded him of the class nerd—the one all the guys had secretly lusted after but had been too intimidated to ask out on a date. The professor had unusual violet-blue eyes that showed clear signs of a sleepless night. He would have felt guilty, but more than one person had told him he was a heartless bastard who didn't have a conscience. A sociopath by any other name.

He didn't give a shit, so they were probably right. Hell, she should be thanking him. Being tied up and threatened sure beat the hell out of a trip to a Black Camp or a lifetime in prison—and those were the more civilized options.

Audrey Lockhart wore ubiquitous jeans over Birkenstocks and a tight white tank top that molded her breasts in a way that left little to Killion's undeniably vivid imagination, all topped off with a thin purple shirt that she left open. She wasn't carrying a weapon—unless she had a frog in her pocket. "I'm Dr. Lockhart, I study anurans and my specialty is the family *Dendrobatidae*—poison dart frogs."

For all intents and purposes she appeared to be exactly what she said. A scientist, dedicated to her research. He rarely trusted appearances. That's what data analysts, surveillance, and background checks were for—not to mention interrogation.

"I thought captive ones weren't poisonous?" Killion pointed to a little guy about an inch long that was sitting at a precarious angle on a large green leaf. The creatures didn't look real—they looked like miniature plastic toys. They certainly didn't look like the deadliest creatures on the planet. He placed his hand lightly on the redhead's back, and she sank against him, proving her taste in men was as terrible as his taste in clothes.

The professor's eyes ran over him and his new squeeze, then away, dismissing him as just another tourist.

She didn't recognize him from last night. There was no obvious guile in her gaze. No deception.

"You're right in that individuals bred in captivity have no toxicity, but *these* specimens were pulled straight from the nearby rainforest where they are endemic and, trust me, you wouldn't survive a close encounter." Her voice was husky, sexy enough to raise his awareness of her as a female rather than a target.

He'd always had a thing for voices. And nerds.

She continued, growing more serious, "It takes years for them to lose their toxicity, and even touching a paper-towel that has been in contact with the skin of these particular individuals can kill you. They are *extremely* dangerous."

"Death by frog." His smirk didn't reach his eyes. "Bet that ain't pretty."

The redhead laughed. The professor did not.

"We're very careful how we handle them." She looked stern now, like she was the teacher and he was the naughty schoolboy. And there was his vivid imagination going nuts again.

"Have you ever seen someone die after touching one?" asked his new friend.

"Thankfully, no." The professor's gaze was open and sincere.

What did he expect? Skull and crossbones instead of pupils? He'd been with the Company long enough to spot an operative with one quick glance, but this woman was an enigma. Either she was an incredible actress, or he was way off base in his assessment of the facts. Hell, maybe she was just another enviro-nut trying to save the planet—or, in this case, frogs.

"Do they taste like chicken?" he joked.

Those violet-blue eyes flashed. "I don't know," she bit out. "Would you like to try one?"

Ouch.

Her fiery response was hot as hell, but obviously she didn't appreciate his sense of humor—he'd been told it was an acquired taste. He didn't look away, instead used the opportunity to study her carefully. Her gaze was determined, but he could see fear at the edges—from the scare he gave her last night? Or did she live in constant fear, waiting for her time between the crosshairs? He didn't figure being an assassin was particularly good for your long-term health. Someone, somewhere was always trying to tie up loose ends.

The information he had on Lockhart was solid, but facts didn't necessarily add up to truth—something he'd learned during his time in Iraq. He needed to dig deeper, get closer. But didn't dare tip her off. Hence his little tourist trip today. Like Lockhart with her frogs, he wanted to study her in her natural environment.

"Aren't you scared, working with them?" His new friend asked in a voice that was as thin and high as her heels. "I mean, what if one hopped on you?"

"I'm more scared of people than I am of frogs." Sadness touched one side of the biologist's stern mouth.

Join the club, sister.

"I'd be terrified." The woman shuddered beneath his palm and relaxed back into him. He removed his hand. God, he hated using people, and yet he was so fucking good at it.

"What d'you feed 'em?" He searched for questions a normal tourist would ask, rather than "do you stay and watch your targets die, or do you take off early to avoid traffic?"

"Ants, beetles, some plant material. We go out and forage in the jungle for fresh food every few days," the professor told him.

"You go into the rainforest alone? Aren't you scared of being kidnapped?" he asked.

K&R was a lucrative business throughout South and Central America, as well as many Middle-Eastern countries. One of his best friends was a former SAS soldier who worked full-time as a negotiator for the families of kidnap victims. This was prime territory for those who liked to extort a little extra pocket money with relatively low investment, so why was Dr. Lockhart immune? Were the local bad guys more scared of her than she was of them? Was she connected in some way? None of his sources had any information on the professor that he hadn't already gleaned for himself.

"I don't go into the jungle *alone*." Lockhart's gaze skewered him, seriously questioning his intellect—he got that a lot. "I'm extremely careful, obviously, but it's no more dangerous here than in some parts of the States. I've never had any trouble in the rainforest."

She'd experienced trouble somewhere though and not just his visit last night—he could see the echo of experience in her eyes. Men like him exploited weakness like that.

"You studied these things for long?" He sought to distract her from her memories.

She made direct eye contact this time in a way that told him she didn't like him very much. Ignoring his question, she checked her watch and called out to the others to begin her demonstration. Four o'clock on the dot.

Killion moved closer, close enough to catch the scent of lavender on her skin and to see her gaze flick warily over him. Her complexion was pale, skin fine-grained. Lips soft and deliciously pink.

She was delicately-boned, petite, but not skinny. Even so, he'd had a hell of a time holding onto her last night and had almost got his balls twisted off. He wouldn't underestimate her again.

He brought his attention back to the talk.

The teen asked a lot of questions. Maybe the kid was a wannabe frog geek. Or maybe he liked listening to the doc's voice as much as Killion did. She had a wicked chuckle that seemed to affect a certain part of his anatomy that should know better. He shifted uncomfortably.

If her career in science fell through, she'd make a fortune doing phone sex.

The fact he was thinking about phone sex when she was talking earnestly about chytrid fungus and climate change being the biggest global threat to frog populations, combined with habitat loss and over-harvesting by the pet trade, suggested he was long overdue in the getting laid department. He now knew far more than he'd ever wanted about frogs and the effect of Audrey Lockhart's voice on his libido.

Talk about torture.

She knew her stuff, but then this was her field. His was finding people who didn't want to be found and extracting information they didn't want to reveal. His expertise usually garnered those he captured some quality time in a US institution. The really lucky ones got to travel the world, although it was hard to be a tourist with a bag over your head.

Audrey Lockhart, PhD, looked squeaky clean, but she'd been in Kentucky the day Ted Burger had been murdered with batrachotoxin—a deadly alkaloid secreted in the skin of *Phyllobates terribilis*, the golden poison dart frog. Murdered by a woman pretending to be the maid, of the same general height and weight as the good professor. Eye and hair color were easily altered, but how many women knew how to handle these suckers without dropping dead on the spot? Not many.

Coincidence?

Not likely.

Problem was Audrey Lockhart wasn't throwing off operator vibes, and that bothered him. It bothered him a lot. Whoever killed the VP had waltzed past security into his fancy house, served high tea, and then walked calmly away as the guy lay frothing at the mouth on his study floor. It took either balls or a sociopathic coolness under pressure. And he wasn't seeing it. Not last night, not today.

Lockhart looked innocent. Actually she looked almost too innocent, all perky frog geek, which automatically raised red flags for him. How could anyone be that innocent after the last fourteen years? Or maybe he was getting soft. The current shit-storm in the Middle East had him questioning what all those years in the sandbox had been for. Bin Laden was dead, but the situation was more fucked up than ever with extremists trying to initiate Armageddon—and not figuratively. They were literally trying to instigate the end of times, as if the world wasn't fucked up enough.

What was wrong with these assholes?

People in the US had no idea how lucky they were, and it was his job to make sure they continued to thrive in blessed ignorance. He should be out there, figuring out a way to help moderate people regain control of their countries and reduce the threat to his homeland. That's what he should be doing.

Instead he eased to the back of the crowd, pulled out his cell phone and snapped a photo of the group. He'd seen enough, but he waited until the professor finished her spiel and he drifted away with the others. No drawing attention to himself. No standing out. He even bought a frog T-shirt from the gift store, and said a warm goodbye to his new friend from Miami and her family.

It was late afternoon and the sun went down fast in this part of the world. It was already getting dark. He started the engine of his rental, but hesitated as a small sedan pulled up in front of the ecological center. Killion took a photograph of a man getting out of the car before he headed quickly through the entrance—a definite player judging from the bulge near his left shoulder. The guy left the engine running, and if that didn't scream "quick getaway" Killion didn't know what did. Was this Audrey Lockhart's ride? Maybe the guy had her new identity tucked into the pockets of his bad boy leather jacket.

Killion dialed a number he knew by heart. "Crista. I need an ID on the photograph I just sent."

There was a pause. "Running it through facial recognition programs. How you doing, babe?"

"Been better. How's the new boyfriend?"

"A jerk. Ex-boyfriend."

"Give me his number; we can start a club."

"Oh, please. You are so *not* an ex-boyfriend."

"I seem to remember doing some very girlfriend-boyfriend activities with you a few years back." He rubbed his chin, only half concentrating on the conversation.

"The fact you think sex is the same as dating just proves my point. Have you ever actually been intimate with a woman?"

"Don't tell me you slept through some of the best experiences of my life?"

"*Intimate*, jackass. Not *inside*. We all know you're an expert on what to do with a woman's body, but do you ever dare to try and figure out their minds?"

"Hell, no. And what do you mean 'we all know'?" He was still watching the gate. "Did you go and start your own club?"

"Not yet, but I'm thinking about it."

He turned his mind back to the conversation. "This guy really did a number on you, huh?"

"I guess."

"Bastard."

"Kill him for me?"

"As soon as I get back," Killion promised.

"Sorry I was bitchy—but I kind of meant it about your inability to do more than connect physically when you're in a relationship."

"I don't do relationships."

"Exactly. Hey, before I forget, Maclean was looking for you."

"What did you tell him?"

"Nothing."

The last thing he needed was his boss suddenly poking his nose into his business while working this particular mission. "Thanks."

"You're welcome, darlin'. Okay, I have a name for you. Hector Sanchez. Listed as a known associate of *El cartel de Mano de Dios*."

Killion's eyes widened. He'd heard of good old Hector. The guy was an aficionado of the art of tying the Colombian necktie. Audrey Lockhart sure had friends in low places. She'd fooled the hell out of him.

It wasn't the first time, but he didn't like being conned by a pretty face.

"Thanks, Crista. Gotta go."

"Be careful," she told him.

"Always am."

"Liar."

He grinned as he hung up, then stared thoughtfully at the entrance to the park. What was taking Lockhart and Sanchez so long?

AUDREY WALKED BACK to the lab wishing she could shake the low-grade anxiety that had plagued her since the attack last night. All she wanted was sleep, but the idea of going home to bed filled her with dread. Her PTSD had reduced over the years, but being assaulted last night had brought back the symptoms in huge crashing waves and she knew she had weeks of flashbacks and nightmares to look forward to.

She hated living in fear.

The detectives who'd come to take the report last night had been more interested in her body than in the threats her assailant had made. They'd taken her statement, but made no effort to look for evidence and hadn't even bagged the plastic ties that had cuffed her wrists and ankles. She hadn't been raped, robbed or beaten and they didn't seem to know why she'd called them. When she had the energy she'd get in touch with the embassy in Bogota, but right now there was nothing to do except jump at shadows and scream like a weenie whenever something moved in her peripheral vision.

The Gateway Project. What the hell was the Gateway Project? She'd googled it and got nothing but computers.

Her phone rang. She checked the caller ID—Devon Brightman. If he were just her ex or her sister's new boyfriend she'd blow him off. But he was also Rebecca's younger brother and because of the grief they'd shared, no matter how she was feeling on any particular day, she would always pick up.

"Hi."

"Hey, how's my favorite nerd?"

"Said the techno-geek."

"Techno-geeks are way cooler than nerds."

"Only they and their toys think so." She laughed. When Devon wasn't being over-demanding and possessive, he was actually a good guy.

"You back in Colombia?" he asked.

"Yep." She removed glassware from an autoclave and stored it on a rack.

"You cool with me dating your sister?"

"Sure." She stopped for a moment and realized she was cool with it. Devon and Sienna were closer in age, both being a few years younger than she was, and had a lot more in common. "Just don't screw it up."

He laughed. "Everything going okay down there?"

She opened her mouth to tell him about her attack last night, but stopped. He might tell Sienna and her sister would definitely rat. The thought of giving her mother something real to worry about was enough for a vow of silence. "Everything's great, but I have work to do. Gotta go." Not wanting to linger, she hung up.

Pleased with how maturely she'd handled that transition, she got down to work. Shakira played loudly on her music system and her hips were swaying as she measured out Ringer solution. Her work revolved around examining how high levels of batrachotoxin in the indigenous frog's skin affected the fungus that was wiping out their brethren worldwide. It might give the wild poison dart frogs an advantage in an ever more challenging environment. Or not. She tried to be optimistic, but it was hard to protect the environment in the face of big business. She often argued with Rebecca and Devon's father, Gabriel Brightman, about how he ran his massive pharmaceutical company. He occasionally listened to her, but he listened harder to his shareholders.

Even though the fungus was naturally present in the environment, she didn't keep it on site. She wouldn't risk it escaping into the wild and being responsible for more deaths. Instead she used a level three laboratory in the city and at her home university in Louisville, Kentucky to conduct the exposure experiments under controlled conditions. Here she collected eggs and samples of the toxin.

The public displays and guided talks at the Amazon Research Institute were a way of educating and inspiring locals and tourists to engage with their environment and support conservation efforts. It was also a way of giving back to the community. She usually enjoyed sharing her knowledge and enthusiasm with people, but not today. After last night she just wanted to fade into the background.

She pushed her reading glasses up her nose. Maybe she could scrounge up some company to go to a bar for a few drinks tonight. Then she thought of her sister and decided relying on a chemical depressant to numb herself into oblivion might not be the smartest idea.

She doubled up on latex gloves and pulled her lab coat sleeves down over her wrists before putting her hands inside the terrarium. Using a sterile cotton bud she swiped the tip over the back of the nearest frog. She was gentle and he didn't seem to mind too much, but she did have to prod him a little to secrete more toxin. It beat shoving a stick through his body and out his hind leg the way the Embera tribe did when they wanted poison for their arrows. Still that was their culture—who was she to judge? Their environmental impact was minimal. She didn't want to think about the damage her culture had inflicted upon the world or she'd spend all her time running in circles screaming, "We're all going to die."

Having collected a bunch of swabs from several different individuals she placed the Q-tips in pre-labeled sterile containers and secured them. Then she noted a fatality in the corner of the tank. The lifeless body was a reminder of all the things she couldn't control, like her sister's drug addiction and a stranger attacking her in the dark. She picked up the limp body of the dead frog. The sound of the main door opening and closing had her glancing around. She hadn't realized anyone else was still here. A man she didn't recognize walked into the lab and turned his head this way and that as if looking for someone. He had jet-black hair and bullish shoulders beneath a tight T-shirt and heavy leather jacket. His eyes were black as coal and when their gazes met, his locked onto her. He gave her a smile that drove stakes into her spine.

Was this the man from last night?

"¿Quién es usted?" she asked. *Who are you?*

He didn't answer, nor did he stop walking toward her.

"Can I help you?" she asked, her voice rising in panic. No response. He just kept coming. *Oh, God.* Considering the look on his face and lack of greeting she wasn't hanging around to find out what he wanted. She took off running. When he started chasing her she knew she was in serious trouble.

She darted through the door that led into the park and screamed for help, but there was no one to hear her. The receptionist who also sold the tickets in the kiosk always left at five sharp. Audrey had given her student the day off, and most of the local scientists were still on vacation. The place was deserted. Darkness had fallen. *Good.* Plenty of places to hide. Her white coat made her an easy target but the man was so close on her heels she didn't have time to take it off—and she was still wearing her gloves and clutching the little dead frog in her hand. She needed to remember what she touched so she could clean up later. She almost laughed. Stupid what went through people's minds during moments of extreme duress— Rebecca had lain dying in her arms pleading over and over to make sure her cat, Marley, was taken care of.

The memory ripped through Audrey's mind like a machete.

She was *not* going to die.

Her feet pounded the concrete. If she could get to the area where they hatched the butterfly chrysalises, she could lock and barricade the doors, then use the landline to call for help. Her cell was in her purse back in the lab.

She dashed nimbly down a small path that wound between different enclosures. There were no lights because they didn't want to disturb the natural rhythms of the animals, but she knew the way. She heard the man stumble and swear, falling farther and farther behind. Good. Exhilaration filled her. She was going to make it.

Her sandal caught on a piece of hosepipe and she flew through the air, losing her glasses a split second before she smacked her head on a post. Pain and disorientation exploded inside her skull. The sound of labored breathing brought her back to the present. A dark shadow dropped to his knees beside her. The smell of cigarettes on hot rancid breath turned her stomach.

"What do you want?" she asked weakly.

Something sharp pressed against her side, and she tried to pull away, but it didn't stop coming. Pain was all consuming, and shock crashed through her as a knife slid deep. Her mouth went wide in astonishment and she grabbed the man's wrists, nausea rolling through her body. She struggled frantically to push against his arm.

"W-why are you doing this to me?" she panted. Agony streaked along her side. She could barely breathe, let alone think. "Help," she begged someone, no one. "Help me."

He said something indistinguishable in Spanish, but after a few seconds he loosened his grip on the knife and fell backward to the ground. All she could think about was the fact this man had *stabbed* her and it *hurt*. Then she understood what had happened. The neurotoxic steroidal alkaloid from the frog's skin had transferred from her gloves and was now making her attacker's heart beat too fast as the poison irreversibly opened the voltage-gated sodium channels of his body's cells. She dragged herself to her knees, tugging off the lab coat in case she'd got batrachotoxin on that too. The man needed immediate medical attention if he was going to live. Ignoring him and her own wound, she carefully peeled off her gloves, balling them inside out before tossing them aside.

Blood ran down her hip in a hot, slick trickle that streamed down her leg.

Holding onto the fence she dragged herself to her feet and staggered along the path. She knew she shouldn't remove the knife, but it cut into her with every step. Blood soaked her jeans, making the denim feel wet and heavy against her leg. She swayed unsteadily, clinging desperately to the fence. Her assailant thrashed on the ground behind her, having a seizure.

The equivalent of two grains of salt could kill a man. She doubted he'd last until she called the ambulance, but she had to try.

The sound of footsteps made her freeze in fresh horror. He had a partner. She wanted to scream with frustration at the unfairness of it all. She couldn't run. She could barely walk. The beam of a flashlight hit her full in the face, and she tried to shrink back into the shadows.

"Come to finish the job?" she bit out. The pain in her side was so intense she couldn't concentrate, but the lightheaded feeling from losing too much blood was more worrying. The beam of light swung from her to the ground where her would-be killer lay prone on his back with his mouth wide open, eyes staring fixedly into the sky. If he weren't already dead, he soon would be. The newcomer bent to check his radial pulse.

"Don't," she warned sharply. "Poison on gloves." Her words came out in short gasps. "Transferred to skin." A throbbing wave of hurt pulsed through her. "I-I didn't mean to hurt him." Why was she warning the guy? So he could finish the job his buddy had started? But avoiding the inherent danger of the frogs was so ingrained she couldn't keep her mouth shut. "If you touch him you might die, too." She spoke in English because her brain wasn't up to translating into another language, but he seemed to understand. Her thought processes were dulled from blood loss and shock. Her entire left side was hot, sticky, and numb. She stumbled away along the path.

She didn't get far. At first she thought she'd fainted. Then she realized the dizzy sensation was her being scooped up in strong arms and carried along the path. Her cheek nestled against a hard male chest and she could feel his heart beating against his ribs. Something about his scent teased her senses, but its significance drifted away as she slipped into unconsciousness.

CHAPTER THREE

KILLION DIDN'T KNOW what the hell was going on, but he hadn't expected to find a known enforcer for *El cartel de Mano de Dios* in convulsive death-throes after trying to take out Dr. Audrey Lockhart. Any doubts as to her involvement vanished along with Hector Sanchez's ability to breathe.

Did she work for the cartel? They'd assumed the murder was something to do with the now disbanded Gateway Project as a couple of known murderers had been poisoned in a similar fashion and it fit their MO. But could *Mano de Dios* have ordered Ted Burger's assassination in retaliation for their leader being locked up in a US maximum-security prison? And were the cartel now cleaning house so no one else figured it out?

He rolled the idea over in his mind. It could fit. The vice president had been relentless in going after the illegal drug trade after his son had died of a cocaine overdose. It made a pragmatic kind of sense. Use a hired assassin unassociated with their group to get rid of the problem without anyone suspecting they were involved and bringing down the wrath of the American military on their organization—not to mention getting their faces on their own personal deck of cards.

He hefted the professor higher in his arms, careful of the jutting knife. She wasn't very big. She wasn't very heavy.

At the entrance of the park he glanced about to make sure there was no one around. It was full dark now. Streetlights were few and far between in this non-residential area. He strode up the hill, past Hector Sanchez's idling sedan, and placed Lockhart awkwardly in the backseat of his rental. Her eyes were closed.

"Hey, wake up!"

She opened her eyes.

"Keep pressure on the wound," he told her sternly.

He headed back to the parking lot, leaned inside the enforcer's sedan, and turned off the ignition, pocketing the keys. He closed the door, making sure he didn't touch anything with his bare skin. Langley wouldn't appreciate having one of their operatives linked to a messy murder. Confident no one had seen him, he got back in his car and started the engine. Lockhart was lying in the darkness, panting to control the pain. The handle of the blade protruded just above her hipbone on her left side. At least it wasn't in the gut or the chest, but knife wounds hurt like a bitch. Hector Sanchez had a sadistic reputation, and probably intended to play with Dr. Lockhart for as long as possible, to make her bleed and scream.

The world was a better place without Sanchez in it.

Killion put the car in drive and headed slowly down the hill and through town, past local bars, and the darkened police station. He dragged his orange T-shirt over his head and tossed it to her. "Use that to try and stem the bleeding." He drove calmly, doing the speed limit in a part of the country that generally didn't bother. He adjusted the rearview, saw that her eyes were now closed and she appeared to have passed out.

"Hey, Lockhart! Wake up," he yelled.

Her eyes flicked open. "H-hospital."

Their gazes met briefly. "You know I can't do that."

She didn't have many choices—not in this town, not with a cartel knife sticking out of her side. It wouldn't be long before *Mano de Dios* started looking for their pet killer, and when he turned up dead they'd scour the entire country for this woman. If they found her, they'd make her pray for a swift end.

"Why not?" she croaked.

Jesus. "You know why not." Was she really gonna continue the charade?

Her features twisted as she pressed the T-shirt against her side. Her face looked clammy, her skin pale. "If you don't take me to the hospital, I'll bleed to death."

"If I take you to the hospital you'll be dead before sun up."

"They're not that bad."

He frowned and concentrated on the road ahead of him. Did she mean the cartel? Or the doctors? His fingers tightened on the steering wheel. Was she so confident in her ability to handle the drug smugglers even after an attempted hit? Did she have dirt on them? Maybe she was fucking one of them— she was attractive enough, but Hector Sanchez didn't freelance. If he'd tried to kill Audrey Lockhart it was at his lord and master's bidding. Raoul Gómez—the brother of Manuel Gómez who was serving life in a California federal prison— was an evil sonofabitch and had no qualms about murdering women and children to maintain his iron grip on his organization. Killion wasn't getting on that rat-bastard's radar until he'd figured out who'd ordered the hit on the VP because *that* was his mission. And his mission was paramount, even if his methods were a little unorthodox, if not downright illegal. Nothing was going to sidetrack him from his purpose.

Audrey Lockhart could help him. In fact, she was probably the only one who could help him figure out the truth. He needed her alive.

She cried out as he rumbled over a pothole, but things were going to get a hell of a lot bumpier from here on out. He had few options. He could take her to the embassy in Bogota, but then this fracas became official. Considering cartels owned half the cops and politicians in South America, the diplomats might decide that releasing Lockhart into the custody of local authorities to face the justice system here was more expedient than protecting her rights as an American citizen. And no way could he reveal classified information about the importance of this mission even to other CIA agents, hell, not even to his boss. In theory, he was due to head back to HQ in a couple of weeks to receive his next assignment, which in all likelihood would be a temporary duty overseas—TDY. In reality, his current mission was going to take a while.

Aside from himself, the president, and a handful of Lincoln Frazer's FBI BAU-4 team, no one knew Burger had been murdered. Official reports were the guy had suffered a heart attack and the nation had grieved for the elder statesman. Killion didn't know how many bad guys knew about the assassination plot, but at least one person did and he'd bet his government pension she was bleeding out in his backseat.

He gritted his jaw as he realized something else. Lockhart could not be allowed to talk. Ever. If the world discovered Burger's murder had been covered up, the man's life and actions would be put under the microscope. Burger had been up to his eyeballs in dirty deals and international terror plots. The fact they'd deceived the public about his murder would be the least of their problems. World War III was likely if the truth got out.

Thoughts raced through his mind as he assessed options. Plan A had been making sure the assassin knew the vigilante organization—The Gateway Project—was now defunct. Frazer's people had been monitoring Audrey's communications to see who she contacted and where she went, hoping to backtrack to the mastermind behind Burger's murder. Killion glanced at the woman in the backseat who was panting heavily while gripping the knife in her side.

Time for Plan B.

He drove a few more miles and then swung west. Over the last twenty years the drug situation in Colombia had changed. Nowadays it operated on the same principles as a terror network with small groups only knowing about their piece of the operation. That way, if they were arrested, they couldn't sink the entire cartel. Farmers cultivated small plots of coca in dense forest regions, easier to hide from spotter planes and government officials. Marxist rebels still controlled large swathes of land that were no-go areas. Colombia might be opening up to the tourist trade, but so was Mexico, and anyone who didn't think that was a dangerous place to visit outside the hotel resorts had their head up their ass.

He pulled down a quiet dirt road surrounded by plantations on both sides and parked up on the side of the road. There were no streetlights here. It was all dense vegetation and thick darkness. Locals barely had electricity. He climbed into the backseat and made room for himself by shifting Lockhart's legs to the side. She cried out, but he didn't have time to be gentle. He flicked on the overhead light. "I'm going to remove the knife and bandage the wound."

"No! That could increase the bleeding." Her voice was a

hoarse whisper that was too pained-filled to be even remotely sexy.

"Lady, we don't have a choice." She'd already lost a lot of blood, but there wasn't a damn thing he could do about it. "I need to get the knife out so I can get you away from this area before every member of *Mano de Dios* comes looking for us."

"The cartel is after you?"

Time to cut the crap. "The clown you took out with your poison glove routine was Hector Sanchez—chief enforcer for Raoul Gómez, head of *Mano de Dios*." Like she didn't know. "And he was after *you*. Now that *I* rescued you, he'll be after me, too." Basic psychology. Reminding her she owed him for saving her life. "If you want to live you're gonna have to do what I say."

Her brows drew together. "I don't understand."

Jesus. "Sure you don't."

"You're the tourist from earlier."

Tourist? Like he didn't have "Spook" tattooed across his forehead?

"You were with a family. Girlfriend."

"I don't have a girlfriend." He had hookups, contacts, assets, and coworkers, all helping him fight the seemingly endless Global War on Terror, whether they knew it or not.

He reached into the rear compartment, dragged his bag over and dumped it in the front passenger seat. A professional assassin could pull the knife and fillet him like a damn fish if she wanted to. But she must have understood the implications of the man she'd killed being *Mano de Dios*. She was fucked if she stayed around here. She was pretty much fucked if she went with him too, but she didn't know that yet. Right now she needed him. He was her only hope. Just call him Obi-Wan

Kenobi. He grabbed the emergency first aid kit out of his duffel and another shirt. The orange T-shirt was dark and heavy with blood. He tossed it to the floor.

He grabbed a package of QuikClot out of the medical kit and ripped it open, then pushed her hair back from her face. The fear and vulnerability in her eyes caught at him unexpectedly. A surge of sympathy shot through him. No one wanted to die.

"This is going to hurt." Even as he said it he eased the blade out of her flesh and then poured powder onto her wound. "The good news is the knife didn't sever any arteries." If it had, she'd already be dead.

"I don't think I want to know the bad news." Sweat gleamed on her skin.

That the knife might have nicked an organ and you might already be bleeding out internally? Going into sepsis or shock? "Probably not," he agreed.

He pressed the fabric of the clean T-shirt hard against her side and watched her eyes bug with pain. Then she squeezed them shut and finally went lax—all without uttering a sound.

Out cold. Good.

Fifteen years ago, during his first TDY, he'd spent time north of the Darien Gap in Panama, figuring out the Colombian cartels' distribution networks. Small, unregistered airfields had played a major role in getting the farmers' product to the factories where it was refined into crack cocaine. Those airfields were everywhere, but he'd used one around here, many years ago, with a bunch of DEA agents and Navy SEALs who'd been actively hunting narcos.

Monkeys howled in the trees around him, warning him that this wasn't his territory. He changed into a black, long-sleeved T-shirt and BDU pants, slipping his SIG in a shoulder holster and extra clips in his pocket. There wasn't a lot of space but he'd changed in worse places. He got back in the driver's seat and rumbled down unpaved roads half washed away by the monsoon rains. He crossed a river, hoping to hell it wasn't too deep for the rental. He gunned the engine and water streamed up the side of the windows. They made it across— just. Audrey cried out from the back seat. He gritted his teeth to silence any reassuring platitudes that wanted to spring loose from his lips. Everything was not all right, and the whole situation was her own damn fault.

Ten minutes later, he killed the lights and drove wearing a pair of night vision goggles. Another four miles and he cut the engine, coasted down a small hill, and then pulled over onto the side of the road before tugging on his leather gloves. The airfield was still there. A small turboprop plane sat just inside the open doors of a new looking hangar. Whoever ran the place wasn't worried about thieves—probably because no one was crazy enough to steal from the cartel.

No visible activity in the hangar, but he didn't kid himself the airfield was empty. He climbed into the back seat to check Audrey's wound again. The bleeding had stopped. For now. He unbuttoned her jeans and dragged them low enough to bandage her up. It was impossible not to notice her body, but the fact she was covered in blood meant he was more concerned about keeping her alive than admiring the view.

Emotional detachment was his thing.

Mind fucking was his thing.

Ogling unconscious women was not his thing.

He grabbed gauze and a bandage from his kit, wrapped it carefully around her, lifting her hips and pulling the dressing as tight as possible before securing it into place. Finished, he sat back and took a breath, finding his focus.

Good intelligence officers thrived on ambiguity, on devotion to mission and on ideals greater than themselves. Good intelligence officers had to figure out what decision to make when all decisions contradicted their values and obligations—and when no decision was right. Intelligence officers often failed. Thankfully failure was a better teacher than success. Killion was a damn good intelligence officer because he'd failed a lot. He didn't intend to fail tonight.

He eased out the door, having disabled the interior light—tradecraft 101. Plan B wasn't going to be very popular with the CIA, but if he played his cards right the CIA would never know. He took his duffel bag with him, easing the car door silently shut because noise carried in this part of the world. The NVGs made it easy to make his way, but flattened the landscape so he had to be careful to not scuff his boots on the dirt. He kept to the edge of the field, hugging the darkness until he reached the hangar. A quick inventory revealed two small aircraft and a jeep inside. Light came from a small room at the back of the hangar—probably an office of some sort. It was eerily quiet. He raised his NVGs and tried the door of the plane—unlocked—keys in the ignition. He silently placed his bag in the passenger seat. The rear seats had been removed but the cargo space was empty, which meant they probably weren't doing a drug run tonight. Good news. He took out his SIG P229 and crept noiselessly through the darkened building with its cavernous corrugated metal roof that would make even the slightest noise reverberate like a drum. A cockroach scuttled beneath his feet. He checked the second aircraft, reached inside, and quietly pocketed the keys.

The sound of a chair scraping against the floor had him freezing in place. After a minute of silence he crept closer to the office until he could peer through a crack between the door and the jamb. A man was bent over a computer, pecking away at a keyboard, muttering under his breath in Spanish. Silently Killion moved in and tapped him on the temple with the butt of his pistol. The man slumped forward and Killion grabbed duct tape off a shelf and bound his wrists together behind his back then taped his ankles to the chair legs. He wrapped tape around the man's eyes and mouth, making sure he could still breathe.

He searched the rest of the building, but it was empty of people. A beat-up truck sat out back that probably belonged to the man in the office. Killion jogged to the SUV where Lockhart was still unconscious inside. He drove them closer, parking in the shadows beside the hangar.

He popped the fuel cap and put papers from the glove compartment into the pipe. He opened the rear door and dragged Lockhart across the seat.

"Ow." She woke up protesting.

"Quiet," he ordered. Although he hadn't seen anyone else guarding the area he didn't want to announce his presence until he had to. She swayed on her feet and he caught her against him. Soft and female. He turned her away from him, hitched up her pants and closed the zipper and button. The pants helped keep pressure on the bandages but doing them up probably hurt. He propped her against the hood while he checked to make sure there wasn't any damning evidence left behind.

She raised a hand to her face and left a streak of blood on her cheek. "I've never had a nightmare this convincing before."

"Keep the noise down, Dorothy. We're not in Kansas anymore."

"Am I dead? Because if I were going to be stuck in purgatory I'd rather be with someone hot and funny like Dean Winchester. No offense," she whispered, proving she hadn't totally lost her mind.

"I'm saving your ass, in case you didn't notice," he muttered quietly, watching the airfield for any signs of activity. "Think I could get a little gratitude?"

"It feels more like an abduction than a rescue," she muttered.

He'd rather she didn't think too much about being abducted in case she implemented her own Plan B. "Hey, some women think I'm hot."

"No one is as hot as Jensen Ackles."

He looped an arm over her shoulders, and she surprised him by grabbing his waist with firm, strong fingers. "What happened to Dean?"

"Jensen, Dean, whatever." She grimaced and her fingers tightened on his shirt as she took a step.

"Fickle. My favorite kind of woman." He was almost certain this conversation was the only reason she hadn't collapsed in a heap. "I'm hotter than both of them." He'd never had any complaints in the hotness department. It was "emotional availability" and sticking around that he sucked at.

"Men always think they're hot. It's like an inheritable trait attached to the Y-chromosome." She switched to lecture mode, which was a definite weakness of his. "Even fat, ugly guys think they're hot, whereas amazingly gorgeous women worry about not being perfect or having stomachs that aren't taut as drums."

He shrugged. "So I'm fat, ugly, *and* hot."

"And my stomach is taut as a drum."

He grinned. She was funnier than he'd expected. Definitely sexier. He could use that and hated himself for thinking that way. But his job wasn't all bullshit and bullets. Sometimes the sacrifices didn't have to feel like sacrifices at all, and they beat the hell out of the days when it felt like his heart was being ripped out with pliers.

She hissed in a breath as they took a step.

"Hang on a moment." He propped her against the side of the hangar and took a lighter from his pocket. Walked back to the SUV and lit the papers in the gas tank. He went back to where he'd left her, gripped her high around her waist to avoid her injury, holding his gun in his other hand. "Okay, let's book it."

He couldn't afford to drop his guard. She could be playing him with her apparent cooperation, waiting for the best opportunity to betray him to those inside—which would be right about now. A CIA operative might be valuable enough to exchange for her life but he doubted it. No one crossed *Mano de Dios* and lived to tell the tale.

They shuffled awkwardly through the door. The place was quieter than a cemetery but that was about to change. Killion opened the rear door of the Cessna and pulled down the steps, bundling the professor quietly inside. He turned on the floodlights outside so he could see the runway, and then climbed in the pilot's seat, running a quick pre-flight check. The gas tank on the plane was full—always a bonus.

A loud *whoosh* came from one side of the building as the rental car caught fire. Hopefully there'd be little left by the time someone got around to dousing the flames. They'd easily track it to the rental company and a useful alias he'd used for years was now burned. He started the engine, watching the propellers catch and speed up. Keeping an eye on the mirror he began taxiing forward. Orange flames glowed on one side of the hangar and licked at the timber frame. His SIG rested in his lap. Lockhart was trying not to make a sound as she writhed in pain on the floor behind him.

Headlights appeared along the road in the distance. Shit. Somebody new was arriving at the party. The plane gathered speed as they bumped across the dirt toward the makeshift runway. A jeep screeched around the corner and gave chase.

Killion accelerated faster, hoping he had enough speed and enough airstrip left to get this baby off the ground. There had to be. He eyed the distance to the trees, knew it'd be close, and knew they'd only get one chance.

"Come on." He pulled back on the throttle and suddenly they were airborne, but with nowhere near the altitude they needed to clear the trees. He held his breath as the forest loomed closer. Shit. He was going to die from his own ineptitude and take Audrey Lockhart with him. He wrestled the controls and pulled back harder, banking to the right. Finally, the aircraft responded and they cleared the rainforest, scraping the leaves of the upper canopy with the wheels.

"Woohoo!" Adrenaline raced through him as he checked the airfield below. Tiny figures ran about frantically, trying to put out the fire, hopefully delaying them long enough for him to make his escape. He tossed the SUV and other plane keys out the window, the sharp breeze making his eyes water before he closed it again.

"We made it," he said cheerfully to his companion. But

43

Audrey Lockhart had passed out on the floor of the cargo space and only the steady rise and fall of her chest told him she wasn't dead.

He pulled out his NVGs. Her being unconscious was a good thing. Now he could concentrate on navigating nearly a thousand miles over the Amazon rainforest at night and hopefully, when he got where he was going, he'd remember how to land one of these suckers. After that he had a decision to make. Assuming Audrey survived the journey, what the hell was he going to do with her?

VIBRATIONS FROM THE aircraft buzzed through her bones and made her teeth rattle. Audrey didn't know what was going on except someone had stabbed her, and the blond tourist had come to her rescue. Tears pricked the corners of her eyes, not just from the searing pain that streaked through her whenever she moved, but from the shock of everything that had happened. She was grateful to still be alive. Another wave of agony crashed through her and a moan escaped.

"You okay back there?" asked her unlikely rescuer.

Stupid question. "Where did you learn to fly a plane?" Her voice was like a metal rasp in her throat. There were a million things she wanted to know, but she didn't have the energy to figure out which was the most important. This whole episode seemed like some surreal nightmare.

"Here and there."

Who was this guy? Why had he helped her? Her mind jumped around the idea of some Special Forces soldier on vacation—Jason Bourne does South America. Maybe the guy had been on holiday and heard her scream back at the research station and run to her rescue? Frankly, he could be anything from a serial killer to an Indiana Jones wannabe. Until she could take a breath without being cut in half with pain, she was at his mercy. And if he was correct about her attacker being a member of the local cartel then they had to find a hospital out of the region.

She was powerless. She had to trust him. "Do you have any water?"

He fiddled with something in the front seat and took a long swallow from a plastic bottle, then recapped the lid and tossed it back toward her. It rolled across the floor. She reached out and grabbed it as the bottle moved closer. Shaking as she twisted off the cap, she couldn't believe how weak she was. She took a swig of the lukewarm water and carefully replaced the cap. "Thank you," she whispered.

"You're welcome." His eyes held a glint as he turned toward her. "Try to get some sleep. I'll wake you when we land."

She nodded and her eyes drifted shut. The craziness and confusion of the last few hours slowly slipped away. The last thing she heard before she fell asleep was the sound of whistling coming from the pilot's seat. At least one of them was having fun.

"YOU'RE TELLING ME a woman barely five-foot-two inches tall took out your best hit man with her bare hands?" And *Mano de Dios* were supposed to instill terror in the local population?

"Hector stabbed her before she killed him. She bled like a stuck pig—she might already be dead. Her accomplice took her. You never told me she was working with someone." The tone was accusing.

"Audrey isn't working with anyone." Audrey was clueless.

"Then who was the man who stole my aircraft and flew her away? You owe me a new plane, *amigo*."

He didn't owe Gómez a damned thing.

But what were the chances this was a coincidence? Someone warning her about The Gateway Project one night and then snatching her out of Hector's grasp the next?

Not likely.

Mano de Dios had been too slow to get rid of the problem. Now, presumably someone from the CIA—or whoever was secretly investigating Burger's death—had intervened and spirited Audrey away.

Why hadn't they let Hector finish the job? He'd have thought getting rid of Audrey would have worked to their advantage. In fact, why warn her at all? The answer was blinding in its simplicity. They didn't want the assassin—they wanted whoever hired her. Thankfully Audrey didn't have a damned clue.

Would they torture her? Lock her up? The idea was enticing. Would her obvious ineptitude persuade them she was a patsy, or would they just work harder to break her? He wished he could afford to wait; to let her suffer, but there was too much riding on this.

"Once Lockhart is confirmed dead you'll get your money, Raoul, but I want proof. Not hearsay. And if you kill whoever took her I'll double the reward."

Raoul's tone turned sly. "They won't get out of the country. Everyone is looking for them now."

So the Colombian had orchestrated some sort of plan.

Hopefully it was more effective than his last one.

"Thank you, my friend. This won't affect the shipments?"

Raoul's tone grew menacing. "The shipments go on as planned. No delay."

"Good."

They said goodbye and he dialed another number.

"I need to see you in my office." He could no longer afford to trust the Colombians to get the job done.

A few minutes later there was a knock on his door and a woman entered. Attractive, mid-thirties, blonde. Tracey Williams, Head of Security. Tracey Williams wasn't her real name.

"We have a problem," he said before she mistook this summons for pleasure rather than urgent business. "The Colombians screwed up. They say they can fix the problem, but I'd like you to go down there and check it out for me."

Her red painted lips parted in surprise. "She got away?"

"She had help."

Her brows rose.

"I need you to give it your *immediate* attention," he said when she still didn't move.

Her expression tightened, but she nodded. "I'll be on the next flight out."

Some of the tension eased from his chest. Unlike the Colombians she'd never let him down.

CHAPTER FOUR

I T HAD BEEN a long time since Killion had flown anything and flying a stolen plane below radar at night over the jungle had been a hell of a refresher course. He was exhausted, running on adrenaline fumes and pure nerve, but finally, after many hours, they'd reached their destination—another unmarked airfield on the outskirts of Cartagena on the northern Caribbean coast of Colombia. The plane rumbled along the landing strip, making him glad to be back on solid ground even if the situation was a little shaky. It was still dark as he headed to the farther-most corner of the small airfield where a tall man leaned nonchalantly against the wooden hull of the hangar. Killion slowed his speed and taxied inside before stopping the plane and turning off the engine. He glanced over his shoulder into the cargo space. Lockhart had slept most of the journey. Either that or she was dead. He was almost too tired to care.

The door opened and a man he hadn't seen in two years grinned up at him. The former British SAS soldier took in everything with a quick glance. "You've looked worse, but I doubt she has." He gave Killion a wink and climbed inside the aircraft, putting his fingers to Audrey's throat.

Logan Masters and a few of his Brit pals had set up shop in South America a couple of years ago. Their company, "Penny

Fan," sounded like a Chinese piano protégé, but was actually named after the infamous Welsh Mountain that formed part of the SAS's Selection process. They consulted on security issues for corporate businesses: hostage negotiations, kidnap and ransom, threat reduction of a permanent nature. Killion knew they did other things, secret things, operations that couldn't be tied to their government. Like most operators in the clandestine service, Killion believed in the three wise monkeys approach to doing business with allies—see no evil, hear no evil, speak no evil.

"Is she still alive?" He found himself holding his breath, hoping she'd survived his clumsy rescue.

"Pulse is thready and rapid." Masters quickly checked her wound and still, the woman didn't wake up. "Looks red and inflamed. She needs IV fluids and antibiotics." He speared Killion with a look. "Assuming you don't want to take her to hospital?"

"No hospital. I've got to get her out of Colombia without anyone knowing she's alive."

"Destination?"

"Good question." He laughed. "I'm working on it."

Masters climbed out of the aircraft and pulled out his cell, pressing a button before putting it back in his pocket.

Killion tossed his SIG in his duffel and climbed out of the machine, feet hitting the ground with a thud. They shook hands. Then Killion stretched out his arms and back until his vertebrae cracked and the tightness in his muscles eased. He needed food, water, and sleep, but first he needed to take care of his captive.

The word was an ugly one. It reminded him of some of the other things that had been done in the name of God and

Country.

"I'm not going to get a call from someone wanting to hire me to help find her, am I?" Masters asked carefully.

"Only if you've started working for Raoul Gómez."

The Brit's eyes hardened. "That asshole? Did you hear he's started wearing bulletproof pajamas to bed? I keep hoping for an invitation to test how well they protect against a double-tap to the head." His teeth gleamed in a predatory smile.

Killion knew exactly what Masters would do if he got close to the cartel leader; it wouldn't be pretty, but it would be fast and it would be terminal. It was the main reason he'd chosen to come to these guys instead of using his other contacts. The cartel leader had killed two SAS men more than a decade ago. The Regiment knew how to hold a grudge and would never sell them out to the guy. That old saying about revenge being a dish best served cold?—He was looking at a world-class practitioner of that particular adage.

"'That asshole' isn't very happy with my passenger. And it's possible I accidentally borrowed his plane without asking permission when I rescued her. It might have a tracker on it," he warned.

"The hangar is cloaked from any unauthorized electronic signals." The Brit's brows pulled together as he eyed the small aircraft. "I can make the Cessna disappear—on paper anyway." He grinned. "It might come in handy at some point in the future. You have alternate transportation arranged?"

Killion shook his head. "I have people working on it. My escape plan involved getting the woman out of his territory. It was a spur of the moment intervention."

"You're not using Company resources this trip?"

"This one's below radar." He'd contacted Frazer from the

plane, but the guy was on medical leave. The FBI agent was pissed he wasn't available to help, but he'd arranged for a former CIA operative and cyber-security specialist, Alex Parker, to work with him on this. Parker was good—but even better news was the fact Jed Brennan was back at Quantico, riding a desk, and running the FBI's BAU-4 until Frazer returned to work. Killion trusted Brennan, and his buddy was working on finding him and Audrey a safe house. Hopefully one that didn't involve a remote cabin in the Northwoods of Wisconsin with Brennan's conspiracy-nut father watching his back. If it did, Killion was liable to get a bullet in his skull because the old man didn't trust anyone, but Brennan's father certainly didn't trust the CIA, and in particular didn't trust him.

Ideally, they'd find something on a beach somewhere. Killion preferred hot to cold. Sun to snow. Brunettes to redheads...

"Noah's on the way with our ride. I'm assuming you can cope with a little British hospitality for a few hours?"

"I'd appreciate it."

"Gómez wouldn't risk the wrath of the CIA just to get his plane back." Masters' eyes sparkled with curiosity. "What's the story with the woman?"

"Gómez doesn't know the CIA has the woman. He doesn't know the CIA is involved at all and I want it to stay that way. The asshole sent Hector Sanchez after her. Hector came off worse during the encounter. I happened to be in the area at the time and got her out."

The Brit's eyes widened with grudging respect. "Company business?"

"She has information I need." Killion hedged.

Masters held up his hands. He knew all about the three wise monkeys. And all about Killion's primary skill set.

The noise of a car engine had Killion turning toward the door of the hangar. A black SUV pulled up inside and a dark-haired man jumped out and walked over, sporting a cocky grin.

Noah Zacharias—another so-called *former* SAS trooper—held out his hand. "Good to see you, mate."

Noah and Logan were part of a cadre of soldiers Killion had been lucky enough to save after a logistical fuck up had almost cost the elite warriors their lives. It wasn't every day he got to do the right thing. Now he was cashing in his chips.

"Noah," Killion acknowledged with a smile. "Still writing cheesy love songs for the ladies?"

Noah snorted. "Only when I'm not kicking some crazy American's ass. You still causing trouble?" It was a rhetorical question. Noah's eyes flickered over Killion's shoulder to the aircraft. "Don't bother to answer that. Looks like your lady friend just woke up."

AUDREY STARED OUT of the open doorway to find three men staring at her with expressions that ranged from concern to speculation to curiosity. Details from the night before were fuzzy. Her skin felt sizzling hot. Mouth scorched. She had no idea where she was, or even what day it was. It looked dark outside. Nighttime. Between blood loss and lack of her reading glasses her vision was blurry. She was inside the small aircraft the tourist had stolen earlier. She staggered to the open doorway and sat on the edge as white-hot agony ripped through her side.

"How're you feeling?" asked the tourist.

"Like death, only in excruciating pain." She panted as she shifted her left leg. She'd never experienced anything like this before. Had Rebecca suffered this much after being shot, or was that even worse? Audrey didn't want to think about her friend. Even after five years it still hurt and right now she had to get through her own trauma. "I need to get to the American embassy. I don't have a passport and I need to tell the police what happened at the research station."

The men's expressions were masked now. Closed down. She swallowed nervously, realizing that although these men didn't radiate an obvious threat, they weren't necessarily her friends. Fortunately, they'd shown her nothing but kindness.

"Where am I?"

"Still in Colombia," said her hero whose name she still didn't know.

"Can you get me to the embassy?" All she wanted was to go home, but she didn't know if the airlines would allow her to fly with no passport and a stab wound.

Her rescuer nodded. Thank goodness.

Her head started to pound. As if reading her mind her rescuer held a bottle of water to her lips. She tipped her head back and felt moisture flood her tongue. The water had a bit of a tang but she put that down to the warm plastic bottle. When she was finished she wiped a drop from the side of her mouth. She wasn't sure how much blood she'd lost, but enough to leave her with zero energy.

"Who are you guys?" Her hands started to shake from fatigue. No one answered. "How did you know I was in danger yesterday?" She assumed it was yesterday that she'd killed a man. The realization she'd taken someone's life made her feel awful. Then she pushed the guilt aside. The fact a man had died was terrible, but it had been his own fault. He'd attacked *her*. It was only by a twist of fate she'd survived to regret any of it.

She tried to stand, but pain streaked white-hot through her body. The skin around her wound felt both fragile and blisteringly hot. The man who'd saved her moved quickly to help, sliding his hands under her back and knees and lifting her against him. She barely had the strength to thank him.

Even her untrained eye could spot the military bearing of the other two men, but the tourist possessed a different aura. She frowned. Not military. Not a rule follower—if torching the rental car and stealing the plane were anything to go by. He was quick, sharp, confident. Was he a criminal? Her head fell against his chest. Even if he was an axe murderer, right now, she didn't have the strength to do anything except take comfort in the care he offered. His warm scent enveloped her. His heartbeat drummed against her cheek. She snuggled deeper.

He slid into the back of an SUV, holding her tight. Probably not an axe murderer. One of the men got into the driver's seat and they pulled quickly away. The second man stayed behind. There was nothing she could do right now except recover and regain her strength. She slipped in and out of consciousness. The idea of a dreamless sleep was so tempting; she welcomed it, even wrapped in a stranger's arms.

NOAH SKIRTED THE city itself and drove out into the country.

Founded by the Spanish in the Sixteenth Century, the port city of Cartagena was a tourist Mecca in South America, with the fortress of Saint Domingo being its most impressive landmark. They skipped the sightseeing tour. The Brit seemed to sense his exhaustion and didn't bother making idle chitchat. Maybe he realized most of what Killion had to say was best spoken out of earshot of petite brunettes, even those who were seemingly unconscious.

Killion welcomed the darkness that pressed around him like an old friend. Daylight revealed too much—exposing all the cracks and flaws of his profession, making it hard to deny the cruel reality of what he did. Rendition tore families apart. Even when the detainee was a radicalized terrorist intent on harming others, the families were often clueless as to their relative's actions. In the age of the Internet the problem was no longer confined to those who attended mosques run by extremist clerics. Nowadays potential recruits could be groomed and manipulated online, thousands of miles away from the Middle East and a designated war zone. Funds could be transferred anonymously at an event using Q-squares, making it impossible to track. Kick-start campaigns and pop-up charities in the wake of natural disasters meant illegally funneling money was now easier than ever.

The key had to be controlling the World Wide Web, but governments were reluctant to do that. Nations had to balance personal freedom with the needs of national security, and none of them were particularly good at it.

Audrey snuggled against him like a warm puppy but he couldn't afford to fall for the act of innocence. Truth was if he hadn't seen Hector Sanchez's body with his own eyes he probably wouldn't have believed she was the assassin, and he was probably the most jaded and cynical intelligence officer working for the Agency. Her hand gripped his shirt reflexively. He pressed his lips to her forehead, not to kiss her but to assess her temperature. She was hot, and not just in a good way.

She had a fever and the wound was infected.

Damn.

Maybe he should have taken her to the hospital and called in the political attack-dogs to kick up enough fuss to whisk her back to the States where he could question her in a federal facility. But it was just as possible the powers-that-be would deny all knowledge and hang them both out to dry.

It was easier to simply disappear.

Killion regularly went dark during missions. This was nothing unusual. The clandestine service did not want officers who needed their hands held. But if McLean had started asking questions he was probably needed for an assignment, and that meant American lives were in danger. However, for this particular mission he'd been sworn to secrecy by the President of the United States himself and, while there was nothing on paper from POTUS, it was hard to renege on that sort of promise and maintain your reputation, not to mention your federal job.

Usually Lincoln Frazer dealt with the political bullshit and Killion dealt with information retrieval. They trusted each other to cover each other's backs. But Frazer was out of the picture for now and, even if he wasn't, his network wasn't as global as Killion needed it to be. If the local cops caught him or Audrey here in Colombia, it would be game over for getting the information he sought. Game over for Audrey, too.

Which is why he'd come to Masters and Zacharias for help. Few people knew his connection to the Brits. Those who did were either Agency, or part of the same brotherhood he'd embedded with back in Afghanistan. He trusted them. More surprisingly, they trusted him.

Noah drove for another fifteen minutes before turning into a large estate on the outskirts of Cartagena complete with a crumbling mansion and twelve-foot high stone walls. Heavy wrought-iron gates closed solidly behind them. Motion sensor controlled floodlights lit up the grounds as they approached.

He eyed the entrance and exit points and knew the Brits would have additional security in place. "Nice digs."

Noah grinned in the rearview. "Beats that shit-hole we were in in Helmand. We actually have electricity, running water, and comms here."

"No local warlord trying to mortar your ass?"

"Ah, those were the days." Noah smiled reminiscently. "They prefer semiautomatics around here."

"Nothing says class like an assault rifle," Killion agreed.

They pulled under a carport next to the house. It was covered in enough vines to obscure them from aerial view. The bright yellow of the mansion shone like Inca gold in the security lights.

Noah checked his phone and got out of the vehicle, grabbing his friend's duffel as Killion slid out with his arms full of soft warm woman. He followed Noah to a side-door and they walked through a stone-flagged utility space and into a brightly lit kitchen with oak cabinets and marble countertops.

Killion followed Noah farther down another corridor. They stopped in front of a plain white door.

"Guest bedroom." Noah opened the door. Inside was a twin bed made up with clean white sheets, a chair, a small bathroom off to one side. No windows. Camera over the door, facing the bed.

Killion raised his brows in question.

"It's usually reserved for unwelcome visitors, but it's the closest place we have to the kitchen and we need to keep an eye on your friend here until the fever clears. Plus, if we have to leave the house for any reason, we know she'll be safe." And contained. Killion nodded. It was about time he started treating Audrey like his prisoner and not his girlfriend.

Noah checked a drawer and came up with an over-sized white T-shirt. "Strip her and get her cleaned up. Wound is infected. I'll get the stuff for an IV and stitches."

When Noah left, Killion grimaced. The Brit was right, he needed to wash all the dried caked blood off her body and see exactly what they were dealing with, but he'd slipped a mild sedative into the water bottle and she was going to be out for hours. Shit. He maneuvered them both into the bathroom and eased the purple shirt off Audrey's shoulders and tossed it in the sink. Then he did the same with her pants, pushing them along with her panties down her legs, tugging when the blood stuck them to her skin. They jammed on her ankles so he sat her up against the wall, unhooked her sandals and trousers and panties and tossed them all in the sink. He turned on the shower and tested the temperature until it felt right. Even that didn't wake her. He glanced at the spray of water and the almost naked woman lying on the floor of the shower and realized the water alone wasn't going to get her clean. He toed off his boots, pulled off his T-shirt and trousers, and climbed in beside her. Grabbed soap and then hooked his hands under her arms and hauled her carefully to her feet. She was like a rag doll in his arms, the white cotton tank top doing precious little to cover anything now that it was wet. He tried not to notice.

Tried to pretend she was just some skanky terrorist he'd picked off the streets.

Didn't help.

Great.

The idea of being attracted to his captive didn't sit easy. He reminded himself she'd killed the VP with sociopathic coolness, and downed an experienced operator like Hector Sanchez without even a handgun for self-defense. But the woman he'd rescued hadn't been cool or competent. She'd been floundering. Desperate. Confused.

Hell, maybe she was just better at this shit than he'd ever be.

Or maybe she was innocent?

That was the real soul eater. What if he'd been wrong about Audrey Lockhart?

He anchored her with one arm and washed her from the top down, soaping her skin, making sure he was thorough and as clinically detached as possible—which wasn't very clinically detached at all.

Killion loved the female form and he'd have to be a monk not to appreciate the slim, but curvy figure she'd hidden beneath practical clothes. He wasn't a monk. Not even close. His wet boxers clung to him uncomfortably. He was supposed to despise this woman but it didn't seem to matter. If anything he grew more aroused.

Great. Just great.

He unpinned the bandage he'd put on her way back when on the side of the road and unwrapped it from around her waist. The bleeding had stopped and the wound had started to knit, but one part of it was an angry red and obviously infected. The skin around the wound seared his fingertips.

Okay, so it was official—he was a dog for lusting after a sick woman, but what else was new. He wasn't gonna get any awards for good behavior. Not in this lifetime.

Irritated with himself he turned off the water and wrapped her in an enormous towel. Then he picked her up and carried her to the bedroom, leaving a trail of water in his wake. Noah stood waiting for him, which killed any arousal stone dead.

"Let's get her wet top off and the dry shirt on instead."

And now Noah was going to see Audrey naked, too. Killion didn't know why he was pissed at that thought. Removing a prisoner's clothes was usually the first step of a rendition, but there was nothing usual about any of this. Audrey chose that moment to sigh in his arms.

His throat got tight and he couldn't speak.

Killion laid her gently on top of a couple of bath sheets Noah had spread out on the bed and adjusted the towel she was wearing so it draped over her lower hips, keeping her decent. Noah raised her arms and started to ease the top higher.

Killion grabbed the bottom of the shirt and held on. "I'll do it. Turn around." He told the other man.

"Hey, I'm a professionally trained medic." Noah shook his head, but turned away, clearly amused by Killion's attempt to preserve Audrey's modesty. Killion got rid of Audrey's top and bra and pretended he didn't see small perfect breasts with tight rosy nipples. A clean T-shirt smacked him on the side of the head and he jerked back to the moment. Crap. He eased it over Audrey's head and pulled her arms through the armholes, covering her so only her midriff was bare.

Noah was now looking at him with a curious smile, as if Killion had revealed more than he wanted to. Bottom line was, he wasn't as callous and ruthless as he'd once been. He'd learned caution and a measure of respect for those in his custody. He hadn't gone soft or grown a conscience, he'd just refined his methods. Experience told him being kind to Audrey would get him a lot further than being a hard-assed prick. The best intel came when people trusted one another and both had something to gain from the exchange of information.

Not soft. Smart.

Noah inspected her injury and inserted an IV needle into her arm. "She's burning up, but this should help."

Killion turned away from the sight of the ugly wound against such pure white skin. He cleared his throat. "I'm going to shower and crash. Need me?"

Noah glanced up at him absently. "No, mate. We'll see how she is after the first dose of antibiotics and try and get this fever down. She might still need a hospital."

"No hospital."

Noah's lips tightened.

Gómez had a long reach and a simple phone call could lead to an injection of something deadly and that would be all it would take to get rid of this woman and the information she held.

She let out a deep sigh and turned her head away from him. Her cheeks were flushed compared to the rest of her face. Her hair was a tangled mess of dark wet silk against the white cotton. Killion told himself not to look. Not to care. If Audrey died at least he'd tried. Her odds were far better with him than alone against the cartel.

Ironically, Audrey's rescue—if that's what anyone could call it—followed the KUBARK human resource interrogation manual's recommendations for a successful rendition. It had achieved surprise and maximum discomfort, an intense feeling of shock, insecurity and psychological stress. Audrey was suffering, confused and didn't know who had her or where she was.

Gold star for Killion.

He grabbed his bag and gathered up his clothes, walked into the bedroom next-door, taking the key out of the lock. He jumped in the shower and scrubbed himself with soap. He rinsed and dried off just as fast. Wrapping a towel around his hips, he stuck his head back into Audrey's room.

"Call me if she wakes."

"Gotcha."

"As soon as. I mean it," he said sternly.

Noah eyed him narrowly. "I heard you the first time. You look like shit, mate. Get some sleep before you fall over. I'll look after your date."

Killion fought the urge to stay and watch over her, and that told him he was already too invested. But he could get the information he wanted by being charming as easily as by being a prick. The knowledge left him a little hollow, but he put that down to being too world-weary to whore himself out for his country.

The memory of holding a dead child in his arms flashed through his brain but he pushed it away. No more guilt for fulfilling the oath he'd made to his country. He went next-door and crashed. Wishing he was too tired to give a damn.

CHAPTER FIVE

N EXT TIME AUDREY surfaced she was lying on a bed with a strange man leaning over her.

"How you feeling?" The stranger had the prettiest gray eyes, surrounded by thick black lashes and spoke with a sexy British accent. A shard of memory drifted through her mind. He'd been in the hangar when they'd landed.

"Like someone stabbed me." She tried to lift her hand but even that was too much effort.

The Brit pressed a straw against her lips and cupped the back of her head so she could drink. "Just a sip until your stomach gets used to it."

At least that sounded vaguely optimistic that she might live. The pain in her side had eased, but she still felt like she was burning up from the inside out and was incredibly weak.

"Where am I?" Her voice was a dull rasp.

"Somewhere safe."

"How long have I been here?"

"Not long." Those pretty gray eyes were smiling, but she didn't miss the fact he wasn't answering her questions. "How you feeling? Headache? Nausea?"

"Both." She nodded, and then winced as the motion set off a gyroscope inside her skull.

His hand touched her arm as he adjusted her IV. She

wasn't used to being so utterly dependent on anyone, especially not a stranger. "Are you a doctor?"

"Medic."

She shifted in bed and realized that under an unfamiliar white T-shirt she was naked. Embarrassment crept into her cheeks. Someone had stripped her and changed her clothes. A feeling of vulnerability and helplessness swept over her.

"I didn't see anything. Promise." His gray eyes twinkled. "Your guard dog protected your modesty. I'm Noah, by the way. My mum always said that she should never have called me that because all I ever said when I was little was 'no.'"

"I can think of a few things she should have called you," came a familiar voice from the open doorway. Her eyes darted to her rescuer who leaned a shoulder against the frame. "But I probably shouldn't use them in polite company."

She was polite company? A confused half-naked, half-dead frog biologist?

The blue eyes were bright and piercing, but there were shadows in their depths. His blond hair could do with more than a trim and there was a light scruff on his jaw. He wore a dark T-shirt with black canvas pants, but his feet were bare. Whereas the Brit, Noah, was tall, dark and charming, this guy was lean, blond, and exuded confidence like a pheromone.

When he'd been at the visitor center yesterday she'd assumed he was part of a family and hadn't paid too much attention, as she didn't make a habit of ogling other women's husbands or boyfriends. But at some point he'd told her he didn't have a girlfriend so she must have been mistaken in her assumption.

Intelligence gleamed in the blue eyes that scanned her face. Enough intelligence to make her nervous.

She forced some moisture onto her tongue. "And what did your mother call *you*?" she asked pointedly.

His eyes narrowed for a moment before the smile returned. "On a good day she called me Patrick."

Noah's expression was flat, but even that was telling her something. These men were being careful with the information they shared with her. Were they some kind of criminals? But they hadn't hurt her and would criminals really go to this much effort to help a woman they didn't know? If Patrick was correct about the man who'd stabbed her being part of the *Mano de Dios* cartel, he'd saved her life at great risk to his own.

She owed him.

Another wave of pain hit and she lay back on the pillow and stared at the ceiling. She wished she could wind the clock back twenty-four hours and start the day over. "Where are we?" she asked. "Have you contacted the embassy for me? I need to talk to my parents. My mom is going to freak."

Noah pushed to his feet. "I'll make you both a cuppa."

Patrick moved farther into the room as Noah left. Her injury was neatly bandaged, but she was well aware her midriff was on display. She inched the T-shirt down and his gaze rose guiltily to meet hers. Was that interest in his eyes?

"Feeling any better?" he asked.

"Compared to yesterday when someone tried to kill me? I feel better. Compared to the day before that? Not so much."

He nodded. Those eyes of his watched her with some kind of an agenda but she had no idea what that might be.

"I don't understand," she said, finally.

One brow rose. "Which part?"

"Any of it. Why I was attacked?" Her voice rose in agitation. "Why you brought me here?" A man like him didn't need to kidnap a woman to have sex. Even some sort of perverted serial killer would have easier ways of finding his victims than stealing planes from drug lords and flying across the South American continent. His actions didn't make sense. "I don't understand why you haven't taken me to the hospital. It's almost like you're holding me captive but there's no reason for you to do that."

Patrick continued to search her face, as if looking for an answer to some unspoken question. He shook his head. "I can't take you to the hospital."

"But why not? Surely the cartel doesn't have spies everywhere? Surely when they figure out they made a mistake attacking me they'll just leave me alone?"

He sat on a chair beside the bed, leaning forward, legs spread, elbows resting on his knees. Even though she felt like crap she was uncomfortably aware of him as an attractive male, sitting close beside her, as she lay half-naked in bed.

"Why would the cartel leave you alone?" he asked quietly. "They have billions of dollars and fingers in every imaginable pie. If they want you dead why would they *ever* leave you alone?" His anger echoed softly off the plain white walls.

She swallowed. "But I haven't done anything wrong."

His lip curled as if he thought she was lying.

"Honestly." Why didn't he believe her? How insulting was that? "Look, they've made a mistake. That man who stabbed me also attacked me the night before. Told me 'The Gateway Project was over' and I was to tell my boss. But my boss didn't have a clue what they were talking about, either."

"Were you hurt the first night?" The expression in his eyes was guarded, like he didn't trust she was telling the truth, which was crazy. If she had the energy she'd roll her eyes. Why would she lie about any of this?

"He tied me up, scared me to death, but didn't hurt me—not then anyway. He obviously came back to finish the job." Her energy started to lag. Her eyes felt heavy. "I reported it to the cops who were probably scarier than the perp."

Her brain grew fuzzy. She had a suspicion there was some sort of painkiller and sedative in her IV because she wasn't hurting anymore but couldn't keep her eyelids open.

"Patrick?" she asked drowsily.

"Yeah?" His voice sounded close, as if his lips were next to her ear.

She turned her head toward the sound, opened her eyes to find him an inch away, staring at her with an expression she couldn't read. "Thank you for saving my life."

TRACEY WILLIAMS SAUNTERED into the Colombian police station and smiled at the bored young officer who sat behind the front desk. He wasn't wearing a wedding band and he had that amped up male vibe about him, all testosterone-driven virility. One of the easily manipulated. She was older than he was, but she kept in perfect shape. She crossed her arms under her breasts, drawing attention to her impressive cleavage displayed by the deep vee of her tight white blouse. Then she bent just a little to smooth her hand down her just-above-the-knee dove-gray skirt. His eyes flickered. Good. Now she had his proper attention. She smiled straight into his dark chocolate eyes and watched his pupils heat.

"*Hola, mi nombre es Meredith Childs. Trabajo con la com-*

pañía de seguros." My name is Meredith Childs. I'm from the insurance company. Another false identity. In truth, she had so many she'd almost forgotten her real name—it was better that way. *"Necesito ver el carro de alquiler que se quemó anoche para evaluar sus daños." I need to see the burned out rental car from last night to assess it for damages.* Her Spanish held just the barest trace of an American accent but, to her annoyance, he replied in perfect English.

"Trust me, *Señorita*, the car is a write off."

"I understand, Officer, but if I don't personally set eyes on the vehicle, I can't process the claim for the rental company, and then they can't press criminal charges for destruction of property against the renter."

A look of amused disbelief crossed the young man's face.

She pushed. "My firm will send somebody else until one of us actually lays eyes on the car. You know how insurance companies are." The same the world over.

The young man gave a heavy sigh and shouted through an open door to some cops in the back room. The place was hopping after a murder—Dr. Lockhart's student to be exact. Apparently *Mano de Dios* had thought the kid might have an idea where his supervisor had gone and had tried to beat it out of him. They'd discovered absolutely nothing. The cartel operated on violence and intimidation, but not smarts. They also operated on bribes.

She'd bet her new BMW Z4 Roadster that the investigation into the student's death was already written up and the cops had concluded that Dr. Audrey Lockhart was the prime suspect. Poor Audrey, all she'd ever tried to do was beat back the disappointments and tragedies of her life by burying herself in her work. The biologist's future looked increasingly bleak. So sad. Too bad. Life happened and you adapted. Or died.

The uniform led her out through the front door and around the side of the low squat building. She maneuvered carefully over the hot, cracked, pitted concrete in her four-inch, black, patent leather pumps.

He pulled keys from the belt at his side and said something about the weather. She smiled with just the right amount of sparkle. His expression was more relaxed now. Attentive. Interested. All because his Tab A might fit into her Slot B. It was the only form of biology that had ever interested her.

They approached a large lot filled with cars and boats, surrounded by a ten-foot high chain link fence. The acrid stench of smoke and gasoline tainted the air. A burned-out SUV sat on the back of a flatbed tow truck. The cop swung up inside the cab and started to slowly lower the SUV to the dusty ground. She peered closer as the vehicle dropped to her level. Gas cap was missing. Small pieces of what looked like incinerated paper were stuck inside the pipe. Definitely a torch job. All the interior upholstery had melted away and the inside was a twisted mess of carbonized plastic and steel. Just the skeletal frame of the seats remained. Whoever lit it up had done a good job.

The car came to rest on the ground with a bump and a groan.

"Did they find any prints?" she asked when the cop turned off the winch.

"*Nada.* We sent a knife and samples of material covered in what looked like blood to the crime lab but it might not be possible to get DNA." He shrugged in that sexy arrogant way some Latino men had.

The blood probably belonged to Lockhart. From the information she'd received Lockhart had miraculously killed one of the cartel's trained monkeys, but had been stabbed in the process. What Tracey needed to know was the identity of the mysterious white knight who'd ridden to the biologist's rescue.

Despite the public cover up, someone was actively investigating Ted Burger's death—probably someone in the US government. Tracey would be more concerned if it were The Gateway Project, but that shadowy vigilante organization had unexpectedly shut down in December, and the secretive cabal had disbanded without her or her boss learning their true identities. Burger had been pissed by the decision, but he'd also been afraid. She'd enjoyed the look in his eyes when she'd told him The Gateway Project had sent her to exact revenge, but she had no real desire to come to their attention.

Tracey was smart enough to tread lightly. Once she figured out who was involved, then she'd know where to start looking for Little Miss Lockhart.

A dead "assassin" suited everyone. Especially her. Tracey had wanted to kill Audrey before this, but her lover hadn't let her. A mistake. Tracey didn't like mistakes.

She eyed the cop up and down. If she couldn't get what she needed out of this guy she'd have to risk going to the car rental company and try to bluff her way into seeing their records. She took photographs of the vehicle from all angles, and wrote notes on her iPad as he eyed the outline of her flat stomach and full breasts under her business attire.

She bit her lip and frowned. "I need the vehicle identification number to confirm this is the right car and then I can close the case from my end." She gestured to her clothes, which were not suited for exploring a burnt out vehicle, and pouted. "I don't really want to get too close."

He raised his eyes, gaze shrewd and calculating.

Come on, pretty boy. Give me what I want and I might do the same for you. She smiled.

"I have the information inside," he said.

"Thank you."

"I'll get it for you."

He was young, fit, good-looking—unlike some of the people she'd screwed for information. Back inside the police station, the officer went through to the rear of the building and returned with a thick file.

She eyed it avidly and he saw her interest. She bit her lip and raised her brows. "I don't suppose you have anything in there that might save me a trip to the rental office, do you?" She leaned over the counter, providing a nice view of her breasts enclosed in a lacy bra. "I have to be at the airport by three and can think of better things to do with my lunch hour."

"*Señorita*, that is not possible I'm afraid," he said loudly. Then she watched him photocopy the entire contents of the file before he returned it to the officers in the back.

He made a big show of putting the photocopies into a large envelope while she watched his every move. He thought he had all the power here, all the control, not realizing she was leading him around with a firm grip on his hefty young balls. He held out the envelope and she went to take it, but he didn't let go. His dark eyes smiled and he tilted his head slightly, not threatening, but arrogant enough to know he held a few cards of his own. "Perhaps I could take you to lunch before you have to catch your flight?"

"That would be very sweet of you." She fluttered her lashes. "But, considering my boss is an ass, it depends on what's in the envelope." She flicked long blonde hair over her shoulder. "He won't be happy if I don't get the information I need and I can't afford to get fired."

He let go of the envelope and she quickly peeked at the name and signature on the rental agreement. She recognized neither. The photograph on the driver's license, however, made her whole body freeze. His identity shouldn't have shocked her. But it did.

She should have known. A ball of hatred rose up inside her. The person responsible for her fall from grace. A man whose pretty blue eyes and irreverent grin were as famous at Langley as his unconventional way of doing things. The thought of ruining his legendary reputation, of making him look like an incompetent fool sent a thrill rushing through her blood.

She shivered with anticipation. After all these years she could finally make him and the CIA pay for ruining her life. But could she do it without getting caught? A challenge, she conceded, but not impossible. Not if he wasn't expecting it. The idea of getting the better of a man like that was both tantalizing and seductive.

The cop walked around the counter to guide her out of the building to her car. Along the way he whispered in her ear, "I know a motel nearby. Perhaps you'd like a different kind of lunch today?" The chocolate eyes held a dark promise.

"Maybe I would." The information he'd given her was worth celebrating. Giving her the opportunity to destroy the man who'd ruined her was worthy of a reward.

He walked to his own car with a male swagger in his step and she almost laughed. Men were so predictable—except for her boss, her lover, her partner in crime. She never knew what to expect from him, which was probably why she'd fallen for him quite so hard.

He might not let you take the revenge you want to take, a little voice inside niggled. *And he might not know until the dust settles*, she argued back. She'd take her chances. And as unpredictable and brilliant as he might be, right now, he needed her more than she needed him.

The cop rolled up beside her in his shiny gray muscle car as she started her rental's engine. A huge rush of adrenaline surged through her. She was buzzing with pent up energy and the burning desire to show her true colors if only to a strange man in a paid by-the-hour motel room. Having a connection inside the police station could prove useful.

She waved her fingers at him and put her car in gear, following him out of the parking lot toward the outskirts of town. Romeo better make getting sweaty and naked worth the effort. She didn't deal well with disappointment, as the spook and Audrey Lockhart were about to find out.

KILLION STARED THOUGHTFULLY as Audrey drifted off into another drug-induced coma. Why would she mention The Gateway Project in her report to the cops? Why the hell would she do that? No one involved in that organization would want it to be a matter of public record.

The facts didn't make any sense. The situation didn't make sense.

The night that he'd grabbed her and tied her up, she'd told him she didn't speak Spanish, but he'd *known* she was lying.

Right now if someone asked his professional opinion as to her veracity, even though he'd watched Hector Sanchez die at her hand, he'd say she was telling the truth. It raised the awful prospect that she might actually be innocent.

If she was innocent—huge *if*—but if she was, it was possible the police report she'd filed about his little warning visit two nights previous had spooked someone into sending Hector Sanchez to permanently take care of the problem. And, if Killion followed that line of reasoning, it meant that he was indirectly responsible for the attack on her yesterday and, therefore, the death of Gómez's chief enforcer.

He could live with the latter. The former, however...

The thick bandage on Audrey's waist, the smooth curve of her cheek and the idea she might be blameless made a wedge of remorse lodge in his throat. He *really* didn't want to believe she might be innocent, but he'd seen that kind of denial before—in people who'd crossed so far over the line they couldn't afford to admit they might have made a mistake. Or maybe his radar was off because of his attraction to her?

He didn't know—and he wasn't used to that either.

He watched the gentle rise and fall of her chest as she slept. There was an air of naivety about her that was hard to fake. But there was too much evidence and too many coincidences to believe this woman was uninvolved. She was either playing him like a maestro—because he was ready to wrap her up in cotton wool and personally take care of her in *every* way—or she'd been set up and he'd foolishly swallowed a line attached to a big fat juicy hook.

Neither was palatable.

The first priority was keeping her alive. The second was interrogating Audrey Lockhart-of-the-trusting-violet-blue-eyes-and-tremulous-smile because, whether she knew it or not, she held the answers to his questions.

He couldn't afford to let down his guard. There was still the very real possibility she was playing him until she got the chance to put something appropriately noxious in his coffee. She wouldn't be the first woman to want him dead, but she would be the first frog biologist to ever go there.

"She out of it?" Noah came back into the room with a mug of hot tea. Killion hadn't drunk the brew until he'd been stuck in the middle of the desert with a bunch of tea-swilling Brits. He'd figured out that the quickest way to defeat the British Army would be to put an embargo on Tetleys.

"Totally. What'd you put in her IV?"

"Morphine. She's responding well to the IV antibiotics but she's going to need to be on them for another forty-eight hours at least. Stitches will come out on their own. I'd recommend keeping her lightly sedated until the infection clears up, otherwise she's going to be trying to get out of bed and generally be a handful."

"She's going to be a handful all right." Killion dragged his hand through his hair. Damn. This wasn't part of the plan.

He walked into the kitchen where Logan was dishing up lunch. The TV on the kitchen wall was switched to the local Spanish news channel.

Logan thrust a bowl in his direction and tossed him a bread roll. "We've got a job that's just come up. Have to head out tonight. You can lay low here with your friend if you want."

"'Preciate it." Killion dug into his stew, knowing Logan was a good cook from their time together in Afghanistan. His encrypted phone rang and his one hand paused with his spoon halfway to his lips as he checked the screen. He hadn't realized how hungry he was until he'd started eating.

It was Jed Brennan.

"You missing me already?" Killion said and then carried on chewing.

"Like a dose of the clap. Vivi says 'Hi' too, by the way."

"Sure she did." Jed's new squeeze was slowly coming around to Killion's special brand of friendship, but she wasn't quite there yet. "You got anything for me?" He stole another mouthful of stew and chewed fast.

"I'm going to send you some coordinates," Jed said.

He swallowed. "I thought these phone lines were secure?"

"Yeah, but when you get the coordinates you'll understand. You've got free run of the place for two weeks before the owner returns."

"Security?"

"Tight as a duck's ass," Jed said.

"It isn't Wisconsin, is it?" Please, God, don't let it be Wisconsin.

"What the hell is wrong with Wisconsin?"

Killion had known Jed would take the bait. "Nothing, if you're a cheesehead—"

"Kiss my—"

"And then there're the Packers…"

"Hey, buddy, don't cross a line that can't be uncrossed," Jed warned. "Anyway, it isn't the Badger State. We begged but they wouldn't take you."

Killion grinned and ate.

"So two weeks," Jed continued, "is that long enough to, er…get the information you need out of the woman?" His words were measured.

Killion shook his head. It pissed him off that his friends believed he might be a party to torture, but he did perpetuate the myth, and he did get results. "Depends on when I drag out the thumbscrews."

"You could seduce it out of her. Shouldn't be a problem with your good looks and winning personality."

Killion's levity instantly evaporated. "Screw you." He let out a tired sigh. "Something feels off. I'm not a hundred percent convinced she knows anything."

There was a long pause. "You said it had to be her. You said you were certain."

"She's involved, I just don't know *how* she's involved."

"What about the bank account? The poison?" He heard the resignation in Jed's voice. Then the guy swore. "Why couldn't the killer have just shot the bastard?" Jed sounded dog-tired all of a sudden. No doubt Brennan had come back to work too soon after nearly dying in the line of duty.

But right now Killion was grateful. He needed all the help he could get from people he trusted. "Do me a favor, see if there's any way of getting hold of a police report Audrey Lockhart says she filed the night before last."

"The night you warned her off?"

"Yep. She says she reported it. I want to know exactly what she said and what the detectives did with that information. How's Frazer?" Killion changed the subject.

"Bitten by the love bug apparently."

"Are you kidding me? This is worse than losing George Clooney. It's like a contagious disease. All my bachelor icons are falling."

"Pretty sure you'll never have that problem."

Hurt flashed quick as lightning along his nerves. He hid it

under his usual banter. "Because I could never deprive the female population of their favorite stud?"

"Because you're never in one place long enough to meet a woman." There was another short pause. "And you never let them closer than your bed."

He felt tightness in his throat. "That's close enough for what I have in mind."

"Don't be an ass."

"Seriously?"

"Sorry, I forgot who I was talking to." Jed laughed but Killion heard something behind the humor. Frustration, because Killion didn't talk about personal shit with anyone.

He wasn't some teenage girl. He was an Intelligence Officer for the Central Intelligence Agency. "It's safer not to go there in my profession. For their sake and mine," he blurted. Where the hell had that come from?

"Sounds like a crappy profession."

"Like the feebs have it any better."

"I've got it pretty good." He could hear the smugness in Jed's tone.

"That's because you have a good-looking redhead to climb into bed with every night."

"Not every night." Jed sounded pissed now. "She's in Fargo packing up her and Michael's things and putting her house on the market. I was going to help, but with Frazer out of commission we're short-handed here. I even have a rookie to break in."

"Frazer will be back before you know it."

"I'm more worried about Vivi and Michael."

"Worried she might leave you for someone better looking?"

"With nicer friends," Jed agreed.

Killion felt a pang of envy at Jed's life. The guy had been shot and almost died, but he had a fiercely loyal woman in his life and her very cute kid, and the lifelong gratitude of the President of the United States. He also had a job he loved with colleagues he didn't mind seeing every day.

Most of Killion's colleagues were grounded at Langley for a reason. Aside from Crista, his favorite people were the ones assigned overseas—like the Station Chief of the Pakistan field office who'd helped Killion through numerous inter-agency fuck-ups including one time when the State Department accidentally released all the names of CIA personnel operating in South East Asia to the Press Corp. And another time where a team of Navy SEALs were deployed to rescue three female hostages who'd already managed to escape with the aid of a CIA asset Killion had activated. Thankfully, the bad guys hadn't discovered the SEALs or the hostages and everyone had come home alive.

The last couple of years he'd been attached to the Joint Terrorism Task Force, followed by this collaboration with the FBI. It was as close to freedom as he'd ever known with the Agency and he liked it. But he had a feeling the autonomy was about to end, just as soon as he figured out who was behind Ted Burger's untimely demise.

"I've gotta go," Jed said suddenly. "I've got an agent in New York State and he's on the other line. Series of killings at an exclusive university. Pissed off rich people and slaughtered co-eds don't go down well. Shit hitting the fan from all directions."

Maybe Jed's job wasn't all it was cracked up to be. "Don't forget to look into that police report for me," Killion reminded him.

"On it. I'm sending those coordinates right now. Two weeks. Parker cleared it with the owners."

They hung up and Killion dug into his stew again, appetite renewed, until Logan grabbed the remote and boosted the volume on the TV. Audrey's passport photo appeared on the screen, and that of some young guy, a student apparently who'd been found dead in his apartment early that morning. Killion stopped eating. Damn. The reporter was talking excitedly at the camera. Professor Lockhart had disappeared and it was unclear at this point whether she was a killer or another victim. No mention of Hector Sanchez or stolen airplanes. Gómez must have gotten rid of Hector's body because he wouldn't want to look weak to his competitors.

Killion stared at the screen, not really seeing it anymore. Gómez had gone after Audrey via her student—but if she was the assassin someone wanted Killion to believe she was, why bother? A professional would be long gone and her student wouldn't know a damn thing about it. Anyone who'd hired her would know that. It was another "fact" that didn't add up to the whole picture of this frog biologist being a cold-hearted killer.

His phone beeped with the coordinates of the safe house. Killion grinned and shook his head when he checked the GPS and saw the location was right in the middle of the ocean.

He turned the screen of his cell toward Logan whose brows rose. "We've got a destination, but I'm gonna need a ride."

CHAPTER SIX

THE SITUATION DIDN'T seem quite so amusing five hours later. As soon as the sun dropped from the sky, they packed up and drove to another airfield. Killion held Audrey's unconscious form in his arms in the backseat of the SUV. She looked pale and there was a fresh sheen of sweat on her brow.

"I don't like moving her," Noah said for the tenth time as he twisted around in the front seat.

"We don't have much choice. Gómez framed her for the murder of her student. Cops aren't going to listen to any alternate explanation when they have their prime suspect wrapped up with a nice pretty bow." His arms tightened on his charge. "I can't protect her if she's in custody."

"She's getting worse," Noah persisted.

"The last thing you need is the cops turning up on your doorstep and finding you harboring a wanted fugitive."

"They won't find her." Noah's chin jutted out.

"How will you know?" Killion challenged. "You won't be there."

"He doesn't have a choice and neither do we." Logan backed up Killion from the driver's seat. "She has to get out of the country and this is the fastest, most efficient way to accomplish that."

"You gave me the instructions to keep her fever down, the

medicine and antibiotics." Killion tried to reassure the younger man.

"That doesn't make you a bloody doctor." Noah did not look happy.

Killion wasn't exactly dancing a jig himself.

"We can get her to a clinic somewhere off the mainland." Noah divided a look between him and Logan.

They all knew it wasn't possible.

"As soon as she goes in the system she's as good as dead," Killion stated baldly.

Noah held his gaze. "She might die anyway."

"I won't let her," he snapped. He pressed his lips together to bite back anything else. He was slow to lose his temper but once it was gone it was hard to stuff back into its box. These guys were helping him and he owed them, but he didn't see any alternative that didn't involve sacrificing Audrey to the cartel. He wasn't willing to do that, not at any price. She had information he needed. "I've got a backup plan if she gets any worse." Not that his friends in the FBI would be that keen to secretly smuggle Audrey into the US for emergency medical treatment, but Killion was the master of getting his own way. He'd make it happen.

Noah kept quiet this time. Logan turned off the main road and drove down a dirt track so narrow the trees touched the SUV on either side. They pulled up sharply and Noah got out to open a gate.

"This is the place?" Killion could just make out an opening in the canopy that was about the size of a basketball court. "Please tell me we aren't hot air ballooning to the Caribbean?"

Logan grinned. "Don't be a pussy." He drove the SUV into a large garage. They got out, Killion still carrying Audrey in his arms. Logan and Noah grabbed his duffel and heavy kit bags for themselves, and locked the garage behind them. Killion hadn't asked where the former soldiers were going—he'd just taken them up on their offer to drop him and Audrey off along the way.

A hum vibrated through the night sky, distant but growing steadily louder. Killion recognized the sound from his days in Afghanistan, and shifted Audrey higher in his arms. What was she going to think when she woke up?

"Pretty fancy transportation you got, fellas. Private work must pay well."

Logan's grin burst out. "Better than government spooks."

"That's for damned sure." Killion laughed, then realized Audrey's glazed eyes were open and blinking up at him. Logan winced in apology. They'd let their guard down and forgotten there was a possible hostile in their midst. But it didn't matter. Her eyes were already closing again and he doubted she'd remember any of it.

The noise of the approaching helicopter got louder and louder. Finally a dark shadow appeared over the top of the forest. The rotors beat at the leaves of the surrounding trees and the downwash had them all bracing against the wind and flying debris. The bird landed gently in the middle of the field. Killion kept his eyes on the pilot who was lit up in the front seat. Once the guy gave the signal, they all hurried across to the sleek black chopper. Inside, six men were kitted up in a similar fashion to Logan and Noah, heavily armed, their faces blackened. Even if Killion knew these guys he wouldn't recognize them tonight. Probably a good thing.

One of the men took Audrey from his arms and laid her on the floor between two rows of ATAC boots. Someone else put a blanket under her head and another man held the IV bag so it dangled between his knees.

Killion strapped himself in and pulled on a headset.

"Slight detour, boys," Logan announced to the others through the comms. "Gotta drop these two lovebirds off at their honeymoon suite along the way."

Noah smirked.

"It's a tough job but someone's gotta do it." Killion grinned back even though he wasn't relishing what lay ahead with Audrey.

White teeth flashed in the darkness.

"If you want to swap places…" Noah offered with a glint in his eyes.

"Maybe next time." His grin was sharper. Noah's reputation with the ladies was probably worse than his. Noah would never behave inappropriately when she was sick, but when she recovered? Hell, yes, he'd be as inappropriate as she was willing to get.

Then they were airborne and everyone grew quiet, watching the lights of Cartagena getting smaller and smaller to the west as they headed northeast. Suddenly they were out over the ocean, blades slicing the air and making an urgent pulse throb against the water. His gaze turned back to Audrey who lay unmoving and vulnerable on the floor of the aircraft.

Did she realize her life as she'd known it was over? Or was she too sick to appreciate anything except for pain and discomfort? If she was guilty she probably had a thousand options lined up to disappear. But if she was innocent…if she really was some biologist battling to save frogs, her world had just collapsed and she didn't even realize it yet.

———————

AUDREY LAY IN darkness pretty sure she'd descended into the pits of hell. It was pitch black but the flash of a red light glanced off the silhouette of a man wearing dark military clothing and face paint. Her eyes rolled in her head and she barely kept herself from sinking back into oblivion. Something moved and somewhere in the dim recesses of her mind she registered there was another man, then another. The loud throb that encompassed her was a helicopter. She was in a helicopter and they were flying...

She tried to shake her head and felt a hand on her shoulder.

"Hold still," someone shouted above the din. She recognized the accent—it was the Brit from before. "You're going to be okay, but don't shift around or you'll pull out the IV. The antibiotics are helping to fight the infection." The fingers squeezed her shoulder in reassurance then let go.

Not dead, yet, then.

She was beginning to wish she were.

She felt so ill she didn't care about all the pairs of eyes on her. She didn't care that she was lying on the floor of a helicopter between the feet of what looked like a casting call for a Tom Clancy movie.

Her gaze searched for and finally found a familiar pair of eyes glistening in the darkness. He was still here. Her savior. She swallowed the unexpected burst of relief. Her heartbeat leveled off as she took a deep calming breath. Her rescuer was still with her. Still trying to get her to safety. She didn't know what was going on or who these people were, but she trusted this enigmatic stranger who was doing his utmost to make sure she survived.

———————

HE EYED THE screen and checked the manifests of two shipping containers headed from Colombia to Australia. He had key figures planted strategically within his organization, people who were paid handsomely to make sure certain special cargo items looked exactly like the real deal. They also made sure no one noticed when some of the inventory disappeared at the other end. Tracey took care of anyone who proved intractable.

This shipment contained enough crack to keep his Colombian business partners happy even though they'd so far failed to find Audrey Lockhart.

The Mexicans were tough competition, and together with the Dominicans pretty much controlled New York and much of the Eastern Seaboard's drug supply. The DEA were concentrating on watching the old shipping routes—the mules, the tricked out vehicles crossing from Mexico, or coming in via the thousands of miles of unguarded Canadian border. They weren't looking at highly respectable businesses shipping manufactured goods around the world.

He called his PA and had her book dinner at a fancy restaurant for tonight. Life had to go on as normal, which is exactly what he had to pretend it was.

His burner phone rang. He answered but said nothing. She'd taught him well.

After a few moments Tracey Williams spoke, "She's in the wind."

Shit. His fist tightened. Audrey couldn't get away. He'd

spent too many years plotting his scheme to fail now. "She's wanted for murder," he said. "How far can she get?"

"Well, that depends on who's helping her and how lucky they are."

Something in her tone made his pulse jump. Tracey was smart and bloodthirsty. He'd discovered her true identity years ago and had been using her for his own ends ever since. She was in love with him and thought they'd be together one day. He was careful to perpetuate the myth.

"You know who she's with?" he asked.

"Yes." The word was careful. She was always careful.

"But you don't know where they are," he concluded.

"It's only a matter of time before I find out."

He was sick and tired of waiting. Audrey should have died years ago. He uncurled his fingers slowly and looked at his computer screen. The screensaver showed two girls, Audrey and Rebecca, grinning at the camera. It was taken the same month Rebecca had been shot dead in the street. His mouth went dry and a quiet rage filled him. "I want this finished."

"It's not a problem."

It was his damn problem. He rapped his knuckles on the desk. "Do it." He hung up and stared out of the window. The sooner Audrey Lockhart joined Rebecca six feet under the better, just as she should have done five years ago.

CHAPTER SEVEN

T HE PEOPLE WHO'D told him he was a jackass and had his head up his ass may have had a point. Right now Killion would barter just about anything to rewind his choices and take his pretty little frog geek to a real hospital with real doctors. For the past thirty-six hours he'd done nothing but fight to keep her alive.

The water was icy cold as he climbed into the enormous bathtub with his arms full of delirious female. A female who'd just spiked a temp of 105 F. He knew there was a risk of cardiac arrest from what he was about to do, but it was the only thing he could think of to stop her brain from being fried. He eased into the freezing depths and felt his balls retract to the point of no return.

"Holy mother trucker." *Goodbye manhood, it was fun while it lasted.* He gritted his teeth as the water climbed higher, creeping closer to the top of the tub, almost to the edge but not overflowing. Audrey's head rested on his shoulder, lolling in a way he didn't like. He did not want her to die.

They were both naked. It was easier this way and she was too out of it to give a shit. Anyway, his dick was now a worthless icy nub that would probably never recover from this experience, which served him right for believing he could handle everything himself. He shivered but Audrey's skin sizzled to the touch. He'd run out of IV antibiotics four hours ago, so he'd crushed up tablets and put them on her tongue. Now all he could do was keep her hydrated and try to keep her body temperature within the normal range—normal for raging fever, anyway.

"Don't die," he whispered in her ear, hugging her closer and trying to ignore the fact he had an unobstructed view of her naked breasts. He'd taped plastic over her wound and was careful not to disturb that area.

He wasn't an asshole, but he wasn't blind, and he didn't know whether to be grateful or horrified when his dick stirred. At least it hadn't snapped off down there.

What the hell had he been thinking? Playing God with someone's life? But no matter how much he berated himself he knew it had been the only choice.

"Please don't die." He already had a village full of dead people on his conscience. He couldn't take any more. He stroked the hair off her forehead. Then picked up her wrist and searched for her pulse near the delicate blue veins. Fast, racing, scaring the shit out of him.

He pressed his lips to her temple; she was still searing hot while his teeth were starting to hammer. She let out a little moan and started to twist in his arms. He held her tighter.

"Come on, Aud. Fight this. Stay alive and if you're innocent I swear to God I'll do everything in my power to get you out of this mess."

After another five minutes, his arms were shaking so badly he was worried he wouldn't be able to lift her out if he waited any longer. He pulled the plug with his right foot and clambered awkwardly to his feet using his elbows for purchase.

He found a big fluffy towel and wrapped it carefully

around the woman in his arms. Barely five-two and yet she was hanging in there valiantly, fighting for life with everything she possessed. She reminded him of his grandmother—diminutive, but feisty, just like he'd told her when he'd had her bound on her kitchen floor and she'd still gone for his balls.

He laid her on the bed and grabbed another towel, using it to squeeze the water out of her hair, then patted her dry, doing his damnedest not to think about the fact she was a living breathing woman. He removed the plastic covering her injury and examined the jagged wound closely. It was healing nicely. There was nothing weird or sexual about his actions—he was trying to keep her alive. Even so, as soon as she was dry he grabbed a baggy T-shirt that belonged to the owner of the house and eased it over Audrey's head and arms—no easy feat—and adjusted the sheet to make her decent.

He'd never been offended by anyone who wanted to walk around naked, but that was a choice, and right now Audrey didn't have a choice about anything that was happening to her.

He dried himself off and pulled on boxers from his duffel bag. A rattling noise startled him, and he realized Audrey was shivering so badly her teeth chattered. Shit, had he cooled her down too much too fast or was this a natural progression of the fever? He had no clue. He stood there stupidly wondering what the hell to do. Then he crawled into the big ass bed, wrapped his body around her much smaller one, warming her as best he could. She burrowed back against him, a perfect fit.

"Come on, Aud. You can do this, baby."

She trembled in his arms, and he found his eyes slowly drifting shut, his brain finally dis-engaging from the craziness of the last three days. Sleep came, surrounded by soft white sheets and the pure clean scent of a woman. It didn't even matter that she might be a cold-hearted killer; he just wanted her to live.

————————————

TRACEY WILLIAMS HAD traveled back to the States, heading for Patrick Killion's last known address though she wasn't stupid enough to break into the place. A man like Killion would be prepared for intruders and probably wouldn't leave anything useful around anyway. As far as she could discover the guy had no family. He'd just been spawned one day for the sole purpose of ruining her life.

She sat in her hotel and had been scouring the news coming out of South and Central America, looking for clues as to where Killion and Lockhart might be. She stared again at one news report that made her senses tingle. A large oil tanker approaching the Panama Canal from the Caribbean had reportedly been hijacked a couple of days prior and the hijackers had threatened to ram into the gates of the canal unless the Panamanians paid a fifty-million dollar ransom. Peanuts compared to the cost of shutting down that shipping channel for even a few days. Panama had apparently worked with Colombia to retake the vessel and—so sad, too bad—all the hijackers had been killed during the liberation.

Wouldn't want any would-be terrorists thinking this was a smart idea.

But the thing was, Panama wasn't usually that chummy with the Colombians and the situation rang alarm bells. She picked up the phone and called a contact, Peter. They made small talk and arranged to meet for a drink while she was in town, then got down to business. "Can you get me details on the company used in the rescue of that oil tanker near Panama?"

Her questions wouldn't seem too outlandish. The company she worked for shipped billions of dollars of goods around the world annually. Piracy was a big deal.

There was a long pause as Peter accessed information. "It was an outfit called 'Penny Fan Solutions.'"

She felt like she was missing something. "I don't suppose you know who owns it?"

She heard tapping. "There's a shell company, but," more tapping, "As far as I can tell it's registered to some guy called Logan Masters."

She leaned back in her chair and stared at the ceiling with a smile on her face. She should have known. Killion turned to his old SAS pals to get him out of Colombia. She rolled her eyes at herself for taking this long to figure it out. Had he taken Lockhart with him? Of course he had. If she weren't with him he wouldn't need covert ops.

"Anything else you need?" Peter asked.

"Yes, actually." She leaned forward in her chair again. "Do you know if they flew straight from Colombia to the tanker?" This was a bit of a weird question, but she'd make it worth his while.

A moment of silence before he said, "No. They approached the tanker from a US naval frigate based in the Caribbean. Hmmm."

She waited, nerves plucking like guitar strings. Would Killion have boarded a naval ship with a wanted fugitive? Possibly, if he knew the captain. That would make Lockhart virtually untouchable.

"I'm looking at some satellite data we had on aircraft in

the region. We focused extra resources on it after the ship was jacked. Looks like the helicopter made a detour north before heading to the frigate. Maybe refueling or picking someone up?"

Or dropping someone off.

"Can you tell me where it went?"

"Tiny island also owned by a private security company but this one based in DC—Cramer, Parker and Gray. Security Consultants—sounds more like a law firm. I'm obviously in the wrong business."

She laughed. "No kidding. I owe you."

Peter sent her the coordinates of the island. "See you soon."

"Looking forward to it." She thanked him and put down the phone and punched the air. The guy wasn't great in bed, but he gave good information and he'd always been kind to her, unlike certain other people she could mention. She usually had to get him drunk because he was squeamish about his wife, but she never put pressure on him and always made it about old times and a bit of harmless fun. She needed to keep him on her side. Sure she could blackmail him, but dinner and blowjobs were a lot less effort.

By keeping a broad perspective she'd narrowed down Killion's exact location even though he thought he was so clever. He was predictable in the fact he used his friends and connections rather than striking out on his own. She looked up the island on Google Earth. Completely isolated and vulnerable. She wished she could be the one to do this job, but it was logistically impossible. And who knew what a Colombian drug lord would do to an active CIA operative? She winced. Whatever it was, it wouldn't be pretty. *C'est la vie.*

She picked up the phone and passed on the information to her partner who was in boss mode and obviously worried by the level of incompetence being shown by his Colombian friends.

He didn't ask when she'd be home.

Pissed, she tossed down her pen and picked up her purse. She was about to go shopping and buy something nice as a treat for herself, and he was going to pay the bill. Diamonds, she decided, for all the men she had to screw and assholes she had to kill. She deserved something pretty, something eternal, something that reflected her true value, even when the rest of the world was determined to take her for granted.

CHAPTER EIGHT

A UDREY'S FEVER HAD broken a few hours ago, and now she slept peacefully as Killion watched from a nearby chair. Her skin was pale and she looked about fifteen as she lay there with her dark hair spread over the snow-white pillow, dark lashes draping the heavy circles under her eyes. He'd barely left her side over the last two days except to scope out supplies, make sure there wasn't any indication of where they were or whom this place belonged to. He didn't want any blowback from this operation if Audrey Lockhart turned out to be the assassin he'd initially suspected.

It was nighttime with the moon silvery bright in the navy sky. He stared through a picture window where the orb was reflected in the calm Caribbean ocean.

The place was paradise. Perfection. Tranquil, indolent, and rich. The house was built into a hillside on the leeward side of an island about a mile wide by two miles long. It had its own beach, its own helipad and according to all sources of information he'd located and removed, belonged to someone called Haley Cramer, one of Alex Parker's partners in his exclusive security business.

The house had running water, electricity from solar panels, and an emergency back-up generator. The pantry was full and the freezers well stocked with everything from milk to steak. The main deck had a fantastic sunset view Killion hadn't yet been able to enjoy.

It was *Nim's Island* on steroids.

He went and grabbed a fresh T-shirt from his duffel. His gear was here in the same room because that had been the easiest way to nurse her and also get some rest. Thinking about it, she was the first woman he'd slept with in over a decade. It had felt surprisingly good to hold someone in his arms. Of course, she'd been comatose.

His usual encounters with the opposite sex—outside work—were more of the hit and run variety. It was for their own good. He was upfront about what he wanted, some fun, a little downtime, and no expectations beyond some naked tangoing of whatever variety the woman preferred. He didn't have a normal job. He didn't have a normal life. Nor could he advertise his trade to excuse his bad behavior. His life was a series of secrets stacked upon secrets like a thousand cobwebs, each layer intricate and discrete. Build enough lies and eventually even you forgot where you came from—and it was better that way. It protected the few people in the world he cared about.

He yawned widely. Logan and Noah had helped him carry Audrey and their gear up a series of steep steps from the helipad. Killion and Audrey were stranded on the island until someone arrived in a chopper or they flagged down a passing boat. Great for privacy, not so great in an emergency, as he'd discovered about a day too late.

Still, he was pretty sure she was over the worst. She looked like she'd probably survive. Not that it mattered. She was just a suspect. A "detainee" until he said otherwise. His hands clenched into fists. He eyed the sweet bow of her lips and reminded himself not to get played, else he might find himself drinking arsenic with his next cup of joe.

Exhausted, he rested his eyes for a moment.

When his body jolted awake in the leather recliner hours later, the room was bathed in weak golden sunlight. He didn't know what had woken him until he glanced at the bed and found a pair of violet-blue eyes staring straight at him. He'd never seen eyes that color before, like some sort of exotic flower.

"Hey. You're awake." Relief flooded his veins.

"Patrick." Audrey's voice was scratchy, her smile pale and tired. She touched her forehead. "I feel like I went ten rounds in a UFC cage."

His lips kicked into a grin. "Me, too."

A line cut between her brows. "You've been looking after me?"

Killion nodded.

"Just you?" She glanced around in confusion and then down at the clothes she was wearing. Her eyes widened as they cut back to his.

"Just me. And, yep, I've seen you naked—thank you. I did not close my eyes, but I did behave as a perfect gentleman even though there were no witnesses." He crossed a finger over his heart. If errant thoughts had entered his mind it wasn't his fault. It was biology. If anyone understood that it would be Audrey. "Hey, we even slept together, but you managed to control yourself."

She nodded, looking more resigned than unhappy, then glanced around the huge bedroom with the flowing net drapes that opened out onto a wide deck.

"Where are we?" She blinked as if trying to focus. He'd

forgotten she usually wore reading glasses. He knew from his research she was a little long-sighted—just enough to look cute when she squinted.

"Somewhere safe." He leaned over and put his hand on her forehead as he'd done countless times over the last few days. This time she pulled away and her eyes dilated—definitely back in control of her faculties.

He felt a pang of unexpected loss. *Idiot.*

Now the hard stuff began.

The key to a successful interrogation was to understand the emotional needs of the subject and to relieve the fear they felt when being questioned—not to increase it. He had to establish a rapport and figure out the motivation of the person he was questioning. A good interrogator made the subject want to tell him what he wanted to know.

So how did he get Audrey to want to tell him what he needed to know?

And what if she didn't know anything?

She shifted uncomfortably. He'd been staring at her stupidly, trying to figure out a way to dig inside that brain of hers.

"Do you want to sit up?" he asked, stalling for time.

She nodded and he reached over, grabbed the pillow he'd been using and slipped it behind her upper back. Her hair brushed his hand—soft and tangled. He already knew he was going to miss the satiny texture of it as it sifted through his fingers, and he was going to have to compartmentalize those thoughts to get his job done.

"How's your side feeling?" The stab wound had healed nicely, forming a thick scab over her skin. The two stitches had held up well and he'd kept it clean and dry.

"It's a lot better than it was. Sore," she admitted. "But not painful."

"It healed okay, but you came down with a fever. You seem a lot better now."

She nodded.

"So why did Hector Sanchez try to kill you?"

She shook her head. He passed her some water, suddenly aware of the sound of the air conditioner kicking on, and her small hands wrapping around the cup. Her nails were short, and she wore a gold signet ring on the pinkie of her right hand. Her cheeks hollowed out as she drank through the straw. She'd lost weight during her battle with the infection and there hadn't been much of her to start with. He didn't like it. Didn't like the idea of her suffering, didn't like how frail she looked. Even sitting up seemed to tire her.

He didn't like that he didn't like it.

"It must have something to do with the attack from the night before." Her voice regained some of that huskiness he'd noticed during the talk she'd given on frogs. He'd forgotten the effect her slight Kentucky accent had on him.

"The one you reported to the cops?"

She nodded.

"No police report with your name on it was filed that night."

"What?" Her surprise looked genuine. No micro expressions of deception.

"I checked," he added.

"How?" She frowned.

He shrugged. "I asked around."

"But why wouldn't they file the report? I was with them for *two* hours."

No record of that either.

Her confusion turned to anger. Righteous indignation rising to the surface with every breath. "The caretaker warned me the cops might not take me seriously."

"Can you remember the detectives' names?"

Her lips were dry and cracked as she pinched them together. He passed her the salve he'd already applied several times and she took it with a cautious expression. "Thank you."

He avoided looking at her mouth when she put it on. Obviously he was suffering from whatever the reverse of Stockholm syndrome was, where the captor felt sympathy for their captive. His subjects were usually stinky, ugly, hairy guys, much easier to detach from, but he hadn't rescued and repeatedly saved them from death, nor bathed with them naked—thank God. Maybe this was a biological thing—his wiggly DNA wanting a chance to divide and conquer.

As long as he recognized the issues he could deal with them, and use them to his advantage.

She frowned as she struggled to remember. "One guy was called Ortez, he gave me a card which is in my purse in the lab."

Or more likely in evidence—or destroyed—but he didn't tell her that. Interestingly a detective called Patrice Ortez had been on duty that night, alongside a guy called Diego Torres. Alex Parker had gotten the names of all the detectives working in the area, now he'd hopefully be able to pull the right phone records. Apparently it wasn't as easy as it sounded—and it sure as hell wasn't legal.

Audrey didn't know about her dead student yet and he wasn't about to enlighten her. He was saving that information for when he might need leverage, or to knock her emotionally off balance. Yep, he was a real prince.

He crossed his arms and leaned back in the chair. "Like I said, nothing was filed. There is no report."

"I don't know if they're corrupt or incompetent." She put the glass on the bedside table. "I should get to an American police station immediately and tell them exactly what happened. Can you call someone for me?"

"No." He let his eyes get hard. It was time to get down to brass tacks while she was still weak from her illness and vulnerable from the uncertainty of her situation. "Time for the truth, Audrey. I know who you are."

She blinked twice. "I didn't realize who I was was ever in question." Her tired features pinched further. "I want to make a phone call and talk to someone official." She pushed the bedclothes off and swung her legs carefully over the edge of the bed.

It took every ounce of self-control to force himself to sprawl back in his chair and let her struggle. "Knock yourself out."

As she placed her toes on the sheepskin rug she tugged the T-shirt as low as it would go—mid-thigh. Her legs wobbled as she pushed to her feet and staggered to the doorway that led to the deck. The fresh sea breeze swept through the room and cleared out the scent of the sickroom, but the effort was obviously too much for her. She sagged against the doorframe as she looked outside. "Where are we?"

He moved to stand behind her. She swayed and he scooped her up when she would have collapsed to the floor. She grabbed onto his shirt, fingers curling tight over his heart.

"Just tell me who you work for and I'll get us both out of here." Up close her eyes were almost lavender. The fire in them told him exactly what she thought of answering his questions when he wouldn't answer any of hers, but she surprised him.

"I work for the U of L and hold adjunct status at the university in Bogota. My boss is the head of department, Professor Paula Renault. Now I've told you what you wanted to know. Get me out of here."

Killion shook his head and carried her out onto the deck and spun them in a slow circle. "See this?" She clutched his shirt tighter, holding on as if dizzy. "There's no one here except us. There's no one to talk to except me, and we're not going anywhere until you tell me the truth about who you work for." The sky was so blue and the sun so strong Audrey tucked her face into his chest, and he hated how the action affected him. His voice grew softer. "I'm all for hanging out until you tell me who hired you. But you aren't fooling me. I know what you did. I know who you killed, and I don't mean good old Hector. So let's cut to the chase and get this over with."

Her mouth dropped open as she looked up at him.

"Hey, I'm not judging you." He tilted his head and gave her his best smile.

"You know who I *killed* but you're not *judging* me?" She gaped, then took a swipe at his cheek with her open hand.

He easily avoided the blow, and laughed. Mistake. She started to struggle, so he gripped her tighter and returned to the bedroom. He laid her down carefully on the crumpled sheets and leaned over her, staring deep into those indignant eyes.

"I mean it when I say we're not going anywhere until I get the truth."

She opened her mouth to say something and then stopped,

biting her lip in a way that flipped his small brain to the "on" position. No doubt about it, he needed to burn off a little steam in the sex department.

She frowned thoughtfully, as if replaying something in her mind. "Spook."

Uh-oh.

He blanked his features.

"Someone said you were a government spook."

Something a good operative would never call another on. He straightened. "You're mistaken."

"No, I'm not. It was that other guy. The big Brit." Her eyes grew huge. "He thought I was asleep. You're not a tourist at all, are you? You're a spook. A CIA agent." She said it like it was akin to being a child molester. Her pupils flared and she shrank back against the pillows. "What do you want with me? Why have you kidnapped me? I'm a frog biologist, for God's sake."

Boom.

She'd been awake ten minutes and he'd already lost control of this interrogation. Never underestimate smart people. Rather than screw it up further by trying to regain the upper hand, he turned on his heel and left. He didn't bother locking up. There was nowhere for Dr. Audrey Lockhart to go.

———————

AUDREY LAY IN bed with her heart hammering like a hamster on a red-hot wheel. This wasn't a rescue. This was a kidnapping.

As soon as "Patrick" left, Audrey rushed to her feet and headed for the garden doors. She was wearing nothing except a long T-shirt, but if she flashed the neighbors while trying to escape she didn't really care. She had to get away.

Her wound was healing, but she was careful not to jar it as she staggered out onto the balcony. The sun reflected off the surface of the topaz ocean so brightly tears stung her eyes. The house was perched near the top of a steep hillside covered in dense forest. She looked around frantically. There wasn't another house in sight, nor were there any people visible. She thought about shouting for help but didn't want to attract the wrong sort of attention until she knew exactly what she was dealing with.

A wave of wooziness flowed over her and she clutched the railing until it passed. The heat sapped her meager strength and even this short walk to the balcony left her tired and breathless. The deck didn't lead anywhere. There were no steps and nowhere to go unless she wanted to climb thirty feet down a sheer rock face.

Not today. Not any day for that matter.

Surely, if she went out the front door there would be a road and she could flag someone down for help?

One thing was for certain, she wasn't sitting around for the insane government agent to come back with more of his ridiculous accusations. She went to the bedroom door and peeked out along the corridor toward a living room with hardwood floors. The house was constructed with beautiful clean lines of pale wood and white-washed walls and if it wasn't for the fact she was being held captive when she should have been at work, she might have paused to admire the architecture of this tropical paradise.

"Patrick" wasn't anywhere to be seen. If he was a spook—and there had been no reason to lie as they'd thought she was unconscious at the time—she doubted Patrick was his real name. It felt wrong not even knowing his name when he held her life in his hands, but even more disorienting was not knowing where on the planet she was being held. She didn't even know what day it was. Did her parents know she was missing? She hoped not. Her mother would freak. Her mom and dad were already run ragged keeping Sienna from going off the rails and looking after their grandson. It wasn't fair to put them through anything else.

Using the wall for support, she made her way to an airy open-plan living room and staggered past a large center island that marked off the kitchen. It was empty, thank goodness. There were huge seascapes on the walls, but no personal pictures anywhere. Was this a rental cottage? She couldn't imagine it was a CIA safe house, but if it was, it certainly explained her taxes.

Her head started to pound. What was she doing here? She had a busy schedule, experiments to run. Students to teach. Frogs to care for. Things like this didn't happen to her—then she remembered her friend, Rebecca. They'd been walking home from a club one night and a mugging had turned into murder when their attacker had pulled a gun.

So things like this *did* happen to her.

Maybe she was jinxed.

A cell phone sat on the living room coffee table and she snatched it up, turning it on and finding to her amazement it actually had a signal. A toilet flushed somewhere in the house. The sound spurred her into motion.

She was out of breath and sweating by the time she reached the front door. The elaborate electronic lock surprised her, but the door opened easily. She eased the solid oak door quietly closed behind her and dialed nine-one-one. The call rang endlessly and she gave up and dialed her parents instead. She looked out at a thick canopy of trees and frowned in confusion. No road. No vehicle. Not even a bicycle to borrow. Where was this place?

Her call again went unanswered.

She tried their cells. Maybe her parents were at the police station filling out forms about their missing daughter. Maybe they were printing flyers or posting on social media requesting help in finding her. Frustrated, she hung up and dialed Devon. If anyone had the wherewithal to track her whereabouts it was her ex, or his and Rebecca's father, Gabriel, who was very fond of her.

Again the call rang endlessly, seeming to echo incessantly over the fiber optics network of the world.

A steep path led down toward the beach. Even looking at it sucked the energy from her marrow, then she remembered she wasn't a guest here, she wasn't on vacation. Instead, she was the prisoner of a delusional, if handsome, lunatic. She took a step forward and found herself once again swept up into strong arms. With her free hand she grabbed onto his shirt for balance, recognizing his scent before she even saw his face.

He plucked the cell out of her fingers and pocketed the phone. "For the love of Christ, you've been awake fifteen minutes and you're already a giant pain in my ass."

She fought to get out of his grip, but she had no strength left. Patrick had about seventy pounds of muscle mass on her, plus he hadn't almost died from a fever.

"You're going to hurt yourself and put your recovery back another week. I've already wasted enough time trying to keep you alive," he bit out.

The callousness of that comment hurt. "I didn't plan to get stabbed."

He strode through the house and dumped her on the bed. She lay there too exhausted to move. Tears pricked her eyes and she turned away, not wanting him to see her so vulnerable. She'd been kidnapped by a rogue agent who'd mistakenly thought she'd killed someone—which should have been laughable except here she was being held captive in a strange house at an unknown location. He'd been watching her. Following her. Stalking her. How else had he been on hand to "save" her? Sure, he'd nursed her for days and probably saved her life, but who knew what else he'd done when she'd been unconscious. A rush of revulsion shot through her. She adjusted her shirt to cover more of her thighs.

His eyes narrowed as if reading her thoughts, a touch of temper spiking those cool depths.

"Just tell me who hired you, Doc, and I'll arrange transportation back to the mainland ASAP. Getting you out of my hair will be a pleasure, believe me."

They were on an island? She tried not to give away her surprise or unease. "And what happens when I can't tell you what you want to know?"

He stared at her with a hard expression. Nothing like the nice guy who'd slept in the chair beside her bed earlier. There was nothing *nice* in his expression and a little shiver of apprehension slipped down her spine as she realized this guy had total control over every aspect of her life.

The moisture in her mouth evaporated as her fear increased. "What are you going to do if I don't tell you what you want to know?"

"Oh, you'll tell me eventually."

And despite his default laid-back persona, she believed him. This man was not some beach bum, surfer dude. The harsh set of his features told her he'd done things and seen things that would make her cover her eyes in horror. The trouble was she didn't know the answers to the questions he posed.

She reached for her water but her hand was shaking too much to actually pick up the glass and she almost knocked it over. He grabbed it and held it to her lips. She reluctantly took a sip wondering why she trusted him on one level and thought he was dangerous on another.

The water eased her dry throat. His face was only inches from hers, so close she could see the white gold of his eyelashes. She pushed the cup away. "Are you really CIA?" He said nothing and she could read nothing from his expression. "Are you a spy?"

His lips tightened. "I'm not a spy."

"So CIA, but not a spy. What do you do for them?" Her breath hitched as she remembered all the times the CIA had been on the news in the last few years. "Were you one of the people searching for Bin Laden? An analyst?"

He shook his head and put the cup on the side table. "It's classified."

She'd followed the hearings of the Senate committee and knew some of what the CIA had done in the name of democracy and freedom. "Oh, my God." She sucked in a breath. "Did you torture detainees?"

His eyes were icy cold now and he didn't answer. *Shocker.* Instead he said, "Just tell me who hired you and you won't have to worry about any of that."

She shivered, but refused to be cowed. "Are you going to

waterboard me if I don't tell you what you want to hear?"

A half smile played on his lips, a smile that hinted at knowledge, experience, and a measure of absurdity. "I already tried that in the shower. Didn't work."

Her eyes flashed to his in alarm. He'd showered with her?

"Hey, it wasn't that bad. I kept my pants on. Although I admit to being naked in the bathtub because I ran out of dry clothes." He was searching her face now as if looking for her sense of humor, but she was so beyond finding this situation funny.

"Who do you think I killed?" she asked. It sounded so ridiculous.

One cocky brow rose. "You mean apart from Hector Sanchez?"

Her hand flew to her mouth. She'd forgotten she had actually killed a man. Nausea roiled in her stomach. But Patrick was trying to rattle her, determined not to answer her questions even though he demanded she answer his. She'd killed a man while fighting for her life—it wasn't the same as being a killer.

"Is your name really Patrick?"

"That's classified."

God, he was insufferable. "I *need* to know."

"What part of classified don't you understand?"

"And what part of decent human being don't you understand?" she snapped back.

He flinched. A chink in the armor. A hole in the wall. It wasn't much, but it proved he was at least human. She had to keep him on the defensive.

"You're one of the people who tortured prisoners during the Iraq War, aren't you? How'd that make you feel, Patrick?

Like a big man?"

His lip curled. "How'd it make you feel lying safe and snug in your own bed while others sacrificed themselves for you? Easy to blame the foot soldiers when the smoke clears, isn't it?"

"You can't just ignore the law."

He pointed his finger at her. "Trust me, I know more about the law than you've even begun to process." A furious light shone in his eyes. "And if I deny 'torturing detainees,' who are you going to condemn next? The Counterintelligence Officers? The military interrogators? The drone pilots? Who gets the blame and who gets the credit?" He paced. "It was a shambles after 9/11. Utter chaos. We were all just doing our jobs with fuck-all guidance from back home except to make sure there was no imminent threat to the American Homeland. And in case you didn't notice, we did a pretty bang up job of that at the time."

She narrowed her gaze. "It doesn't make it right."

"It's hard to play the game with one hand tied behind your back."

"Tell that to the people you tortured." Audrey believed in right and wrong. There was no moral ambiguity here.

"You think terrorists follow the Geneva Convention when they're sawing off aid workers' heads?" He leaned closer and she wanted to pull away but she held her ground. "You think they worry about being condemned for war crimes when they make women and young girls their sex slaves and rape them, repeatedly, until they're either dead or pregnant? Those bastards deserve a bullet in the head at point-blank range for what they do, not a fucking lawyer." The muscle flexing in his jaw mesmerized her, as did the masculine scent of his skin.

He drew back and lowered his voice. "You know the safest place for any terrorist? FBI or CIA custody. And they know it. They aren't scared of us because we might 'torture' them." He jammed his hand into his too long hair. "They're laughing their fucking asses off because they know we can't touch them, not the way we'd like to."

"Unless you whisk them away to some Black Camp location." She looked around pointedly.

He snorted. "You're out of your mind, lady. This is nothing like a Black Camp. But keep up the denial and maybe you'll get to see the real deal—and I'd strongly advise against that option." He clamped his lips shut. He must have figured he'd said too much.

The sudden silence buzzed with anger. She'd rattled him, which had been her intent, but she liked him more for his honest reaction than for the annoyingly honed veneer of cynical amusement. Then his expression changed and his eyes drifted slowly over her body. She tugged the hem of the T-shirt lower.

She glared back, recognizing the predatory gleam in his eyes. "Touch me and I'll scream," she warned.

"Oh, you'll scream all right." His grin was sexy rather than threatening, which probably wasn't the effect he was going for. Her nipples tightened and her breath caught with a shot of anticipation. No doubt about it, the guy looked like he knew his way around the pleasure spots of the female body. She hated herself for letting him get to her.

A flicker of self-satisfaction touched his lips, and she realized he'd purposely turned the tables on her once again.

"Is this how you normally get women into bed?" she muttered irritably.

"Trust me, it's not something I usually have to work at." His expression became one of supreme self-confidence. "Hey, don't get me wrong. Under normal circumstances I'd do you." Those blue eyes of his were boring into her again, trying to upset her and doing a hell of a job of it. "You're female and not dead, and frankly I'm not that fussy. But I like my women willing and enthusiastic, and preferably not with a killer frog in their pocket."

Killer frog? Was that his idea of a joke? Considering how Hector Sanchez had died it wasn't funny. If she'd had the energy she'd have smacked him. "You've got some nerve, you know that? Why don't you run along and poke bamboo under someone's fingernails."

"Good tip. Anything else you'd like to pass on?"

"I hate you." She hugged her knees to her chest, but judging from the way his eyes widened and nostrils flared she'd flashed more than she'd intended. She glared. So what? He'd already seen her naked.

He looked at the ceiling and muttered, "If anyone is a professional torturer around here it would be you."

She licked her lips nervously.

He watched her mouth and then met her gaze. "You can play the seduction game if you want, Aud. Despite what I said before I'm totally up for it. But it won't change the outcome of our time together. Don't say I didn't warn you."

She let out a choked laugh. She'd been stabbed, kidnapped, and comatose for days, and she was playing the seduction game? *Seduction game?* Was he out of his ever-loving mind? She looked like death. Her hair was a wild scraggly mess. She hadn't brushed her teeth in days.

"I'm keeping you here until you tell me who hired you."

He went over and picked up a duffel bag she hadn't noticed from the top of a chest of drawers. "You and me are stuck together until I get the information I need, and that's true even if you force me to have sex with you."

Her mouth dropped open.

He did *not* just say that.

He thought she was trying to seduce her way out of this? Who the hell was she supposed to be, Mata Hari? Red-hot rage surged through her like molten lava. She grabbed the water cup and threw it at him, but it was plastic and fell short. She was so angry her vision blurred and her jaw locked. In the past she'd never wished anyone ill but if he stuck around that could change.

His expression had regained its annoying arrogance and that told her he had her back exactly where he wanted her, acting on instinct, not logic. Not asking him the tough questions.

She took a calming breath. "You're making a big mistake, *Patrick*. I'm an American citizen. People will be looking for me. My parents, the university I work for."

He weighed her words for a moment. "They'll look for a while. Then they'll forget all about you. That's the reality. Trust me, I know."

He turned and left. This time she heard the lock turn.

CHAPTER NINE

KILLION WAS PISSED. He was pissed that he was pissed. Audrey Lockhart had knocked him sideways. First, the expression on her face when she'd guessed he was CIA, like he was some sort of sexual deviant, rather than a respected and upstanding member of the intelligence community. Then she judged him and all his co-workers by leaping to conclusions about the kind of work he did.

"Fuck."

He went to the window and stared out at the miles of glistening water. His job was classified. He didn't talk about it, period. Not even to defend himself. But he wasn't a whipping boy who'd stand around letting others take potshots at him, either. He was a decorated patriot who fought for his country in a covert war that never ended. This was what he did, this was what he was good at. What the hell would he do with himself if he wasn't picking up bad guys and squeezing them for information?

Audrey Lockhart had no right to judge him. Sure, she'd suffered. Being attacked and nearly dying wasn't a picnic. But if she'd murdered Ted Burger then certain risks had to be anticipated.

If...

His problem was this ever-growing tendril of doubt.

Doubt about her involvement. Doubt in himself. She wasn't behaving like an assassin should, on any level. She wasn't following any of the unwritten rules. She was just being her wide-eyed ingénue self and if it was an act it was a damn good one.

Interrogation required the same skills as a good case officer handling an asset—except an asset was a willing participant whereas a detainee was generally pissed. But it was an intense relationship where trust was critical.

When interrogating detainees in Abu Ghraib—after the terrible events that had *preceded* his arrival in the country—he hadn't worried about uncertainty. He'd been sent to glean as much information from key prisoners as possible. Contrary to what everyone thought and accused him of on a regular basis, he hadn't used "enhanced interrogation techniques." He hadn't needed to.

His hands weren't clean. He didn't condone torture, but he'd been complicit in watching other CIA and military personnel question suspects and he'd seen them go hard on one captive in the early days of the Iraq war. He'd been too green to know better, too low on the rungs to alter the course of events, but it hadn't taken long to figure out that it wasn't the way he wanted to uphold his vow.

At the time the operators had felt justified. They'd been searching for information on a particular high-value target who'd been on everyone's shit list and they hadn't been shy about extracting it. The operators hadn't cared about rules of engagement, they'd been desperate, believing the US was under imminent threat. They'd gained the information they required and Killion had no doubt they'd saved lives. The operators had fast-tracked the interrogation process, but it could have gone either way. The real key lay in the fact they'd scooped up the right person off the street, someone who'd known the relevant information.

Killion might not believe in torture, but he wasn't about to condemn the people on the ground who'd been part of the most ill thought out military campaign since the trench warfare of WWI. Actually, no, that wasn't fair. The campaign itself had been masterful. It was the lack of planning for the aftermath that had been a goddamn disaster.

Despite the early hour, he poured himself two-fingers of bourbon then hunted in the freezer, pulling out a large steak and finding potatoes in the bottom of the fridge. Audrey probably wouldn't eat much, but cooking eased his mind and he hadn't eaten a decent meal since Logan's stew a couple of days ago.

No matter what Killion threw at Audrey she never dropped out of character—that of being an innocent biologist caught up in something she didn't understand. She'd gotten him to spill his guts. Not operational details, but he usually kept his mouth shut, period.

She pushed his buttons.

It would be hard to break her—mainly because he liked her too much. Maybe he should pass her over to someone who could do the job they were being paid to do.

His phone rang. The island had its own satellite connection. He checked the number. Jed Brennan. He'd been expecting the call.

"How's the va-cay?" Jed asked.

"About the same as yours was before Christmas, except for the getting laid by a good-looking woman part."

Jed had helped Vivi Vincent and her young son escape

from terrorists during a mall attack last year. All three of them had come close to death and Jed could have lost his career over some of the choices he'd made. Thanks to Professor Lockhart, Killion understood Jed's decisions a little better now. Not the playing happy families bit, but the running-and-hiding and assessing your position part.

"Win some, lose some." Jed laughed.

"Smug bastard." Killion looked out the window at the spectacular view, but all he saw was Audrey's pretty eyes turning a distinct shade of disappointed. He jammed his fingers into his hair. "Honestly, I'd rather be stranded in Wisconsin eating raw turnips."

"Because that's what we eat. I take it she's still alive?"

"Alive and well. But now I'm tempted to smother her with a pillow."

"I'm sure she feels the same way."

"She practically accused me of being a pervert." Killion complained as he put the steak in the microwave and programmed the defrost option.

"You *are* a pervert."

Killion laughed. "Yeah, but *she* doesn't know that. I've been the perfect gentleman." He remembered her naked body and the memory was enough to make him hard. Dammit. At the time he'd been strictly professional, but now that she was recovering his subconscious seemed to have decided she was fair game. Not what he needed, although as he'd told the woman herself, he'd use it if he had to.

Big sacrifice—he rolled his eyes at himself. "So, who'd she call?" The cell phone had been left lying around as bait but she'd gotten to it way faster than he'd anticipated. Parker was tracing any numbers she called, though she'd been blocked from actually making contact.

"Nine-one-one, her parents, and an ex-boyfriend."

Killion didn't like the unpleasant surprise of the latter. He hadn't thought there was anyone special in her life from the background checks he'd run on her. "Who?"

"Devon Brightman."

She'd dated Devon for a few months more than four years ago. Why call him?

"Interestingly Devon's father was a friend of Senator Burger's. So we're going to look into him further."

They finally had a tangible link between Audrey and Burger, even if it was a tenuous one. So why did he feel disappointed?

"What's the plan?" Jed asked. "You letting her sweat?"

Killion thought about the way her damp hair had stuck to her forehead when she'd been delirious with fever and closed his eyes. Crap. He'd really thought she was going to die for a while there. He hadn't liked the idea. Not at all. "I don't think sweating it out will work with this one. She's pissed. Already figured out I was CIA."

"But you still think she's innocent?" Jed sounded dubious.

"She's whip-smart and overheard a conversation she shouldn't have. Put two and two together. It was sloppy. Nothing I can do about it. What's the other news?"

"The Colombians have issued an international warrant for her arrest for the murder of the student."

Ah, shit. Audrey was fucked.

"So what *is* the next move?" Jed asked again.

Killion heard the uncertainty in Jed's voice. Did the guy really expect him to make her hold a stress position when she could barely walk ten steps? Maybe force the truth out of her by threatening the people she loved? He'd done plenty of things he wasn't proud of but he couldn't do anything like that to Audrey—and she sure as hell better not figure that out or he was screwed.

Bottom line was, he'd never physically hurt a woman. He wasn't about to start now. "What's the profile of your typical hired killer?" he asked instead.

"You actually want me to do what I'm paid for?"

"You're talking to a spook who is playing nursemaid to a sick woman, so stop whining."

"Murder-for-hire. There's no general psychological pro-file. Despite what you see on TV most murderers for hire aren't that bright. They don't cover their tracks, they brag about their kills and then they get caught. They tend to be men, younger than the so-called mastermind and often have criminal records. Whoever killed Burger doesn't fall into that category. Firstly, the killer was female, which is unusual. It was more like a targeted political assassination and the killer was a professional—probably government trained?"

But which government?

"Could the killer be cartel?" Killion was searching for a way for this to make sense.

"Sure, but I don't see them training a woman like Lock-hart. I mean, when? Where?"

Frazer's team had gone through Audrey's background in intricate detail. She hadn't had time to fit assassin training into her academic schedule. But backgrounds could be faked. The CIA did it every day.

"Maybe they threatened someone she loved?" Parents, sister, nephew?

"Because she just happened to work with the deadliest

119

creature on earth and her former boyfriend's dad was a friend of Senator Burger? Seems like a stretch." Jed paused. "The best bet for finding a killer is usually by looking at the victim. But Burger had so many enemies that doesn't help us."

There was also the five hundred grand in the Caymans registered to an account in Audrey's name, but that could also be a set up. Frankly, Ted Burger had been such a world-class asshole a lot of people would have killed him for free. And surely a woman with a Ph.D. would be smart enough to use a shell company to cover her tracks?

Killion tossed back the rest of his drink. "I need a few more days. Maybe spending time with me will make her so desperate to get out of here she'll confess to everything."

"As good a plan as any."

"Thanks for the ringing endorsement, pal."

"You getting itchy feet?"

Downtime was not something Killion did well. Last time he'd taken time off was for a broken ulna. He'd lasted twelve hours. "I think we're missing something and being purposely misled. Rather than being able to track down information I'm sitting here with my thumb up my ass, playing nursemaid."

"We're working all the angles."

Killion grunted.

"What's the problem?"

Killion poured himself another shot of bourbon. There were too many problems to count. "All the facts point to Audrey."

"And?"

"Even the facts that we know aren't true point to Audrey."

"Like the dead student?"

Who she still didn't know about. "Yeah. And if I hadn't

been Johnny-on-the-spot when Hector tried to off her we'd probably have believed any tale they spun. If they can set that up, maybe they can set up the rest." He stabbed two potatoes with a fork, wrapped them each in tin foil. He didn't know how much Audrey might be able to eat but she had to try to regain her strength—probably so she could verbally beat the shit out of him. "Something about this whole thing isn't adding up." And it bothered him too much to ignore. The microwave dinged for the steak. "Make sure you tell that beautiful interpreter of yours that it's not too late to have a chance with me if she's changed her mind about you."

"You've got more chance of leading the Mars mission."

Killion grinned. Thinking about it, when they first met, Vivi had looked at him the same way Audrey looked at him after she'd realized he wasn't taking her to the cops or letting her go. Like he was something nasty that needed scraped from the sole of her shoe. It was not the usual effect he had on women. Women liked him. He had a smile that promised a good time and the patience to deliver. Apparently Vivi and Audrey were both immune to his charm. Smart ladies.

He said goodbye to Jed and tossed back the rest of his drink. The heat of the liquor warmed his throat and the relaxed feeling it evoked made him want to pour himself another and just get trashed. Instead he checked the steak. He'd need all his faculties to get through the next few days and figure out exactly what information his captive held. Guilty or not, he had a feeling Audrey's life depended on him finding the answers.

AUDREY PUSHED HERSELF up in the bed and blinked herself awake. She'd slept most of the day and felt more refreshed than earlier, less blitzed. Before going to sleep she'd found underwear and a pair of workout shorts in the dresser and borrowed them with a silent apology to the owner.

She needed all her wits to cope with this man and couldn't afford to be distracted by her lack of clothes. He was scary intelligent and not afraid to break the rules to get what he wanted. She wasn't used to dealing with this sort of man on any level, she hadn't even had a boyfriend in eighteen months. Her last long-term relationship had been a disaster when the guy had turned out to be screwing a summer student even though they were dating. Before that had been Devon. It had taken months to realize they were drawn together by loss and grief, and had zero chemistry. Not the healthiest of foundations. She was grateful they were still good friends, especially now that he was dating her sister, but she wished that part of her relationship history had never happened.

Relationships came with too heavy a price and she wasn't willing to pay it anymore. Nowadays, Audrey preferred to be alone.

Why was she thinking about *relationships* and *dating*?

The sound of the lock turning, followed by a knock on the door startled her. Patrick stuck his head in warily as if expecting her to throw something at him again. His hair was a little rumpled as if he'd been napping too. Bed head suited him. She suspected there weren't many situations where the spook didn't look like some purposely ruffled model from a men's cologne ad.

Patrick had said he wasn't fussy about the women he slept with, but she knew the type of women men like him dated.

The beautiful ones, the ones who worked out daily and got their faces airbrushed into place every morning. She rarely even bothered with make-up. Her frogs didn't care.

Why was she thinking about looks? Heat flooded her cheeks and she gripped the sheets. Looks were irrelevant. First chance she got she was going to scream bloody murder to anyone who'd listen.

"Truce?" He was clearly feeling out her mood.

She glared at him then remembered that old saying about catching more flies with honey than vinegar. Plus, she didn't have the energy to fight. She had nothing to lose by putting away her hostility as long as she kept up her guard. "Fine."

"I made dinner."

She hugged her knees tight to her chest. "I'm not hungry."

Beneath an unbuttoned shirt, a rumpled tee stretched over his well-defined chest. She tried not to notice.

"You've gotta eat. Build up your strength before you waste away."

"You sound like my mother." Her poor mother fussing over her sister who'd rather smoke crack than eat a proper meal or look after her two-year-old son. Sadness settled under her ribs. Audrey wasn't big on self-pity, but after being stabbed and abducted—by a helicopter full of black ops soldiers she remembered suddenly—she'd earned a little feel-sorry-for-herself time.

And now it was over. Time to move forward, stop moping and figure a way out of this mess. The only person going to take care of her was her and she'd better start now. She threw back the covers and Patrick took in her new clothes with a carefully blank expression. She was beginning to see he revealed more in those moments when he hid everything, than in the rest of their time together.

"I'm just going to use the bathroom." She went to turn away but a memory stopped her cold. He'd helped her to the bathroom on several occasions, waiting outside the door before helping her back to bed. She glanced back over her shoulder, seeing him differently this time.

He'd taken care of her.

Memories flooded in as she stared at him. The endless sips of cool water. Sponging her brow with a wet cloth. The feeling of flying when he carried her because she was too weak to walk on her own. The tired lines around his eyes were from lack of sleep because he'd been by her side the entire time she'd been sick. The *entire* time.

"It was cold," she said.

A slight crinkle formed between his brows. He didn't understand.

"When you put me in the tub the water was cold…" She swallowed her confusion.

"You were burning up. I didn't know what else to do." From the wary expression in his eyes he thought she was about to get mad again.

She remembered something else. Pressing as close as she could get to a big warm body, and that body wrapping around her until heat suffused her bones and her teeth stopped rattling.

He'd saved her life. For all the wrong reasons, but he had saved her life. Maybe it was a starting point.

"Thank you," she said slowly. "For taking care of me."

He watched her, eyes guarded. Gave her a small nod. "Come on out when you're ready. We can eat in the kitchen."

Audrey went into the bathroom and closed the door. She

didn't know what to think anymore. Snippets of memory were reappearing and they didn't jive with someone about to force information out of her.

He'd never admitted to being an interrogator.

He'd never admitted to being anything at all.

She used the facilities and washed her hands. The mirror over the sink revealed a gaunt oval face. Messy hair. Dark circles under her eyes over ivory pale skin. She squinted. She looked exactly like what she was. A serious-minded scientist recovering from a severe illness. She didn't look like some crazy killer.

Why did he think she was? There had to be a logical explanation.

Why had someone from the *Mano de Dios* stabbed her? It had to be a case of mistaken identity, right? Excitement burst through her. This was something they could fix. And she could go back to her life as soon as the misunderstanding was cleared up.

She splashed her face with cold water and her stomach growled. For the first time in days she was actually hungry. Drying herself she padded barefoot into the bedroom. Already feeling tired from this small exertion, she headed through the door and found her captor in the kitchen, buttering a piece of toast. It was dark outside. They must have both slept the day away. He'd laid out two place settings. One had a glass of water and a plate with half a potato and three thin slices of meat. The other had a large steak, loaded baked potato, and peas. A bottle of beer was front and center.

"Take a seat." He indicated a stool at the kitchen island and plunked the buttered toast beside her plate. "I wasn't sure what you might want."

"This is great. Thanks." She climbed gingerly into the chair and looked around. "This is a beautiful place. Is it yours?"

He shook his head. "You want anything else to drink? There's juice, milk, tea, coffee. I'm withholding alcohol until further notice."

She smiled even though he avoided answering her question. She wrapped her fingers around the cool glass and tried not to resent him. "Water's fine."

He sat kitty-corner to her and it felt weird. Like they were suddenly supposed to pretend to be two normal people when everything leading to this moment had been extraordinary.

The silence got louder and louder until she couldn't stand it any longer. "So, where'd you grow up?"

He swigged his beer. "California. You?"

She picked up the toast, wondering if he was telling the truth and how you'd ever really know with a man like him. "I assume you know. In fact, I assume you know everything about me from my dental history to my menstrual cycle."

He winced. "Not quite. But I know a lot. Born in Montana, moved to Kentucky when you were twelve. Still living and working in the Bluegrass State except for when you're down in Colombia doing your funky frog thing."

"I explained my work with the frogs during my talk the other day. You were too busy feeling up that poor tourist to pay attention to what I was saying."

He shook his head. "Harmless flirtation. And I was listening. Frogs are dying and you're trying to help them. I paid attention, but didn't know I was gonna get a test on it." He sliced into his steak and started eating.

She bit into her hot buttered toast and her toes curled as

the salt from the butter dissolved on her tongue. She wiped the crumbs from her lips. "This is delicious."

"Cheap date. Good to know." He smiled, a dimple flashing in his chin. "You took a gap year after high school. Where'd you go?"

"This sounds like an interrogation but as I've got nothing to hide I'll tell you." She took another tiny nibble of toast. "I went to Europe, then Thailand, then Australia and New Zealand."

"Your parents didn't mind you taking off on them?"

The reminder of her parents brought a flash of remorse. They'd already suffered enough. Picking up her glass and taking a sip of water, she pushed the worry away. One stressor at a time. Once she convinced Patrick she wasn't a killer, she'd find a way to contact her parents and let them know she was alive.

"They weren't happy about it, but I needed to get away. I'm pretty sure I'd literally have gone insane if I'd stayed home." She'd been suffocating on the inside, desperate to escape the pressures from school and her home situation. Full of a burning desire to travel and see the world.

"I take it your sister's drug addiction has been hard on your family." It was a statement, not a question.

"I had no patience with Sienna when she started using." The inner anger that lived deep inside her broke free. "Honestly? I was mad with all of them. My sister was a screw up but my parents let her be. They indulged her from the day she was born. If she was sick she stayed home from school. If she didn't do well in class it was the teacher's fault. If I said anything I was acting out, being mean, jealous." She wasn't usually this frank about her family dynamics, but Patrick apparently knew more about her than anyone else on the planet. She'd give him some meat to go on those bones. "I needed to get away from everyone and everything to save my sanity."

"Did it?" he asked.

"Some days that is debatable, but yeah." She nodded. "That year taught me a lot about myself and what I was interested in. My passion. I came home with more patience and maturity than when I left."

He watched her with those blue eyes of his that missed nothing but never looked wholly convinced she was telling the truth. Normally people assumed she was as transparent as glass and as interesting as drying paint. A small part of her enjoyed being an enigma for once.

"Do you have a family?" she asked.

He shrugged.

"You don't want to talk about them in case my frogs and I go on a rampage?" She sniggered, holding her side. Maybe the joke was in bad taste, but so was being stabbed and abducted.

He wiped at a ring of condensation on the wooden countertop. "On your world adventure, which was your favorite place to visit?"

She eyed him over the top of her glass, telling him she knew he was trying to control the conversation and that she'd let him, for now. "I take it you've traveled?"

He nodded.

"Could you choose a favorite out of Venice, Paris, Rome?"

"Anywhere people don't try to kill me goes on the happy list." The look in his eyes told her he wasn't kidding. He surprised her by continuing. "I guess if I had to pick one, I'd choose the desert somewhere. Australia, maybe. Utah, North

Africa—I like heat, and the colors. The quiet." He shrugged and she thought he might actually be telling the truth. "You must have a favorite place," he persisted.

"I loved Australia. The wildlife there is phenomenal."

"Bugs." He pulled a face. "You're a crusader. Trying to save the world."

"I thought you said I was a murderer?" She arched a brow.

"People can be both." Patrick looked like he'd met quite a few of them.

"Who exactly do you think I killed?"

He took a swig of beer. "It's classified."

She laughed, and then realized he was serious. "Seriously? How am I supposed to defend myself against a crime when you won't tell me what the crime is?"

"Tell me every crime you've ever committed and we'll go from there." His smile promised many things and Audrey didn't trust it even a little bit.

She was suddenly unwilling to do this dance when all he really wanted was to pump her for information. She put down her toast.

"Hey," he raised his hands in surrender. "I'm just making conversation. You need to eat."

"Fine." She sipped her water and wished she didn't feel so weak and helpless. "Let's see. What's the worst thing I've ever done? In Venice I found two hundred dollars and I didn't hand it in to the authorities. I was broke and that money lasted me an entire week. It was wrong and I'm assuming illegal, but I did it anyway because I didn't want to have to beg my parents for help when I'd told them I could take care of myself. What else? I once went skinny dipping in New Zealand, which was a huge mistake given how cold it was. I used to get into bars when I was underage with a fake ID. I jaywalked in NYC—"

"Everyone jaywalks in NYC."

"And while I try to stick to the speed limit I admit that I've occasionally put my foot down on long wide open stretches of highway."

He cut into his potato, then pointed at her plate with his knife. "Eat."

"What about you, what crimes have you committed?"

He chewed and swallowed, then grinned. "Aside from leaving the scene of a suspicious death and stealing a plane from a Colombian drug lord? Nothing recently."

"What about kidnapping?"

He looked startled by that, then one side of his lips curved. "You got me."

She ate more toast and managed to finish one entire slice before pushing the plate away.

"Do you work on live frogs back in the States?" he asked.

She tilted her head at him. Surely he knew this? "I ship samples and specimens back home, but I try and do as much of the work as possible in Colombia." She grimaced. "That way I can avoid all the admin hassle associated with my job."

"Aren't you young to be faculty?"

"Thirty." She nodded, but a chill swept over her arms. Would she be fired over this debacle? She'd worked hard for everything she'd achieved. Goose bumps formed on her skin and she rubbed at them. He obviously noticed because he shrugged out of his cotton shirt and handed it to her. She slipped it across her shoulders, grateful for the extra warmth, but wishing it didn't smell so much like the man himself. The black shoulder holster he wore on his T-shirt was an unwelcome surprise. She hadn't known he was armed.

She was completely at this guy's mercy and she mustn't forget that, despite the pretty face and disarming grin.

Crumbs fell onto the table and she swept them up and put them on her plate. "Why do you think I killed this person?" But the mental light bulb flashed, bleaching her brain and bringing clarity to her thought processes. "Ah... Someone was killed with batrachotoxin." She frowned. "You know that can be synthesized, right?"

His gaze remained steady on her face. "It was analyzed and there were indicators it came from a natural source in the region you work in. DNA."

She felt almost light-headed with relief. This was how the CIA conducted operations? On evidence that flimsy? "Anyone could have put on some gloves and gone and picked up a frog in the rainforest. You just need to know where to look. I can't believe you used that as grounds for accusing me of murder." Then she frowned. "This can't be why the cartel tried to kill me. They'd know better than that. And they'd know exactly how to get hold of a native frog. Am I a scapegoat? The convenient clueless white girl?"

Those blue eyes drilled into her, but he kept his thoughts to himself.

"There's more, isn't there?" Her heart gave a little flutter. "But you're not going to tell me, because it's *classified*."

He broke the connection, looked down at his plate and carried on eating. Audrey lost the little appetite she'd had. She pushed her plate away and stood. "Thank you very much for dinner. Now I'm going to bed." She went back to her room and slammed the door. The sound echoed hollowly throughout the house and reminded her that it didn't matter how much noise she made, there was no one around to hear.

CHAPTER TEN

KILLION JERKED AWAKE and realized he'd fallen asleep on the recliner in the lounge. He held still as he listened for whatever had woken him.

There it was again.

A cry. Audrey.

He rocketed up out of his chair, SIG in hand as he sprinted to the bedroom. He paused with his hand on the door handle, listening hard and heard the cry again. He eased open the door. The bathroom light was on and the door ajar.

She was alone.

Audrey lay twisting in the bed, fighting with the covers. There was no attacker except in her dreams. He felt a pang of guilt that he might be responsible for these nightmares.

She started sobbing and wailing. Damn. What the hell was he supposed to do? Hesitant, he went inside, and sat on the edge of the mattress. Sweat glistened on her brow. Had her fever returned? He put the gun down on the bedside table and pushed her dark hair off her forehead. Not feverish, thank God, but hot and sweaty.

"Aud," he called gently. He'd missed sleeping in here with her he realized. It was a weird thought for a man who preferred his own company.

She rolled her head in the opposite direction. "Rebecca.

No. No!"

The sobs twisted him up inside.

He'd had these sorts of dreams for a few years. He'd been embedded with an SF unit, negotiating with the local elders for tribal support of the new Afghan leader, looking for help rounding up any Arab fighters passing through the region. Although the elders hadn't been convinced they should openly defy Mullah Omar, Killion had earned their trust after weeks of cultivating the relationships. He was invited to attend a wedding there. Another intelligence officer, a woman who'd been competing with Killion since their days at the Farm, had received conflicting intel from a source Killion had known was fundamentally unreliable and out to make a buck. The source had convinced the female IO that fugitive Taliban leaders were holed up in the village right under Killion's nose, preparing to take him and his group hostage. She'd used her influence to have the place bombed. He'd tried to stop the attack, but it was too late. Two airstrikes had reduced the place to smoking rubble.

The images of broken humans, some of them friends, some of them children, had haunted him for years. There were days when he was angry that the dreams had faded—that the memories of those people and the culpability of his own agency had diminished over time.

Trust was an ephemeral thing, but once gone it was gone forever. Needless to say they'd lost the support he'd worked so hard to establish. The US Government had later apologized for any civilian casualties. The female intelligence officer had been shipped back to HQ and had eventually resigned.

"Rebecca!"

He snapped back to the present.

"Don't die! Please don't die."

He put a hand on each of Audrey's shoulders and squeezed gently.

She jerked awake and grabbed hold of his forearms. Her eyes were wild and he could see the pulse beating strongly in the base of her throat. She blinked, seeming to come into herself.

"Patrick." His name came out as a sigh and her grip on him tightened. Why that felt like coming home, Killion didn't know.

He tucked her hair behind her ear. "You had a bad dream. You're okay now."

She nodded, but her pulse jumped crazily beneath her skin. The thought of placing his tongue on that exact spot made something curl in his stomach, something hot and sensual that had no place on this assignment. But he wasn't a eunuch and he was only staring at her neck for chrissake.

"Who's Rebecca?"

She relaxed back into the pillow and let go of his arm. She stretched out beneath him and he tried not to think about that soft female body just inches away.

"She was my best friend in college." She closed her eyes and when she opened them her lashes were damp. "Five years ago, we went out clubbing and were mugged on our way home. The guy shot her. Tried to shoot me, too, but his gun jammed."

How had they missed this?

He ignored his own pounding pulse. "I don't know if that makes you the luckiest woman on the planet, or the unluckiest."

Her answering smile dissolved into tears. "Me neither."

She quickly wiped her eyes. No breaking down for Audrey Lockhart. "Rebecca died in my arms at the scene. I tried to save her, but the doctor told me later the bullet nicked her aorta. She never stood a chance."

"I'm sorry." He'd held people when they died. Soldiers. Friends. Kids.

Bearing witness to human mortality was the most sobering experience imaginable, especially when it came about through violence.

Her pink lips pressed together. And now he was thinking about what she might taste like while she was reliving her best friend's murder.

He was going to go to hell.

He reminded himself he had a job to do. "What was her surname?"

The light in her eyes altered when she realized he wanted this information for work and he didn't like the disappointment that flared there.

"Rebecca Brightman. It was big news at the time because her father is the big industrialist Gabriel Brightman."

He frowned. "You dated her brother, right?"

She nodded. "After Rebecca died."

And she'd called him earlier, so they were still close. Did they still have feelings for one another? The idea didn't sit right, but it had nothing to do with the mission.

He frowned. "Why didn't I know you witnessed your friend's death?"

"Did I forget to mention that on our first date? Sorry." Her voice had that husky amused quality that turned him on like a freaking light switch whenever he heard it. Not what he needed when his brain was supposed to be engaged in prying out relevant information.

"Don't go firing your analysts just yet." Her eyes rolled tiredly. "I was the only witness, but I never saw the guy's face. He wore a mask. The cops and DA kept my identity secret because they wanted to pretend 'the witness' knew more than she actually did and I refused WitSec because I was halfway through my Ph.D. and no way was I throwing that away for some stupid mugger. They set up a sting operation with a woman police officer as a decoy, but they never caught the guy. The case is still open, but no one thinks they'll find him after so many years."

She sat up and reached for the water. By the time he realized she wasn't going for the cup he was staring down the barrel of his own gun. The space between heartbeats felt like an eternity.

Well, hell.

"I need you to back away from the bed, Patrick." The heavy gun wavered in her one-handed grip. Her finger was hooked around the trigger.

He could lunge and maybe knock the weapon out of her grip, but taking a bullet from that gun at close range meant he'd bleed out before he even made a phone call.

He raised his hands, palms facing forward. "Careful, Aud. That thing is locked and loaded." He eased his weight from the bed and backed up a half step. "You don't want to do something you're going to regret."

"Shooting someone who kidnapped me and held me against my will?" Her bottom lip wobbled. "What US court would have a problem with that? I don't even know if you're really CIA because it's *classified* and I only overheard part of a conversation when I was almost unconscious. For all I know you made that up, too." The gun wavered and she wrapped both hands around it, but it was still unsteady.

Killion eyed her narrowly. He wasn't a big fan of having a loaded weapon pointed in his direction, but a professional assassin would have already pulled the trigger.

"No court in the country would convict an innocent woman on that basis," she told him.

He edged to his right. "Unfortunately they might not be so understanding toward a woman already wanted for murder."

Her eyes widened. "They think I murdered Hector in cold blood? Oh, my God." He didn't correct her assumption it was Hector they thought she'd killed. She looked like she was going to start to cry again. "I have to talk to an American official." Her voice rose in bewilderment. "I need to tell them the truth. You have to help me!"

He crossed his arms over his chest and eyed the weapon in her hands. "You gonna shoot me or not?"

"No!" She lowered the gun so it rested on her thighs. "Any sane person *would* shoot you. You're arrogant, annoying and so goddamned secretive. *And* you could be a deranged serial killer for all I know." She wasn't making a lot of sense. "But I don't care what anyone says or thinks, I'm *not* a killer." She wiped her eyes. "I just want to go home."

"I'm beginning to see that, Dr. Lockhart." He reached out and lifted the gun out of her lap and stuck it back in his holster, feeling like a damn fool. His heart regained its normal sinus rhythm and a sense of relief filled him. Not just because she hadn't shot him, but also because any doubts to her innocence had been obliterated.

"Remind me sometime to show you how to take the safety off a SIG—just not today, okay?" He leaned down and dropped a kiss to her forehead. The desire to climb in beside her and hold her close almost overwhelmed his good sense, so he stood and backed away. She was no longer someone to be played for information. She was an innocent who needed his protection.

"Go to sleep." He paused on his way out of the room. "And call me Killion. Only my grandma calls me Patrick, and that's only when she's pissed."

KILLION PICKED UP his satellite cell phone and punched in Jed's number. "I've got good news and bad news."

"What's the good news?" It was the middle of the night and he'd obviously woken the guy, but Jed didn't complain.

"No way is Audrey Lockhart our professional assassin."

"What's the bad news?"

"No way is Audrey Lockhart our professional assassin."

"Dammit. You're sure?"

"I'd bet my reputation on it."

Killion expected a joke about that not being much to lose, but Jed took him by surprise and grunted. "Good enough for me. So why were we led to this woman?"

They'd been fed just enough information to find her before someone had tried to take her out of the picture, permanently.

"I just found out Audrey was Gabriel Brightman's daughter's best friend when the daughter was murdered during a mugging a few years ago. Audrey survived because the guy's gun jammed."

"Why didn't we know about this?"

"Cops and DA kept her name out of the reports to protect her identity," Killion told him.

"Audrey dated the brother, right?"

"Yeah, but I didn't know about the friend/sister connection until tonight." He was kicking himself for not knowing something so vital.

"What happened tonight?" asked Jed.

Killion's career was built on passing along information and Jed was someone he trusted with his life. This wasn't gossip. It was data. *And how'd you like it if your nightmares ended up in a database, asshole?*

"Her friend's death came out in conversation. Cops never caught the guy. You gotta get Frazer or Parker digging into Gabriel Brightman. He sounds like a perfect candidate for The Gateway Project. Friend of Burger's. Getting revenge for a dead kid? Maybe involving the cartel? Maybe blaming Audrey for surviving when his daughter didn't, so setting her up to take the fall?"

"It's the closest we have to a motive, although why take out Burger if they were supposed to be friends?"

Killion shrugged. "Maybe he figured Burger had gone too far?" The VP had helped fund a terrorist attack in some twisted effort to increase the fight against them. "Maybe Brightman figured if Burger got caught he'd bring him down, too?"

"I suppose." Jed sounded tired.

"You all right?"

"It's four AM." Jed's voice held an edge.

"I forgot you feds were nine-to-five government employees."

"Said the man living it up in the Caribbean."

"Which reminds me. I need to get off the island. Now that we know Audrey doesn't have information to squeeze, I need to keep searching for the assassin." And the more time he spent with Audrey the more involved he became. He didn't like it. Didn't want it. She wasn't the kind of woman he could walk away from without one or both of them getting hurt, and he always walked away.

Time to move on.

But no matter how many reasons he came up with for ditching the biologist the idea still felt wrong. How about the fact he'd attacked her that first night? And that his attack and her subsequent report of the attack probably got her stabbed the next day and her grad student murdered—not that she knew about that yet. Another fact that would make her hate him if she ever found out.

"What about Lockhart?" asked Jed. "We can't just turn her loose, she's wanted for murder. Even if the truth comes out the cartel still wants her dead for reasons unknown."

Audrey was definitely in danger. "We have to assume either Brightman or the cartel masterminded this whole thing, or they're working together. We need more people on them. See if there's a connection between Gómez and Brightman." Killion scrubbed his face. "Did you check the phone records of those two detectives?"

"Yeah." Jed sounded like he was working on a computer now. "Detective Torres called a burner cell located out the outskirts of Bogota. Parker is trying to pin it down because that same burner cell was used to call a number in Kentucky. The burner is now turned off and if the person they called has half a brain they'll have ditched it."

"Keep monitoring it. Plenty of smart people do stupid

things." He thought of all the things he wanted to do to Dr. Lockhart even though she didn't have a clue. Smart people. Stupid things.

He mentally kicked himself. He shouldn't be having these thoughts about someone under his care and supervision. The situation had changed.

"We're gonna need documentation to get back into the country. We'll stash Audrey in a safe house somewhere. As long as no one spots her arriving she should be safe until we catch up with the guy pulling the strings."

"It's going to take a while to set up transportation if we want to keep this below the radar. Unless those Brit friends of yours can give you another ride? Chatter is someone took out some terrorists who hijacked a vessel heading toward the Panama Canal. Think that was them?"

Killion smiled. "If it wasn't us, it was them. But I'm not pulling them back into this unless we have to." He wasn't jeopardizing their base of operations in Colombia. There were other ways to move around that raised less red flags than dead of night helo flights. His reluctance had nothing to do with the way Noah had looked at Audrey back in Cartagena. "Know anyone with a boat?"

Jed laughed. "It's only thirty nautical miles to the nearest airstrip. You could swim over and steal another plane. All very Indiana Jones by the way."

Killion rolled his eyes at the ribbing.

"It's going to be forty-eight hours before we can get a chopper out there," said Jed. "I just texted Parker. His security firm is all tied up, helping us out on a case in upstate New York. Unless you want to bring in someone else?"

"No." The risk of someone blabbing about Audrey's identity was too great, especially with her face on every newspaper in South America.

"Think of it as a weekend—remember them?" said Jed.

Killion ignored him. "How's Frazer?"

"Getting better. He arrested the serial killer and got the girl this time."

"He's definitely keeping her?"

"Looks that way."

Killion grunted.

"That's it, isn't it?"

"That's what?" Killion growled.

"The problem I can hear in your surly tone. You like her. You like Dr. Audrey Lockhart and spending time alone with her is scaring the shit out of you."

"Fuck. Off."

"Not your usual type, buddy. She's got that nerdy thing going for her."

"Up until ten minutes ago I thought she might still be a cold blooded killer."

"Which made the attraction safe because you'd never betray a mission." Killion was flattered for all of a millisecond. "Now you're trying to run away as fast as you can."

"Don't be an asshole."

"Hey, that's your job."

"Bite me." Killion hung up and closed his eyes. Dammit. He hated that Jed was right. This was why he worked alone. It was much easier alone.

———————

AUDREY LAY IN bed staring at the streaks of sunlight playing over the ceiling. She was so mad at herself. She'd had Patrick Killion at her mercy last night but she'd managed to blow it by breaking down like some pathetic weenie. There was a knock on the door and the man himself opened it wide and stood wearing jeans, a faded blue T-shirt and sun block, which she could smell clear across the room.

"Time for some PT, Lockhart."

She hadn't been sure how he'd react after she'd pointed his gun at him last night. The kiss he'd placed on her forehead had been unexpected, and sweet. It made her uneasy now—too gentle, too tender—reminding her of the fact he'd taken care of her when she was sick, and rescued her when she would have otherwise died.

A hero.

Their dynamic had changed, but he was still an operator on a mission, doing dangerous things on behalf of his country. And she was still a frog biologist.

Even if he *was* a government agent, James Bond did not live happily-ever-after. When he did fall in love, the woman generally died a painful graphic death, and she had no intention of dying for at least another seventy years. And she couldn't afford to believe she was anything other than a job to a man like this—no matter how "sweet" those tender little kisses were, or how they made her heart squeeze.

Audrey pushed herself up in the bed and winced as the healing skin on her side tugged. "I don't think I'm ready for sit-ups just yet." But she was fed up of lying around like a slug.

He grinned and she was startled by how much younger he looked. How less world-weary.

"How about a swim?" he suggested.

The idea of getting into the ocean was appealing, but there

was a problem. "I don't have anything to wear."

He went over to the drawers and started searching through them until he came back with two turquoise pieces of string. "Unluckily for me this looks like it might fit." He spread the triangle of material over his own chest.

"I've seen bigger post-it notes." She leaned forward and snatched it out of his grasp. "I can't believe they let you loose with a gun." She cocked a brow. "And what are *you* wearing?"

His mouth twisted. "Seriously? There's no one around for miles, and, trust me, not even the most advanced military satellite system can spot a man's dick from space."

She raised another brow at him, and he pushed out a heavy sigh. He went to the other side of the room and dug into another set of drawers. Whipped out a pair of red board shorts. "These big enough to preserve your modesty?" He quirked a brow back at her.

"Only if you can squeeze them over your ego."

The smile got hot and dangerous. "I do have a big ego."

"No kidding." She slung a pillow at him, clutching her side as much to stop laughing as to stop from hurting herself. "Out."

He looked genuinely pained. "I hate to tell you, but I've seen you naked—three, maybe four times if we count—"

"This is not helping your cause."

"Hey"—he hung onto the doorframe, clearly reluctant to leave—"what kind of costumes do frogs wear on Halloween?"

"You really think there's a frog joke I haven't heard? Jumpsuits. Ha ha."

His eyes got a wicked gleam in them. "What did one lesbian frog say to the other?"

She shook her head. "Lesbian frog?" The guy was incorrigible. "Fine. I don't know, what did one lesbian frog say to the other?"

His smile was pure devilry. "They're right. We do taste like chicken."

Oh. My. God.

Heat rushed through her in a wave that had nothing to do with terrible frog jokes and everything to do with the way Patrick Killion was looking at her—like tasting her was on today's menu. Thankfully he left before her knees went weak and she dropped back onto the bed.

Would he have taken that as an invitation? Probably.

And for the life of her she couldn't quite remember why she was supposed to say no.

CHAPTER ELEVEN

AUDREY MADE QUICK use of the bathroom and smoothed the sunblock she found in the cupboard over every inch of her pale skin. She pulled on the bikini that was a little loose but felt like it might stay in place if she tied the laces super tight. She removed her bandage and checked the wound. No inflammation or pain. The skin itched beneath the flaky scab, which was a good sign. The stitches should fall out on their own soon. Ugly as hell, and a vivid reminder that she'd almost died.

She left the bandage off to air the wound. Grabbed a big beach towel out of the bathroom and wrapped it around herself. Then she headed into the living room.

Killion was in the kitchen, wearing nothing but the low-slung board shorts. His washboard abs had a thin smattering of golden hair that arrowed down from his navel and looked like it would be fun to follow.

She watched him as he packed stuff out of the fridge—food, water bottles. She hadn't hung out with a guy who looked this in shape since she'd dated a lacrosse player during her freshman year in college. The guy had turned out to be a jerk, but as far as eye candy went... She pushed the thought out of her head. Killion was a dangerous operative. He kept in shape to steal airplanes and seduce information out of unsuspecting women.

She bet he was good at it, too.

The atmosphere had shifted from captor and captive to something a lot more friendly. A lot more. Either he was playing her, or last night's ineptitude with the gun had finally persuaded him she wasn't the hit woman he was looking for.

She hoped it was the latter, but didn't really know why it mattered. She was stuck on this island regardless.

He handed her a glass of cold milk. "Did you know people froze milk?"

She blinked. *What*? "Sure." She took a sip and it was delicious. She tipped it back and drank the whole glass.

"I didn't."

"So you've learned something new on this adventure. Not a complete bust after all."

He stared at her intently and said nothing. Then his gaze lowered to the towel, putting her under the microscope again. "Why are you so self-conscious about your body?"

She tugged the knot higher. "I'm not."

"Well, you shouldn't be." He pointed toward some flip-flops near the door. "Put those on." Then he grinned again. "Do you remember when we stole that plane?"

We?

"You were out of it, but you told me even gorgeous women worry about not being perfect, whereas us fat ugly dudes think we're sex on a stick?"

He was sex on a stick, and he knew it. "It's a bit blurry, but it sounds like something I might say."

"Oh, you said it." He draped a pink towel around his neck and strapped the bag of supplies over his back. A proper boy scout. "And you kept going on about some guy called Dean

Winchester."

Her face heated. "I did not." The fact she had a crush on the actor was not something she advertised.

He guided her out the door and closed it. It locked behind them. Talk about security conscious.

"You did. So I looked him up online when we were in Cartagena. You're a *Supernatural* fan, and you like blonds." He said it with such a self-satisfied grin she wanted to smack him.

"No," she corrected him. "I like specific people, not generalized swathes of the population."

The path was steep, and she was already feeling tired just looking at it. Still, she wouldn't get stronger if she didn't push herself. Then she yelped in surprise as Killion swung her up into his arms—again. Her fingers curled over his heart. No shirt to hold onto this time, just sleek hot muscle.

She swallowed nervously and raised her eyes to meet his. "I can walk you know."

It felt weird to touch him skin on skin. Intimate. Considering the complicated nature of their relationship, she probably shouldn't enjoy feeling the beat of his heart against her palm, but she did.

"A day ago, Professor, I didn't even know if you were going to make it through the night. Swimming was my idea, but let's take it slow, okay? I don't want you to suffer a relapse. Anyway, you can carry me back." His grin told her he knew the effect he was having on her libido.

She sighed.

It didn't seem fair that he held all the aces. She was hardly some simpering female, but she was completely out of her element.

The blue eyes were serious for a moment, and his face was a lot closer to hers than she'd realized. His gaze dropped to her lips. There was attraction there, but she didn't know how real it was.

Maybe it didn't matter.

Maybe it didn't have to be real. Maybe until she found her way back to civilization she should just take advantage and enjoy herself…

"So what happens next?" she asked rather breathlessly.

"We need to wait for transportation to the mainland and then you need to lay low until I can figure out who set you up and why *Mano de Dios* tried to kill you."

"So you finally believe me?"

He nodded.

And because he didn't try to elaborate, she actually believed him.

"That could take months." She had a job, a life.

"Hey, look at me," he demanded. "We'll figure this out. The most important thing is you're safe. The frogs will wait." His arms squeezed her tighter against his chest and, even though she didn't necessarily agree, she didn't argue.

They followed the dirt path, passing under the dappled canopy of deciduous trees and coconut palms. A lizard darted into the bush, but it moved too fast for her to be able to identify it.

"It might take a day, a week, or a month. But I will get them and I'll figure out a way to clear your name," he murmured, almost to himself.

A lump formed in her throat. This man had saved her life even when he'd thought she was a killer. Despite everything, she realized, subconsciously she'd always trusted him. "I guess

I owe you my life. I'm sorry I pointed your gun at you last night."

"If I'd been in your position I'd have shot me days ago." His irreverent grin made her pulse skip. "Just don't do it again. And next time I say skinny-dipping we go skinny-dipping. Got it?"

"You are incorrigible."

"Clothes are overrated," he insisted.

"Stubbornness is a flaw, you know that?" He opened his mouth, but she beat him to it. "As is always needing to win an argument."

He shook his head. "Jensen Ackles. Unbelievable."

She grinned. "He's hot. You're jealous."

"We've been over this." Finally at the bottom of the steep hill Killion placed her carefully on her feet. Then he took her hand and she couldn't remember the last time a man had been this considerate. She should get abducted more often. "Beach is just around this corner," he said. "Come on."

As suddenly as he started walking, he stopped and raised his free hand in warning. A snatch of sound drifted on the breeze. Voices.

Her eyes shot to his. From the tension in his grip they weren't expecting visitors. He put his finger to his lips and spoke just above a whisper. "Could be day-trippers taking advantage of an empty private beach. Or it could be bad news. Let's assume the worst." He slipped off the backpack and retrieved his weapon, drawing her deeper into the shadows of the trees.

"We need to lose this." He tugged the white towel off her shoulders and balled it up and stuffed it under a bush, sweeping dust and dirt over the top. He didn't comment on her bikini, but his eyes went to her stab wound. He draped his dusky pink towel over her shoulders and gave her a tight smile. "Healing nicely. Now keep completely still. Movement attracts the eye."

The voices seemed to be getting closer—men creeping along the path speaking Spanish. Killion drew her behind a large palm tree. Him facing the path, covering her with his body. They were hidden in dappled shade beneath dense coconut palms. Hard to spot unless someone was actively looking for them. The sound of a weapon being cocked sent a spark of fear straight through Audrey and she startled. Killion pressed his body more firmly against hers in warning. Out of the corner of her eyes she counted six men inching furtively along the trail.

"Okay. Plan B." His words were a brush of air against her ear. "You okay?" he asked when the men were out of sight.

His fingers gripped her upper arm, and she realized she was shaking. She looked up at him. "Just tell me what you want me to do."

"That's my girl." He took her hand and led her through the woods so they could see the beach from the safety of the trees. A guy sat in the sand guarding a small inflatable boat that had been pulled up out of the surf.

"Wait here."

She sat motionless, crouched in the bushes, feeling pathetic and needy. All these years she'd preached equality, but she wasn't holding up her end of the bargain. But she was a biologist, not some government agent or member of a criminal gang. She'd hinder rather than help if she started giving Killion orders.

He was back. "There's a fishing boat anchored just offshore. How far do you think you can swim?"

"Normally I can swim for at least a mile, but…" She held out her fingers, which were trembling "…I don't have a lot of strength, so it depends on how strong the current is."

From the tight expression on his face the currents were pretty strong. "Plan C. Give me ninety-seconds to get around the other side of the beach and then you drop into the surf when the guy isn't looking. Stroll up onto the beach as if you've just come in from a long swim. I need you to deliberately draw his attention to you and away from me. Take off your top."

"Seriously?"

"Trust me. All I need is a five-second distraction and your breasts will get me that."

She instinctively held her hands over her boobs. Her cheeks were hot, but she could do this. Hopefully. "How should I act? Sophisticated or shy?"

"Men are idiots, so a little strutting would probably work best. But it doesn't matter. He won't notice anything except for your body. Not at first."

And then he was gone.

Shit. Audrey couldn't do this. She was not a Bond girl. She looked down at her chest. She was a shy person. Private.

Crap. She was supposed to be counting.

She started at ten because he'd probably been gone that long. She eased Killion's towel from her shoulders and laid it in a neat pile in the sand. The idea of getting naked in front of a stranger made her feel sick. But these people were not day-trippers, they were here to hurt her and Killion. She wasn't about to let a little natural reticence get them both killed. She might not be able to fire a gun, but she could show her breasts to some moron too stupid to know she was part of the plan. She got to seventy and pulled on the tie at the back of her bikini top, slipped it over her head, and dropped it to the ground next to the towel. At eighty-five she climbed gingerly down the rocks into the swell of the surf out of sight of the man on the beach. The water wasn't cold, but it still took her breath. She struck out gingerly toward the beach and knew the moment he spotted her because he stood, resting one hand on his handgun. Even the short swim made her limbs quiver with exhaustion—or maybe that was fear. Her feet hit the sandy bottom and she stood, water streaming over her breasts and down her stomach. She grabbed the bikini bottoms as the weight of the water threatened to drag them down her legs. Crap. Now *that* would be a distraction.

She smiled at the guy and kept walking toward him, putting a little sway in her hips.

"Can I help you?" she asked in English even though she knew he probably didn't speak the language.

She kept her eyes off the flash of movement behind him, just let her mouth open in shock as he grabbed his crotch and leered at her.

"*Ven acá, nena.*" *Come here, baby.* He reached toward her with grabby hands and she took a step back. He caught her wrist, dragging her toward him, eyes latched onto her jiggling breasts.

Killion grabbed the man from behind and twisted his neck sharply to an unnatural angle. The man fell dead at his feet. Bile seared her throat.

"Get in the boat." Killion was ripping the dead man's shirt from his body and putting it on, along with the greasy Panama hat and mirrored sunglasses. He stuffed the revolver in the back of his shorts.

Audrey ran to the boat and started pushing it into the surf, trying to be more than just a distraction. Strong hands gripped her hips.

"In the boat, Aud, now. Do as I say and we might get out of this alive."

His fingers sent a shockwave of heat through her. Maybe it was being topless in broad daylight. Maybe it was knowing Killion had just killed to protect her—because she knew instinctively he could have swum as far as was needed.

She climbed into the boat and sat quickly as he shoved the craft back into the surf. Once they were floating clear of the breakers he jumped in and started the engine.

"Sit up front and hold your hands behind your back as if you're tied up."

Audrey did as she was told, painfully aware of the cold breeze scraping her exposed skin, her nipples beaded and goose flesh pebbling her body.

"I'd cover you up, but I need to use the distraction technique again."

"What if someone finds the dead man and radios the trawler?" she asked, glancing back at Killion. The guy had seen her naked so often now she didn't know why she even worried about clothes anymore.

Next time she'd make sure he got naked too, just to even the score. The idea made her tip her chin defiantly. Beat the heck out of vomiting over the side of the boat the way she wanted to.

"We need to take over the fishing boat before they make contact. These guys aren't going to let us take it from them without a fight. The cartel will probably kill them if they fail."

The cartel? *Mano de Dios* had followed her all the way to this tiny island? What the hell was going on?

Killion pulled his gun and handled the boat with one hand hidden behind his back. A man popped his head over the side of the fishing trawler. Audrey forced her chin up and chest out. If she was going to be the token female she was going to play the part to the best of her ability.

A radio squawked.

They got closer and while the man was leering at Audrey, Killion shot him in the head. Audrey flinched at the spray of blood and watched him fall dead into the water. Her mouth went dry and nausea stirred in her belly.

"Hold it together, darlin', or we're both going to wind up dead."

Their inflatable bumped into the side of the trawler, and Killion grabbed one of the floats, quickly tying their rope to it.

"I'll be right back." He tucked the gun into the waistband of his shorts—good thing they hadn't decided to go skinny-dipping—and monkey crawled around the side of the boat toward the prow.

Audrey felt ridiculously vulnerable standing there almost naked. Was there anyone else on board? She stood up on tiptoes. A loud bang had her dropping to the floor as a bullet whizzed overhead. *Dammit*! Footsteps made her look up and another dark-haired man peered over the side. This one didn't look entranced by her boobs. His eyes narrowed, and he swung a big black gun toward her.

Oh, hell.

She threw herself overboard just as he pulled the trigger.

———————

"AUDREY!" KILLION RAN to the side of the boat and looked into the inflatable, frantically searching for the woman he was struggling to keep alive.

He'd taken care of a guy in the wheelhouse who'd been trying to raise the troops attacking the house, but the geniuses had left the radio in the boat. Then he'd turned around and seen another man leaning over the railings with a bead on Audrey. The guy got a shot off before Killion managed to send him to hell. But there was no sign of his brave, nerdy, frog friend.

Shit. Where the hell was she? He needed to search the trawler for any other bad guys, but he couldn't let Audrey drown—assuming she hadn't been killed. The thought made something desperate twist inside him. Then a hand reached over the side of the inflatable and a dark head emerged from the water. Her eyes met his, haunted, scared. Still alive.

Sweet Jesus. She was going to be the death of him.

"Can you climb up without my help?" His voice came out meaner than he'd intended, like he wanted to rip off someone's head. She gritted her teeth and nodded, flinging her arms over the side, hooking her leg over until she rolled virtually naked into the bottom of the boat.

No bullet holes, which was a blessing, and her stab wound hadn't reopened, *bonus*. He closed his eyes in relief. Then he reached down and gripped her hand, hauling her aboard the trawler, and pulled her close for a quick, wet hug. She was shivering and had her hands crossed over her breasts. The woman had spent more time naked in his presence than any other woman he'd ever met, and he hadn't even kissed her properly yet.

Yet?

He tore off the stolen shirt and dragged it over her shoulders, pulling it closed at the front. "I've gotta make sure there's no one else on board. Come on." He took her by the hand. Her teeth chattered, and she was shaking, probably from shock rather than cold. Inside the wheelhouse he showed her the lock. "Don't let anyone in except me, okay?"

She nodded, those violet eyes of hers huge now. He stepped over the body of the captain, took the man's weapon, and pressed it into her palm. "Safety is off this time." He gripped the back of her neck and drew her close, kissing her on the lips. "Don't shoot me."

Killion went out the door and made sure Audrey locked it after him. As soon as he heard the click of the latch he began a systematic search of the vessel, checking every inch including the stinking cargo hold. He found enough weapons to start a war, but no other would-be killers. He went up on deck, got his pack from the inflatable, and eased the body of the man who'd shot at Audrey overboard. With luck he'd never be found. Killion went back to the wheelhouse and knocked loudly. "Aud?"

The door opened immediately, and she held out the gun to him with the barrel pointed to the deck. "Take it. I'm scared I'm going to accidentally pull the trigger."

Killion didn't argue. He tucked it in the waistband of his shorts, along with his own weapon, and both dug uncomfortably into his butt. He went through the captain's pockets until he found a cell phone. He took it, then picked up the dead captain by his feet and dragged him over the lip of the door and down the steps onto the deck. He shoved the man over the side with the others. When he turned around, Audrey was staring at him from the wheelhouse door with a look of abject horror on her features. Shit, she looked like she was about to fall over, and no wonder. She was barely out of the sickbed and forced to run for her life again.

How had they found them?

He went over and took her hand. Led her down to the small bathroom. He turned the temperature of the shower to warm and held her trembling form in his arms. When the temperature felt okay he started to slip the shirt off her shoulders. She went stiff with resistance for a second, then her shoulders relaxed and she rested her forehead against his chest. A lump the size of Arkansas wedged itself in his throat as he eased off the shirt and tossed it on the floor.

"I'll find you something clean to wear."

She shuddered and he pushed her under the spray wishing he could join her, knowing he didn't deserve an invitation. Not that it would have stopped him under normal circumstances, but this wasn't normal. She had just watched him kill four men and he had a horrible feeling he was responsible for a lot of the things that had happened over the last week.

She turned her back to him, but the view was good from any direction. He felt himself getting aroused and curled his fingers into his palm.

For some reason Audrey thought she came up short in the body stakes. She was mistaken, but then everyone was fucked up one way or another. The fact Audrey was hung up about her body just showed she was correct about her fat bastard inequality theory.

He shook himself out of his daze and went and rifled through lockers, looking for the smallest, cleanest clothes he could find. He bundled them up and put them and a clean towel just inside the door of the bathroom. Audrey was still turned away from him, washing her hair. He dragged his eyes away from those tantalizing turquoise bikini bottoms and headed back to the deck where he started the engine and motored slowly away from the island. He retrieved his cell phone, grateful he'd put it in a Ziploc before heading to the beach. Despite his unkempt appearance, taking care of the essentials was one of the tenets he lived by.

He pulled the captain's cell out of his pocket and called Jed's number.

"Agent Brennan."

"It's me."

Jed understood the significance of him calling from another cell. "Ah, shit. What happened?"

"Find out who owns this phone and a fishing trawler called La Santa Anna."

"You guys safe?"

"Let me call you back on my cell." Killion scanned the horizon as he headed north. Jed answered again before the phone completed its first ring.

"There are six armed men trying to break into the place where we were staying." If not for his need to get out of the confines of the house and some lucky timing, they'd have been trapped. "How the hell did they find us?"

"I'm going to patch Parker into this call."

Killion didn't know if he trusted Parker or not—they'd never actually met and he knew that at one time the guy had worked for CIA on projects so sensitive they'd never be subject to the freedom of information act. His buddy Lincoln Frazer trusted him though, and Frazer was a hard sell. It would have to be enough.

Parker didn't waste time on small talk. "Do the attackers

have any other way to pursue you?"

"Pretty sure I just confiscated their only means of transportation. But they probably have cell phones so they could call for help."

"Give me a sec." Parker came back a few moments later. "I turned off the signal tower just in case one of them has a sat phone. They won't be talking to anyone. There's a camera system that shows them camped outside the front door, trying to figure a way in. The door is bulletproof and it looks like one of them already shot himself in the leg."

"Bet they weren't expecting that." Killion's smile felt as thin as a blade. "Does your friend Haley have some sort of end of days mentality? Is that why she has so much security?"

"Nah. She bought the house off some Russian gangster when I was in a Moroccan prison. I stayed there for a few weeks after I got out and suggested a few upgrades. It's possible I was a little paranoid at the time. We use the place for sensitive jobs where people want to drop off the grid—usually to avoid the press. But Haley fell in love with the place and decided she should have it." Parker laughed softly. "You don't argue with Haley once she's made up her mind about something."

"Sounds like my sort of woman."

"They're all your sort of woman," Jed interjected.

Not really, Killion realized.

"Those goons are going to take a few hours to even figure out you've escaped," Parker said. "The place is built like a fortress. Why didn't you stay put?"

"For the first time since we arrived I thought I'd take the professor for a swim to try and build up her strength. We were already at the beach by the time we realized we had company."

"How is she?" this from Jed.

"Scared. Traumatized. Look, I want to know how the hell they found us when as far as I know you guys were the only ones privy to that information."

"Only you and I knew from this end, right, Alex?" Jed was talking to Parker.

"No one else needed to know. Don't worry, I'll figure it out," said Parker. "I don't like finding holes in my security protocols. Could the Brits have given you away?"

"Possible, but not likely," Killion had to admit. "Could someone be tracking this cell?"

"CIA and NASA can track it."

"Can you track it?"

Parker kept quiet for a long moment, and then admitted, "I could if I had to."

"Can you make it so they can't?"

Another few moments of silence. Killion didn't think Parker was thinking about the technicalities, more the legalities of doing this for a federal employee.

"It's possible your phone could malfunction and start popping up in other parts of the globe, all at the same time." Thus confusing the trail. "Langley won't appreciate losing track of one of their top officers though."

"Better to disappear temporarily than permanently. See if you can figure out any other way we might have been compromised so I'm not making the same mistake twice. And I'm going to need travel documents to get back to the States. Where do I head from here?"

"Your trawler is out of Honduras. Captain Tippitat was probably one of Gómez's many smuggling conduits." Parker relayed the information in a thoughtful voice. "Head north to

Jamaica. Sink the trawler offshore, find a small hotel somewhere and call Jed again. Someone will deliver the documents you need."

"Someone trustworthy?"

"You bet your life on it."

"I am." There was a beat of silence. "What about the idiots camped out on the island. Do we let them starve to death?"

"They can sit tight for now. I'll see if I can hire your buddies from across the water to go pick them up," said Parker. "Let Gómez remain ignorant about what's happening out there for as long as possible while we figure out who tracked you down and how."

"We'll get you out of this," Jed promised.

"I appreciate it. And I hope your friend's home is still standing by the end of it." Killion wasn't happy about the damage those guys might inflict when they figured out they'd been stranded.

"We can fix property," Parker said, his voice serious. "We can't bring people back from the dead. If Audrey Lockhart is innocent—"

"She is."

"Then we need to figure out who the real bad guy is and finish this thing."

Killion couldn't agree more.

They hung up.

He'd find out exactly how far he could trust them when he hit Jamaica. A figure moved silently up to the wheelhouse door and Killion rested his hand on the grip of his P229.

CHAPTER TWELVE

H E PACED HIS corner office. Why the hell hadn't he heard anything yet? It would have been faster if he'd swum to the island and took care of business himself.

Finally the burner in his pocket vibrated and he pulled it out, making himself take a calming breath before he answered it. "Is it done?"

"We've lost contact with the people we sent," admitted Gómez.

"Lost contact?" What the hell did that mean?

"The radio is probably broken and there's no cell phone coverage out in the middle of the ocean." Gómez laughed but it sounded forced.

He held onto his patience. "So what is the plan?"

"My people will continue trying to raise our *hermanos* on the radio. There's another boat we can send but it's eight hours away. It is a big ocean. *Si?*"

Eight *hours*? He didn't think he could wait that long. He had the horrible feeling Audrey had once again slipped through his fingers, or maybe everyone was screwing with him, trying to milk him for more money.

"You know I'm a rich man, *amigo?*"

"*Si.* We are both rich men."

"About to get a lot richer, huh?"

"*Sí.*"

"Unless this woman gets away," he hissed.

The silence on the other end of the line told him Raoul had definitely underestimated what this meant to him.

"If this woman escapes, our association will be forfeit." He spelled it out so there would be no misunderstanding.

"She'll be taken care of. She's probably already dead." The Colombian tried to sound nonchalant, but he heard the edge of uncertainty.

"The stakes are too high to make assumptions." He calmed himself before he continued. "Hear me, friend, and hear me well. No product moves *anywhere* until this thing is finished. Understand me?"

"I understand, *amigo*. Don't worry. I understand." Gómez finally had a note of urgency in his voice.

"Send a helicopter to see whether or not your men failed you." He allowed a beat of silence to follow his order. "And if they did, they die. Every single one of them."

AUDREY STOOD QUIETLY and listened to Killion on the cell phone. She heard him talking about the house they'd just left and then a cryptic "she is."

She is what? Clueless? Terrified? Oblivious?

After a few moments he hung up, tossed the cell on a small shelf. A decidedly unhappy expression twisted his features. He had just killed *four* people. She'd have been worried if he'd been jolly and smiling.

She hadn't thought he'd noticed her until his hand went to his pistol and he turned and looked her straight in the eye without any outward sign of surprise. But then it would take a lot to surprise a man who relied on his wits to survive.

"She is what?" she asked.

His face crinkled in a smile though his eyes didn't change. "Innocent."

They locked gazes. "Do you have any idea how they tracked us down?"

"Not yet," he said.

"It might have been my fault." She chewed her lip and clasped her hands together. "I tried to call for help when I took your phone yesterday. Could someone have traced those calls?"

He tilted his head to the side. "None of this is your fault."

She crossed her arms over her chest, trying to disguise her shaking limbs. Despite the near scalding temperature of the shower she couldn't get warm.

"But maybe they traced the signal."

"They didn't trace the signal. This isn't your fault," he repeated.

"How do you know that? Yesterday you thought I'd murdered someone. I must have done something, somewhere to make you and the cartel think that."

"Someone left enough crumbs of evidence to persuade me you were the killer I was searching for. But once I caught up with you they didn't want you alive to defend yourself. They sent a cartel hit man to shut you up. But rather than dying like a good little girl, you killed their chief enforcer."

She opened her mouth to protest, but he cut her off, "I know it was self-defense, but in their eyes you made them look like idiots and believe it or not, leaders of drug cartels can't afford to look weak or stupid in front of their competitors."

He was right. No way would the cartel ever let her get away with what she'd done. They'd hunt her to the ends of the earth. Maybe Antarctica would be safe, but there weren't exactly many amphibians on that continent.

Her life had been turned upside down with no warning, and no grand announcement. Just BOOM! Now she had to adapt and survive, or roll over and die. She wasn't ready to roll over and die, not yet. The fact Killion seemed to take the loss of life for granted made her wonder how many of these situations he'd faced over the years.

His job was dangerous. Who could live like that? Who would want to?

She pulled the white and burgundy plaid shirt tight across her chest. Beneath it she wore a man's baggy gray tee and a pair of worn denim shorts, which she cinched around her waist with a leather belt she'd found in a locker beside a narrow cot. She tried not to think about whether or not she was wearing a dead man's clothes. It was irrelevant. She couldn't wander around naked no matter how much Killion might approve.

There was sympathy in Killion's eyes as he watched her, but also a measure of male appreciation. Did he find her genuinely attractive or did he just want to get laid because adrenaline was running high? Why was she even thinking about that?—Except it was better than remembering someone had not long ago pointed a gun at her and pulled the trigger. Instead of her dying, he'd had his head blown off.

She nodded toward the phone. "Do you trust your contacts at the CIA?"

"I'm not working for the CIA on this one." His gaze held hers. It was more than he usually admitted. "And yes, I trust them. Frankly, we don't have much choice."

That answer made another shiver crawl up her spine. "So what's the plan?"

He pointed at a rack on one side of the cabin. "See if you can find any charts of the area. I've got a good idea on how to drive this thing, but we need to know of any hazards in the water, any rocks or reefs. And figure out a good spot to anchor when we need to sleep. I'll set a course straight north for now. The water's deep around here so hopefully we won't hit anything."

Grateful to be given a real job to do, she went to the table where a map was already spread out. She stuck her finger on the small dot in the top right-hand corner in the middle of a huge expanse of blue sea. "This is the island we were on?"

"Yeah."

It was tiny. How had someone tracked them down? It couldn't be random.

"Look for charts north, north-east of that one. We're going to head to Jamaica and from there back into the States."

"Won't I be arrested at the border?"

"Audrey Lockhart would be arrested on the spot. You won't be Audrey Lockhart."

"And the fake ID will hold, even through customs?"

"If it doesn't we have a lot more to worry about than drug cartels. It'll hold."

She nodded slowly. If he was wrong they were already dead.

The idea of traveling under a false identity scared the crap out of her. Killion was probably used to it. "Killion" probably wasn't even his real name. That made her feel cheated somehow. Now wasn't the time to worry about this. Now was the time to prove she was good for more than being the sparkly assistant who distracted the crowd. She was smart and a team player, more than capable of contributing to their quest for survival.

She tipped large scrolls of paper out of metal canisters. She discarded one after the other and finally found the charts they needed by figuring out the matching lines of longitude and latitude. She waved him over and pointed at the map. "It would be shorter to head to the mainland."

Killion grunted. "Except Honduras and Nicaragua aren't particularly happy to accommodate the needs of the CIA, and they'd probably stuff you in jail for a year before they decided on whether or not to send you back to Colombia."

"By which time Gómez would find me and arrange a little prison fight where the stupid white girl gets shivved."

He raised a brow. "You catch on fast."

"I watch a lot of TV." She rubbed the goose bumps from her arms. "Do my parents know I'm wanted for murder?" The thought made the slight ache around her heart burn. How would they cope with this extra pressure? They had enough worries.

He took her by the shoulders and when she looked into his eyes, she found the craziness making sense in a way she didn't want it to.

"As much as I'd like to, I can't turn back the clock, but I can help make it right. It just might take a bit of time to figure out who is behind this, and out how to get the cartel off your back. Trust me." He tipped her chin up and stared down into her eyes.

What was he trying to distract her from this time?

"You say that a lot, you know."

He frowned. "What?"

"'Trust me.'" Her fingers tingled with the need to touch him. "It's usually a sign of deception."

His eyes twinkled. "Is it?"

"Usually, yes." She didn't think she'd ever been this physically attracted to a man as she was toward this one. She tried to move away, but he shadowed her until her back was pressed against the corkboard.

He moved a strand of her hair off her forehead and his voice dropped lower. "You don't *have* to trust me."

"I know." The constriction in her throat was back and her heart began beating so hard she was sure he could hear it. Her words came out in a whisper. "But for some inexplicable reason I do."

His eyes darkened and his gaze drifted over her lips, which parted.

"You want me to kiss you," he said in surprise.

A small laugh burst out and she rested her hands on his chest. "*You* want to kiss me."

"I'd be a fool not to."

"So do it." She held her breath.

"I'd be more of a fool if I did." His cheek buzzed hers and a shiver curled her toes.

"Since when did that stop you?" she said.

She felt his lips curve against her cheek. "Okay then." He touched his lips to hers, keeping the kiss closed-mouthed and chaste, more an exploratory touch than a real kiss.

Rules didn't seem to apply to his job, but she'd bet kissing someone in his custody probably crossed the line and broke a few rules. Considering what had happened to her life it seemed only fair to stir things up even just a little bit. She was a frog biologist, he was a CIA operative, but in this one thing they were equal.

She wrapped her arms around his neck, inhaling the masculine scent of him. She licked along the seam of his lips and felt his resistance melt away as he opened for her, letting her control this particular adventure.

She sank her fingers into his overlong hair, loving the texture of it. She moaned softly, stretching her body against all those hard muscles, feeling his arousal against her stomach and reveling in the fact she'd done that to him. She'd turned him on and she wasn't even naked.

Then something changed.

The air sizzled, the oxygen evaporated and it was suddenly difficult to breathe. What had started slow and languorous, exploded. He angled his mouth over hers, and started kissing her like he was starving, striving to get as close as physically possible. Her blood heated. The needy ache grew until she just wanted him inside her, right now, as fast as humanly possible. No foreplay, no teasing.

He dragged the shirt she wore low enough to expose her breast, and raised her taut nipple to his mouth. The sensation of his teeth on her flesh almost made her knees give out. Her fingers bit into his shoulders.

He blew cool air over the tight rosy peak and she was instantly wet. "You have no idea how long I've wanted to do that." His voice was gruff. He didn't give her time to respond, just switched his attention to her other breast while she tipped her head back against the board at her back and sank her fingers into his hair, holding him to her. Desire shot from her nipples to the apex of her thighs. Apparently Patrick Killion knew exactly how to deliver on all those arrogant promises and heated looks.

She gasped as his teeth nipped just a little. Oh, God, that felt good.

The sight of his blond head against her flushed skin was erotically beautiful. Desire consumed her. She couldn't remember a time when she wanted anything more than to have this man sink deep inside her.

The thought had her pressing her thighs together as a shiver of anticipation shot through her core. Was she really going to do this? Was she really going to have sex with a man who until a few hours ago had thought she was a cold-blooded killer?

God, she hoped so.

For the last few days her life had sucked, and escaping that reality even for ten minutes would be a welcome relief.

He licked and nibbled his way back to her mouth. She ran her hands over his flat stomach, and downwards over his shorts, stroking the hard length of his arousal that pressed against her stomach. Touching him made her desire grow stronger. She wanted to examine every inch of him, but he reclaimed her lips and kissed her some more. His arms tightened around her and she found herself lifted and pressed up against the wall, his thighs wedging themselves between hers.

"Ouch," she squeaked into his mouth.

He pulled back in alarm and then blinked as if he'd forgotten where he was. She would have been gratified by his obvious concern, but she didn't like the way he quickly disengaged their bodies and let her slide to the floor.

"Did I hurt you?" he asked.

She put her hand on the side of his face and turned him to

look at her. "No. It's okay, there was just a twinge in my side."

"Shit." He dragged up her shirt, but not in a way that screamed "I want you naked so I can take you fast and hard against the wall."

Once he reassured himself she wasn't bleeding, he stepped back and she let out a frustrated breath.

He dragged his hands through his hair. "I'm sorry. I can't believe I did that. Your life's a mess and you're still recovering from being stabbed."

She snorted at his lack of tact.

But he wasn't amused. He swore and moved away to stand beside the wheel. The look on his face screamed remorse and the death of desire.

She cleared her throat as she straightened her clothes. "It's okay, Patrick. My 'seduction games' are pretty hard to resist." Mortification at being so thoroughly rejected when she so obviously wanted to screw out his brains crept in. "Sorry. I shouldn't have—"

"Stop." He pointed his finger at her but refused to actually turn around and look at her. "You've been attacked multiple times and barely managed to survive. Finding an outlet for all that adrenaline is a natural part of the process. *I'm* the one taking advantage."

"Well, I was enjoying you taking advantage."

He glanced at her and his mouth twisted with regret.

A horrible thought shot through her. "Is there someone waiting for you back home?" Why hadn't she thought about that before she'd gone after him like a rabid beast? Why wouldn't he have a secret wife and kids back home?

He shook his head. "There isn't anyone—"

"But you'd say that anyway, to protect them—"

"Yes." His eyes looked a little wild. "Yes, I would. But I wouldn't be desperate to nail you against the wall if I was married!"

Her lips parted at the revelation. "Then what's the problem?" she asked slowly.

His eyes widened and, for a moment, she thought he was going to take her up on her obvious invitation. Instead he scrubbed his hands over his face and took a deep breath. "There are things I haven't told you."

They both knew there were a lot of things he hadn't told her.

Okay then. "Like what?"

His expression blanked the way it did when he was hiding something important. "The Colombians don't want you for the murder of Hector Sanchez."

She scrunched up her brow and opened her mouth to ask the obvious question but he beat her to it.

"They want you for the murder of Mario Aguilla."

"That's impossible." Her brain scrambled. Mario was her student. He was twenty-four and full of more charm than any young man had a right to. She'd met his parents. She had high hopes for a career in science for the young man. "That doesn't make any sense. Mario isn't dead." But from the look on his face she knew it was true. Numbness encased her. "Why? How?"

"We think the cartel went looking for him after I dragged you away from the institute."

It felt like a wide gaping hole had been blown in her chest. She looked down, half expecting to see the damage he'd inflicted to her heart. There was nothing visible, but on the inside she felt like she'd never be the same again. A young man had been murdered because she had defended herself and Killion had rescued her.

"This isn't your fault."

"Then whose fault is it?" she snapped.

"Raoul Gómez and whoever the hell set you up for this huge fucking fall, that's who."

She narrowed her gaze. "And you?"

He nodded. "And me."

They stared at one another for a full ten seconds. Part of her wanted to dissolve into a puddle of tears, but that wouldn't get them out of here, and it wouldn't bring Mario back.

"His parents think I killed him?" she asked in a thin voice.

He nodded.

"Do mine?"

He nodded again, looking stricken.

A lump of anguish grew inside her. People had been told she'd murdered a young man she liked and respected. Family. Peers. Did they believe it?

Why wouldn't they?

Everything she'd worked for had crumbled to nothing, but Mario's life had been stolen from him immutably. She had no career to go back to. Not anymore. Not until she cleared her name and got justice for her student. The only way to do that was to help Killion find out who was the mastermind behind this wretched scheme. Find them and expose them.

She walked over to the table and scanned the charts. "There's an atoll to watch out for, just over there." She scanned the horizon and pointed out a small rock jutting out of the ocean about a mile northwest.

Killion put his hand on her shoulder, but she stiffened at his touch. "I'm sorry I didn't tell you earlier. I needed to be certain you weren't involved."

"It's fine." She shrugged out of his grip.

From the look on his face he understood that "fine" didn't necessarily mean "fine." It meant, *"Back off before I scratch out your eyes."* He was smart enough to let it go.

After everything that had happened, her heart felt as if it were frozen solid in her chest and her blood had stopped pumping. Grief and rage coalesced into something bitter and angry. Focused too. Honed like a dagger. She needed to hold onto that focus because she intended to claw back her life. Even though the odds were stacked increasingly against her, she would exonerate herself and get justice for her student. No matter the cost.

CHAPTER THIRTEEN

I T TOOK A full twenty-four hours for them to make it to Jamaica. Now the sun was sinking in the western sky and a light breeze was starting to whip up the white caps. The sea and sky merged in a pale shimmering gray that he hoped would help hide them as the twilight deepened.

"Got everything?" he asked Audrey.

She nodded with a cold detached expression that had been the only emotion she'd shown since he'd told her about the dead student. He could tell she was devastated and furious and using that fury to carry her through this nightmare. Killion got it. He even appreciated her calm, precise help with piloting the boat and getting them this far. But he missed the other Audrey. The funny one. The one who argued with him. The one who'd said she trusted him and sounded like she meant it. The one who'd kissed him as if he were water in the desert and clung to him like shrink-wrap.

Even the memory of that kiss had him shifting uncomfortably. The woman was distracting him from the mission and her life depended on him getting everything right.

What he needed was someone to meet them on the island and take Audrey to a safe house while he took off and did the job the president had tasked him and Lincoln Frazer to do. Find the person who'd hired an assassin to murder a sitting vice president. So what if the guy had been an asshole? They didn't get to make that decision, and they certainly didn't get to murder Dr. Audrey Lockhart just because they wanted to. He'd underestimated his enemy once and they'd caught them unaware. No more assuming they were safe. No more blind trust.

He left Audrey in the inflatable and went back and opened the hatch to the dank hold, inserted an earplug into each ear and picked up an AK-47 by the strap. He fired a full magazine into the bottom of the boat, spent shells flying around like popcorn in a skillet. He switched the cartridge and aimed at the same spot, watching splinters of wood spit and spray around the enclosed space. Impressed by the strength of the hull he changed the magazine a third time and this time was rewarded by a spout of water. He kept firing until the small trickle turned into a steady flow.

Convinced he'd done enough to scuttle the vessel, he tossed the now empty submachine gun to the deck, picked up his beach bag and slung it over his shoulder. He climbed over the side of the trawler and hopped into the inflatable, casting off before settling in beside Audrey on the bench seat.

"You good?" he asked, starting the outboard. She had a canvas hat pulled low over her eyes and wore a pair of crappy men's black sunglasses that kept slipping down her nose. He didn't want anyone with a telescopic lens getting a good look at her face when they got closer to shore.

"I'm fine." She kept her eyes on the horizon, voice clipped, body rigid.

Sure. He blew out a frustrated breath and pushed away from the hull of the trawler, then motored around the old fishing boat. It was a waste, but keeping Gómez and his co-

conspirator in the dark was worth it, and should help to keep Audrey safe. Plus, any forensic evidence that they'd been onboard would be at the bottom of the ocean.

The boat was beginning to sit lower in the water. They were about four nautical miles north of Montego Bay. There was no one visible on the horizon, and he'd obliterated the name and number of the vessel where it had been painted on the hull. He just hoped the boat sank before anyone spotted it. He hadn't wanted to attract attention by setting it on fire.

Using the compass on his watch, he directed the inflatable west. He needed to find a beach quiet enough for them to land without anyone spotting them, but close enough to some small tourist spot that they could easily walk to a hotel.

Audrey was much better than she had been a few days ago, but walking more than a mile was going to tax her strength. Thankfully they'd had a good supply of fresh water and food on the fishing boat, but she hadn't eaten much, and he was worried about her. It wasn't an emotion he usually allowed himself to feel, but it had been a constant since he'd stepped in after Hector's attack.

He lived in a gray world that was multifaceted and obscure. Moral purity was a lie. There was no such thing as good and evil, or right and wrong. He did the best he could do, keeping his oath at the forefront of his mind. A good interrogator—like a good case officer—had to be capable of deep sincere attachments while at the same time maintaining a cynical detachment.

Usually he excelled at cynical detachment, but somewhere between Audrey warning him not to touch Hector Sanchez's skin because of the poison, and her getting the drop on him with a gun she obviously had no idea how to handle, he'd lost that cynical detachment and started to care. To really care.

She hated him for lying to her—imagine if she knew the full extent of his deception?

As a Company man his commitment was to his oath—to protect integrity and defend the US Constitution without losing sight of human decency. He was often asking people to commit treason against their own countries to get the information he needed, and that required a measure of compassion and understanding. But his country and his mission were always paramount in his mind, which was why he was so successful at what he did. For the first time since he'd joined the Agency, he wasn't sure he could make an objective decision for the good of the mission. He'd invested too much in Audrey's survival. She wasn't an asset. She wasn't a detainee. She was someone who'd been targeted by the person who'd murdered Ted Burger, and that made her valuable to him. But she meant more to him than that and those were feelings he couldn't afford if he wanted to do his job properly.

He motored onwards, looking for just the right spot to haul out. There were lights strung across most of the beaches, hotels just in the distance. Couples walking hand-in-hand along the sand.

He carried on past the big resorts. The area became dark and wooded.

He was so attuned to Audrey's wellbeing that he noticed immediately when she hunched her shoulders and began to shiver. He shrugged out of the fleece he'd picked up on the boat and handed it to her. She shook her head at first.

"Put it on," he told her sternly.

She took it, pulling it over her shoulders, pinching her lips in annoyance at what she probably considered a show of weakness. *Hell.* She had no idea how strong she was. Most people would be flailing about complaining bitterly about how unfair life was for treating them this way, but she seemed to have accepted the shitty situation. He'd be lying if he said he wasn't worried about just how fiercely she was holding it all together though. Even a trained operative would struggle after what she'd been through, especially with no end in sight. He wanted to tell her he'd be there for her, but that was a lie. Jed Brennan would find her a safe house and whisk her away.

She'd cease to be his problem.

But what if the safe house wasn't so safe? Like the place in Minneapolis where the US Marshals had put Vivi Vincent and her son before Christmas? The house had been attacked and two marshals killed. It was a miracle Vivi and Michael had survived.

Audrey had already experienced two miracles, three if you counted the experience on the island. How many more times could she cheat death? But he couldn't just quit the mission. Until they caught the mastermind behind this, Audrey was always going to be in danger. So far the perp had used smarts and ingenuity to attack her multiple times while remaining incognito.

His fingers tightened on the rudder.

It was almost full dark now, and he was thinking they might end up going around the entire island before he found somewhere suitable. Then he caught sight of a group of hotels about a half a mile down the coast, and spied a curving sandy cove just off to his right. There weren't any lights, but a pair of car headlights swept along a nearby road, and no way would a spot like that not have a point of access. He angled the inflatable until they were perpendicular to the waves and headed for the pale sand.

"Hold on." It was high tide, which was good news, but the surf was rough closer to the beach, throwing the boat around. He accelerated through the big waves then lifted the propeller out of the water and jumped over the side, hauling on the rope to move the boat up onto the sand.

Audrey had removed her sunglasses and looked like she was about to jump out and help him.

"Stay put," he ordered sternly.

She kept forgetting about the newly healed knife wound, just the way he'd forgotten it when he'd been trying to get inside her yesterday. Only her gasp of pain had stopped him from dragging her clothes aside and thrusting deep.

At the time she'd been wild for him, needing a distraction from the horror and fear she'd endured. That moment of madness was over and done with. Now the only thing she wanted to nail to the wall was her student's killer. Sweat formed on his brow and not just from the exertion of pulling the heavy boat up the beach. She'd been so sexy. So sweet. Another wave broke against him and the cold water doused any sexual fires that might have started to burn.

He kept hauling on the rope, fighting the undertow. When the surf was ankle deep he went to the side of the boat. "Come on." He waved her over. "Grab the bags." He held out his arms.

"I can walk," she protested.

"Just put your arms around my neck and stop being a pain in my ass."

Her eyes flashed. *Finally.* She slid her arms around his neck and he pulled her against his chest, gathering her to him in a way that felt too familiar. He dropped her a few feet beyond the reach of the water and then concentrated on hauling the boat out. It was fricking heavy, but he put his whole body into moving the dead weight past the water line, until the muscles in his arms and shoulders burned. Audrey followed him up the beach, an insubstantial shadow in the darkness, but even so he knew exactly where she was. Finally he was satisfied. He dropped the rope and delved into his bag for a flashlight.

They both wore flip-flops, though Audrey's were three sizes too big for her and she kept tripping. He took her arm to try to prevent her falling on her face. "Careful."

He flicked on the light and swept the beam over the vegetation that edged the pale sand, searching for an opening in the greenery.

Audrey grabbed his wrist. "There." She pointed with the flashlight.

The woman had good eyes. He waved her ahead of him, and they tramped through the sand, which turned into a dusty path that ran through the trees. He kept the beam just in front of Audrey's feet in case there were any snakes around.

She stopped abruptly, and he put his hand on her shoulder to prevent bumping into her.

"What is it?" he whispered, alert for danger.

"Hear that?"

Killion listened hard for some indication they weren't alone. "I don't hear anything."

"A tree frog. It's a tree frog singing." He felt the shudder move through her. "My old life. Did you know 'amphibian' means 'living two lives' in Latin?"

She went to walk on but he pulled her back against him

and turned her around. "You'll get your old life back. We'll beat these bastards. In the meantime we just need to keep you safe."

"You don't understand." She swallowed audibly. "All these years, my sister's addiction, Rebecca dying…" She tried to pull away, but he wouldn't let her go. "My work, my *research* was the one thing I had control over. Now someone's taken that away from me and hurt people I care about in the process." Her voice shook. "I'm angry. I'm so *damn* angry."

He got it.

Her head dropped, and she rested her forehead against his chest. He wrapped his arms tight around her, relief smothering him that she was back with him, finally. Maybe he could make it happen on the research front—there were military bases with lab facilities. When he found the person who'd arranged the assassination plot, POTUS would owe him a favor, and getting Audrey's life back on track would be his number one priority.

Emotion gripped his throat. How had this woman come to mean so much to him in such a short time? The answer was simple—Audrey was good and kind and pure of heart. A living and breathing ideal. Exactly the sort of person he'd joined the CIA to protect. Even as he held her close he knew walking away was going to be a bitch. He released her and turned her around to face the path again.

"Okay, let's move it. Remember our cover. Newlyweds, but you hate our hotel because you just found a cockroach and freaked the hell out. Be as high-strung about that as you want. I'm the doting husband who just wants to keep you happy so I can get laid ten times a day."

"Only ten?" He gave her points for trying to get into her

role.

"If I was on my honeymoon with you, Lockhart, I'd want to have sex at least ten times a day. If not eleven. Which is probably a few down from when we were living in sin."

"What if I'd refused to live in sin? Perhaps I said I needed you to put a ring on it before we had sex ten times a day?"

"In that case we've got a lot of catching up to do."

She laughed the way he'd hoped she would, but the words did something weird to his insides. They made him wonder what having a proper relationship with this woman might be like. His profession was too treacherous to put anyone in danger, but Audrey was already running for her life...

And that *was his idea of a proper relationship? With someone on the run?*

Jesus. He was too messed up and too cynical for romance. Bad guys were always plotting against the US and people died every day. He had the skills to prevent that and a relationship never measured up when stacked against those opposing factors.

He ignored the inner voice that wanted to argue that maybe it was someone else's turn to fight. He wasn't ready to retire yet. What the hell would he do? Sell insurance?

They came out of the forest onto a gravel road. He shone the light first right then left, took her fingers in his and headed left. "Drivers around here are nuts so stick to the side of the road. Keep your hat pulled low in case anyone sees us. I reckon we have a ten minute walk to the nearest tourist trap."

"Do you have ID?"

"Yep. But I don't want to use it. Hopefully we can find some mom and pop deal that'll let us stay a couple of nights for cash. Just let me do the talking—"

"Unless I'm moaning about cockroaches."

"I knew you were a quick study."

"They don't just give Ph.D.'s away you know."

"I know, darlin'. I know." He smoothed his hand up and down her back to calm her agitation. He needed to get them somewhere safe before Audrey hit the tears part of the grieving process. Right now she was stuck on anger, but once the floodgates opened the storm would unleash. The last thing he wanted was to be around when it did, and yet, he didn't want to be anywhere else, either.

THE WEATHER IN Virginia was the usual lousy January mix of freezing rain and overcast sky. It was early evening and Tracey Williams sat at a table in the mall coffee shop. A pretty blonde with a cappuccino took a seat nearby and pulled out the most recent copy of *People* Magazine.

Killion and Lockhart had disappeared, as had the idiots Gómez had sent to take care of them. Last night Tracey had gone to dinner again with her Agency contact, Peter. They'd eaten too much, drunk too much, talked for hours, and then fucked like bunnies.

And Peter had been very informative as to agency gossip.

The girl she was following, Crista Zanelli, had a reputation as some kind of brilliant analyst, but like most geeks she had her head up her ass when it came to personal security. Apparently a former girlfriend of Patrick Killion's, Crista was the person he turned to when *he* needed information. Crista was Tracey's best hope of finding out where Killion had gone to ground, unless he or Lockhart surfaced of their own accord.

Crista—bless her heart—had stopped on the way home to pick over the ragged remains of the January sales. Tracey sipped her coffee and avoided staring directly at the girl. Animals knew when they were being hunted, that elusive sixth sense honed for survival.

She broke off a corner of a large chocolate chip cookie and nibbled.

Killion really was the perfect choice to lead a covert mission tracking down Ted Burger's killer, and one of the few Intelligence Officers to make her nervous.

She'd done the world a favor getting rid of Burger, even if her boss's reasons were less than altruistic. They'd bugged Burger's computer and discovered he'd somehow been involved in the terror plot that had recently gone down in Minnesota. They'd already known about the old man's involvement with the shadowy vigilante organization called The Gateway Project. After Burger's failed assassination plot against the president, they'd decided it was time to get rid of the old man before he was either caught or became too powerful to touch. She'd removed all trace of the bugs from Burger's computer and disappeared.

The Secret Service hadn't been happy, but she'd dealt with those clowns before.

Her boss had come up with the idea of using frog poison after visiting Lockhart in Colombia. It was a stroke of genius. Two birds. One stone. Gaining them a scapegoat if their crimes were detected.

Patrick Killion had obviously fallen for the bait, and he'd traced that poison all the way back to the Colombian jungle and sweet little Audrey Lockhart just as planned.

Would the biologist be able to convince him of her innocence?

Tracey pouted as she pondered the question, drinking her coffee and nibbling her cookie. Killion was susceptible to a pretty face and went through women the way most men went through razorblades. Of course, they had to be beautiful. She had no doubt he'd seduce Lockhart to get the information he needed. And, unless he'd lost his touch, he'd have figured out the truth by now, which meant he'd be continuing his search for the real assassin.

Crista Zanelli checked her phone and smiled whenever a text came up. Tracey had hoped the girl was meeting Killion here, which was why she'd followed Crista inside the mall rather than just following her car home.

So far, no sign of him or Lockhart.

Tracey sipped her coffee. She'd been here too long. If Killion was around she didn't want him to spot her, not that he'd recognize her with her sleek figure and long blonde hair. She got up, put her napkins in the garbage and left the coffee shop to browse the window of the jewelry store opposite, checking out the rings. When Crista still didn't move she went inside and looked at some earrings.

Crista finally finished her coffee and placed her magazine carefully in her Kate Spade tote before clearing away her table.

Such a good little drone.

Crista headed back to her car, and Tracey hung around for another five minutes, lucking out when Crista popped up at the mall entrance at the same time she did—the woman had picked up milk and bread from the supermarket. It was dark outside but the area was well lit. Not many people were around and those that were had their heads down to avoid the light drizzle that had started to fall.

Tracey got in her car and pulled slowly out of the parking lot, turning onto the highway and keeping three or four cars back from the other woman. She was in no hurry and knew where Crista lived. She just wanted to see if she took any side trips or if Killion made contact.

Her work cell rang, and she put it on speaker.

"The idiots haven't got a fucking clue where their people disappeared to." He sounded on the verge of losing it and needed to calm down or he'd get them both caught.

"I have a lead on something," she said.

"Seriously?"

"I'm shocked you have so little faith," she teased.

"Sometimes I forget how amazing you are."

"This is true. You do."

He laughed, sounding calmer. "I should have let you take care of her the way you wanted to last month."

"Yes, you should have," she said primly.

"Next time I'll listen. I promise."

No, he wouldn't. It was part of the reason she loved him. The other was he knew her darkest secrets, but accepted her anyway.

"Maybe you and I can sneak away for a vacation when this is over," he said, surprising her.

But if everything went to plan they'd be too busy for a vacation. Didn't matter. They'd be together eventually.

"I just want to be alone with you," she told him honestly, "just for a few hours."

"As soon as you get home," he soothed.

They were both so busy having sex with other people for the sake of this scheme she'd almost forgotten how good it felt to be held in his arms.

"Come to the office as soon as you get back. I feel a very important meeting coming on."

Her heart stuttered. He rarely touched her at the office. Said it was too risky, but she craved those stolen moments. He had a way about him. Genius, good looking, and rich. If it weren't for his general lack of conscience he'd be the perfect man—and wouldn't look at her twice.

"I'll be there as soon as I can."

"What would I do without you?" He sounded calmer now. Less on the edge of losing it. She'd done that for him. She'd done much more than that for him.

Tracey was behind Crista at the lights, but she carried on straight through when the woman hooked a left. She drove to the next junction and doubled back to where Crista had turned off. A few hundred feet into a nondescript housing estate, Crista was unloading shopping bags and walking into her neat little bungalow.

Tracey never slowed. She'd be paying Crista a visit in the near future. Wouldn't take long to find out everything the analyst knew.

She smiled. This would hurt Killion. He had such a soft heart beneath that cynical smile. It was probably bleeding all over poor little Audrey, right now. She hoped he fucked her every which way, so that when he ditched her Audrey would be devastated. She'd hate him.

But every woman should have a man like Patrick Killion at least once in her life. It was only fair, especially when death was just around the corner.

AUDREY FOLLOWED KILLION into a small rustic-looking lodge down one of the side roads in a small tourist town. They'd walked past gift shops, bars, and restaurants all plying their trade as if the world hadn't gone to hell in a hand basket. She just wanted to find a safe spot to curl up and sleep. The last thing she wanted was to watch people going about their normal business while her life disintegrated around her in ruins.

This lodge was quaint, not one of the big chains. Potted ferns grew profusely outside the entrance. Inside the reception area, a desk and computer sat on the left side, and a wicker love seat bracketed the right. Dimly lit for ambiance, with racks of brochures on the walls, promoting zip lines and horseback riding, scuba and snorkeling trips. Normal things for vacationers. Safe, healthy adventures. A bit of an adrenaline rush before they returned to their everyday lives. She wondered if there was a brochure that contained information on what to do when evading the authorities while running for your life.

Killion probably knew it all by heart anyway.

Through the window, a dark blue swimming pool glistened through iron railings and she wanted to slide into its depths and forget her troubles. But her troubles weren't the kind to go away if she ignored them. The longer she ran, the more whoever was behind this shored up their position and made her look like a criminal.

But right now she was too tired to fight.

She waited near the door while Killion sweet-talked the girl behind the desk.

Exhaustion ate at her, making her vision blurry, her balance off, and her thought processes slow. She and Killion had spent most of last night each taking three hour shifts to pilot the boat so they could put as much distance between themselves and Gómez's thugs as possible.

Even when it had been her turn to rest she'd laid in the cot and stared at the rough wooden boards above her, thoughts of Mario running through her head. A young man. Beautiful, dedicated, and smart, really smart. He'd only been with her since September. He was her grad student and she'd somehow managed to get him killed.

Emotion threatened to overwhelm her.

As if sensing her impending meltdown, Killion slipped his arm around her shoulders. "It's just for one night." He worked the receptionist, who was a pretty teenager with dark skin and eyes the color of bitter chocolate. "Actually make it two. Just while I sic my lawyers on the hotel we booked our honeymoon with. Trust me, they'll be begging to give us the presidential suite by the time we're done, won't they, baby?"

"Even then I won't go back." Audrey produced a mechanical smile as his fingers massaged the knots in her shoulder.

"The snooty woman at reception was a bitch and I'm going to make sure she doesn't treat some other poor sucker the same way. We should have come to a place like this instead of some anonymous hotel."

"I don't care where we stay as long as it doesn't have roaches. You don't have roaches, do you?" she asked the girl, more sharply than she'd intended if Killion's tightening fingers were any indication.

"No, ma'am." The receptionist gave her own shudder. "I hate them, too. My father sprays regularly to make sure we don't have them around here." Her smile was warm and welcoming. "We have one vacancy." Her eyes ran over her computer screen. "And it just happens it's the honeymoon suite, which has its own hot tub."

"Perfect." Killion's eyes glowed as he smiled at her, and Audrey would give anything to know what he was really thinking. But with a man who could lie as easily as Killion, how would she ever know for sure?

The girl behind the desk gave them a price, and Killion handed over the cash.

"Where's the best place to get a meal around here?" he asked, although the last thing Audrey wanted was food, or to go out. "We haven't explored much, yet. It's actually the first time we've left the hotel room—pretty much the first time we've left the bed." He winked.

Audrey elbowed him in the gut, but his grin was Cheshire cat wide. The man was truly irredeemable.

The receptionist blinked rapidly and her cheeks flushed.

"That's because he tires easily." Audrey scooped up the key the girl placed on the counter. "Thanks so much." She headed off in the direction the girl had indicated, along a path decorated with shells.

The greenery was lush and hung over the fence surrounding the property. The honeymoon suite was around the corner from all the other apartments, in a secluded bay filled with potted plants, and enough vegetation to make it very, very private. The hot tub sat on one side of the deck. Killion moved like a panther but she could feel him following behind her. In fact she was achingly aware of every move he made. She unlocked the door into a beautiful room that looked like a tropical paradise. A massive four-poster bed occupied the center of the room, its sides draped with mosquito netting. The floors were a dark wood that matched the bed frame, but everything else was blindingly white, from the walls to the linen, to the towels she could see in the en suite bathroom.

Hands pushed her forward. "Go grab a shower. I'm going to make a phone call and come back with something clean to wear and warm to eat."

"We're not going out?" Relief filled her.

"I'll make it up to you some other time."

"No, you won't." She turned to face him and her mouth went dry. "Once this is over, you'll move on and I'll never see you again."

He flinched, but didn't speak. Answer enough.

"Go make your phone call," she said tiredly. "Would you mind bringing back some deodorant and toothpaste? If you have enough cash…"

She knew he wouldn't use a credit card.

He avoided her gaze and looked at the floor. "No problem. Lock the door after me. I'll take the key."

"Okay." She frowned.

This tension between them had come out of nowhere. His expression suggested he wanted to say something, but he remained silent. He simply left and Audrey fought the urge to cry. Moving slowly she forced herself into the bathroom and stripped off the disgusting reminder of the men who'd tried to kill her. Under the hot spray tears came and she let them—for Mario, for her stolen life, for the shock and horror of being stabbed and almost dying, for being shot at and accused of murder. But most of all for the loss of a man she should never have met. She didn't really know anything about him, but he'd saved her life, over and over again. It wasn't surprising he'd wormed his way into her heart. It would be more shocking if he hadn't.

Warm tears continued to flow down her cheeks as sadness enveloped her. When this was over he would walk away, and no matter how deeply he affected her, she'd have to let him.

CHAPTER FOURTEEN

K ILLION SCANNED THE area as he walked through one of
the big hotel complexes to the beach. Part of him didn't
want to make the call to Jed. He trusted the guy but what if he
was wrong? What if there was a security breach in the FBI's
BAU-4? What if Alex Parker wasn't as shit-hot with cyber-
security as he thought he was?

It wasn't just his life at stake, it was Audrey's too.

Trouble was Killion didn't really have a choice. He was
down to five hundred bucks cash and even though *he* had the
means to disappear he didn't have the means to take Audrey
with him. She probably couldn't wait to get rid of him. Sure
she'd kissed him, but she knew he wasn't good for the long
term. Once this case was over he *would* move on and never see
her again. It shouldn't have cut so deeply that she knew it too.

Bob Marley sang "I Shot the Sheriff" on the patio. It jerked
him back to the moment.

Killion wandered down to the water, the sand warm
against the soles of his feet. Stupidly, he'd made a promise not
only to keep Audrey alive, but to restore her reputation with
the authorities, which might be at odds with completing his
mission as ordered. Trapped between a rock and a hard place,
he dialed the number on his encrypted sat phone.

Jed answered straight away. "Acting SSA Brennan." Which

suggested he wasn't convinced someone couldn't be listening in on their conversation either.

"We're here."

"I'll take care of it." And Jed hung up.

Killion stared at the phone. "A little light on instructions there, pal." *Well, hell.* He stuffed the cell in his pocket and caught the aromatic scent of baked fish on the night air. His stomach growled. He hadn't realized how hungry he was until his stomach threatened to rip out his throat. Time to get some supplies and plan their next move.

IT WAS LATE when Tracey knocked on Crista's door. It was pitch black outside. She could have bypassed the pathetic alarm system installed in Crista's house, but she had a different plan in mind for now.

The sound of footsteps and then a flicker in the lights behind one of the glass panels in the door told her someone was approaching. The lock turned and the door opened.

"Hi?" Crista asked. "Can I help you?"

Tracey held up her collector's badge. "I'm collecting for heart disease."

Crista's face cleared. "Oh, okay. Hold on a moment." The woman turned and walked down the corridor, presumably to get her purse. Tracey let herself in and closed the door quietly. Quickly she planted a listening bug under the hall table.

"It's freezing out there. You deserve a medal for collecting in this kind of weather."

"Actually, I lied." Tracey stood by the door and pretended to be nervous.

Crista froze.

"Look, I'm sorry. I, uh, I have something really embarrassing and private to confess."

Crista picked up her cell and let her finger hover over what had to be emergency services on speed dial.

"I didn't know what else to do." Tracey let tears fill her eyes. "The thing is, I'm pregnant." She let her hand cup her empty belly. "And I don't know how to get hold of the father because he's blocked my calls."

"What's that got to do with me?" Crista had a glint in her eye that said she didn't believe her. The woman better believe her.

"We were only together for a month, but I know you guys are friends."

Crista rolled her eyes. Not as stupid as she looked.

"I looked at his phone one day while he was in the shower and saw your name and number." Tracey looked at the floor as if ashamed. "I was jealous of all his secrecy, but when he found out I'd looked at his phone he left the same night." She swallowed tightly. "I thought at first he was married and you were his wife."

"Who was it?" Crista demanded, her hand still hovering over that damned button.

Tracey reached behind her for the doorknob and shook her head. "It doesn't matter. He wouldn't be interested anyway."

"Not interested in his own kid? What kind of asshole were you dating?"

Tracey hesitated and let her lip wobble. "He told me his name was Killion, but I'm not sure if that was his real name."

Crista's eyes went wide.

Tracey opened the door as if to leave. "I'm not expecting anything from him. I can support myself and the baby financially." Her voice broke. "I just thought he should know." She began to slip out into the cold night.

"Hey. Stop!" Crista rushed toward her. "Come in. I'm sorry. I'm pretty suspicious by nature."

Tracey forced a laugh. "Me, too." A couple of tears streaked her cheeks and she swiped at them. "I can't believe I let the guy charm me into bed. I really can't believe the damn condom broke."

Crista took her by the arm. "There are a lot of condom babies out there." She drew her into the immaculate white kitchen. "I'll call him for you."

"No!" Tracey swallowed hard and shook her head. She needed time to get a fix on his GPS coordinates. "No. I mean this is huge news. I really need to tell him face-to-face."

Crista stared at her, hesitating. "So what do you want me to do?"

"When I last saw him he said he was leaving the country. I know he could be gone months." In reality he'd be back very soon to pick up his search for the person who killed Burger. "I want the chance to tell him in person that I'm having his baby. See if we can maybe make this thing work." She pulled her card out of her pocket. "When he gets back to the country would you call me? Help me arrange a meeting?" She wore wool gloves and had made sure there were no prints or DNA on the card, just the number of a burner cell. If Crista got suspicious she'd probably assume Tracey was CIA or NSA. "I grew up without a father"—she knew Crista did too—"I'd like my baby at least to have the chance to get to know his or hers."

Crista nodded.

"I won't put you out any longer. Thank you." Tracey turned and headed back to the front door.

"He's a good guy, you know." Crista's voice made her pause. "He'll be there for you and the kid."

"I hope so." Tracey smiled tremulously and let herself out. The bitch was so fucking sentimental and stupid. She got in her rental and decided to head home. Everything was set up for her plan. There was nothing to do except wait, and for the first time in what felt like forever, she wanted to be wrapped in the arms of the man she loved.

———————

WHEN KILLION GOT back to the honeymoon suite, the place was cloaked in darkness. He knocked on the door, announcing himself though it went against every instinct to make a noise. He unlocked the door and went inside.

A sliver of moonlight showed Audrey stretched out beneath the sheet, seemingly fast asleep. Crap. She looked so pretty lying there. Funny how some women managed beauty without the aid of makeup or fancy clothes. Audrey pulled off "natural" with an unconscious grace and she probably didn't realize most men preferred women that way.

He turned away. He'd wanted her to eat a decent meal but she was completely out of it and no way was he waking her up. He went over to the small kitchenette and put the take-out boxes inside the small refrigerator.

Then he stretched out his arms over his head and heard his back click into place. Damn, he was stiff and sore and fucking exhausted.

As quietly as possible, he moved a heavy chest in front of

the front door. Nothing he could do about the windows except close the blinds.

Still in the dark, he took stock of his weaponry. He had his SIG, the captain's old colt '45, and another 1911 he'd taken from the boat. All locked and loaded with several clips of spare ammunition for each. He put one handgun on each bedside table—if Audrey had wanted to shoot him she'd have done it days ago—and kept his SIG with him.

In the bathroom he eyed the tub. It was tempting, but considering how tired he was he'd probably drown. While most days he'd take his chances, he had Audrey to think of. So he turned on the spray in the glass shower and tried not to imagine his pretty biologist in here earlier. The knowledge that he was going to have to sleep next to her made the memory of her naked body more arousing and he gritted his teeth as his dick went stiff as a police baton.

He bumped his forehead against the glass in defeat.

No way was he getting any sleep like this.

He slid soap over his body and, unable to resist, slid it over his own length, trying not to imagine Audrey's hands on him, or her legs wrapped around his hips, but doing it anyway.

Part of him knew he should feel some shame fantasizing about her like this, but that's not how his brain worked. She was safe and sleeping and he wasn't compromising anyone. He wasn't crossing lines or making false promises. He wasn't making the bond they shared even stronger—because there was no doubt they shared a very real connection no matter how temporary or inconvenient.

And if it was her lips around his cock he was imagining when he threw back his head and came, that was his business. He was taking care of a craving that needed satisfied, like hunger or thirst. Filling an emptiness that needed to be filled. There was no harm being done to anything except his sanity.

———————

AUDREY WOKE AS the mattress dipped. It took a nanosecond to realize Patrick Killion—she still didn't know if that was his real name—had slid between the sheets beside her.

"You're back."

His big hand cupped the back of her head in a gentle squeeze before releasing her. "I didn't mean to wake you. Go back to sleep."

All her life she'd been the strong one, the independent one, and the one who didn't need any help from anyone. Now her world had spun completely out of control and she needed this man to keep her alive. Maybe that was why she wanted him sexually too—maybe it was a biological imperative for the female to take care of the alpha male's sexual needs. Or maybe it was because beneath the laid-back, wisecracking exterior, he was kind and thoughtful and generous.

He smelled like soap and clean male skin. The moonlight caught the edge of his jaw as he lay on his back and stared up at the ceiling. Her fingers curled against the need to touch him. There was only one thing she wanted to do right now and he was lying right beside her.

"Will you hold me?" she asked.

He reached out over the sheet and dragged her against him. It was only when her back connected with his front that he realized she was naked.

He groaned and moved to release her, but she grabbed his hand and squeezed it over the top of the sheet, her nipple pebbling against his palm.

"I can't hold you like this without getting a raging hard on, Doc." He pressed his hips against her ass to prove his point.

"Good, you're going to need it." She turned in his arms and touched his now clean-shaven face. It was dark except for moonlight, but her eyes had adjusted to the shadows. "I want to be with you, Patrick. I know you're going to walk into the sunset as soon as you can hand me off to someone else. But I want this."

His fingers flexed on her hip. "The next guy might be a keeper."

She pressed her thumb to his bottom lip and felt it open. "If we don't do this I'll always wonder what it would have been like to make love to you…always."

She heard him swallow.

"This is a really bad idea. I told myself I wouldn't touch you. I'm trying to keep you safe."

"I want you to touch me." She arched against him.

"I don't want you to hate me." His voice sounded rough in his throat.

"I won't hate you—not for this anyway." She gave a half snort, half laugh.

That made him pause for a second. He ran his hand up her body and his thumb found the center of her nipple with unerring accuracy. He scraped his nail over the sensitive flesh and her sex contracted, hard and sharp. "Might spoil you for every other man, Aud."

God—that ego. "It's a risk I'm willing to take."

His mouth dipped to hers. "Don't say I didn't warn you."

His lips were warm and firm against hers as he rolled her onto her back and took the kiss deeper. It was an exploration of her mouth, a journey around her lips. She tried to touch him, but he held her free hand flat against the covers. She moaned as his lips slipped lower, down her neck, over her collarbone and down to her breasts. Her back arched up off the bed, nipples aching to be tasted. He complied, grazing the tight buds with his teeth, taking her to the edge of pain before pulling back. Then his head slipped lower, down to her navel, tongue dipping inside.

He shifted down the bed and moved her knees apart, blowing on her sensitive skin. Her breath stopped when his tongue slid along her opening. Her body moved toward him like it was coming home.

She grabbed the pillow, needing to hold onto something. "This is kind of advanced stuff for the first time, don't you think?"

"Go big or go home, baby." His mouth found her center again, and her hips rose of their own volition and she squeaked. She grabbed his hair when he zeroed in on a particularly amazing spot and her vision blurred. She found herself dragged up his body, her knees over his shoulders as he gave her his full attention. An orgasm was winding up inside her and she was desperate to reach it, closer and closer, the coil contracting tighter and tighter until she exploded into tiny pieces of sparkling pleasure. She cried out his name before floating quietly back to earth. He let her legs drop and crawled over her body to kiss her on the mouth.

She tasted herself on his lips and pulled back. Blinked because he was so close and unfocused. "Weird."

"*Great*," he corrected.

She could hear self-satisfaction in his smile.

"Weird," she reasserted. She kissed him again because she

loved his mouth. He lay on one side of her, tracing his fingers slowly over her body, his arousal hot and heavy against her thigh. Holding back. Slowing them down when she wanted everything frenetic and fast.

"Do you have condoms?" she asked, already desperate for him to be inside her.

He pulled back. "Will you think less of me if I say yes?"

"The way I tried to climb onboard you when I kissed you on the boat? You'd have been a fool not to buy a truckload."

He rolled out of bed and retrieved a box and gave it a shake. "I wasn't raised to be a fool, but I wasn't thinking you were a sure thing either. I want you to know that. I just like to be prepared…"

She wasn't going to think about that statement. He came back to the bed and tossed the box on the side table.

She pulled him down beside her and then pushed on his shoulders until he was on his back.

"Is this how you want me?" He laughed up at her.

Damn, he was gorgeous. She swallowed against the tightness in her throat as she looked at his body in the dim light. He was all lean muscle and toned, warm skin. "For now."

She caught the flash of teeth as he placed his arms behind his head, cocky as always. They were both being careful about making this a sexual hook up to work off some tension. She knew it wouldn't take much to fall in love with him, and she didn't want to be one of many women who probably begged this man for more than he was willing to give. So she'd give him this. Take this. Good sex to distract their minds and make them forget the terrible things they'd had to deal with recently. And the difficult things that lay ahead.

She ran her hands down his body, the taut pectoral muscles, flat belly, delving into the crisp hair surrounding the hard length of him. She knelt next to him then ran her hands over the strong thighs, sensitive knees, then back up the inside of his legs, feeling the quiver in his muscles as she approached her target.

She cupped his balls and then took his length in her other hand, leaning down to add her mouth to the mix.

His hands fisted in her hair and she heard him swallow, then whisper, "Good thing I took the edge off in the shower."

"Did you think of me?" She took him again before he could answer. *Stupid question.* She didn't want to know if he was thinking of someone else, and he was too good a liar for her to know the truth.

She had to make this just about sex. Anything else would rip her apart.

She leaned over to pluck a condom off the side table, ripped it open, and slipped it carefully in place.

"Keep your hands at your sides," she told him.

He eyed her balefully in the darkness. "But I want to touch you."

"I want to fuck you first," she said.

She heard his sharp intake of breath. "Audrey," he admonished.

"Don't make this into something it isn't." She drew her knee across him. "It's basic biology and I'm an expert at biology." She took him inside her, huge, hot, and wonderful. His hands grabbed her thighs, but they didn't move from there, didn't touch or caress. He was giving her this so she gave it back, drawing up so only the tip of him was inside her, and thrusting back down, taking him all. He felt amazing, but this suddenly didn't feel amazing. It felt mechanical and empty.

She increased the pace, and he rose up to meet her, his breathing changing, getting shallower and faster. She added a twist and felt him tense beneath her.

Then his grip on her changed as he gritted out. "You're not there, yet, Aud."

"I already came, remember?"

"Fuck that."

She opened her mouth to argue, but his fingers found her clit and started circling that small nub of flesh, and stars flashed in front of her eyes. Then he cupped her breast and pinched her nipple and his thrusts got wilder. She lost all control of the rhythm she'd established, she just held on as he pounded into her, destroying her from every different angle until her body convulsed and exploded around him.

"Hold on," he warned.

He turned them so they were on the edge of the mattress and her legs were spread wide and he was driving into her, but she was coming again, over and over in endless waves that crashed through her so hard she screamed as she felt him climax inside her, sending even more waves of pleasure through her body.

The world spun like she was being thrown around in an amusement park ride. Even as she lay there with him collapsed on top of her, her brain swirled. She'd never come like that before, repeatedly and forcefully, like the rolling surf. She had never been with anyone even half as good at sex as Killion. She'd never been in a relationship even remotely as intense as this one. And it wasn't even real. It was a trip, a fantasy. Some crazy adventure that had blindsided her.

Emotions pounded her. She brushed his hair off his ear. "Is your name really Patrick Killion?" she whispered.

"Yep." His voice was muffled in the sheets. "Give me a minute and I'll move, I promise, but right now I can't. You killed me."

A weird laugh moved through her and she wrapped her arms and legs around him, holding him tight. "Thank you. For letting me have my wicked way with you."

"I took an oath to serve my country."

"One woman at a time?"

"It's a tough job, but someone's gotta do it."

She thumped him in the arm and he rolled off, laughing. And as he disappeared to clean up she told herself she wasn't going to be sad about this. Sex didn't have to mean anything except fulfilling a basic need for connection and pleasure.

When he came back, he climbed into bed and dragged her close, resting his chin on her shoulder as they both stared at the patterns the moonlight made through the closed wooden slats.

"What do you normally do after shagging someone's brains out?" he asked.

She huffed out a quiet laugh. "It's been a few years, but normally I'm in a relationship and I either go home or I go to sleep." He'd opened the door with his question. "What about you?"

"Leave." His arm tightened around her.

There was something sad about the way he said it. It gave her the courage to raise his hand to her mouth and kiss his knuckles. "Part of me feels guilty you don't get to run away, and another part is glad you're forced to stay here beside me," she said honestly.

His arm tightened further. She didn't think he was going to reply but he buried his nose in her hair. It felt wonderful.

"Being here isn't exactly a hardship," he admitted. "Now go to sleep."

Night settled around them. She pushed away the ugly memories and concentrated on the lingering pleasure that fluttered inside her. The warmth of his body and slow pulse of her blood dragged her slowly toward sleep. For the first time in days, she allowed herself to think about something other than grief or fear. Instead, she thought about the man whose breath brushed her ear and whose legs tangled with hers. She thought about his relentless pursuit of her pleasure and knew he'd been right when he'd said he'd spoil her for any other man.

If she lived long enough, she had a nasty feeling Patrick Killion was probably going to break her heart.

"I can hear you thinking, Aud." His arms squeezed her again. "Go to sleep."

CHAPTER FIFTEEN

Killion drifted in and out of sleep with a dick as hard as the Washington Monument, although perhaps a little less impressive in terms of being an international tourist attraction.

A little morning wood wasn't an unusual occurrence. What was unusual was the hand that curled around him and stroked him, while lips kissed his back and more fingers sank into his hair. Maybe this was the reason people had relationships. Morning sex. It wasn't something he'd enjoyed in too many years to remember.

But most people didn't live his life. Being an undercover operative wasn't about pretending to be James Bond. It was about being nobody. Ceasing to exist as a normal person. Even during his more recent assignments he hadn't changed how he lived his life. He didn't have a real home, he had an apartment where he occasionally slept and kept his stuff. He'd distanced himself from his family years ago because by the time he'd realized some of his targets might have the capability to strike back, he'd already been in too deep.

This was his world and he'd made peace with walking through this life alone. Except the damn hand on his cock was reminding him of all the things he was missing out on. As was Audrey's warm heat pressed against his back.

She did seem determined, and she knew this was temporary. What harm could it do?

He cracked an eyelid and listened for any sounds of disturbance outside. Birds sang and the sun was up. The sound of laughter rang out in the distance.

What the hell. He wasn't going anywhere during the daylight hours, and neither was the surprisingly intrepid Audrey Lockhart. Her fingers squeezed and he groaned as he stretched out in the bed. And there went all his arguments against getting more involved with this woman, in less time than it took to order a cappuccino.

He turned and rolled on top of her, taking her by surprise. He nudged her knees wide until he lay cradled between her thighs, his erection stroking her core.

"What's a frog's favorite drink?"

He pressed against her.

"Oh, God! I have no idea." She laughed and arched up beneath him. He loved her voice, but, even more, he loved making her laugh.

"Croak-a-cola." He moved his body against her and wondered why they fit so perfectly. "What has more lives than a cat?" He didn't wait for an answer. "A frog—they croak every day."

"Those are awful jokes, you know that, right?"

That sexy laugh of hers made him ravenous for her. "I have a thousand more."

"Kill me now." Sunlight sifted between the blinds, bathing the room in a golden hue. Her hair was mussed, violet eyes crinkling at the corners.

She was enjoying this. Them. He assumed it helped her forget their reality and until he heard different he was going to keep her too entertained to think about anything except making love with him, bad jokes, and possibly food.

He held her wrists and pressed them to either side of her head. Then he nuzzled the skin beneath her ear and he could feel her toes curl into the mattress as she quivered against him. He nipped her earlobe and worked his way to her lips, tasted her quickly but thoroughly. There were so many places he wanted to explore. And the more he got of her the more he wanted.

He took her nipple between his teeth and rolled its twin between his thumb and forefinger. He'd already figured out she liked a slight bite to sex. Not rough—he wasn't the rough sort. Hard, yes, maybe with a little edge, yes, but always watching out for her because she was so much smaller than he was. It was easy to forget a man could hurt a woman if he wasn't careful.

He wasn't going to think about what they were doing in terms of emotions. She'd tried to turn it into a clinical encounter last night, but he couldn't do that—not with her. It didn't mean they'd forgotten their reality. She didn't need him in her life. She was fine on her own, or at least she would be when they cleared up this mess. He moved against her core and her thighs widened as if to take him.

Oh, boy. Now that was temptation.

A shudder moved through him as he grabbed a condom and slid it on. He'd had all these great intentions of taking his time with her, but one shift of her hips and he was a goner.

He pushed inside her slick heat and wondered how the hell people stopped doing this? Why do anything else? She shifted beneath him, taking him deeper and at an angle that blew his fucking mind. Then she wrapped her legs around him, crying out, and all he could do was drive deeper and deeper until his world went white and the earth shattered and he roared out a sound as a corner of his brain realized that walking away from Audrey Lockhart was going to be the most difficult thing he'd ever done.

His heart hammered and even as he supported his weight on his elbows, his hips sank farther into hers and his hips kept thrusting like he didn't even control them anymore. She continued to shudder around him, head thrown back, clearly still in the throes, and he just kept moving until her breathing calmed and she opened her eyes.

They both stilled, staring at one another guardedly.

"Morning, Gorgeous." *Keep it light.*

She grinned. "Good morning."

He pulled out carefully, and got rid of the condom. He put on coffee and remembered he'd bought her a present last night.

"Got you something." He grabbed them out of a bag and came back and perched a pair of tortoiseshell reading spectacles on her nose.

"I can see!" She grinned and then pulled a face at him. "Man, you're a lot better looking without glasses."

The sight of her peering at him through those lenses had him hard as a rock even though he'd only just had her. Nerd-porn. It took another twenty minutes before either of them came up for air.

He got up to pour them coffee, put two mugs on the bed-side table. He was about to make breakfast when she pulled him back down into bed.

"Stay here for a while?" she asked.

There was no resistance as he climbed in beside her. He

lay on his back and she lay half draped over him, her head on his chest.

"What would you have done if you hadn't been CIA?"

His lips curled. "Not that I'm confirming anything…but I was on track to be a Wall Street guy."

"Seriously?" She looked like he'd said trophy hunter.

He laughed. "I know, right? But I have an MBA and an uncle who was in finance. He offered me a job, but I needed a little adventure in my life so I turned him down and joined…the government." He grew quiet for a moment, and then shared something he didn't usually talk about, not with anyone. "My uncle died during the attacks of 9/11. I was in Manhattan that day. I was supposed to meet him for lunch." The feeling of guilt and grief and rage had dulled over the years, but never completely went away. The good guys had died that day. The bad guys had won. He and his colleagues had failed the nation. "It was my first leave since I'd joined the Company and I was hung-over in bed with some cocktail waitress I'd picked up the night before. Figured I'd earned a little time off, a little R&R. I never saw the towers collapse, but I saw the smoke pall over the city. I was called straight back to work and basically haven't stopped since." That was the last time he'd spent the whole night with a woman before Audrey.

"I'm sorry," she said quietly.

The tightness in his throat made his eyes burn. Impossible to remember that day without his chest cavity being scraped raw.

"That's why you joined the CIA."

He shrugged, neither confirming nor denying, then stalled some more by taking a sip of coffee. "My life was altered that day, same as every other American. It made me dedicate myself to stopping these assholes. Not just put the time in, but to give it everything I had—no half measures and no excuses."

"You gave up everything."

He shook his head and avoided her gaze. "Others gave more. Way more. I've never regretted the choices I made." He regretted it now, and didn't want to think about why that might be. "It made me a better person. Someone I can stand to see in the mirror."

"You mentioned a grandmother... Do you have more family?" She touched his face.

His heart pounded. He caught her hand. "I don't talk about them."

"Do you ever see them?"

"Occasionally." He pressed his lips together, shook his head. "Not for a while."

"You don't have to sell your soul to serve your country."

"Sometimes you do." He changed the subject. "Did you always want to save frogs?"

She laughed, but it sounded a little lost. "Couldn't save my sister so I moved on to something more achievable." She lifted her coffee cup off the side table, blew on it before taking a drink, and then carefully set it back down. "We've lost one-hundred-and-twenty species of amphibians since 1980 and the rate of disappearance is increasing. Frogs are also an indicator species for an ecosystem and things aren't looking good for the natural world right now."

"Saving the world's species from global extinction is more doable than saving your sister?"

"She got into drugs in high school. She never found her way out."

Now it was his turn to give comfort. "I'm sorry."

"I know her addiction issues are probably in whatever file you have on me, but what isn't is the fact I loved her so much. I tried my best to help her, but she wasn't interested." She shifted uncomfortably, hiding from him now, the way he'd wanted to hide from her when she'd asked about his family. His parents mourned his loss even though he wasn't dead. They missed him.

"I was the good kid, the one who was never any trouble," Audrey continued. "I overcompensated for her screwing up by being the most well behaved teenager ever." She ran her fingers over the light sprinkling of hair on his chest. "Which made her resent me even more."

"You can't win over people like that," Killion told her. "They screw up and they blame you. You do well and they think you're fucking the boss."

She nodded and bit her lip.

"So you threw yourself into your work as a way of escaping your home life." He guessed.

"It's important work," she argued, and then groaned. "Why did you remind me of my family and my job and what I'm trying to achieve with my life?"

He tucked her hair behind her ears. "You fight for frogs, but you gave up on your sister. Why?"

He watched grief move over her features.

"Have you ever known an addict?"

He shook his head. "Known a few alcoholics…"

"It's pretty much the same thing. They want what they want when they want it." She pursed her lips. "No one can really help someone until they're ready to ask for help. I thought Sienna was in that place when she got pregnant and had a baby a couple of years ago, but no. She overdosed again before Christmas—swore it was accidental."

"That's why you were in Kentucky, right?"

"Yeah." She looked at him, those pretty eyes almost purple in this light. He could see her wondering how he knew she was in Kentucky and just how long he'd been following her. He couldn't tell her. It was classified. And now that he knew Audrey was innocent, it was an important part of the investigation.

She curled her knees into her chest. "Fighting for frogs is a lot easier than trying to get Sienna to stop doing drugs. Or maybe it just hurts less."

The words were heavy, and he refused to let them settle in and ruin the fun. Audrey deserved a little fun after all the crap she'd been through.

"What about all the climate change naysayers?"

She pinched him. "Doesn't matter if people agree or disagree about the cause of the loss in biodiversity. We can still join together to try and protect habitats. That's the key. The estimates are we're losing over 10,000 species a year. We're losing species we haven't even discovered yet."

He shut her up by moving to third base without a warm up. Not because he wasn't interested in her work, but because her passion was a turn on. They both fought for the causes they believed in. They had both dedicated years to their personal battles. He intended to use all the skills he'd ever learned to get her back in the game even though it meant he'd never see her again.

AUDREY'S STOMACH RUMBLED. "I'm starving." But she was too

lethargic after marathon sex to get out of bed and do anything about it.

Killion rolled to his feet and went to the fridge. "I picked us up sandwiches last night. Tonight we can go out and explore a little. Maybe go for a moonlit swim."

They were both avoiding the subject of what would happen when his compatriots showed up.

She watched him move naked around the kitchenette. "Be careful with that knife," she joked.

His eyes went to the ugly scab on her side. "Your side still okay?"

His concern made her choke up a little. He was always looking out for her. She hid her reaction and nodded. He went back to making lunch with the supplies he'd picked up last night.

Spending a day in bed with this man had beaten the hell out of staring at a wall feeling sorry for herself. She had a horrible feeling it wouldn't be long before someone stuffed her in a safe house and she went insane from boredom.

Assuming the bad guys didn't find them first.

She pushed the thoughts out of her head. Maybe she could catch up with her academic reading. Or find a new hobby. Her hands sank into her hair. She had no idea how she'd cope with being anything other than a biology professor. Since going to college, it was all she'd wanted to do. Make a positive contribution to the education of others and protect the natural world.

Now she just wanted to survive long enough to clear her name.

A soft knock on the door had her freezing in place. Killion reached for the weapon on the bedside table before grabbing her hand and tugging her into the bathroom. He pressed the heavy gun into her palm. "Stay here. Use this if you have to. Aim and squeeze the trigger. Safety's off."

He went back into the bedroom and swept another gun off the nightstand along with his cell.

The knock came again. "It's Parker."

She peeked around the doorframe, and Killion glared at her. She pulled back but surreptitiously watched him peer outside through the slats of the blind. Then he moved around to the other window and repeated the process.

Apparently satisfied with whatever he saw, he went to the shopping bags he'd brought home with him last night and snatched up one and tossed it to her. "Get dressed."

Gone was the lover. Here was the operator back on the mission. She'd known they had to end sometime, but hadn't expected it to be so abrupt. She dug into the bag and pulled out a bikini and a pretty black halter neck dress. An emotion that felt a lot like grief locked down her throat, but she ripped off the tags and pulled on the clothes. Killion stepped into his board shorts, but never let go of his gun.

His eyes ran over her covered form, and his expression went carefully blank. It caused a shot of warm anguish to rush through her.

"Lock the door and stay in there until I tell you to come out. If I don't tell you, don't come out."

She nodded and backed inside, wrapping her fingers around the grip of the gun, praying she didn't need to use it.

KILLION HADN'T REALIZED how desperately he'd wanted to

stay in this room and pretend the world wasn't out to get them until he heard that knock on the door.

Even though he'd been expecting it, the intrusion was unwelcome. Time to go back to being an Intelligence Officer rather than messing around with a smart, beautiful woman. Time to make sure Audrey got out of this mess alive.

Keeping hold of his pistol he dragged the heavy chest out of the way of the door. Then he opened up, just an inch, to find a guy of similar height and build as him, lounging against the post that held up the small veranda. The man had a scar cutting through his right eyebrow and close-cropped hair. Alex Parker. Like his photograph suggested, he looked less like a desk jockey and more like a cage fighter in a suit.

Killion's operator radar, the one that had been so dormant around Audrey, was practically electrified standing this close to Parker.

Alex Parker was former CIA, but he'd never been on the books. Off the books operations usually meant assassinations although the government always denied their involvement in such matters. The fact Parker had ended up in a Moroccan prison suggested at some point he'd been hung out to dry by his own people. Killion was good at putting pieces of a puzzle together, and these pieces of Parker were jagged and potentially dangerous. It was a professional courtesy not to dig too deeply into that quagmire, but it didn't mean he'd drop his guard.

"Afternoon," said Parker carefully. His hands were visible. From the way his pants hung he didn't look like he was carrying. Maybe he didn't need to. Killion checked around without taking his eyes off the man. The guy exuded a relaxed air, but it was an illusion. The situation was too tense for anyone to relax.

Parker eyed his pistol. "Nice piece. I haven't fired the SAS GEN-2. Keep meaning to try it."

"Maybe we can go to the range sometime." Killion smiled tightly and stood back to let him in. He had to trust Parker and yet it wasn't just his life at stake. It was Audrey's too. And whose fault was it she was even in danger? If he hadn't acted so rashly and warned her off, maybe he could have backtracked and reexamined the evidence. Found the real culprit without involving her and destroying her life. His actions had catalyzed the shit-storm she now found herself in, and he'd forgotten to mention *he* was the guy who attacked her that first night before he spent the last twelve hours burying himself inside her as often and as deeply as possible.

She was going to kill him.

At some point he had to tell her the truth, but he'd wait until she was somewhere safe, somewhere where walking away didn't mean he was leaving her unprotected.

Parker sauntered into the room and Killion became aware of the rumpled state of the sheets and the scent of sex in the air. The fact it reflected badly on him wasn't the issue. He didn't want Parker getting the wrong idea about Audrey.

He closed the door behind the newcomer. "I didn't expect you to come yourself."

"I wasn't sure who else to trust."

That was a little ominous.

"I assume Dr. Lockhart is in the bathroom?" Parker asked.

Killion nodded, but didn't move to tell her to come out.

"You don't trust me?" Parker asked quietly.

"Someone tracked me to an island in the middle of nowhere and very few people knew about it." He was the one holding the gun, but something about Parker made the spot between his shoulder blades itch.

Parker's eyes were watchful. "I don't blame you for being cautious." He held his arms aloft and turned slowly in a circle to prove he wasn't armed. "But I have a woman I love back home, pregnant with my baby, and just out of the hospital. I only left her side because I wanted to help Dr. Lockhart and find this assassin. I promised Mal I'd come home to her safe. I get that you're uncertain about what's going on—we all are—but you need to put the gun away."

Killion held his stare for a few more seconds then relented. He shoved the weapon in the waistband of his shorts, walked over to his duffel to find a T-shirt. He pulled it on, strapped on his holster and covered it with an unbuttoned shirt. He pushed his feet into the cheap sneakers he'd bought yesterday.

Alex Parker paced the room, helping himself to a drink of water. "Jed and I *were* the only ones in the BAU who knew exactly where you were. I checked out your buddies from across the pond and there is no record of communications that suggest they contacted Gómez, but it's impossible to know for sure. What I did discover was someone inside the Agency accessed the flight plan of the helicopter the Brits used and checked out the satellite images."

"Inside the Agency?" Killion gritted his teeth. "Who?"

"I don't know," Parker admitted. "Some bright young thing realized I was in the system before I could dig too deep." A line cut through his cheek when he smiled. "That doesn't happen to me very often. I was impressed."

Killion raised a brow. "They know it was you?"

Parker rinsed his water glass and put it on the drainer. "Nah. The feds are going to pay a visit to a man called Hugo

Lutz. And while they're looking at his PC for evidence of hacking into a government agency they'll find thousands of images of child pornography."

"Planted?" Killion asked.

"Nope. Hugo has a sickness that involves underage kids. If he stopped at just looking I might not have lured the feds to him." Parker shrugged. "I covered my tracks and gave the authorities one of the bad guys to chew on. Frazer was in on the decision. There's a dark webmaster Lutz works with whom I'm hoping he'll give up for a little less jail time…"

"Not my problem." Killion eyed him narrowly. "I only care about getting Dr. Lockhart to safety and tracking down whoever is behind this thing."

"You're right. The webmaster can wait." Parker checked his watch. "I've got a private jet waiting for us on the tarmac. We can discuss it there."

The bathroom door opened, and there stood Audrey, her hair nicely brushed and pulled back in some sort of improvised ponytail, looking like little orphan Annie, holding her toothbrush in one hand, deadly weapon in the other.

"Dr. Lockhart, I presume?" said Parker.

She nodded, looking too damn good in the sundress he'd picked out for her.

"I'm Alex Parker." The guy didn't move. Probably a good thing as Killion was so tense the air in his lungs felt like it was brushing up against an electric field. The woman had totally messed with his objectivity. Great. Just when she needed him most he was at his weakest.

Audrey's eyes were wide and scared, but she straightened her spine and gave Parker a nod. "I wish I could say it was nice to meet you, but under the circumstances…" She moved into the room and handed Killion the handgun. Then she turned and reached out to shake Parker's hand. Killion held his breath. Alex gave him a pointed look as he calmly shook Audrey's hand.

Killion grunted. His tension was contagious and he was behaving like the greenest rookie. He had to get over his fear for Audrey and do his job before he did something stupid and got them all killed.

"There are some sandals in the bag over there." Killion pointed to the chair farthest away from Alex Parker.

Parker smiled and went and sat in a wicker chair in the opposite corner of the room, leaning forward and immediately making himself look less of a threat. This guy was good. Killion watched him like a damned hawk.

Parker concentrated on Audrey as she put on her shoes with shaking hands. "I know what it's like to be scared, Dr. Lockhart. I was in a Moroccan prison for a time and scared was my first name. My last name was witless."

"How did you get out?" asked Audrey.

"You don't wanna know."

"You said someone in the Agency tracked the helicopter flight plan?" Audrey asked.

"We can't talk about that here—"

"Okay," she interrupted the guy, "I'm used to people not answering my questions." She shot Killion a pointed look. "But what's to stop them doing the same thing with your airplane?"

Parker grinned and Audrey seemed a little blindsided.

"Move it, Aud," Killion interrupted. A person would have to be dumb as a rock not to see Alex Parker's charm. Bastard. "We'll discuss it on the road."

Parker rose to his feet. Killion grabbed their stuff. "Let's go. We've already been here too long." He held the door wide for Parker to lead the way. Audrey followed but before she could exit, he stopped her with a gentle touch on her arm, leaned down and whispered close to her ear, "Thanks for the best honeymoon, ever."

CHAPTER SIXTEEN

THEY SAT ON a private jet that smelled of leather and money. Audrey couldn't help but admire the gleaming interior and the crew who wore blue shirts and crisp black pants as they busied themselves for takeoff.

Once they were in the air, Alex Parker waved away the stewardess who joined the pilots in the cockpit, and then made everyone coffee. He pulled a keychain from his pocket and tossed it on the table. A little red light lit up on it. "Now we can talk without being electronically monitored."

"It doesn't affect the plane's computers?" she asked.

"I guess we'll find out." Parker quirked a brow.

Audrey's mouth dropped open.

"He's messing with you." Killion shot the guy a look. "Or he better be."

Parker took three mugs to the cockpit and then again closed the door on the crew. When he came back he filled three more mugs. "I am messing with you. The signal blocker has a clearly defined radius of three feet, so huddle up."

Audrey leaned in. "Why won't whoever was checking us out in the CIA connect us with you and this jet?" She'd had her ear pressed to the bathroom door and had heard every word. "I'm assuming they could link you to the island in some way?"

Parker put a hot drink on the table in front of her along with a small carton of milk. "If they had the right resources theoretically they could. If it was me, I could and would. Which is why Frazer used one of his contacts to lend us one of their jets, and I sent the company jet to Alaska on another project."

He poured milk into his coffee and sipped. "So our being on this airplane could be tracked, but it's a long shot and I don't think it will be. Short of an invisibility cloak this was the best way I could figure to get you back onto US soil without leaving a trail."

"What about when we land?" asked Killion. He'd become distant since leaving the hotel. His comment about the honeymoon had taken her by surprise, but it almost seemed to bookend what had happened between them. Now he was back to cold and clinical. Clearly only the mission mattered.

Parker dug into a bag on the seat and tossed them both passports.

Killion looked at his and then picked up Audrey's and passed it to her. "Not bad."

She looked at her unsmiling photograph and new name. It was of her, but it wasn't a photograph she'd ever had taken.

"Computer generated," said Parker. "Feebs have their own people."

"Traceable?"

Parker shook his head. "These guys don't even exist in the system."

Killion grunted. "Good."

"I don't think I can do this," she realized suddenly. "I'm a terrible liar."

Parker held her gaze. "All you need to do is look the border control guard in the eye and remember your new name and what you were doing in Jamaica. We used the newlywed theme. Allows for a little name confusion and it means Killion can keep his arm around you the entire time—sometimes we all need that extra bit of support."

There were lots of secrets in Parker's eyes, but there was kindness too.

Killion was focused on the details. "What about biometrics?"

"I took care of it."

Killion looked disgusted. "You better be the only one able to access those databases."

"One of my firm's contracts is Homeland Security and Border Protection. I've set this up as a demonstration as to how current loopholes in the system could be exploited by the right hacker." He crossed his legs at the ankles and clasped his hands together. "They didn't believe I could do it so I'm proving them wrong. It's one of the things they pay me to do."

"So they're effectively paying you to smuggle a wanted fugitive back into the country?" Audrey was both impressed and horrified.

"We discussed the options. With a potential CIA breach we had to run this far below the radar until we know for certain exactly what we are dealing with."

"Do you have a chief suspect yet?" she asked, crossing her arms as both men looked at her with decidedly guarded expressions.

"Gabriel Brightman," Parker revealed, shooting a glance at Killion.

"Rebecca's father?" She sucked in a breath. "No. You were wrong about me, you must be wrong about him, too."

Both men's expressions turned implacable, but they didn't know Gabriel. "He wouldn't do that to me. He's supported my studies, he even created a scholarship program in Rebecca's name and made sure I was the first recipient."

"He fits the profile," Parker said. "Powerful businessman who has been affected by personal tragedy and whom the justice system failed. Someone in his company *is* in regular contact with *Mano de Dios.*"

She processed this. "But why would he want me dead?"

"You lived while his daughter died." Killion didn't cushion the blow. "He might have presented a loving and sympathetic front, but inside it's possible he hated and resented you for being the one to survive while the child he loved died."

Audrey shivered and Killion dug into his duffel and pulled out a hoodie for her. Their fingers brushed as she took it and their eyes connected. He blanked his features before he looked away.

God.

"How do we figure out who in the CIA might be dirty?" asked Killion. "To connect the Brits to Audrey means they figured out I was the one who stole Gómez's plane." Audrey could see Killion's brain working and it was fascinating. "They either checked hotel security cameras and got a picture of me checking in or got hold of my driver's license from the car rental company, and ran it through the database."

"No one ran your photo through any database," Parker told him.

There were a few seconds of tense silence, although she didn't know what that meant.

"So someone recognized a photo of me. Someone I know personally or that I've worked with in the intelligence community."

"You have any enemies?" asked Parker.

"Are you fucking kidding me?"

Parker shrugged. "So it could be anyone, but we have to assume the worst and that someone within Langley is feeding information to the bad guys."

Killion looked thoughtful for a moment. "Or some analyst is fulfilling requests from an Intelligence Officer they trust in the field."

Audrey had a thought. "You said you thought it was me because they used batrachotoxin, correct?"

Killion tilted his head as he looked at her. He was so familiar and handsome she felt a quiver around the region of her heart.

"Well?" she prompted.

"It wasn't just because they used batrachotoxin. It was batrachotoxin with DNA traceable to frogs you worked on in your lab." His lips pulled back. "University security is lousy by the way."

"You broke into my lab at the university?" Her lips parted in surprise.

Killion gave her a thin smile that was scary rather than reassuring. "And your office. Gabriel Brightman is a regular visitor to the campus."

"He gives a lot of money to the college." She felt numb and huddled into his hoodie and wished she could get the other Killion back. He kept pushing her away, probably so when he left she'd be happy to get rid of him. What he didn't seem to understand was, she'd known from the start he'd never stay.

"Your computer could do with a better firewall," added Parker.

"Great." She crossed her arms over her chest. "You two have no appreciation for the law."

The two men looked at one another.

Killion leaned forward. "We couldn't get a warrant because we can't admit a crime has been committed. We're working on time sensitive information with the sort of stakes that start wars. In this instance I'll do whatever it takes to get the information I need."

"Does that include sleeping with your prime suspect?" she asked silkily.

Parker winced.

Killion narrowed his eyes. "Probably, darlin', but by the time you and I got together it was painfully obvious you were nothing more than an ordinary frog biologist."

Hurt froze her in place. She hadn't expected his casual dismissal to sting so much.

Killion ran his hands through his hair and closed his eyes. "Okay, back up. That didn't come out the way I meant it."

"We were all convinced you were involved, Dr. Lockhart." Parker cut into the conversation that had gone from big picture to personal in a blinding flash. "It wasn't just the poison."

Her heart felt like it was stuck a few beats back. She inhaled and tried to listen to what Parker was telling her.

"The murder took place while you were in Kentucky and not long afterward, we found a large amount of cash transferred to an account registered to your name in the Caymans."

Her hands clenched into fists. "I don't have a Cayman Island bank account."

"According to the bank you have half-a-million dollars," Killion corrected.

"What?" Audrey couldn't believe it. No wonder Killion had thought she was guilty. But there was a flaw in their thinking. "You said I was in the right place at the right time, but they couldn't have known I'd be back in Kentucky for Christmas. I only went home because of a family emergency."

Killion's sharp blue gaze softened, and he moved close enough their knees bumped. "Audrey." He reached for her hand and squeezed her fingers.

Oh, my God.

"You mean someone made Sienna overdose?" Her voice broke as something snapped inside. She wanted to throw up. All the time she'd spent blaming Sienna for her weakness and the whole thing was Audrey's fault. "Someone almost killed my sister just so I'd come back to Louisville?" She stood and paced to the cockpit door and back. "Who hates me this much?"

Killion rose and drew her against him. At first she fought him because she was still so angry at him for the cold indifference he'd exuded. Then she gave in and wrapped her arms tight around his waist, wishing she could keep this version of the man—the good one she bet very few people knew existed.

"How do we get information on Brightman?" Killion asked over her head.

She couldn't believe it was Gabriel. He'd always been kind to her. Generous even. Wanting to know how she was and what she was doing. Keeping a benevolent eye on her achievements—or so she'd thought. She couldn't believe that under that altruism ran a vein of hatred so deep he wanted her dead. But who else did she know who had the power to set up this kind of operation that included paying off an assassin, a

CIA analyst, not to mention placing half a million dollars in a bank in the Caymans?

No one. Except maybe the cartel and she'd never done anything to them until Hector Sanchez had shown up.

Killion sat and drew her onto his lap.

Parker massaged his temples. "Brightman has top of the line security—both physical and cyber. We can break into his system or his house, but he'll know within seconds. His IAS is top of the line. Intruder Alert System," he explained at her confused look. "I can't find a direct link to *Mano de Dios*, but someone at his company HQ is in regular contact with someone down in Colombia according to cell tower information."

She shuddered as she remembered the moment when Hector had slipped that blade into her side. Pain and hellfire, fear and confusion. Not only that. The terrible feeling of impotence, of not being valid or necessary. Of her life being worthless.

Killion's hand ran up and down her spine, trying to soothe her. "I can get in, but it'll take a few days to set up. Get me the floor plans and—"

"I'll do it," Audrey said suddenly.

"No," said Killion.

She pulled out of his arms. This was something she could do. This was where she could contribute not only to her own survival, but to helping these men catch a dangerous killer.

"You don't understand. He's always pretended to be like a father to me. He'll let me in. He'll help me even if behind my back he's plotting to kill me. I know he will."

"Over my dead body," said Killion. "Tell her, Alex."

"There would be dangers to going in alone," Parker

agreed, "but it isn't a bad idea."

"What the fuck?" Killion swung to face Parker.

"If Audrey is willing to risk being alone with Gabriel Brightman for a couple of hours—"

"It's too dangerous," Killion cut in.

"It might allow us to get inside the family home and search for proof as to his involvement without him knowing about it."

"It's too dangerous," Killion repeated again, louder, in case she and Parker had gone deaf.

"I want to do it. I'm telling you, there's no way he'll confront me directly."

Killion's expression got downright mean. "What if he calls the cops? What then?"

"You wait outside in the getaway car and we escape into the sunset?" she suggested, only half joking.

"You're wanted for murder, Audrey," he said harshly. "This isn't a laughing matter."

She seethed although she knew he was being a bastard because he was worried about her. "Someone stole my life, *Patrick*. I'm not going to sit around staring at some lonely farmhouse walls, wasting my time and other peoples' when we could get a head start on this by me being proactive."

"And what's your cover story, Madam fucking genius?" Killion's eyes flashed bright angry blue. "You just happened to get out of Colombia and back into the US without anyone seeing you?"

"I crept onboard a cargo ship and stowed away. Really, how is that any more fantastic than what actually happened?" The realization he had so little faith in her abilities hit her hard. Her mouth went dry. She was done with being the victim

233

who did what everyone else told her to do. She wasn't a dummy. She stood and headed for a room at the rear of the plane. "I'm doing this. Unless you intend to tie me up, you better get used to the idea."

————————————

"I CAN TIE her up, right?" Killion said to Parker as Audrey stormed out of the cabin. "Lock her in a padded cell somewhere so she doesn't get to endanger herself?" He raised his voice so she could hear him.

Parker drank his coffee as Audrey closed the door with a definitive snick. "Gabriel Brightman has been extremely careful to avoid direct confrontation during this little enterprise. He's not going to start now."

"If it was your woman you wouldn't let her do this." Killion didn't even question the fact he'd just claimed Audrey as his. During this op, she was his.

"Mallory would have my ass if I tried to stop her from doing anything just because she's a woman, mine or otherwise." The slight twist of Parker's lips suggested he'd tried on more than one occasion. "But I get why you're pissed. You care about her."

Killion dropped to the seat and planted his forehead in his palm. "Of course I care about her. I got her into this mess. It's my fault Brightman sent the cartel after her. I promised I'd get her life back for her. Shit."

"You promised you'd get her life back? What are you gonna do? Blow up Gómez's compound and dismantle the entire *Mano de Dios* drug operation south of the Equator?"

"I was thinking more along the lines of destroying the evil

mastermind, putting the real assassin out of business and just hoping the cartel faded away." Killion rolled his eyes at himself. "If Brightman *was* part of this Gateway thing why did he want Burger dead?"

Parker shrugged. "Maybe he wasn't part of it. Maybe Burger tried to recruit him but the guy said no. Maybe Brightman was involved and discovered Burger's involvement with last year's attack on the shopping mall in Minnesota and thought Burger had gone too far? Or maybe Burger found out about Brightman's connection to the drug cartel and threatened to bring him down?"

"Long on theories, short on fact?"

"Absolutely." Parker nodded. "But one thing I do know, using a professional assassin to kill Burger and at the same time framing Audrey took some serious planning. Mix in *El cartel de Mano de Dios* and we are dealing with some very dangerous individuals, with serious high stakes." He grew thoughtful. "But not people who want to go down in flames for first degree murder. Not people who want to draw attention to themselves in any way."

"That is not making me feel better about Audrey getting anywhere near Brightman."

"She won't be alone for long."

"She almost *died*, Parker. When I first met her I thought she was the assassin and I didn't give a shit about her. But I was wrong." He shuddered at his callousness. "I drove her through the jungle and flew her across the entire continent of South America while she lay bleeding in the back of the aircraft from a serious stab wound. After that little adventure I refused to take her to the hospital and she almost died of fever. Then I take her somewhere I promise is safe and we almost get butchered by a bunch of crazy Honduran fishermen." He rubbed his hands over his face. "The thought of putting her in danger again…"

"She wants this over with."

"And I want her to survive long enough to slap my face when she finds out I'm the guy who threatened her that night," Killion bit out.

"We'll keep her safe." Parker didn't react to his temper.

Killion narrowed his eyes. "Let's keep her safe in an S-A-F-E house." He spelled out the word for emphasis.

Parker watched him with eyes that looked like they'd seen everything. "Dr. Lockhart isn't going to sit idly by while we spend weeks looking for ways to get into Brightman's mansion. Not to mention Gabriel Brightman might not be involved in this any more than Audrey was, in which case we could waste days investigating him while the real players escape unnoticed."

Killion swore and eyed the other man sharply. "Would you let Mallory do it?"

Parker grinned and tipped his face to the ceiling. "Not even for a moment."

Killion drank his coffee and wished it were something stronger. Wished he could drown in a bottle. "There you go then."

"We also need to figure out a way to draw out the source inside the CIA."

Killion's lips twisted. "I'm thinking it's someone who knows me personally. Someone I've worked with."

"You have any enemies at Langley?" Parker asked.

"Who doesn't?" Killion countered.

Parker didn't rise to the bait. "Anyone who hates you

enough to sell you out to a Colombian drug lord?"

He pressed his lips together. "There was one woman, but she left the agency years ago." He rubbed his fingers over his jaw. "June Vanek. She went through the Farm same time as me. She was pissed to be stuck in Islamabad, but military support was limited in the early days and many of the tribal leaders wouldn't deal with a woman. She persuaded the brass to bomb a village near the Pak border."

Parker nodded. The guy had received the Distinguished Service Cross for his actions in Afghanistan and not long after that had started working covertly for the CIA. Parker understood the nuances and politics of war.

"I'd told her the informant was full of shit. I'd told HQ we were getting somewhere with local people, but rather than listening to the man on the ground they trusted an unreliable source and an inexperienced field officer." His mouth went dry. Kids had been among the victims killed. "Needless to say, she seriously fucked up our efforts to gain support in the region." He gave Parker a tight smile. "I reamed her out in public, then laid it all out in dispatches. I was surprised they didn't fire my ass for that one."

"She resent you for it?"

"Hated my fucking guts, but she wasn't the only one." Killion's methods were a little unorthodox and he bent noses out of shape.

Parker frowned. "Make a list of the people who dislike you most, or the ones you think could be bought. I'll investigate them all."

Killion didn't want to wait that long. "I could make a mistake that lets someone know where I am. Nothing too obvious. I'm not an idiot, no point pretending to be." His gave his trademark cocky grin but wasn't sure who he was trying to sell it to. Parker wasn't buying, and Audrey wasn't here. What the hell was she doing back there?

"You have anyone you trust at the CIA?"

"A lot of the best people retired in the last two years." Burned out after fourteen years of grueling stress and unrelenting tension. "There's Crista Zanelli. She's an analyst. We had a thing years ago but we're good friends. She said my boss has been asking questions about where I am. I could call him." He *should* call him.

Parker nodded carefully. "Or we could organize a call from some payphone to your boss or Crista and see who runs a search on the number. If no one takes that bait we'll make the next move a little more obvious, like an email asking for a meet."

"Might work." He climbed to his feet and went to the door of the room Audrey had entered earlier. What the hell was she doing in there? He opened it carefully and saw she was curled up on the bed, fast asleep.

Something wrapped around his heart and squeezed tight. He wanted to climb in beside her, but that part of their relationship was over. Emotion crowded through him. The thought of never touching her again made his fingers clench in reaction. Loneliness at the realization he'd already lost her was like a physical ache. But the idea of her being hurt was worse.

It was over. His only job now was to get her through this alive.

CHAPTER SEVENTEEN

THEY DROVE THROUGH the icy streets of Louisville in the back of a van that had a phone company logo emblazoned on the side—courtesy of a group of mysterious FBI agents who'd left it waiting for them in a parking lot at the airport. Audrey wriggled into a pair of jeans that were tighter than she normally wore and tried not to fall over as they went around a corner. Alex Parker was at the wheel in the front cab, leaving her and Killion alone in the back. Every mile closer to their destination seemed to prize them farther and farther apart. Killion's expression grew increasingly cold and forbidding.

She hastily pulled off her halter dress and the bikini top beneath and tossed them on the floor. She was more worried about the temperature than the idea of Killion seeing her naked again, but he wasn't even looking at her. He was checking his weapon, pissed because she wasn't doing what he told her to do. She pursed her lips and narrowed her eyes.

Getting through customs had been easier than expected. Killion had kept his arm around her and she'd pasted a tired smile whenever the border control guy had glanced in her direction.

"I don't want you to do this." He finally broke the fraught silence.

He'd been trying to sway her decision ever since she'd announced her intentions. If Parker hadn't agreed with her she was pretty sure she'd be locked up in a trunk somewhere.

"I heard you the first forty-seven times." She thrust her arms into a long sleeved black T-shirt and pulled it over her head.

Killion looked at her now. "I thought we had something special."

She eyed him narrowly. "Are you really going to use what happened between us to try and change my mind?"

"I thought you trusted me?"

Jesus, he was using everything she'd said against her— because that's what a good operative would do. She fluttered her lashes at him. "I do trust you."

"Then don't do this," he said sharply.

"I *trust* you to keep me safe."

"And I thought you were supposed to be smart." Cool eyes skimmed her body. "The only thing you should trust about me is my ability to get you off."

Damn, she'd tried so hard not to lose her temper, but the guy was purposely poking her until she lashed out. "Because that's as close as you like anyone to get, isn't it? Your whole freaking life is 'classified' and you use that to your advantage." But she'd had enough of her chain being yanked. It was his turn. "It was just sex. Get over yourself."

He went to stand up, but there wasn't enough room. "If that was just sex, I'm a used car salesman."

And he'd do very well at that too.

"So what happens next, babe?" She braced her arm on the side of the van to keep from falling over. "We getting hitched and having babies? Shall I pick out the wedding china?"

His jaw tightened.

The pressure in her throat had a lot to do with the fact they'd never have the chance to do any of that. And the last thing she wanted him to realize was the idea of a life with him was ridiculously appealing. Even for a woman like her, smart, independent, self-sufficient and happy with her life—or at least she had been before someone had tried to stab her to death and frame her for murder.

She went on the offensive. "You gonna string me along with false promises?" She sneered. "Maybe you think I'm so desperate for a man you can control me with great sex?"

There was that glint in his eye again. "It was *great* sex."

"That isn't the point." And it wasn't. She wasn't an idiot. He needed to start thinking of her as a partner, not as a potential suspect or victim. She wouldn't be controlled by him dangling their "relationship" in front of her like a heart-shaped carrot. "I'm not yours to take care of, Patrick. You don't get a say in my decisions."

"Really?" A tic worked in his jaw. "Because I could still pack you off to a Black Camp the way I should have done at the start."

"You wouldn't do that to an innocent woman."

His smile was edged with a slice of mean. "Trust me, Doc, I've done worse."

"That's what you tell everyone, isn't it? It's what you tell yourself. That you're some soulless badass."

"The first night you were attacked?" He broke into Spanish, his voice deeper, rougher than usual. "*Yo se cuando estas mintiendo, chica, para que sepas.*"

Her heart squeezed so forcefully she felt a stab of pain. *Oh. My. God.* She sat down before she fell over. It was *him.* Killion was the man who'd bound her wrists and ankles and scared her so badly she'd nearly stroked out. They stared at one another, the knowledge of what he'd done to her, of how badly he'd scared her vibrating between them. She stood and slapped him so hard the sound reverberated around the cab.

They both held their breaths, then he rubbed the side of his cheek. "Assault of a federal officer, sweetheart." His smile moved all the muscles in his face, but didn't reach his eyes. "Now I can hold you indefinitely."

"Yeah?" Her nails cut into her palms. "That ship sailed after you came inside me the first five times, *sweetheart*. And don't think I can't read that carefully blank expression you're so proud of." It was starting to drive her nuts.

His eyes narrowed.

God, she wanted to hit him again, but he'd just sit there and let her. She shouldn't be so attracted to a man who was capable of such deception and violence, but thinking about that first night, he hadn't actually hurt her. He'd never physically hurt her. He was an ass, but he was an ass with a conscience no matter what he claimed. She reached out and smoothed her hand over the skin she'd struck. "Your blank expressions equal having something to hide, and in this case that's your feelings for me."

He captured her hand against his face. "I do have feelings for you."

"I know. I have feelings for you, too. It doesn't matter. I'm doing this anyway."

A rap on the panel made her jump. "We're a block away. Keep it down back there."

Great. Alex Parker had heard every word.

Killion clenched his jaw. Then he indicated she come

closer, so she leaned in. A jolt of surprise shot through her when he lifted her sweater and clipped a tiny transmitter to her T-shirt. Then he dragged her lips to his, pulling her tight against his body in a way that screamed primal possession. The kiss was hot and furious and spoke of all the ways they'd made love and all the reasons they had to stop.

Abruptly he held her away from him and stared deep into her eyes. "Don't fucking die, Audrey."

She swallowed hard. "I'll try not to."

———————

AUDREY WORE A gray wool sweater, jeans, sneakers, and a hooded slicker pulled low over her face. She stood outside the wrought-iron gates and pressed the security buzzer. Gabriel lived in a huge mansion on River Road in the wealthy suburb of Glenview. He also had a horse farm out near Jamestown where he and the family had spent long summers and where she and Rebecca had practiced jumping and going on long carefree trail rides.

She felt like she was betraying all those happy memories by standing here in the rain.

"Who is it?" asked the guard.

A few years ago she'd been a regular visitor, but she didn't recognize the guard's voice, which was a good thing. "Marley. I was a friend of Mr. Brightman's daughter in college—Rebecca. I wanted to talk to Mr. Brightman about an idea I had—"

"Call his secretary to arrange an appointment. Mr. Brightman doesn't like to be disturbed at home."

"No! Wait. Please, just tell him Marley is here. I'm sure he'll see me." She bit her lip.

There was hesitation, then a terse, "Wait there."

Marley had been Rebecca's cat. The sweet creature had died not long after Rebecca. Gabriel had buried it with his daughter. Audrey doubted the security guard would connect the two. But Gabriel should.

Would he call the cops? She hoped not.

She also hoped the guy was alone. Devon lived in a condo downtown. Her parents lived in Fern Creek, about ten minutes' drive from her Jeffersontown apartment on the other side of the city. She ached thinking about them. She ached too, for what her best friend would say if she could see her now. She wouldn't approve. Rebecca had idolized her father, just as he had adored his daughter. He'd taken her death hard.

Audrey pushed the memories aside. Regardless of loss and grief people still weren't allowed to run around trying to kill other people. It was wrong. She tapped her toes with impatience and not a small amount of nerves as she waited.

The cold had been a bit of a shock after the heat of the tropics. But it was a relief to be on home soil. If nothing else, she had a better chance of surviving prison.

She pursed her lips. Dammit. She hadn't done anything wrong. The gates started to open and she jolted.

"Come on up to the front door," said the mechanical voice from the speaker.

"Thanks," Audrey shouted through the rain and hurried up the driveway. The listening device Killion had attached allowed him and Parker to hear everything. Her safe word was "toffee." If she said anything toffee-related Killion had promised to come in, guns blazing. Well, he hadn't mentioned guns, but she was pretty sure that's what it would involve.

Thought of guns and bullets brought memories of Rebecca

crashing back. She clenched her fingers inside her pockets. You never forgot that sort of senseless violence. It was tattooed with photographic-like accuracy on your brain—like Hector with the knife, like Killion breaking that man's neck on the beach under the hot Caribbean sun. Human civilization was supposed to be more evolved but clearly wasn't. It was paradoxical to realize they couldn't live in a peaceful society without strong military and law enforcement institutions backing it up.

A raindrop dripped on her nose and shot her back to the present where she trudged up the ridiculously long drive. The lawn was trimmed. Old stone statues placed strategically around the garden, short hedges adding shape to the landscape. Mature trees lined the mansion from the east side, hiding the house from the neighboring property.

All she needed to do was let Killion into the house undetected so they could find some incriminating evidence that tied Gabriel to the drug cartel.

Sounded easy.

So why was her throat dry and her heart pounding?

Because Audrey Lockhart was a biologist not a government agent. But she wouldn't be a biologist if she couldn't get her life back. And this was why she was standing in the cold January rain approaching the house of a Kentucky billionaire.

She braced herself to knock on the imposing red front door, but it flew open and there stood Gabriel, wearing a black sweater and jeans, tartan slippers on his feet. His face was handsome—eyes just like his daughter's but a little more sunken now, the bones of his skull more prominent than the last time she'd seen him. There was no doubt this man had loved his child—maybe even enough to wish Audrey harm for not being the one to die in her place.

"Oh, my God, Audrey, is it really you?" Joy flashed through his eyes. "When Marten said 'Marley' was here, I hoped it might be you…" He reached out and dragged her against him, wet slicker and all. She held herself stiffly in his arms. "I've been so worried about you." He pulled her inside the warmth of the house, checking over her shoulder to make sure no one had seen her from the road.

Audrey didn't have to fake the tears that welled up. "I'm in a lot of trouble, Mr. Brightman."

"Gabriel," he insisted. "You always called me Gabriel." He put his arm around her and guided her to the den. The room was dark and cozy with a huge TV screen that took up nearly one entire wall and a small fireplace that glowed with heat. Pictures of Rebecca were everywhere, including pictures of her and Rebecca together. "Let me take your coat." He held out his hands and she slipped it off and handed it over, imagining Killion sitting in a nearby surveillance van, biting off Parker's head at the slightest infraction.

"You aren't worried to be alone with a vicious murderer?" Her voice wobbled.

Gabriel shook out the slicker and a thousand droplets of water spun off it. "I know you better than that, Audrey. The girl I know wouldn't hurt a fly. Want a hot drink to warm up?"

Her support team had said not to drink anything in case it was drugged, but this was one of their little rituals and it would look strange if she said no, especially when she was shivering uncontrollably and her lips were probably blue from cold. "I don't want anyone to know I'm here…"

"You and I are the only ones in the house"—she could almost hear Killion's teeth grinding—"except for Marten

246

who's on the gate. He stays in the apartment over the garage."

"Where's everyone else?"

"They worked over the holidays so I sent the cook and housekeeper on a Caribbean cruise." He smiled at her, brown eyes remaining a little sad. "The gardener wanted to visit his parents in Kenya so I gave him a ticket home."

This was the man she knew and loved, kind and generous. Killion and Parker would probably suggest he was getting people out of the way so he could do bad things without witnesses. She hated that she was beginning to think like them, but she needed to be smart.

"What about Devon?" Her voice was hesitant as she followed him toward the kitchen.

"I barely see him. Have you spoken to your parents?" He shook his head. "Stupid question. Of course not. That's the first place the cops would look for you."

Audrey's feet slammed to a stop. "I shouldn't be here. My being here puts you in danger."

Gabriel ignored her resistance and tugged her into the gleaming white kitchen, which had been remodeled since she'd last been here. "In danger? Me? Hardly. And helping you is what Rebecca would have wanted. What do I care about anything else?" His voice broke and he looked away.

"You still miss her." Audrey covered his strong fingers with her own.

He squeezed her hand. "Every day. Every second of every hour of every day."

The silence in the kitchen pressed down on them.

"I miss her, too." She searched his face, looking for some hint of hatred or betrayal. "I wish I'd been the one who'd died that day, not her."

He released her and shook his head as he poured milk into a jug and placed it in the microwave. "She wouldn't have wanted that. She would never have wanted you hurt, and she would gladly have sacrificed herself for you. You know that."

"I know. I know I do." Audrey's voice got tight and she could barely speak. He'd lost his wife about a decade ago. Rebecca had always thought her father would remarry but he never had. He seemed so lonely and Audrey hated being duplicitous. "At least you have Devon."

His lips pinched, then he smiled tightly. "At least I have Devon." He placed the milk back in the fridge. "This will make you feel better, and then you can tell me what the devil happened down in Colombia." He pointed his finger at her. "My lawyers will help you fight this."

Killion and Parker had decided it was best to tell him the truth up to a point.

"A local drug cartel sent someone to kill me. I was at work minding my own business when this horrible man chased and stabbed me." She lifted her sweater and eased down her jeans' waistband. The scab had fallen off leaving a delicate pink scar.

The blood drained from Gabriel's face. "You could have been killed."

"I almost died, but a stranger found me and helped me escape."

"Do you know his name?"

She shook her head. "He left me with a family who nursed me when I became sick. When I could walk they put me on a cargo vessel and helped smuggle me back into the country, but I had nowhere to go. I saw the news about my student when I was in Colombia." Her voice broke. "I can't believe anyone would think I killed him."

"Not even in self-defense?" Gabriel asked quietly.

She thought about Hector. Did Gabriel know about Hector? "We'd all defend ourselves when threatened, Mr. Brightman, but Mario was my grad student. He was a great kid." A ripple of gooseflesh moved over her arms. "He looked after my frogs when I came back over Christmas, when Sienna was in the hospital."

Gabriel's eyes were wide and sympathetic. No guile or malice perceptible. "The police down there obviously made a terrible mistake. I will do everything in my power to help extricate you from this mess, Audrey, but you're probably going to have to turn yourself in."

She nodded. "I know."

"There *is* another option," he said carefully.

Her mouth went dry. "What do you mean?"

He stirred cocoa powder and sugar into the hot milk—she watched him carefully to make sure he didn't slip in any sedatives—and poured out two mugs. He handed her one. "I could get someone to create you a new identity. You'd never be Audrey Lockhart again though. You could never work in science again."

What did it mean that he was willing to offer her this? Did that make him a good man, or a bad one?

"You know how hard I worked for my doctorate. I appreciate the offer, but I want my life back."

He smiled and seemed pleased by her answer. "Come on. Let's go sit in the den. I'll call my lawyers in the morning, but tonight you get to relax in safety and not worry about anything. Okay?"

"I knew you'd help me, Gabriel."

"We've been through a lot together. You're like family

now." And for the first time since she arrived she noticed a twinkle of happiness in his eyes. Because she'd come to him, and he no longer had to search to get rid of her? Or because he was genuinely happy to try to help her?

She sipped her drink. She hated this constant questioning of motive. How could Killion deal with it on a daily basis without losing faith in humanity? She'd been at it for less than an hour and already felt corroded by deceit. Audrey forced herself to harden her heart. If Parker and Killion were wrong she could apologize to Gabriel later. If they were right she'd better hope he didn't figure out she was onto him while they were alone in the mansion. She'd be dead before Killion even reached the front gate.

CHAPTER EIGHTEEN

KILLION SAT IN the van beside Parker, drinking coffee they'd picked up before dropping Audrey off. He'd never been so angry or so scared in his life—and that was saying something.

Parker was on his computer, muttering. He'd found something he didn't like.

Killion's phone rang, and he checked the caller ID. Crista.

"Hey," he said absently.

There was a moment of hesitation before she said, "There's something weird going on."

"Define 'weird.'"

"Night before last a woman came to my door."

Killion found himself sitting up straighter in his seat. He turned the phone to speaker. "A woman came to your door?"

"Yeah, look, it's weird because if she was telling the truth, I'm about to fuck up both your lives, but if she wasn't…"

"What did she say?"

"She said she was pregnant with your kid. Said the condom broke. She'd seen my name and number on your cell when you were in the shower, and she thought maybe you were cheating on your wife."

"Name?"

"She never left her name. She left a card with a number on

it. Burner cell."

Killion's pulse sped up.

"She said you guys were together for a month and that's the reason I had this niggle of doubt that she was telling the truth."

And wasn't that a damning statement. Years yawned in front of him with a string of nameless females when all he really wanted was to get to know Audrey better.

Parker interrupted. "This person was in her house? Is she at home now? Tell her to look for an electronic listening device, but not to move it and not to say anything to give away the fact she's found it. And give me the burner number to run."

A minute later they both heard Crista curse. There was silence for about thirty seconds then she was back on the line. "There's a bug under the table in the entranceway. I'm outside now, in my car."

"Okay, tell her to stay put. I'll get Brennan to send someone over—"

A massive explosion sounded and they lost service.

"Crista? Crista!" Killion called her back. Nothing. "What the fuck just happened?"

Parker was on the phone to Brennan. "Something just went down at a CIA analyst's house. A Crista...?" Parker looked at him expectantly.

"Zanelli." Killion filled in her address. A stab of fear shot through him. No, she was fine. Something must have happened to the signal, that was all.

"It sounded like a bomb. You need to get someone over there ASAP. She called to warn Killion some woman came to her house and claimed to be pregnant with his kid. The woman left a cell number which was apparently a burner phone, but Crista didn't get a chance to give it to us."

Killion sat there feeling hollow. Crista was one of his best friends. She couldn't be hurt. His hands shook. He had to pull himself together. Audrey. He looked up at the mansion and had the door open before Parker grabbed him by the shoulder and didn't let go.

Killion shoved the guy off him. "If Brightman heard that conversation he'll know we're onto him."

"Not necessarily." Parker spoke quietly. Rain was coming through the open door. "Look, chances are that bomb was detonated using a cell phone, but Brightman didn't make any calls. No one inside that house made any calls."

"What about email?" Killion asked taking a deep breath. He closed the door. He couldn't afford to panic, but the idea Audrey might be in danger... But her mike was quiet. There was no sound of any attack, just the rustle of clothes as she shifted position.

Parker checked another file. "Nothing, but I found some unusual electronic activity."

"What is it?"

"I don't know—maybe video surveillance from an outside source. I was just starting to figure it out when your friend called."

Killion forced himself to take a few more deep breaths. He looked at his watch. Ten minutes until he was supposed to meet Audrey and search Brightman's home.

"Keep investigating the signal. Let me know as soon as anyone hears about Crista." His voice broke, but they both pretended it hadn't. "I'm going in."

TRACEY INSERTED A key into the garden doors that led from the conservatory into the den of Gabriel Brightman's mansion, avoiding the security cameras she'd helped install. She couldn't believe Killion had gotten this close to Gabriel already. She'd gotten an alert from the bug she'd planted at Crista Zanelli's and heard her talking to Killion about Tracey's visit the other day.

No matter how hard they tried, they couldn't get a handle on Killion's location from his cell phone signal, which jumped around like one of Lockhart's damn frogs. But as soon as the analyst got in her car and started the engine, Tracey had blown that sucker to smithereens. She couldn't afford leaving someone alive who could identify her. She'd have to get rid of Peter, too, before he heard Crista Zanelli was dead and started putting the pieces together. She'd rigged his car in advance, just in case. It was too bad. The guy had been useful.

Then she'd gotten a message that Audrey Lockhart was inside Gabriel Brightman's mansion. And she just knew Patrick Killion was sitting right outside in the phone company van she'd seen parked around the corner.

Excitement fizzed through her bloodstream as she walked through the den.

The cameras covered the safe, the two main exits, the dining room and the lounge, which housed some very expensive artwork.

Gabriel had balked at having cameras in his private rooms—his den, office, and bedroom. A good thing, she realized now. She wore a stocking mask over her head regardless. She crept up the stairs, avoiding all the boards that creaked. Gabriel would be in bed. She paused. A light shone under the door of the room adjacent to Gabriel's dead daughter's room and her fingers itched.

Poor Rebecca. Poor Audrey. Her time would come, but this was too good an opportunity to miss. After years trying to finesse the perfect crime, it was finally happening.

She held the gun in the air as she edged around the corner. Gabriel's light was off, but she knew every inch of this place, blindfolded.

She went in the main bedroom door because the one to the dressing room squeaked. Gabriel had fallen asleep the way he often did, sitting upright with Rebecca's framed photo in his hands, tearstains on his cheeks.

She moved to stand beside the bed and watched his handsome face, grief-stricken even in sleep. He'd never really recovered from his daughter's death. She angled the gun and pulled the trigger. Recoil buzzed along her forearm, and a hot splash of blood hit her neck. Quickly, she unscrewed the suppressor and placed the pistol in Gabriel's left hand.

Then she smiled. Now it was time for Audrey.

IT WAS TWO AM and Audrey sat stiffly in a wingback chair, waiting for the moment Killion had told her to open the front door. Her heartbeat seemed loud in the silence, racing twice as fast as the second hand on her watch. Deception and covert ops were obviously not her thing. At five minutes to two, she stood, picked up her sneakers in one hand, and went to the door of her room. If the alarm went off, or they were caught, Gabriel was about to find out she wasn't just some waif running from the law, but part of a group of people actively investigating him for murder.

A shiver of guilt rippled over her skin. If he were innocent he'd be furious. After years of showing her nothing but kindness he'd feel used and betrayed. On the other hand, if he were guilty he'd be sly and manipulative, blustering and defensive. She hoped he was innocent. With every cell in her body she prayed he was spitting mad at her for suspecting him of something so heinous.

She eased open the door to the guestroom—the one she'd always used, adjoining Rebecca's bedroom, which was permanently locked up. She had the suspicion it was un-touched from the day her friend had died.

Did that make Gabriel obsessed? Or was clinging to any small comfort understandable when a parent lost a child?

She wasn't a mother. She wasn't a psychologist. She didn't know.

They'd retired to bed about ninety minutes ago. He hadn't drugged her hot chocolate, and she'd refused his offer of anything stronger.

Was he asleep?

She had to pause for a moment at the top of the stairs to just get her breathing back under control. It was dark and Killion had told her not to turn on the lights unless she was being chased by someone trying to kill her.

Reassuring thought.

"I can do this," she whispered to herself. She was more than just the sparkly assistant, distracting individuals cursed with a Y-chromosome with her amazing boobs. She moved down the stairs, holding the bannister, carefully putting both feet on the tread before moving onto the next one. A clock chimed with two clear notes and her heart sped up. Dammit. She was late. She hurried toward the door and tripped over a small step she'd forgotten about. Narrowly avoiding a face plant, she flipped the deadbolts and swung the door open. Killion caught the handle and slipped in with a grunt of disbelief.

"Make any more noise and we may as well put an announcement in the newspaper." He sounded pissed. He wore dark clothes and a black wool hat. He looked like the archetypal burglar. He went straight to the alarm system and entered a code, which shut off the beeping.

"Not all of us are experts in breaking and entering," she retorted in barely a whisper.

"Which is why some of us should have stayed home."

She bit down on what she wanted to say to him. It wasn't polite and it wasn't professional.

He took her hand in his and led her down a corridor to the right. Gabriel's study. The door was locked, but Killion picked it in less time than Audrey could hold her breath for.

"You could make a fortune as a diamond thief."

He shrugged. "Not enough excitement." But his voice sounded flat. He was obviously still mad with her. "Parker took care of the security cameras and alarm system."

So they hadn't really needed her at all. *Great.*

They walked into the office, closed the door softly behind them. Killion pulled a small penlight out of his back pocket. "Stand right there and don't move," he told her.

Audrey froze to the spot, determined she could do her part and not get in the way of his operation. She put on her shoes in case they had to run as he systematically went through each drawer. Checking underneath and behind them. Searching for any hidden compartment in the heavy oak desk. Then he went through a small filing unit.

He came up empty so he got up and prowled the room, looking behind pictures.

"The safe is in a dressing room off his bedroom. There's a door that connects directly to the corridor."

"How do you know?"

"Rebecca kept her diamonds in there."

"Know the combination of the lock?"

"Four numbers. It was her mother's birthday, but I imagine he changed it."

Killion shook his head. "If he did, I bet I know what he uses now. Let's go." He swept a super-sleek, razor-thin laptop off the desk and put it against his chest, zipping his tight black jacket over it to hold it in place.

She caught his arm. "Isn't he going to notice that's missing? And assume I took it?"

"It won't be a problem as you won't be here."

"What if we don't find anything useful in the safe?" It was hard to argue in a whisper but they managed.

"Then we'll look elsewhere, but you aren't staying here," Killion repeated as if she'd gone deaf. Then he disappeared into the hall. She crept after him. He was already halfway up the stairs and moving so quietly he didn't even disturb the particles in the air. How was that even possible?

She started after him, forcing herself to go more slowly when a stair creaked. He paused and looked over the bannister at her.

She grimaced and carried on. Upstairs they turned right down yet another unlit corridor. When Rebecca had been alive this house had always seemed like a gothic adventure, romantic and fun. Now it felt creepy, ghosts and misery marching side-by-side in the gloom.

Killion slowed to let her lead the way, although he obviously knew the basic layout. She slipped in front of him and stopped outside the dressing room door. She held the knob firmly as she opened it, but Killion grabbed her hand when it let out a low groan.

His body was suddenly pressed tight against hers and stirred so many memories her head swam. She couldn't afford to be distracted. His fingers squeezed hers, both in reassurance and in demand to let him do this. She let go of the doorknob and moved out of the way.

He held the knob and did something with the door, but it still squeaked. Then he took a small bottle out of his pants pocket and carefully put a drop of something on each hinge.

"Baby oil," he whispered. "Comes in useful for other things, too." His features were indistinct in the dim light, but she caught the flash of teeth.

She pinched his ass because this was *serious* and he was making sexual innuendos.

This time when he tried the door it swung open noiselessly. They both moved cautiously inside. One entire side of the long narrow room held a rack of shirts and suits. A shelf of neatly stacked shoes sat beneath. Audrey couldn't see a damn thing, but Killion walked straight up to the safe, which was hidden in the wall beside a mirror on the opposite side of the room.

The door to Gabriel's bedroom at the other end of the room was slightly ajar.

Killion turned the dial without Audrey telling him any numbers. Apparently the man had a photographic memory for detail. The place smelled of sandalwood and cedar, but there was also the faint air of dusty disuse.

An echo of Rebecca's laughter and the image of her whirling in front of that mirror holding her diamonds to her ears flashed through her mind. Audrey stumbled and caught herself on the arm of a suit jacket. The metal hanger ground against the rod with a low squeal. They both froze. Killion stopped in his silent perusal of the safe's contents, and went to the door that led into the bedroom.

Killion eased it wider, and that's when Audrey realized he'd put on some sort of goggles that must help him see in the dark.

"Fuck," he muttered.

So much for being quiet. He flicked a light switch on, and Audrey put both hands over her mouth to suppress the scream that wanted to escape. Gabriel lay in bed with a pistol in his hand, half his brain on the wall behind him.

She stood there, staring at him dumbly.

The sound of a distant siren snapped her out of her stupor. Killion was already pulling her through the house at full speed, not worrying about making any noise now.

She stumbled, but he didn't slow down. Out the front door. He drew up short, switched direction and ran behind the house, dragging her along with him even though she could barely keep up. Down a small path between shrubs and bushes. They reached a high wall at the edge of the property. She was panting heavily, the cold air making her wheeze. Killion cupped his hand for her to stand on and virtually launched her onto the top of the wall. She latched on, clinging like a kid on her first pony ride. She leaned down to help pull him up.

"Jump, dammit." He caught the top of the wall just as a

bullet chipped the stone beside her leg. "Go!"

She dropped over the other side, rolling on the ground as she landed. More shots sounded and her heart hammered. Where the hell was Killion?

Then he was at her side, holding her hand and dragging her at a full run through the sparse forest. She tripped over uneven roots, and slipped on wet icy leaves, but he didn't let it slow them down. He slid to a halt when he hit the road, and a pair of brake lights flashed in the darkness up ahead. Still propelling her forward, he opened the front passenger door of the van and pushed her inside and climbed up beside her, even though there was only space for one. He slammed the door shut and pulled her onto his lap.

"Drive," he told Parker. "Just drive."

CHAPTER NINETEEN

"WHY DIDN'T YOU just kill her?" Devon Brightman snapped into the phone. He paced in agitation. Why wouldn't Audrey die? It wasn't natural to be this lucky. He pulled at his hair.

"She went to the front door while I was taking care of your father. Let the spook in before I could get to her room. I couldn't risk him seeing me. The only way we get away with this is if no one suspects either of us. I got out of there and called the cops on a burner from a few miles away, reporting suspicious activity. Then I came home."

"Fuck." His hand formed a fist.

"They disabled the security cameras, but we still have the video feed you set up."

He grunted. He'd set up a camera in his father's home office because he'd wanted to see what his old man was up to. To gain the upper hand and make sure his dad didn't suspect his illegal activities. Now the cameras were going to help Devon get away with the perfect murder. "Did Gabriel say anything before he died?"

"He was asleep. I didn't wake him to ask for any last words. It looks exactly like someone tried to stage his suicide. Audrey is going to be on America's most wanted list. You have your alibi ready?" Tracey asked him.

"She's asleep."

"Go wake her up and fuck her blind. She has to swear you were there. Okay, I have a call coming through on my work cell. Cops will be knocking on your door shortly, but I'll go to the mansion first and confirm before coming to you." She hung up.

Devon slipped the battery out of the burner cell and wandered to the kitchen sink, stuffing the handset down the garbage disposal and grinding it to a pulp. He tried to fathom how he felt about his father's death, but all he felt was the desperate need to get away with it. The guy had never given him any credit. Made him work his way through the company from the ground up. Ironically, Devon had learned enough about the intricacies of the shipping process to instigate his own drug smuggling operation. It probably wasn't what Gabriel had had in mind when he'd started this charade.

His father had never been able to see him for what he really was—a fricking computer genius. He'd always just been second best to his sainted sister. Well, he'd shown her and his old man. Devon had started planning Rebecca's death the day he'd buried his mother. His mother had understood him. She'd loved him. Once his mother had succumbed to cancer, his father had pushed him further away, and Devon had known exactly how to punish him.

Getting rid of Rebecca meant he was also one step closer to getting his hands on his money, all of it. He didn't have to share with Miss Goody Two Shoes.

He'd figured killing Rebecca and Audrey together would make it look less targeted killing, more a crime of opportunity. He'd almost pissed his pants when the gun jammed. He'd never forget Audrey's wide terrified eyes, or Rebecca's screams of pain.

Afterward he'd befriended Audrey to make sure she didn't suspect him. It had been fun stringing her along, then seducing and secretly making a fool of her. And then she'd turned around and dumped him.

Bitch.

He'd hidden his anger and played the long game. He'd worried that if his father died too soon Audrey would figure it out. Now he'd gotten rid of them both with one brilliant move, and no one would believe a word Audrey said.

He walked into his bedroom. Audrey's little sister was stretched out under his silk sheets. He crawled in beside her and trailed his lips up the indent of her naked back. Physically the sisters were alike. But Audrey was such a good girl and Sienna was such a bad one.

He knew how much Sienna's issues troubled her more responsible sister. It had been easy to get Sienna to OD, whereas Audrey would barely drink a beer. He hadn't let Sienna get high tonight even though she'd begged him. He'd wanted her mind clear for when the cops came. She stretched beneath him, and tried to turn onto her back, but he didn't let her.

He gathered her dark hair in his fist and used it as an anchor. He was going to make sure this was a sex session she never forgot, especially if she had to relate it in detail to a bunch of smirking detectives who wanted to know *exactly* what he was doing when poor old daddy drew his last breath.

THEY'D SWITCHED CARS and driven a couple of miles from the

scene. Neither he nor Audrey spoke.

Parker drove. Finally he asked, "What happened?"

"Brightman was dead when I got there. Shot in the head. Staged to look like a suicide." Thoughts and doubts swirled through his mind. He squashed them. "Any news on Crista?"

Parker's mouth pulled back tightly, and Killion knew what that meant. They'd both heard the explosion, listened as the signal was fried. He'd lied to himself earlier so he could do his job, but Crista was dead. And she was dead because she was his friend. A fist of emotion twisted his gut.

Audrey sat silently in the back seat, seemingly in shock.

Those doubts pierced his mind like shards of glass. Could he have been wrong about her? Had she killed Brightman? She could have left the mike in the bedroom, found a gun in the house, killed the guy, returned to get the mike, and then calmly let him in the front door.

She caught his gaze in the mirror, glared at him. "You think I killed Gabriel."

"Did you?" he asked sharply.

"Yeah, I shot your chief suspect—the man *I* said was innocent."

"You insisted on going in alone."

Her eyes narrowed, but her lip trembled. "Yeah. I did."

"You could be cleaning up loose ends."

"Then you're next, big boy. Better watch your back." She stared out of the window, and her tears were reflected in the passing street lamps. He forced himself to harden his heart against the effect she had on him. Circumstantially, she could have committed all the murders. He had to start thinking with his brain and not his dick.

"Who called the cops?" asked Parker.

Killion looked at him. Then closed his eyes. *Fuck.* If Audrey was the assassin there's no way she'd have called the cops while she was still in the building, because she was the one who'd end up in jail. They'd bypassed the security system, and the guard had been oblivious. Therefore, logically, the only person who would have called the cops was whoever killed Gabriel Brightman. Once again they'd set the biologist up to take the fall for a murder they'd committed, and once again he'd fallen for it.

"Shit. Audrey, I'm sorry."

She shrugged, shoulders pulled so tight to her frame they brushed the bottom of her ears. "It's fine." She continued to stare fixedly out the window.

Killion ran his hands over his face. "Did you hear anything? See anyone else in the house?"

She shook her head.

The idea the killer had been so close to her made him feel physically ill. Cold sweat broke out on his forehead, and he wiped it away on the sleeve of his shirt.

"What Killion failed to mention," Parker cut into the taut silence, "is he's worried one of his best friends might have just been killed—probably by the same assassin we're after. He wasn't thinking properly."

Audrey drew her knees up to her chin and refused to speak. Who could blame her? What the hell had he done?

Killion's cell rang. It was Jed Brennan. He knew he didn't want to hear whatever Jed had to say. "Yes?"

"I'm at the scene. It's a mess. I'm sorry, Crista Zanelli didn't make it. She died immediately. Car bomb. No one else was injured."

Acid rose up Killion's throat, burning the lining. Crista

was a great person—generous, smart, and funny. She should have decades in front of her, a decent man in her life, kids. He forced the rage and grief back down along with the bile. He'd find the bastard responsible and put the fucker away.

"I spoke to her boss and told him it was possibly related to one of our cases," said Jed. "Feds are in charge of the investigation, and someone from the Richmond field office is on their way. Her boss promised I'd have access to all the searches she ran over the last few days."

So they could trace the burner number the woman had given Crista. It wouldn't matter. The burner would be as dead as she was.

"Crista died because some bitch decided she was the weak link in getting to me, but she was wrong." He told Jed the other bad news. "Gabriel Brightman is dead."

"Shit," Jed's voice dropped lower. "Look, I'm dealing with some serious interagency politics here. And I can't reveal what you're doing so you guys need to lie low for a while. Regroup so we can figure this out. I'll talk to Frazer."

And Frazer needed to talk to the president to call off the heavily armed cops and feds who'd have Audrey Lockhart targeted as their chief suspect.

"We'll lay low," said Killion. Whoever killed Crista knew about the fact she and Killion were friends, which again pointed to an internal breach. How did Killion protect Audrey from his own people?

"Ah, damn. I just got more bad news." Jed swore bitterly.

"What the hell else can go wrong?" Killion's laugh was mirthless.

"Someone just leaked your face and name to the media."

What the fuck?

Killion turned to Parker. "I thought you turned off the security cameras?"

"I did." Parker frowned. "I guess we just confirmed what the other weird signal was."

Killion sat there stunned. This was the end of his career. "Can you get a news blackout on this?" he asked Jed.

"I'll try, but some hacker put your information on the web along with your name and Audrey's. They're saying you killed Brightman. Sorry, pal, looks like your clandestine days are over."

———————————

AUDREY SAT IN the back of the car and stared out the window, trying to forget the last image she had of Gabriel Brightman. Every time she closed her eyes she saw his dark hair, the bright crimson of blood, and the dirty gray of brain matter dripping down the headboard.

She heard Killion unzip his jacket. "I picked up Brightman's laptop," he told Parker.

"Good. We're going to go get you some transportation. Then I'm driving back to DC to open the laptop and see if I can get into Brightman's files without anyone knowing."

"You're leaving us here?" Audrey didn't like that idea.

"You'll be safe with Killion."

She hunched into herself. She didn't want to be alone with Killion. How could he be her lover one minute and suspect her of murder the next? How could she be so attracted to such a smart-assed, alpha-male who lived amid constant danger and who himself killed with such grim and seemingly casual mastery?

And yet *she* was the one suspected of being the villain? A woman who went out of her way to save anything she damn well could. She hated him, hated his job, hated the fact her life was in ruins. Tears brimmed in her eyes, but she refused to cry.

"Can't you examine the laptop here?" Killion sounded equally thrilled at the idea of being alone with her.

"I could," said Parker, "but I might need backup and equipment to deflect any counter attack. It's possible there'll be nothing more substantial than a Windows firewall, but I don't want to be taken by surprise or lose valuable evidence by rushing it. Someone was spying on Gabriel Brightman, and they might also be spying on his laptop—this could lead us right back to them."

Killion grunted.

"Anyway, you're more than capable of disappearing and protecting Audrey. It's easier if it's just the two of you."

Killion grunted again.

A rough looking roadhouse appeared up ahead, with a line of motorbikes out front and a parking lot full of trucks. Audrey assumed they'd drive past, but Parker pulled in.

"Wait here," he told them.

Parker got out of the car, and the silence he left behind was deafening.

After a few tense moments, Killion bit out, "I owe you an apology."

"Which thing in particular are you apologizing for? Attacking me that first night? Accusing me and Gabriel of conspiring to murder and somehow being wrong about us both? Or accusing me of murder—again?" Rage poured through her.

"I'm *not* the one who came after you with a knife. I'm *not* the one who blew Gabriel's brains all over his bedroom wall."

Her stomach churned, but she would not throw up. "Just be careful who you point the finger at next. Or better still, pick someone you really don't like, because they're likely to get attacked and murdered shortly afterwards."

He turned in the seat to face her, and his expression was closed down tight. "I'm sorry for all of it, okay? I'm sorry I attacked you that first night. I thought I was doing you a favor by giving you a warning. You were supposed to contact your boss and get the fuck out. That's what a professional would have done."

Now it was her fault she wasn't a professional assassin? "Do you even hear yourself? Who in their right mind would have thought a frog biologist would be a likely candidate to be an assassin?"

He turned away to face the front. His voice was flat. "It made sense at the time. Do you need me on my knees begging forgiveness, maybe groveling in the dirt?" Suddenly there was too much emotion in his voice. "I put you in danger, and I got one of my best friends and Gabriel Brightman killed. I'm a fucking idiot. This is not news to me, but apparently it took you by surprise. Again. Sorry. I fucked up."

She twisted the gold ring on her pinkie. She may not be a killer or a government operative, but she was smart. Killion was too. She was furious with him, but he was hurting. The two of them fighting wasn't going to solve anything. "You say they used the poison from my frogs in the lab?"

"Yep." It was tight as a curse.

"And someone put money into the bank to make it look like me?"

"Only half a million dollars."

Who would do that? The only connection between her

and Gabriel was… "It's Devon, isn't it?" He was the only one who made sense.

"He's my next guess," Killion agreed. "But we've already established I don't have a good track record on this case. Why the fuck didn't I just drop it when Frazer told me to?"

She didn't know who Frazer was, but there was a bigger issue to worry about. She leaned forward and grabbed his arm. "Devon is dating my sister."

Killion wrapped his fingers over hers and warmth stole through her. She hadn't realized how cold she was until he touched her.

"She'll be fine, and even if she isn't, there's nothing you can do about it."

Audrey pulled away. "But she's my sister."

"So what?"

"So *what*?"

Killion turned to face her again. "There's nothing you can do. You and I are both wanted for murder and the first place they're gonna stake out is your parents' home and phone lines."

"We must be able to warn her."

"And say what? 'I know the cops said I killed Gabriel Brightman, but it was actually Devon—the guy you're dating.' Well, maybe not Devon himself, probably his hired hand because if he has real brains at all he'll have an airtight fucking alibi!"

Killion's response grated. Sienna was in danger. Devon could threaten her entire family. "We *have* to do something."

"We are doing something. We're regrouping."

"Feels a hell of a lot like running away," she said bitterly.

She watched his shoulders stiffen. "There's nothing you can do, Audrey. Give it up."

"Do you even have a family?

"Yes," he bit out. "I have a family."

"Who you never see."

"Because I don't want shit like this to happen to them." He made it sound like she was the crazy one.

She wrapped her arms around herself and huddled into her seat. "Guess what? That's not being part of a family. That's just being part of the same gene pool."

A knock on her window had her jumping an inch off the seat. Then her door opened and Parker held out a leather jacket and a bike helmet to her. Both were surprisingly heavy. Killion climbed out and stretched as if they hadn't just eviscerated each other with words.

"Got you a ride," Parker said. "Cops won't be looking for you on one of these."

Killion pulled on a leather jacket with some skull design on the back, followed by a black helmet.

"We're going to be bikers?" Audrey was aghast. The closest she'd been to a motorcycle was watching *Sons of Anarchy* on DVD.

Parker tossed the keys in the air and Killion snatched them up. "Which bike?"

"The Royal Enfield."

Killion whistled. "Nice."

"I'm not getting on that thing," Audrey told them.

Parker took the jacket from her fingers and held it out. She put her arms through the sleeves. The jacket was a little big and smelled of beer and cigarettes, but it kept out the biting January wind.

"She's going to need gloves." Killion pulled on the black leather gloves he'd worn when they'd searched Gabriel's house earlier.

"I have some in the trunk." Parker went to the back of the car and rummaged through a gym bag. Handed her some gloves that were way too big for her.

"How'd you get them to part with the bike?" Killion asked as he swung his leg over the saddle of the monstrous bike.

"I offered to pay a guy double what it was worth if I beat him at arm wrestling."

The roadhouse door opened, and two enormous men walked out.

"That the guy?" asked Killion.

"Yep." Parker sounded unconcerned as he slipped the helmet over Audrey's head and tightened the straps.

Sound was muffled inside the helmet. The thing felt strange and unwieldy, like her head might topple from her shoulders.

"Hold onto Killion and mimic how his body moves," Parker told her, seemingly unconcerned about the three other bikers who'd come out onto the porch. "Don't fight the movement of the machine."

Sounded like some crazy metaphor to her.

Killion revved the engine and looked at her. "What's it gonna be, Aud? You gonna trust me one last time?"

She stared into his blue eyes for a long moment not knowing what she was looking for. But one thing was certain, she couldn't stay here. She slipped her leg over the back of the saddle, grabbed onto his waist as he immediately pulled away.

She looked over her shoulder and saw some of the bikers approach the man they'd left behind. "What about Alex?" she asked.

"I'd be more worried about any bastard stupid enough to take him on," he shouted over the blast of the wind. "Alex Parker can take care of himself."

CHAPTER TWENTY

K ILLION RODE SOUTHEAST for several hours, heading toward Tennessee. He took the scenic route toward the Smoky Mountains and kept below the speed limit. There was always the danger of ice, and the last thing he wanted was to drop the bike on a corner. Audrey's grip hadn't lessened the entire trip and as much as he enjoyed the feel of her at his back, he was a little worried she was physically fused to him, and he'd never get either of them off the bike.

He'd hurt her earlier with his reflex accusations, and she'd lashed out at him. He deserved it, and it proved his point about staying away from people he cared about, not that she'd ever admit it. Audrey Lockhart had proven to be surprisingly stubborn in her opinions.

He smiled.

The cold air sliced across his exposed skin, but riding gave him a freedom he relished. He'd always had a thing for classic British bikes. The fact he was enjoying the rush of being on the run from every law enforcement agency in the country with Audrey's arms wrapped tight around him wasn't lost on him. It just meant he was more of an idiot than he'd given himself credit for.

They drove past horse farms and cow pastures in the dark. He needed to think this through and figure out his next move, but all his brain was capable of right now was searching for somewhere safe for Audrey to sleep. He could do with a combat nap himself.

In a small town on the edge of Great Smoky Mountains National Park he maneuvered the bike slowly through quiet streets. In summer and fall the roads around here were packed with tourists trying to escape the crowded humanity of the cities.

Instead they brought it with them.

But the scenery was worth it, and he'd spent some of his best summers of his life out here at his grandma's place. The cottage had been destroyed years ago during a massive storm, and she'd relocated to be nearer her son, his father, out in Arizona.

Audrey's words about family snapped at him. *Gene pool, my ass.* But she had a point; it had been too long since he'd seen them.

The next town was larger, and he turned off the main street and headed south toward a sign that advertised rental cottages. Up ahead was a large lodge constructed of massive logs. As if sensing a change, Audrey's arms tightened around him, and the heat trapped between their bodies was more than a balm on this frigid January morning. He stopped the bike and dropped the stand. They sat in silence as dawn broke over the mountains, the trees coming alive in the sunlight, the distinctive blue haze a welcome reminder of happier times.

The bike engine cooled. He shifted, and Audrey finally let him go.

"Stay here," he told her as he swung his leg over the front of the engine. He didn't look at her. He was scared he'd see that same mixture of distrust and loathing with which she'd

275

looked at him earlier. The crunch of gravel under his boots sounded loud in the quiet morning as he trudged up to the main building to find the reception desk. A tired-looking young man roused himself from a chair behind the desk.

"How can I help ya?"

"Looking for a cabin for three nights."

The guy peered around his shoulder to get a look at Audrey. "Nice bike."

Killion laughed. "Yup. She's a beauty." He didn't know if he was referring to Audrey or the machine—probably both. "Can you help us out? We're touring. Figured we'd stop and check out the area on our way down to the Keys."

The young man smiled a gap-tooth smile. "It's the off-season so we got plenty of openings."

Killion took off his gloves and pulled out his wallet. He had ID that wouldn't be flagged in any CIA or FBI database. Worst came to the worst he'd talk to his contact in Seattle and get something made for Audrey, too. His gut clenched because he didn't want her to have to go on the lam, but right now he wasn't seeing another way out of this mess. He handed over cash, grateful most bikers weren't big on credit cards.

"Number seven." The kid slid a key across the scarred wooden counter and pointed along a side road through the trees. "Take a left. It's the last cabin on the left. Smaller than the others. Here's a map of some walks in the area. There's a scenic waterfall less than a mile away."

Which would be well and good if he didn't have one of the FBI's Most Wanted on the back of his bike. He smiled down at the kid, wondering what his own life would have been like if he'd been content with a simple life. He nodded. "'Preciate the information."

He headed down the path. Audrey leaned back as he swung his leg over the saddle, the two of them in perfect synchrony as if they'd been doing this for years.

He started up the engine, trying not to wince at the noise, and motored slowly along to the cottage the receptionist had indicated. He parked the bike near the front door and out of sight of anyone walking past. Cut the engine and felt cold mist cling to his skin.

Audrey stumbled off the machine, and he leaped off to help her. He wrapped his arms around her and wished things were different between them. That she didn't hold herself stiffly away from him. "Okay let's get you inside." His voice was rough, gritty. She'd put it down to his long night of driving.

He shuffled her to the door, tempted to pick her up, but she was too remote for that now. She needed some space. She deserved some autonomy.

He unlocked the door and swung it wide. The interior was all plaid and honey-colored pine, with a big fireplace and exposed logs on one wall. It looked clean, but was chilly. He left Audrey standing by the door and hiked up the thermostat.

He went over and undid the strap on her helmet, eased it up off her head. Her hair tumbled out in a tangled mess. Those violet eyes of hers squinted at him, bruised with exhaustion and despair. He hated seeing her this way. "Go get into bed. I'm going to go buy supplies. I'll be back in an hour. Do you need any help?"

Her nostrils flared as she appeared to gather her inner strength. "I'll manage. Buy toothpaste."

He nodded, wishing this was all over, but secretly glad she was still here with him. Which made him the most selfish bastard in existence.

All he said was, "Lock up. And stay away from the windows."

AUDREY STUMBLED HER way into the bathroom and shut the door. The effort of clinging to Killion's back all night and not falling off the world's most dangerous means of transportation left her feeling shattered. But, even now, every time she closed her eyes, she still saw Gabriel Brightman's brains spattered all over his bedroom wall.

Nausea boiled inside. She was too empty to cry. She felt numb and hollow. Like someone could stick pins in her, and she wouldn't feel it at all. How had her life gone from worrying about her mother's overprotectiveness to running for her life in less than a week? How had she become so dependent on a man who didn't even trust her?

She'd seen the guarded look in his eyes when he'd gotten in the car after they'd escaped Brightman's mansion—the calculation. He'd honestly thought she was capable of doing *that*. She grabbed onto the commode and threw up what little she had in her stomach. After a few moments she stood and washed out her mouth with cold water. Then she turned on the faucet in the shower and stripped off her clothes.

Patrick Killion was a chameleon. His in-need-of-a-trim sun-streaked blond hair and confident swagger perfectly fitted the biker he was currently pretending to be.

The same way he'd been the perfect honeymooner in Jamaica, and the perfect cat burglar in Louisville, the perfect operative when stealing the plane in South America. He could play whatever character was required at any moment.

Did that include lover?

The idea made her shrivel up on the inside. She stepped into the hot spray and felt the water wash over her skin, warming her frozen flesh. She found soap and scrubbed at her body.

Killion was the only constant she'd had in her life since the day Hector Sanchez had stabbed her. He'd mistrusted her because he thought she might be a killer, but she'd *seen* him kill people—and she'd still fallen for the guy.

Water pounded the top of her head. She was in love with him, she realized in growing horror. Hot tears flooded her vision, and she sobbed. She was in love with a government agent who could kill as easily as any cartel hit man. She wiped her eyes and pulled herself together.

What did she really know about the guy?

He was clever and resourceful. Not afraid to take chances. He carried a gun and was a good shot. He was closed-mouthed and secretive. He had a family he rarely saw.

He worked alone.

But he inspired loyalty.

He was cynical and cold.

But she'd seen in his eyes that his heart was breaking because his friend had been caught up in this mess and had lost her life.

She closed her eyes and swallowed.

He worked alone, but he wasn't as isolated as he made out. He had a network of support. Friends who'd drop everything and ride to his rescue on helicopters and private jets. And he'd stuck by her side not just when he thought she was guilty, but also when he'd decided she was innocent, when the best course of action for him and his mission was leaving her behind in protective custody.

He was cynical and detached, but his touch had been molten hot, and she'd never felt more cared for by a lover or satisfied in bed.

She wished she knew how to defend herself, both from the bad guys and from the emotional pull she felt toward Killion.

Abruptly she turned the taps off and dried herself with a towel, squeezing the excess water out of her hair. She ran her fingers through her disastrous tangles, trying to release any knots. Then she washed out her underwear so she'd have something clean to put on later.

As much as she'd blamed Killion for her problems it was probably Devon Brightman who'd set this up. He was the only link between her and Gabriel apart from Rebecca, and Rebecca was dead. Rebecca and her brother had never gotten on very well. After she died his attitude had changed toward Audrey—or at least it had appeared to.

Devon had been lying and setting her up for years. It was the only thing that made sense. She dragged her T-shirt back over her head and headed into the bedroom. Then she curled up under the covers and sank into oblivion.

———————

KILLION CAME INSIDE the cottage, which was now thankfully warm, and dropped his supplies on the small kitchen table. He'd bought a new backpack, a phone, laptop, enough food to get them through a few days, and some toiletries, including hair dye and scissors.

The cabin was quiet as a church, and his heart raced with

worry until he saw his favorite biologist lying under the covers in the bed.

She was still alive. They were still fighting for survival though the odds weren't looking good.

He eyed the empty half of the bed, then turned away. He shrugged out of the heavy leather jacket and hung it over the back of a kitchen chair, put away the groceries that needed refrigerating, and stuck a chair under the main door handle—just in case. Then he stretched out on the couch and pulled a blanket over himself.

He closed his eyes and let sleep claim him.

———————————

AUDREY CAME ABRUPTLY awake in a cold sweat and sat straight up in bed. Her hands were shaking with the residue of some unknown fear. She heard children's laughter outside and adults joining in. Innocent fun.

She looked at her watch. It was just past midday. She frowned. The bed was empty. Had Killion come back? Had he been caught? Had he abandoned her?

She used the bathroom, dragging on her clean underwear before sliding into her jeans. She hurried into the other room, her heart pounding at the idea of him not being there...

His leather jacket hung over the back of a chair, and a bag of purchases sat on the table—including toothpaste and a new toothbrush. She glanced into the living room. Killion was sprawled out on the couch, feet hanging over the end. A weird ache hit her in the chest. Tension fell away.

The horrible fuzzy feel of her teeth drove her back to the bathroom to clean them. When she came back to the kitchen she tried to move as quietly as possible, but he stirred anyway. He stretched his arms over his head and groaned. "There's coffee and bacon in the fridge if you're hungry."

Her stomach growled at the mention of food. She didn't remember the last time she'd eaten a proper meal.

Rather than speaking she found a pan and got the bacon out, putting it on the burner before figuring out how the coffee-pot worked.

Killion headed past her, presumably to the bathroom. They didn't speak.

She found mugs and plates and cut open four white rolls. The aroma of coffee and bacon filled the air, making her mouth water, reminding her of simpler times. She patted the fat off the rashers and poured two coffees, realizing she didn't even know how Killion took his. Then she turned around and found him standing right behind her, wearing nothing but jeans and wet hair.

Startled, she spilled her coffee over the back of her hand. She set down her mug and sucked the scalding liquid off her skin.

"You okay?" He stared at her through slightly red-rimmed eyes, clearly assessing her wellbeing and sanity. "I mean apart from the running for your life with the world's biggest asshole?"

"Why do you do that?" she asked quietly. "Why do you make yourself out to sound so much worse than you actually are?"

He shook his head and for once looked vulnerable. "I don't want to argue with you."

"This isn't fighting, Patrick. This is talking." Emotions were clearly still too close to the surface. She rolled her shoulders to relieve the tension. "How do you take your coffee?"

"Any way I find it." He picked up both mugs and put them on the table. Then picked up the plates and found paper napkins while Audrey turned off the stove.

They sat and dug into their meal as if they were starving. The taste blew her mind, and she closed her eyes and smacked her lips together. "Best meal ever."

When she opened her eyes, Killion was eyeing her hungrily, and she knew exactly what he was thinking. A curl of sensual desire shot through her. Why she wanted this particular man was an enigma. It didn't matter how much biology she knew, down to the most complex biochemical pathway, the rules of attraction were still a mystery.

"Do you think Parker's okay?" she asked, trying to ignore the pull.

"Parker's fine."

"How do you know?"

Infuriatingly he just shrugged.

"He could be hurt." *He could be dead.*

"Alex Parker can take care of himself."

"Don't tell me, he's got your ninja warrior skills." She crossed her arms over her chest, wondering if she was the only person involved in this whole saga who didn't know how to fight. "What should I have done?" she asked suddenly.

He frowned, clearly not following.

"That night when you attacked me and zip-tied me so fast. How would you have avoided being tied up?"

One side of his mouth curled into a wicked smile. He took a sip of coffee and answered her seriously. "Firstly, the outside light being off should have been a big warning."

"But in the real world that stuff happens."

He shrugged. "There are all sorts of real worlds. Once I got hold of you from behind you should have targeted vulnerable places to attack. Eyes, nose, throat, dick. Shoving your straight arm or elbow into a jaw or nose can kill someone if you get the right angle. Grabbing my balls was a good move, but you should have squeezed harder." He grinned, and her pulse sped up a little. "Depends on what you want."

"I want to not be strung up like a Sunday roast by some asshole."

His brows hitched. "I thought you said I wasn't an asshole?"

"I said you shouldn't call yourself an asshole. *I* can definitely call you an asshole."

"Good to know." He was trying to pretend he wasn't amused.

Dammit.

He climbed to his feet, went into the living room, and moved the coffee table to the side of the room. He motioned her toward him.

"So you come into an environment where you can't see a thing and both your hands are full. First rule is always keep your weapon hand empty."

"I don't carry a weapon."

"That tongue of yours should qualify," he muttered irritably. "Which reminds me—teeth. Teeth are a hell of a weapon and people forget that."

She grimaced at the idea of biting any of the men who'd attacked her recently. Well, except…

Killion came up behind her and she was so completely aware of him as a man that she was shocked when he grabbed her roughly around the middle.

"Fight back, Aud."

She got her mind off sex and remembered what he'd told her. She launched her fist in the direction of his face, felt him jerk away. Then he manhandled her easily to the floor, grabbing one wrist and pinning it with his knee to her back. Exactly as he'd done that first night.

She realized something else. He'd done his best not to hurt her that night, just as he was doing now.

"Let me do it to you," she said. "I want to see how you get out of it."

He nodded and lay face down on the floor.

She placed her weight on his lower back and tentatively took his arm, and promptly found herself flat on her back, staring up into his grinning face.

"What did you do?" she asked, slightly breathless.

"Just swiveled my body and used the momentum to knock you off balance."

Dammit. "So I'm just supposed to accept the fact that if I'm attacked I'm at someone else's mercy." That idea was infuriating.

"Fuck, no—unless there's a reason to believe fighting back is going to get you seriously hurt. Sometimes it's good to wait for the right moment."

He was sitting on top of her chest, crotch close to her teeth.

"How about I take a bite out of this?" She raised her head and opened her mouth to demonstrate.

"Hell, yeah." He shifted back an inch. "That would get them off you pretty damn quick. Inner thigh is highly vulnerable, too. Once they're off use your legs. Kick them as hard as you can." He shifted off her and lay next to her on the floor. "Bottom line is you weigh one-ten soaking wet and I'm a good one-eighty. I have a big weight and strength advantage just 'cause I'm a male. And that's not me being sexist, it's basic biology, which I know you'll appreciate." He stared up at the ceiling for a few beats of her heart, then reached out and took her hand in his, lacing their fingers together. Her mouth went dry. "You didn't stand a chance against someone with my training."

And yet, he hadn't hurt her. She hadn't had a single bruise from the encounter. She lay next to him, aware of his warmth, his scent flowing over her. Of a sense of peace and acceptance for everything that had happened between them. She'd forgiven him, she realized. She knew he did what he did out of conviction and loyalty to his country. How could she not admire that?

She sat up. The man looked ridiculously sexy just lying there watching her. She ran a finger over the waistband of his jeans, stopped on the button.

"I never stood a chance against you. Not from the moment you picked me up and carried me away."

His hand stopped her finger's happy journey. "Don't romanticize it. I kidnapped you, let you almost bleed to death in the back of a stolen aircraft, refused you medical treatment and then struggled to keep you from succumbing to a terrible fever. Don't have any illusions about how many times my actions almost got you killed."

She pulled her hand from his and continued to trace his navel. "I'm not absolving you of your sins."

His eyes darkened.

"I'm just offering to help you commit a few more."

He grabbed her hand before she moved it lower. "You know this can't lead anywhere."

"I'm on the run, Killion. Not expecting flowers or chocolate." She kept her voice light and pulled her hand from his.

He swallowed hard. "My job is too dangerous for—"

She rubbed her hand against his hard length, telling him without words that she knew exactly where this was going.

"Fuck, for all I know I don't even have a career anymore." He climbed to his feet and scooped her up in his arms. "Hey—why did the frog make so many mistakes?"

She groaned and pressed her face to his chest.

"It kept jumping to the wrong conclusions."

She used her teeth as punishment and he swore.

"No more frog jokes," she insisted.

He placed her on the bed and came down on top of her. "I'm making no promises."

And suddenly his words weren't about stupid frog jokes. They were about the two of them, their unlikely relationship.

"I'm not asking for any." She sank her fingers into his hair. "I just want to make love to you without any secrets or lies."

He dropped his head to rest between her breasts. "You know that's impossible, right?" his voice was muffled.

"Then we'll just fuck like bunnies."

"Thank Christ." He tugged her T-shirt up and over her head. He palmed her naked breast with a look of reverence on his face. "I've missed you naked."

She would have made up some amusing retort, but he'd drawn her nipple into his mouth. Her vision blanked, and her heels dug into the back of his thighs as her back arched up off the bed. "Okay."

He pulled back and focused his attention on her other

breast.

"I hope you bought condoms on your shopping trip," she whispered as her fingers dug into his scalp.

He froze with a look of horror on his face, and she wanted to weep.

Then he grinned. "Kidding. But for the record, the only thing I considered a sure thing was my inability to resist you." His fingers slipped into her panties and curled inside her before she could draw a breath. He was stroking and touching and driving her up and within seconds her entire being exploded like the stars. She cried out as she shattered.

When she came back down to earth she opened her eyes to find him staring at her, with a serious expression on his face.

"You're beautiful."

He'd never said anything like that to her before, and she couldn't move. They stared at each other for a long moment. To combat the sadness his words evoked, she pushed him onto his back and used her teeth on his body, though more gently than he'd suggested earlier.

He cared about her. She knew he did. But she knew it didn't make any difference.

Their time together was coming to an end. Assuming they got through this alive she'd go one way and he'd go on to his next top-secret assignment. Her hands smoothed over his skin, and she wanted to show him that she got it. And that she forgave him.

He pushed at her jeans, and they both stripped.

He lay back on the bed, and she bent over to kiss his full bottom lip.

"Where do you take a frog with bad eyesight?" His finger traced the bridge of her nose as he teased. "To the hoptician."

She decided to ignore his terrible jokes. His skin was tanned, the fine hair golden brown. She touched and tasted every inch of him, stroking him gently, absorbing everything she could about this man during what was probably their last opportunity to be together. Finally she found his mouth and he groaned as she kissed him tenderly. His hands were shaking as they skimmed her, clearly terrified of doing something to ruin the moment.

He took his turn with her body, cupping, tasting, stroking. She lay back and closed her eyes and opened herself up to him. By the time he sank inside her, her muscles were melted wax. She cried out as he thrust deep. She wrapped her legs around his hips, and they started a dance that was ancient and elemental and amazing. They moved in perfect harmony, pushing ever closer to that yawning cliff, slowing down, building back up, neither in any hurry, both trying to prolong this moment.

Finally the muscles of her sex clenched and spasmed around him, and she cried out, sobbing his name as he drove into her one last time. Afterward, he rested against her, skin on skin, their heartbeats slowly melding. They held each other for a long while and neither spoke.

CHAPTER TWENTY-ONE

K ILLION WARMED A can of soup on the stove while Audrey got out the remaining bread rolls. What had happened in the bedroom earlier had shaken his foundations. He'd known he'd been missing out over the years, but that connection had damn near blown his mind.

Suddenly she lunged for the TV remote, and he turned to see what the problem was.

"Billionaire industrialist Gabriel Brightman was found dead in his home last night in what police are saying are suspicious circumstances. Police want to question Dr. Audrey Lockhart"—there was a photo of Audrey, smiling this time— "who was a friend of the family and is wanted for the murder of her graduate student in Colombia last week. It's not known how Lockhart got back into the United States. Police are also looking for another man, named online as one Patrick Killion, although his identity hasn't been substantiated."

His image flashed up wearing his burglar gear. Fucking great. National fucking news.

"His exact involvement isn't known." Except to everyone he'd ever worked with, and everyone he'd ever manipulated or conned, or put away. *Fuck.* He closed his eyes until he heard Audrey gasp. She didn't seem to understand his world had shattered, and why would she? He'd never told her a damn thing about his job or his mission. But he didn't need a pity party. He just needed this damned thing over and the bad guys stopped.

Her parents were on TV, begging her to give herself up before anyone else got hurt. "Please, Audrey, we know something terrible must have happened to make you do this."

Condemned by her own family. That had to suck.

Her hand rose to her throat. "Maybe I should give myself up. Give you time to find evidence against Devon or whoever did this."

"The cartel can reach you just as easily in the States as in Colombia, *chica*." God, he was pissed.

The camera panned out and Devon stood there looking rumpled and devastated, his arm around Audrey's sister, his hand resting on a little boy's shoulder as the woman held the kid in her arms.

Could they be wrong about the guy? Sure. But it felt right in a way Audrey had never felt right. And the motive was old as the hills. Money. Goddamn money.

The way the newscaster spun the story made it sound like Audrey was so insane with jealousy over her sister dating her ex that she'd gone on some kind of killing spree.

Audrey stood beside the table staring vacantly at the screen even as they moved on to another story. "No one is going to believe Devon is guilty without a confession, are they?" she asked quietly. He didn't answer. "And there's no way he's going to give it up when he's so close to having everything he ever wanted."

"Money?"

"Power." She nodded. "His dad made him work his way from the bottom up through the company and live off a normal employee wage. Devon resented the hell out of his dad for that. Gabriel said it built character."

Killion snorted. "Hence him getting involved with the cartel. My guess is he's using his dad's business to smuggle drugs around the world. The company has facilities in Colombia I take it?"

"Yes." Audrey bit her lip. He knew she'd put together the rest of the puzzle. "Do you think he's the person who shot Rebecca?"

Killion put his hand around the back of her neck and drew her to him. "Is he the right size and shape?"

She rubbed her arms and nodded.

"Then, yes. Probably."

He watched the anger build in her features as she remembered her past history with the fucker.

"He pointed a gun at me and pulled the trigger. Then he comforted me at Rebecca's funeral and I cried on his shoulder. He knew all about the sting operation the cops were setting up with the undercover police officer."

"Which is why he never touched you," Killion suggested. "No one was supposed to know the identity of the person with Rebecca when she was killed. If he'd made a move on you it would put the killer firmly within her circle of family or friends. A random mugging would turn into a personal assault. Cops would have been onto him."

"And now he has some professional assassin working for him." Despair filled her eyes. "We'll never get him to confess. He's super smart and knows his way around computers—"

"I ever get the asshole alone in a room, I can make him talk," he promised.

She stared at him intensely for a few moments, but he

didn't think she was seeing him. She pulled away, paced the floor, eyes focused inward as her teeth gnawed her lip. He loved watching when that brain of hers went into action.

"We have to kidnap him."

He blinked. "Are you nuts?"

"Why?" Her eyes glowed almost lavender. "You did it to me. Let him think the CIA is onto him and that they've whisked him off to a Black Camp facility."

He just stared at her. His innocent biologist had turned into a strategist.

She put her hands on her hips. "If we don't get to him first the assassin might decide to get rid of him, too. Then no one will ever believe me."

Killion frowned. "A confession drawn out under those circumstances will never hold up in a court of law."

"So what? You said you couldn't prosecute him for the murder you thought I'd committed anyway. You just need to know it was him, correct?"

True. Assuming he could get Devon to confess to what he'd done, it didn't matter whether or not he'd received due process. The president had ordered Killion to find out who was behind the vice president's murder. What they did once they discovered who the mastermind was had always been a little murky. Killion wasn't a cold-blooded killer. Nor had he ever disobeyed orders.

"Shake him up. Get him to confess and tell you the name of the assassin."

He ladled them each out a bowl of soup. "The CIA isn't allowed to operate on US soil or against US citizens."

"Now you're following the rules?"

He laughed. Brightman had to be involved, but who the

hell had done the deed? He was no closer to finding the assassin than when he'd staked out the Amazon Research Institute a millennia ago. "Look, we know it's Brightman—"

"No, we don't." Audrey slipped into lecture mode and damn if it wasn't hot. "We only suspect, the same way you suspected me and Gabriel."

The reminder he'd been wrong stung, as did her lack of faith. But she was right.

"He thinks he's smarter than both of us." A vertical line appeared between her brows. "Doesn't that piss you off?"

Well, duh.

"So we get him to confess, find out who his accomplice is and take them all down." She shook a spoon at him like it was a sword. He wanted to wrap his arms around her and kiss the crap out of her, but kissing would lead to other things, and they needed to figure out their next move.

"You'll still have the cartel gunning for you." He hated to burst her bubble. "You can't just go back to your old life if Devon confesses. And there's that whole wanted-for-murder thing down in Colombia."

Her lip trembled even as she took her place at the table. "I was kind of hoping the CIA might help me with that."

He leaned over and ran his knuckle down her cheek. "I'll do what I can, you know that."

She swallowed tightly and nodded. Maybe she did understand the stakes here. Considering what had happened to her life, she should.

Kidnapping Devon might work, although rendition of an American citizen on home soil was walking all over the constitution. The president might not back him up if they were caught. The alternative was sitting here while the net closed around them. Equally unpalatable. These people had killed Crista, the VP, Gabriel Brightman, and had set Audrey up to take the fall as well as tried to kill her on multiple occasions. They weren't messing around.

A knock on the door had his heart hammering as he pushed Audrey behind him, grabbing his pistol from its holster. *Shit.* "If it's the cops you go with them and call FBI Agent Lincoln Frazer. Don't say anything else to them." He rattled off a number he knew by heart. "*Lincoln Frazer.* Don't forget that name." He'd fucked up this whole mission right from the start.

The knock came again.

Killion checked the window and the wave of relief that rushed through him almost knocked him to his knees. Logan Masters and Noah Zacharius stood on the steps, grinning at him like a couple of fools.

He opened the door and Logan pushed past him. Noah followed and smiled at Audrey in a way that set Killion's teeth on edge.

"Saw you on the news. Thought you might need a bit of help."

Killion crossed his arms. "Yeah? And how'd you find us?"

"Your pal, Parker. Stuck a tracker on the bike and gave us a call."

"He hired you?" asked Killion. Even after what happened at Gabriel Brightman's mansion, he hadn't been one hundred percent certain of the former CIA agent. Now he was ready to kiss him on the lips if he ever saw him again.

"He tried." Masters grinned and punched Killion on the arm as he helped himself to Killion's soup. "We're officially on vacation." The Brit gave him a shit-eating grin.

Noah went over to Audrey. "Hey, you look better." He

held out his hand. "We met before, but you might not remember. I'm Noah."

Killion put his hands on his hips and made himself stay put. No point getting territorial. And if that little voice in his ear said his career was already over so what the hell was the problem with pursuing Audrey, he was ignoring it. He had enemies. He wouldn't bring them to Audrey's doorstep when she'd already endured hell.

Audrey smiled back at Noah, and Killion's heart both expanded and contracted at the same time—not the most pleasant experience. "I remember. You're the one who swore you didn't look when I was naked."

"Unlike some people," Noah said slyly, throwing Killion a look.

Audrey laughed. "Well, he did save my life a few times. I owe you all a massive debt of gratitude."

Noah opened his mouth to say something that would definitely be crude. Killion pointed at the guy. "One word, and I will kill you with my bare hands."

Noah laughed and bent forward to kiss Audrey on the cheek. "There." Audrey looked tiny beside the guy. "All debts are paid. Nothing I wouldn't do for a kiss from a pretty lady, or for you, you big, ugly, jealous jackass."

Killion felt his throat swell because Noah had been poking at him for sport, not to be a jerk. He usually gave as good as he got but recently he'd lost his sense of humor. A feeling of shame welled up inside him. "You don't know what we plan to do yet," he said gruffly.

Noah shrugged and sat down and started eating Audrey's soup. "If it wasn't for you I'd have been dead years ago. Every day's a gift, mate. Let's not waste it."

THE BEST HOPE for success was doing what your enemy least expected. Devon Brightman and the assassin thought they had Audrey and Killion where they wanted them—demonized and on the run. They were taking the fight back to the bad guys.

Killion sat in a white van in the intriguingly named Billy Goat Strut Alley around the corner from Devon's downtown Louisville apartment. It was dark and people were going about their business like it was a normal day.

The four of them were kitted out in jeans, graphic T-shirts, and sneakers. Logan had cut Killion's hair so short he didn't recognize himself in the mirror, and provided Audrey with a short wig of bleached blonde hair with a pink streak.

Killion and Logan both wore Bats ball caps pulled low over their features to evade surveillance cameras without looking suspicious. They were only a stone's throw from the Louisville Slugger baseball field.

Logan was staked out on top of a building with a clear view inside Devon Brightman's apartment. Their target was alone. "He's leaving his apartment, exiting the door now."

Audrey checked her watch. "Right on time."

According to Audrey, Devon usually walked to a Mexican restaurant on East Market Street and cut through this alley to get there.

"He might not keep to his usual routine if he's supposed to be mourning dear old Dad," Noah chimed in. Killion had filled the guys in on everything except the identity of the original high profile target. The three wise monkeys approach to life meant they didn't ask.

"He'll go out. He can't cook worth a dime," Audrey said

with certainty, "but he might go somewhere fancier."

"Then we pick him up afterward." Killion looked at her and willed her to have faith in his ability to do his job.

She bit her lip and nodded.

"Hey, you know Gómez's brother is doing time in a US federal facility?" Noah said suddenly.

"Off topic, but yeah?" said Killion.

"I asked around as to how he was picked up. Anonymous tip. Cartel had some big meeting arranged up in the hills around Bogota and the local *policía* swooped in and cleaned house."

"And?" Audrey asked impatiently.

"Raoul was supposed to be there, but his car broke down on the way to the meet and greet. This was about four years ago."

"When Devon was visiting me?" Audrey asked.

"Couple weeks after."

Killion grinned.

"I don't get it," Audrey said, looking between them.

"You don't have to," said Killion. He'd just figured out how to get the cartel off Audrey's back.

Noah winked at him.

"He's coming out the front entrance." Logan's voice was tinny over the radio. "On foot. Alone. He's rounding the corner. Heading for the alley."

Killion put the van in gear. Noah and Audrey both pulled masks over their heads.

He drove forward. He could hear Logan's progress back to street level. The plan was working.

A cop car went past the west end of the alley.

Killion swore inwardly, but didn't panic. He'd done this a

hundred times, but never while a wanted man, and never on US soil.

"He should come out just over there." Audrey pointed to a small path that cut between buildings.

Killion drove slowly and got to the opening just as Devon Brightman reached it. Killion stopped and waved the guy across in front of him. Then he heard the side-door slide open.

Noah jumped out, moving explosively, and stuffed a bag over Devon's head. He dragged him backwards, flinging him into the back of the van while Audrey shut the door. Brightman flailed his arms and legs in every direction, lashing out, muffled cuss words filling the interior.

Noah sat on him as Audrey prepped a syringe.

"Watch his feet," Noah warned gruffly as Devon tried to lash out.

Audrey nodded and slammed the needle into Devon's ass, pressing the plunger home. As soon as Devon went slack, Noah went through the guy's pockets, found a phone, then a second one. He placed both cells into a box with a signal jammer. It meant they didn't have communications either, but it might be for the best.

Killion drove around the block and picked Logan up at a traffic light. He pulled away from the curb. If he was wrong this time he had no idea how the hell he was going to explain himself to the President of the United States. They'd probably all lose their jobs and would be lucky to escape doing hard time. But for the life of him he couldn't think of a viable alternative. He caught Audrey's tremulous smile in the rearview and felt the sides of his heart crack wide open. God help him if he failed.

———————

TRACEY SAT ALONE at a table at Devon's favorite Mexican restaurant. She checked her watch. Devon was late, but that wasn't unusual. Everything was going perfectly. The grieving son. The betrayed ex-lover. The press was eating out of Devon's hand.

She checked her watch again.

She'd purposely worn a black suit so on the surface this looked like a business meeting rather than a lovers tryst. Her underwear was anything but business though, and she'd unbuttoned her shirt as much as was legal.

She sipped her water impatiently. Where the hell was he? She should have picked him up. Maybe someone from the media or police had delayed him? Maybe that stupid bitch Sienna was crying on his shoulder again. She should just arrange another overdose and put the Lockharts out of their misery.

A horrible thought leaked through. What if he'd stood her up?

Her mouth went dry. The people she'd killed for this man, the people she'd fucked—including his father on a couple of sad lonely occasions. No, she assured herself, he'd been delayed, that was all. She dialed his number again, but this time it didn't even ring. It went straight to voice mail. She frowned and tried his burner cell from hers. The company said the number was unavailable.

Her mouth turned to ash. She sat for a few moments staring at her half-eaten bread roll. Then she jerked out of her seat and left, climbing into her BMW Z4 Roadster and driving away without looking back.

CHAPTER TWENTY-TWO

AUDREY COULD HARDLY believe she'd just helped a CIA agent and two British mercenaries kidnap an American billionaire off the street while wanted for a double murder.

At the facility, they'd stripped Devon naked and left him on a bare concrete floor. He was chained to a wall with a black bag over his head. Some people would think it inhumane, and if he was innocent it would be, but he wasn't. She knew it the way she knew big oil would never support the idea of climate change, the way a Trinity fan would never wear green and gold during the annual St. X-Trinity high school football match.

She shivered despite the layers the men had smothered her in. They were using an empty warehouse on the outskirts of the city, less than ten miles from where her parents lived. The cell phones had been handed to Parker and a geeky-looking dude who looked like he could probably program the space shuttle. The phones should give them plenty of information and evidence even if Devon refused to talk, but they still needed the name of his accomplice.

The urge to reach out to her family was almost overwhelming, but she wasn't about to put this operation or these people in jeopardy. Suddenly she had a much better understanding of the way Patrick Killion lived his life.

"You okay?"

She looked up and there was Noah smiling down at her with his pretty gray eyes. The guy was gorgeous, but all she felt toward him was warm brotherly affection. Killion, she alternated between wanting to drown in the bathtub, jump his bones, or just look at him smile that cocky grin. It was stupid. She was in love with the guy. She'd told him she knew the score, but she'd been lying to them both. All she'd achieve with this weakness was getting her heart broken and hurting him. He didn't deserve that. She didn't want to be some crazed groupie hanging onto his leg as he tried to walk away.

Noah waved his hand in front of her face. "Audrey?"

She blinked. Smiled. "Yes, I'm fine thanks. Just worried."

"It's about to start."

The muscles tightened in her chest. "Okay."

"You wanna watch?" he asked, regarding her carefully.

Did she want to watch Patrick Killion interrogate her former lover? See both men for who they really were? Or would she rather keep her illusions? She pushed to her feet. "Let's go."

———

KILLION'S FOOTSTEPS ECHOED off the bare concrete floor as he walked into the room where they were holding Devon Brightman. Game time.

Interrogations often took months to divine useful information, but Killion didn't have months. Another key to a good interrogation was knowledge. And he knew plenty about this asshole.

The blindfolded man stiffened as he approached. "What do you want?" His prisoner's voice was angry but scared.

"Stand up." Killion spoke with a heavy Spanish accent, but used English as he knew Brightman didn't speak a word of the language except perhaps, *"la cuenta, por favor." The check, please.*

"Fuck you." Devon kicked out at him, but missed and landed on his ass.

It was freezing in here, and Killion's breath froze on the exhale.

Devon was definitely feeling shocked, insecure, and stressed. He'd gone from CEO and heir to a pharmaceutical fortune to naked captive in a matter of hours. It was a by-the-book rendition according to the interrogation manual—aside from the fact it was completely and utterly unsanctioned.

"Where am I? What the hell do you want from me? Money? I'll get you money. Get these fucking chains off me."

"You think this is a kidnap and ransom job?"

Devon climbed to his feet, and Killion moved closer. Devon lashed out at him with his foot again and Killion flipped him so he landed with a thud on his back.

"You think you can mess with *El cartel de Mano de Dios* business and get away with it?" said Killion.

"Cartel? You're fucking cartel?" Devon panted from the floor. He moved carefully as if his ribs hurt. "I want to talk to Raoul."

Killion leaned down and hissed in Devon's ear. "I don't work for Raoul." He backed away and paced. He wished he could see Devon's expression, but he couldn't afford to reveal his identity until he had what he needed.

Devon rolled onto his belly and then up onto all fours, following the sound of his footsteps warily. "Who then?" he demanded.

"The head of *Mano de Dios*."

"Raoul is the fucking head of *Mano de Dios*, you imbecile!"

Killion waited for a few beats then surprised the guy by speaking directly into his ear. "Manuel Gómez."

Devon scooted back until he hit the wall. "Manuel is in prison."

"And he recently discovered that's because of you, my friend. He's not happy. In fact, he is very, very unhappy."

"I didn't have anything to do with Manuel being picked up," Devon defended himself.

"Liar," Killion whispered.

Devon flinched and hunched up against the wall. "That was all Raoul's doing."

"Raoul would never have the balls to betray his brother, not without help." Killion argued.

"Seriously. I went to see Manuel about my distribution ideas, but he rejected my offer. Said I wasn't capable of coming through with everything I'd promised—which was bullshit, obviously. Told me if I teamed up with anyone else he'd gut me. I believed him. The guy scared the shit out of me. Then Raoul drove me back to where I was staying. On the way he told me not to be too hasty about my next decision. A month later Manuel and his cronies were picked up by the cops, and Raoul was king of the cartel."

"You want me to believe that Raoul did this on his own?" Killion pushed.

"Damn straight. He called me up after Manuel was extradited, said we wouldn't have any trouble now that Manuel had been taken care of. But none of it was my idea." He laughed, but it came out sickly and nervous. "Manuel only *just* figured out Raoul betrayed him?"

"Because they're family, *pendejo*. That means something to some people." Killion had what he needed to exchange for Audrey's safety. He dropped the Spanish accent. "I'm going to remove your hood, Devon." He spoke calmly, just an operative now doing his job. "If you try to kick me, or spit on me I'll replace the hood and have your legs shackled, too. You gonna behave yourself?" he asked sternly.

Devon froze, confused by the new American voice. Then he nodded with a swift jerky motion.

Killion undid the ties at the back of the canvas bag. He pulled it off and then moved back out of reach. Devon blinked rapidly, his eyes slowly adjusting to the light and his squalid surroundings.

"You," he said in shock.

"Yeah, thanks for posting my face on the Internet, you prick. It made the decision to finally pick you up that much easier."

Killion could see Devon rapidly running their previous conversation over in his mind, trying to figure out what he'd given away.

He crossed his arms over his chest. "You're going to be taken to a secure facility in an undisclosed location—"

"What? You can't be serious. I know my rights."

"In the US maybe." Killion laughed, planting his hands on his hips.

Devon's gaze swung wildly around. "Where am I?"

"That's classified."

The chains rattled noisily as Devon lurched to his feet. "You can't do this. Do you know who I am?"

Killion gave him a look. "You're a suspected terrorist, and I can do whatever the fuck I want to with a suspected terrorist." He leaned closer to Devon's face. Smirked. "It's my specialty."

Confusion twisted Devon's features. "I'm not a terrorist."

"You were in league with Burger so it's close enough." Killion cocked a brow and checked his watch as if he had somewhere else to be.

"I was never in league with that bastard." Spittle flew from Devon's lips. "The guy was into some vigilante shit. He offered my dad in on it after Rebecca died. Dad refused because he was such a pious asshole. I wanted in, but Burger laughed at me, called me a dumb kid." Devon tried to shrug nonchalantly, but his eyes were red-rimmed, and he was so cold his teeth chattered uncontrollably. "I bugged his laptop. I've got recordings in my safe deposit box. All the dirty shit he was up to, but I wasn't involved."

Killion gave him a shrug like he didn't care even though Devon was giving him everything he wanted. "And then you had him killed."

Devon eyes darted nervously, and he licked his lips, obviously deciding he'd said too much. "I want a lawyer."

"Yeah, I'll get back to you on that."

"What time is it?"

"Time doesn't matter. Not for you. Not anymore." Killion smiled grimly, then added, "A more pertinent question would have been what day is it, but that doesn't matter either. Anyway, I just came to wish you *adios,* I have a new mission. Thanks for getting rid of the VP. Saved us the trouble." He took a few steps toward the exit.

"But I didn't do—"

"Hey, bud, save it." Killion shook his head and smiled. He might be playing this all wrong, but Devon looked ready to piss his pants—had he been wearing any. "You're not listening. We got enough off your laptop to pick up your accomplice. She cut a deal while you were out of it, told us everything. Good looking woman by the way." That was a guess based on descriptions of the maid who'd infiltrated Burger's house. "And I already figured out you killed your sister and daddy." He raised one brow. "Nice touch bagging the biologist after the funeral though. Hit 'em while they're vulnerable. And then setting her up for Burger's murder? Brilliant."

Devon's expression grew bitter. "Audrey has been a pain in my ass for years, but I got some satisfaction from screwing her over."

"Whatever floats your boat." Killion remained impassive when all he really wanted was to wrap both hands around Brightman's throat and squeeze hard for sixty seconds.

"She's a know-it-all bitch. I wanted her to suffer."

Killion took another step away to stop himself from punching the self-absorbed asshole in the face. He still needed the assassin's name. "Well Audrey's in WitSec now. So much for the frog gig, huh? And you have a plane to catch."

"Wait," Devon said frantically. "You're not going to take a statement?"

"We got everything we need for now. There's no rush. Legal process for terrorism charges can be agonizingly slow, especially when the lawyers can't track you down."

"Tracey cut a deal?" Devon sounded incredulous.

"Tracey?" Killion laughed. "We both know Tracey isn't her real name." He was guessing, but he knew he was right. This was someone he knew personally, and he didn't know any Traceys.

"June," Devon's face contorted with fury. "June Vanek."

That *bitch*. "Hey, the one thing she didn't tell us was how you two first met?"

"At work. She's Dad's head of security." Devon looked defeated now, his voice low, obviously realizing he was totally fucked. "Somehow she figured out I was communicating with Raoul Gómez down in Colombia. I thought she was going to tell Dad, but instead she told me if I didn't want to get caught I needed to invest in a shit load of burners. I dug into her past and found out about her CIA background, gave her a cut of the operation. After that all it took was a little male attention, and she'd do anything I wanted. She's the one who killed people. This was all her idea." And there was the bastard finally clinging to a lifeline.

Killion kept his expression neutral as he leaned closer to Devon. "She says you're the one who set the cartel on Audrey."

Devon held his stare. Swallowed noisily. "She wanted to kill Audrey as soon as Burger died, but I wouldn't let her. I *saved* Audrey from Tracey."

Killion's fist piled into Devon's face, and Brightman's nose exploded all over the wall.

"That's for Audrey by the way. And she says you were a lousy fuck on account of your small, limp, self-absorbed dick."

While the guy was sprawled on the floor he stuck another needle in Devon's naked white ass and pressed the plunger home.

———————

AUDREY SAT QUIETLY on a dingy love seat in the corner of a small office they'd set up to watch the interrogation, but her mouth was full of sawdust, and her pulse was revving like that motorcycle Killion had put into storage down in Tennessee. Devon and this woman, June, had murdered a sitting vice president and tried to set Audrey up to take the fall. No wonder the CIA had come after her. Just thinking about it blew her mind. Rebecca and Gabriel would have been devastated by the extent of Devon's treachery. She couldn't believe she'd been so easily duped.

"I was hoping for at least a little good cop bad cop routine." Logan joked as Killion came into the room. "Or some *'you can't handle the truth'* action." He did his best Jack Nicholson impression.

"I'll bear that in mind for next time I have an audience." Killion stopped short when he saw her sitting there. "The things you just heard—"

"Yeah, we know. Everyone thinks Burger died of a heart attack and a cover-up looks bad to all the conspiracy nut jobs," Logan told him.

"You have no idea," Killion said. His eyes never left her, though he didn't come any closer.

"It would take more than that *brilliant* display of bullshit to get anything out of me, mate." Noah thumped Killion's arm.

"You liked that?" Killion grinned.

"Fucking A. Especially the last bit."

Killion's smile vanished.

Part of her was in shock at how easily he'd manipulated Devon into his confession. Part of her was thrilled at how he'd stood up for her at the end.

Parker shouldered his way in the door with his laptop open. "This is our assassin."

Audrey walked over to look at the screen.

Killion followed more slowly. "She's the woman I told you about although she's altered her appearance," he told Parker. "She obviously changed her name to try and outrun her shitty reputation." His expression grew more troubled, which Audrey didn't understand. What had happened with Devon felt like a victory. Now it was turning sour. "She's gonna come after me. She hates my guts, and I just ruined her life—again."

Parker nodded. "I agree."

Audrey couldn't breathe. For some stupid reason she'd thought this would be over now.

"I already called Frazer." Killion worked at a muscle in his shoulder. "He's doing what needs to be done."

They were still talking in code, but after what she'd heard that was just fine. She'd mourned Ted Burger along with the rest of the country and had been saddened by his death. But it didn't sound like he'd been a very nice man.

"What happens next?" Audrey asked, breaking her silence.

Parker's cell rang, and he put it to his ear. "Frazer says to turn on the news."

Noah found the latest breaking news on his laptop and there was June Vanek's picture front and center. The newscaster was declaring that police had discovered evidence pointing to Gabriel Brightman's head of security and son both being the prime suspects in the man's murder, and that Audrey Lockhart and Killion, although wanted for question-ing, were no longer suspects.

She covered her mouth but must have let out a sob. Killion turned and pulled her into his arms. She clung to him, almost embarrassed by her need to touch this man. It felt so good to be wrapped in his arms. After a few seconds she stood on tiptoes and tried to kiss him. He pulled back.

"Thank you," she said. She pushed away her confusion. "You told me you'd do it. You told me we'd get our lives back."

Noah and Logan exchanged a look.

"Yup, I'm that good." Killion smiled into her eyes, not blanking his features the way she hated when he was hiding something. She relaxed.

"But you'll still need security until I can go talk to Manuel and make some arrangements," he told her.

"Can I see my family?" She was desperate to see her parents, sister, and nephew. "My mother will be beside herself. I'm surprised she's not in the hospital."

"Sure." Killion released her and stood back. "Noah and Logan can go with you. I have to wait for someone to take custody of Brightman. Cops can interview you at home. Frazer will arrange a US Attorney to be present. Don't say a word without him. Don't mention picking up Brightman or anything you overheard today."

She nodded. "Are you going after this woman, June?"

Killion shook his head and crossed his arms over his chest, staring at the wall over her shoulder. "I doubt Vanek will hang around here."

"But I thought you said she'd come after you?" Audrey said. His manner was decidedly off.

"She will eventually when she thinks the heat has died down. But the cops will pick her up long before that. I'll have to lie low for a while, that's all."

"But I'll see you again, right?" Her voice climbed a little higher. "Before you go on your next mission?"

"Ah…" He took a half step back and gave her a small *too-*

bad-but-that's-how-it-goes-sometimes shrug. "Probably not."

A cold draft blew over her skin. She looked around at the other men's faces. They were all staring awkwardly at their boots, obviously embarrassed for her. "You're saying goodbye to me here? Like this?"

Logan went to open the door to leave.

"Stay. We're nearly done." Killion looked pained. "Don't make a scene, Aud. You knew this was how it was going to be. It's over. You said you got that when we started up in Jamaica. Now you get to go back to your frogs." He laughed but it was a horrible grating sound. "But I'd avoid Colombia if I were you, even if I can get the cartel off your back." His tone turned patronizing like she was a little slow on the uptake.

She narrowed her eyes, trying to figure out if he was joking about this giant public brushoff. He looked deadly serious though—a little bored, a little impatient, like he had more important things to do.

Her fingers clenched. Emotion swelled inside her, and her blood roared in her ears. God. He was serious. This was it. He was saying goodbye in front of his buddies as if she really were just another cog in the wheel. Tears started to burn, but she refused to let them fall. She was making a fool of herself.

"Come on, sweetheart." Noah took her by the shoulders and started hustling her out the door.

"Keep your eyes peeled for that bitch, Vanek," Killion shouted after them.

Logan gave him the finger. Audrey wanted to give him the finger too. She'd never told him she loved him. She'd never had a chance. But as her heart shattered into a million pieces inside her chest she was glad. One less awful humiliation to deal with.

———————

"YOU OKAY?" PARKER asked when Killion slumped down to the love seat and put his head between his knees.

Fuck. "Yeah. Great." If he didn't count letting the best thing that had ever happened to him walk away thinking he was a fucking piece of shit. He wanted to smash something, preferably Devon Brightman's face.

"I take it you did that for her sake?"

His lip curled in self-disgust as he looked up at the other man. "I'm not that noble. I can't do the work I do with Audrey in tow."

"If that's the lie you need to tell yourself, go for it. We all do what we have to do to get by." Parker's phone rang before Killion had the chance to reply. "Cops are on their way. Let's clear out."

"What about Brightman?"

Parker showed him a live feed on his laptop. Someone had dressed Brightman in his clothes, laid him on a dirty looking mattress. They'd cleaned up the blood, removed the chains and hood, but left drug paraphernalia beside him. "We've got enough evidence for the locals to charge him with conspiracy to murder his father and Audrey, and I'm pretty sure they can probably try him for the murder of his sister, Rebecca, too. And that's not even touching on the narcotics trafficking and other people he and Vanek killed to build their smuggling network."

"What about me kidnapping him and forcing out a confession?" asked Killion.

"Never happened. The drugs we gave him will make him pretty spaced for a while. Come on, I have to figure out a way to get into his safe deposit box before the cops do."

Killion grunted and stood. "Let's get out of here then." He kept his eyes on Parker's back. He ignored the way his brain screamed at him to go after Audrey. She was a weakness he couldn't afford. He had to catch Vanek, and then go arrange a little chat with Manuel Gómez inside Atwater. Audrey wasn't in the clear yet. Not until he tied up all the loose ends. Noah and Logan could keep her safe. Him being an asshole made it easier for her to hate his guts, easier for her to move on. Then he'd have to figure out what the hell he did with his life next.

CHAPTER TWENTY-THREE

I T HAD BEEN three days since they'd arrested Devon and cleared Audrey Lockhart's name. Tracey had known as soon as she figured out they'd lifted Devon that Patrick Killion would get her name out of him eventually. Devon might be a computer genius, but Killion had been trained by the best, just as she'd been. He was the master of manipulation.

She didn't blame Devon, but wasn't going to get caught by trying to save his ass, no matter how much she loved him. He'd betrayed her, and it wasn't something she forgave.

Seeing her picture on the news had been infuriating, but she'd prepared for this eventuality. She'd stashed her BMW away and was driving a non-descript silver sedan registered in a fake name. She'd changed her looks, had new ID, cash, credit cards. She also had access to that bank account in the Caymans that she and Devon had set up to make Audrey look guilty.

She could run.

But every time she started driving out of the city she found herself circling back around.

If Audrey had died the way she was supposed to, Devon would be the head of Brightman Industries and he and Tracey would be together. She needed to punish the bitch for ruining their plans. She also wanted to destroy Killion both personally and professionally. Blowing up his pet analyst had been a start, but killing Audrey Lockhart—who he'd made it his personal mission to keep safe—would devastate him.

She knew Lockhart would be guarded for now, but what about the sister? She smiled. Over the last six months she'd spent many hours tracking Sienna, figuring out her dealer, her routine, the time of the day when her craving overwhelmed her desire to stay clean. Instead of staking out Audrey, she staked out Sienna's dealer. It was only a matter of time before the shallow flake turned up.

It wasn't the best neighborhood, which was good for what she had in mind. People kept their mouths shut in places like this. No one would report her to the cops.

Killion had disappeared off the scene.

She got quite the thrill knowing she'd destroyed his chance of going back undercover in the field again. During their training at the Farm that had been his dream. She yawned widely and opened a bottle of soda, taking just a sip so she didn't need to go pee. As the night grew quiet the players started coming out of the woodwork.

Finally a small Toyota *Prius* pulled in front of the dealer's house. Sienna Lockhart got out and dashed up the front steps.

Tracey watched. She wasn't in any hurry. The loser wasn't going to go home to get high. Sienna came out of the house and trotted back to her car. Jumped in and drove quickly away. Tracey followed her out of town and down by the river to Cox's Park. Sienna pulled up in a deserted parking lot and cut her headlights. Tracey waited at a distance for ten minutes, and then drove closer, stepped out of her car, pulling out her pistol and tapping a false badge on the glass so the girl would think she was a cop.

Slowly the window rolled down. Sienna's eyes were huge

and pupils dilated as Tracey ran a flashlight over her face. The girl swayed in her seat.

"Out of the car, Miss."

Sienna muttered an obscenity and awkwardly pushed open the door. "You can't charge me." She sniffed. She and Audrey looked very alike, but Sienna was a few inches taller and rail thin. And she lacked Audrey's smarts, probably because she'd fried her brain with chemicals.

Tracey patted her down and pocketed the rest of her stash and her cell phone. Then she snapped on handcuffs and helped the strung-out junkie into the passenger side of her sedan.

"I haven't done anything."

Tracey got in the driver's seat and pulled her weapon. Pointed it at the girl who shrank into the farthest corner against the door. "Call your sister."

Sienna's blue eyes bulged. Sweat beaded her forehead. "Oh, God. You're that woman. The security guard from Devon's company."

Tracey grabbed Sienna by the hair and slammed her head against the window. "I was the head of security, you stupid bitch! Devon was only fucking you because I told him to."

Snot and tears smeared the woman's cheeks. Her face was bright white. Eyes terrified.

Tracey dragged out Sienna's cell phone. "Call your sister. Tell her you've done something stupid. Cry and blubber as much as you want. Tell her you need her to pick you up from here. Beg her not to tell your parents." She dug her fingers harder into Sienna's hair.

"You'll kill her. Kill us both."

"I just want to talk to her, but if you don't do it? I'll kill you right now. And later, when they think it's safe, I'll kill that little boy of yours. Shoot him in the head like a fucking rat."

Sienna sobbed and dialed the number. Tracey held the gun beside the girl's nose and never dropped her gaze. As soon as Sienna delivered the message she took the phone and hung up before the woman could betray her.

"Well done, Sienna. You finally did something right." Then she slammed the butt of the weapon into her temple and looked for somewhere to hide the car.

AUDREY WAS ESCAPING the nightmare her life had become by putting her favorite nephew to bed. The fact he was so darn cute was probably a biological imperative—a reason women stuck around even though they knew boys grew into men, and men broke women's hearts.

God, she missed Killion. Missed him and hated him in equal measure.

Redford's warm body curled into hers as they sat in a rocking chair in his room. She'd just finished reading her favorite children's book, *The Wide-Mouthed Frog* to him for the fourth time, and he'd finally fallen asleep in her arms. She carefully lowered the book onto a nearby table, picked him up, and slid him into his cot.

She mentally steeled herself and went to find her parents. "Anything left to clean up?" she asked as her mom wiped down the stove.

"I've got it, honey."

She wanted to rip out her own hair. She'd become "honey." That's what happened when your mother mistakenly thought you'd killed two people in cold blood.

She tried not to grind her teeth. "Is Dad in the lounge?"

That she'd been reduced to a virtual prisoner in her parents' home because her mother refused to let her out of her sight was wearing on her nerves. Noah and Logan were camped out at a neighbor's house across the street with a great view of her parents' home and a surveillance system set up to monitor the backyard. She had a walkie-talkie she carried around with her wherever she went.

Killion was gone. No phone calls—despite the sleek new cell phone Noah had handed her that first awful day when the press had refused to leave her alone. No emails. No messages. Just gone. *Poof.* Like she'd meant nothing to him at all, while her heart lay scattered in pieces between Colombia and Kentucky.

"He's watching the football. Are you sure you're okay? No bad dreams?"

"No, mom, I'm fine." She went over and hugged the woman who'd given her life. She hadn't realized a person could cry so many tears until she'd come home. Her poor mother had been through the wringer. Her dad, thankfully, was much more even-keeled. Audrey had shed her own tears—for Mario, for Gabriel and Rebecca. Most of all she'd cried because she knew Killion wouldn't be coming back. She'd never see him again. Her heart would never race at the sight of his confident grin. She'd never groan at another stupid frog joke. Or lie in his arms and stretch out, trying to touch every inch of her body to every inch of his.

It had been galling to realize she'd been just another job. That when he'd warned her he'd ruin her for any other man he hadn't been lying.

Time to snap out of her funk before her mom latched onto her sadness. She couldn't take another round of over-anxious parenting. Audrey checked her watch. "Sienna not back yet?"

Her mother looked up at the kitchen clock, then straightened the tea towels that hung on the stove handle. "No, but the lines in the grocery store can be bad even at this time in the evening."

Audrey smiled reassuringly but they avoided each other's gaze. It was hard to have faith in someone who'd fallen off the wagon so many times, but they needed to try. "I'm going to go watch the game with Dad." She headed down the corridor toward the den. The university had reinstated her—she'd actually been sacked, which she found kind of horrifying—but they'd insisted she take six-months paid leave to let this whole thing settle down.

She wouldn't last six months doing nothing. She didn't think she'd last another day—not with her heart breaking every time she thought about a certain CIA agent.

Maybe she'd fly to Buenos Aires and volunteer on a biodiversity project they were doing in Patagonia. Maybe find a good-looking Argentinian to take her mind off the American she couldn't stop thinking about.

Her cell rang, and she pulled it from her pocket, barely saying "Hello" before Sienna's voice came over the line. *Shit.* She was high and crying and begging for Audrey to come and get her. She closed her eyes and leaned against the wall. She and Sienna had been getting on better since Audrey got back, but she could see the strain beginning to tell on her baby sister. Hell, she was feeling it too. Sienna babbled out her location and hung up before Audrey could reply.

Dammit.

What should she do? Her mom would have a mental breakdown if there was any more drama around here.

She hadn't left this house since she'd come home to a hero's welcome, escorted by federal agents and her two buff bodyguards. Thankfully, the press had lost interest and gone home after she'd given them a sound bite. It had been patently obvious she wasn't going to say anything more.

She checked her watch. It wasn't late. She could be there and back in under forty minutes. God, Sienna's addiction was frustrating and infuriating and yet Audrey felt the weight of responsibility lying heavily on her shoulders. Even though rationally she knew it wasn't her fault, Devon had still targeted Sienna because of her. It hadn't been easy for Sienna to know she'd been used that way. Audrey knew from personal experience just how much it sucked.

If she took her father's car and left now she could get her sister back before anyone knew Sienna had screwed up. Tomorrow she'd call a rehab center and get Sienna booked in and clean. If it didn't work, at least she'd tried.

She snagged her father's keys and crept into the garage, quietly closing the door. She pulled on her dad's white ball cap and sunglasses even though it was dark. Logan and Noah wouldn't know she was gone.

She sped across town, down Zorn Avenue, taking River Road toward Cox's Park. When she was in high school this was an area where teens had parked, but more recently it was where Sienna went to get high.

High school had seemed like such a zoo at the time. It had often felt like the world was going to end though it never had. Now getting dumped by Patrick Killion felt like the end of the world. It was going to be hard as hell to recover from. Sure, she had her work—to a point—but it hadn't taken many seconds after he'd sent her away so callously to realize she'd never get over him. Bastard.

She swallowed down the sadness.

She didn't really hate him. She just wished she did because the idea of going on without him made the rest of her life loom empty and lonely ahead of her. She loved him.

But she hadn't told him how she felt. She'd been too scared of rejection. Crazy after all they'd been through together. Watching him work Devon with his lies and fabrication had been eye opening. He didn't need to torture anyone to get what he wanted. He twisted words, made his target believe one thing, even though it was patently obvious to the observer that it was a lie…

Her hands tightened on the wheel and she gasped out loud. "That rat bastard."

He'd conned her exactly the same way he'd conned Devon, and she'd been too insecure to realize it. Or he'd been telling the truth…

Her hands shook.

Could he have been acting when he'd rejected her so cruelly? She didn't know. And she had no way of asking him. She could ask Logan or Noah, but that idea made her uncomfortable. If she were wrong about this she'd rather be wrong with a stranger.

She dialed the number Killion had given her in the cabin in Tennessee before he'd realized it had been the cavalry on the doorstep, not the cops.

"Frazer," a deep voice answered.

"Uh, my name is Audrey Lockhart."

"Dr. Lockhart. I trust you're feeling better after your ordeal?"

Her throat felt like she swallowed a mouthful of broken glass. Sienna's *Prius* was parked just up ahead. The wide expanse of the river glistened in the background as it snaked on by. She pulled over. "I was wondering if you could pass on a message to Patrick Killion for me."

"Of course. What is it?"

She thought of all the stupid frog jokes she could send as a coded message, but the bottom line was, "I love him. I know he is way too busy doing important things that we average Americans can barely guess at," her sarcasm came through, loud and clear, "but just tell him that I love him even though he gave me the world's crappiest goodbye. I expected more of him."

She heard the smile in the FBI agent's voice. "I will pass that on. Where are you?"

Just from the way he said it she knew he was watching her phone signal. "You obviously already know. My sister got high. I've come to pick her up and take her home." It was easier to talk to a stranger about this stuff than people she knew, she realized.

"Do you have your protection detail with you?"

"I'm heading right back home as soon as I get Sienna—"

"Turn around and pick up your protection detail."

"I'm right here." She frowned. "Well, that looks odd."

"What?" he asked tersely.

"It doesn't look like there's anyone in the car." She opened her door.

"Get back in the car and turn around. Masters and Zacharias are en route to your location."

She fumbled the phone and jerked forward to catch it just

as the windshield exploded.

———————————

"So you're *really* not planning to see her again? Ever?" Noah asked between bites of a burger Killion had picked up for him on the way over.

Killion had to restrain himself from putting his fist through Noah's face. The Brit's innocent expression failed to disguise his desire to go after Audrey for himself. Killion turned away from his friend. It was going to be up to Audrey whom she dated. His stomach twisted, and he felt sick at the thought of her in another man's arms.

He shouldn't have come here, but he hadn't been able to resist seeing Audrey one last time. Even so, he still hadn't worked up the courage to knock on her parents' door yet.

She must hate him. But another part of him was worried she didn't. That after a few days she'd look back on their time together and realize it was just one of those in-the-moment affairs that meant nothing in the real world.

The fact he preferred hate to indifference showed what a sick sonofabitch he really was. He took a swig of beer that he'd also brought with him for the guys, and downed half a bottle.

Tomorrow he had a new assignment. He'd been put in charge of intelligence operations throughout the Middle East. After all the mistakes he'd made during this mission, it was a dream job. One he was eminently qualified for. A huge responsibility. An important position.

Despondency dragged at his soul.

First, he had to tie up a few loose ends here. Logan and Noah needed an update and a thank you. They'd saved his ass, more importantly, they'd saved Audrey's.

"Manuel Gómez has agreed to the staged escape in exchange for working for the US and the guarantee that the cartel will stop going after Audrey."

"How do you know you can trust him?" asked Noah skeptically.

"We don't." Killion shrugged. "But Manuel's reign was a lot less bloody than his brother's currently is. He knows that Raoul played a part in his arrest. He also knows we know where to find him. I played him a recording of my conversation with Devon Brightman, and I'm betting Raoul won't live past Valentine's Day."

Noah looked disappointed. The Regiment still wanted their piece of Raoul Gómez, but this was the best he could do for Audrey. It had taken all his chips to negotiate this deal. Every piece of goodwill the president and Frazer had for him had been played out. But it was worth it. Audrey would be off the cartel's hit list.

"What happens to Brightman?" asked Noah.

Killion grinned. "He's feeding the cops some bullshit story about this giant conspiracy involving the VP and being kidnapped by the CIA in downtown Louisville. They stopped listening when they matched a gun in his apartment to his sister's murder. Locals are prosecuting the sonofabitch. Every word he spouts makes him look more desperate."

"And June or Tracey or whatever the fuck her name is? Any sign?"

She was the only piece of the puzzle that still bothered Killion. "Not yet. FBI accountants found her money, and it's only a matter of time before she tries to access it. Parker has some people who can take over from you guys in a couple of days, by the way." A second car bomb had killed a data analyst called Peter Fredericks. It turned out he and Vanek were old friends, and he'd probably been her inside source of information.

"Someone's leaving the house." Logan told them from the window. "Looks like the father's vehicle." Logan relaxed but then picked up the walkie-talkie and asked Audrey to confirm her location. There were a few seconds of silence. "She's not answering."

"I'll go over and make sure everything's okay."

"You sure that's a good idea? You were pretty harsh with the brushoff," Noah asked with wide-eyed innocence.

Logan tried to hide a smile. Killion kicked the chair Noah was leaning back on. "Asshole."

Killion left before Noah could pick himself up off the floor. It was crazy that he felt so proprietary over Audrey when he'd dumped her so publicly. *Fuck.* He stopped walking and stared up at the sky for a brief moment before he strode across the street. Time to get this over with.

Before he could knock on the door, Noah was running out of the house, holding his cell.

"Tracker signal has her on the move."

"What?" Where the hell was she going?

"I'm following her, Logan's staying here. You check the house."

Killion shook his head. "I'm coming with you."

They ran to the Brits' rental that was parked in front of the neighbor's house and jumped in. Killion checked his weapon and put it back in his holster.

"She might have just popped out for something," Noah suggested helpfully.

Killion tried to call her, but she was engaged. Dammit. "Whatever the reason I'm going to—"

"You already broke her heart, Patrick. There's not much you can do to top that, mate."

Killion swallowed what he wanted to say. Shit. "I just want her safe."

"We both know no one is ever completely 'safe.'"

"Where the hell is she going?" He stared at the dot on the screen as she headed toward the river. Then his cell rang, and it was Frazer.

"Audrey Lockhart just called me to ask me to tell you you're an asshole, but she loves you anyway. Then there was a gunshot."

Elation then ice filled Killion's veins.

"Where are you?" asked Frazer.

"We're about five minutes behind her." And every second felt like a million years.

"She said her sister was high, and she went to pick her up. Think Vanek set this up?"

"Yes."

"I'm calling the locals for backup."

Killion hung up. "Pretty sure Vanek set her up using her sister as bait."

Noah swore. "That is one sneaky bitch."

Killion didn't say anything. If June Vanek hurt Audrey she wouldn't survive their next encounter. But if Audrey died, neither would he.

CHAPTER TWENTY-FOUR

AUDREY HAD WATCHED enough cop movies to know the best place to hide from a bullet was behind the engine block of a car.

The gunman had shot out both front tires just as Audrey had been about to drive away from this ambush.

God, how stupid could she be? Was Sienna still alive? Probably not, and grief washed over her even as another bullet smashed into the radiator. She gripped her phone in her hand and pressed Noah's speed dial button.

"Audrey?"

Then another voice. One she recognized with every nerve in her body. "Where the hell are you?" asked Killion.

"Cox's Park. Just off River Road. Someone is shooting at me, but I can't see where they are firing from."

"Pistol or rifle?"

"How the heck would I know?"

"Okay. Sorry. We're on our way. Just sit tight. We're five minutes out."

"Okay." She was shaking so badly she could barely grip the cell. She was so sick of this terror that kept following her everywhere. She wanted this over. She wanted her life back.

A voice shouted out of the darkness. "You willing to swap your life for your sister's?" Female.

328

"If you go to her, I will fucking shoot you myself," Killion shouted so loud she didn't need the phone against her ear.

She laughed. "I love you, Patrick. I meant to tell you, but I fell for that act back at the warehouse. I'm so stupid because I'd just watched the full performance you did on Devon. I never for a moment thought you'd do it to me, too."

The rush of the nearby river almost drowned out his words. "I figured it would be easier if you thought I didn't care."

"Easier?" She choked out a laugh. "Having my heart shredded by your professional indifference was supposed to be *easier*?"

"My career makes it too dangerous to have a relationship—"

She laughed harshly. Another gunshot rang out. This one close enough to brush against her hair. She screamed and curled herself into an even smaller ball.

"I'm going to shoot Sienna in her pretty little head if you don't come out," said a sing-songy voice in the darkness.

"Don't you *move*, Audrey." Killion sounded beyond pissed.

She wiped a tear from her face. "I actually figured out you didn't do relationships before we had sex. And you seem to forget I was already in danger *before* you turned up." She heard the swish of footsteps through grass. "Oh, God. She's coming."

"We're almost there."

"So is she." Audrey peeked up over the hood. An attractive blonde woman appeared about thirty feet away, carrying a rifle. If Audrey ran for the road she'd be picked off. Same if she ran anywhere except through the brush down into the river.

She contemplated jumping into the water for three whole seconds, but its treacherous currents would pull her under and suck her deep. She'd never survive, especially when the temperature was close to freezing.

Another shot, and Audrey felt the sting of a bullet across her scalp and the hot rush of blood gushing over her face. She screamed and dropped the phone. Killion was shouting so loudly she could still hear him even though she was sprawled on her back in the mud. He sounded a long, long way away. Wishing things could have been different between them, she closed her eyes and lay there, absolutely still.

———————————

IN ALL HIS years as an Intelligence Officer, Killion had never experienced the kind of terror he felt when he heard the gunshot followed by Audrey's scream that was abruptly cut off.

"She's been hit." He called nine-one-one on his phone and requested an ambulance to go along with the cops. "It isn't far."

The tracker signal was about a quarter of a mile down a gravel road. Noah gunned the engine knowing speed was more important than stealth if Audrey had been incapacitated with a gunshot wound. Finally they came to a clearing by the river and there was Audrey's dad's SUV lit up by the headlights. June Vanek stood beside it, looming over Audrey's prone body, holding a rifle pointed down at her.

Rage overcame him, and he rolled out of the car, coming up in a crouched firing stance.

"Drop the weapon, June. It's over!"

"What's it like to be a few seconds too late, Patrick?" Her voice dripped vitriol. Her finger was wrapped tight around the trigger. If he shot her she'd probably fire anyway and hit Audrey. And just because Audrey looked dead, didn't mean she was. Audrey was a fighter. He ignored the fear that corroded the edges of his heart and stared into June's laughing face.

Victory shone in her eyes.

Suddenly, Audrey kicked June between the legs, and the barrel of the rifle jerked up into the air.

He nailed June between the eyes with two shots and watched with grim satisfaction as she toppled over onto the ground. Audrey was instantly on her feet, crimson blood streaking her face, making her look like the survivor from a horror movie.

"Where are you hit?" Killion ran toward her and started pulling at her clothes to try to find the wound. She shoved him off her.

"It's just a graze along my scalp. We have to find Sienna." She stumbled away and ran toward a stand of trees while he stood staring at her like an idiot.

Noah sprinted after her. Killion shook himself out of his stupor and raced after them both, catching up before they got to the trees. A silver sedan was parked in the shadows, and Audrey's sister lay in the back seat. Killion held his breath as Noah felt for a pulse.

"She's breathing. Gunshot wound to the shoulder." He started working his magic, and Killion called the cops to give them the all clear, making sure his weapon was back in its holster as two cruisers screamed down the gravel road. He waved them over. They radioed the ambulance crew and, after what felt like forever, the paramedics were on scene.

He pulled Audrey away so they could work. She turned and started crying, resting her head on his chest. "Thank you. Thank you for coming and saving me again."

"You were doing a pretty good job on your own."

"No." She shook her head. "As much as you hate praise, I'd have died if you hadn't turned up exactly when you did. It's a habit I happen to appreciate."

"Hate praise?" He attempted a grin. "Are you sure you're talking to the right guy?"

"Oh, you're definitely the right guy."

His arms went around her at that, and he pulled her tight against him. God, he'd missed this. Her softness, her scent, her grit. He closed his eyes and tried to imprint this feeling on his memory. As his heart started to return to normal, he was hit by renewed worry. How the hell was he going to tell her he had to leave tomorrow? How could he return to her arms only to leave again the next day?

She held him so firmly, as if he was her safety line, and he wanted to be. The idea of leaving her again made him want to throw up. But he'd just been handed the biggest promotion of his life, a promotion that could help shape the future of millions of desperate people. He couldn't turn that down even if she begged him.

The medics lifted Sienna from the car and onto a stretcher. Suddenly Audrey ripped out of his arms. "I'm coming with you," she shouted as she ran after them.

"Cops are going to need a statement," he called out, sounding pathetic even to his own ears.

"They know where to find me." She turned and smiled at him, those eyes of hers as beautiful as they were sad. "Goodbye, Patrick."

He opened his mouth, closed it again without saying anything. She climbed into the ambulance, and the paramedic closed the door. She wasn't going to beg. She wasn't going to cling.

It was up to him now, he realized. Their relationship. Their future. Considering how callously he'd walked away from her last time and the fact she'd already told him she loved him, why the hell wouldn't it be his move?

He was flying to Saudi Arabia tomorrow.

And still he stood there stupidly, watching the ambulance drive away. Noah clipped him around the back of the head. "If she was my woman she wouldn't be riding out of here alone."

Killion nodded, and then blinked and looked around at the chaos and carnage of the crime scene. He drew in a deep breath. "Let's sort out this mess."

CHAPTER TWENTY-FIVE

E LEVEN DAYS AFTER Sienna had been shot she was released from the hospital. Audrey stood by the door and watched her mother push Sienna along in a wheelchair.

Sienna paused at the threshold to her bedroom and touched Audrey's hand. "You sure you're okay, Audrey?" The kidnap and shooting had made Sienna more concerned about her than her sister had ever been in the past.

"I'm fine, sweety." She took her sister's cold hand in hers. "You just concentrate on getting better." The shadows under Sienna's eyes looked like bruises, her skin alabaster pale. But there was a determination in her eyes too, a steadfastness Audrey hadn't seen before. Emotion knotted her throat. "I'm proud of you for doing this, Sienna. I am so damn proud."

Her sister took a deep breath and nodded. She'd asked to be put into rehab—especially important with the pain medication Sienna needed to take as her wound healed. "I don't want to die, Audrey." Her voice shook. "It's been a long time, but I finally want to live."

"I love you." Audrey told her and kissed her on the cheek. She'd been saying that a lot lately. Each member of her family heard it at least once a day. She'd even said it to Logan and Noah before they'd headed back to Colombia. She'd never be able to repay them for looking out for her.

There was another person who would have heard it, but she hadn't seen him since the shooting. Some days that made her angry. Most days it just made her sad.

The nurse took over and Audrey pulled her mom away by the arm. "Come on, you. Time to take a break." Her mother had pretty much been going non-stop since the shooting.

"Think she'll be okay?" Sandra Lockhart asked wearily.

Sienna was here for three months without any contact with her family or friends. The hardest part would be the separation from Redford, but everyone knew it would be better to miss three months of his life, than continue this damaging, painful cycle of addiction.

She put her mom in the passenger side of her car and headed back across the city. She was actually driving her own vehicle again and had moved back into her own house. But it didn't feel like home. Not anymore.

She pulled into her parents' driveway. Her father came out with Redford in his arms. He probably hadn't believed Sienna would go into rehab. Audrey turned to watch another car pull up alongside the curb. She smiled and went to meet the young woman who stepped out. She shook hands and introduced the woman to her parents.

"Mom, Dad. This is Frances. Frances Torrino. She's the new nanny."

"We can't afford a nanny." Her mom looked horrified, but her dad frowned thoughtfully.

"Gabriel left me some money in his will." Audrey choked up a little thinking about his generosity and tried to forget how he'd died. Painlessly according to the police officer she'd spoken to. "This is what I'm doing with it."

"We can't take your money, Audrey," her mom objected.

Audrey raised her hands. "It's done, and you'd be a fool not to accept the help. Frances comes highly recommended." She went over and kissed her parents each on the cheek. "I love you, but I can't stay. Not anymore." She pulled faces with Redford for a few seconds and then laughed and went to get back in her car.

The roar of a motorcycle had her looking up the street. Her heart gave one of those painful little jerks that always preceded disappointment. The sun was in her eyes, but that couldn't possibly be who she wanted it to be even though the breadth of his shoulders and lean frame were exactly right. Then the bike stopped at the bottom of the driveway, and the rider lifted the visor of his helmet, revealing a pair of gorgeous blue eyes.

Her heart threatened to burst out of her chest, but she forced herself to remain where she was.

He carefully removed the black helmet and scrubbed a hand over his head. His short hair still shocked her, made his face look leaner, harder, until he smiled up at her with that trademark grin.

He held up another helmet that she hadn't noticed was hooked over his right arm. He swung his leg over the saddle and started walking toward her. "Thought we might go for a ride?"

She forgot to breathe.

"Do you know this man, Audrey?" her mother asked, coming forward. "Isn't he the man whose photo was on the news for breaking into Gabriel's house?"

"Yes, Mom, the same news that had me wanted for a double homicide." She tried to keep the bite out of her tone. "This is Patrick Killion." She turned back to him and found his hungry eyes locked on her face. "He saved my life more times than I remember."

Her father introduced himself, as did her mother, although she looked a lot less certain of the disreputable-looking rogue on the motorbike. Probably because of the disreputable leather jacket, disreputable boots, and disreputable-looking grin.

"We'll leave you to your business," her father insisted, and Audrey was grateful when everyone else went inside. Everything about Killion was precious and painful, and she ached to touch him, but she didn't know why he was here. She didn't think she could glue all the pieces of her heart back together if he broke it again.

"Where'd you get the bike?" she asked. It wasn't the one they'd ridden on before. It was a great big Harley with a cherry-red tank.

"Of all the questions you could ask, you're going with that one?" He raised a brow.

She didn't say anything.

He glanced at the bike. Rubbed his chin. For the first time since she'd met him, he seemed nervous. "Thought we might go on a road trip."

Her heart was so tied up in knots she didn't think it was working anymore. Maybe that's why she felt faint.

"A road trip?"

She watched him swallow.

"They offered me a new job."

"Is this your undercover persona?" she asked.

He shook his head. "I turned them down."

"Why?"

His lips firmed. "Decided to take some time off."

"Why?"

He moved closer until he was standing right in front of her, his toes lined up against hers. She stared at the stitching on his black jacket. He tipped her chin, forcing her to meet his gaze. She was furious because tears were blurring her vision, even more than normal. She hated crying.

"I never had a real relationship until I met you. I never fell for a woman until I met you. The only thing I had in my life was my job. And I couldn't do that because all I kept thinking about was *you*."

"So nothing's changed." She went to turn away but he stopped her by planting both hands on her shoulders.

He leaned down until he was eye-level to her. "Everything's changed, and you know it." He lowered his lips, kissing her slowly. Her arms rose to clasp his nape, and he took the kiss deeper, wrapping his arms tight around her as if he'd never let go. But he'd done that before. And he'd let her go anyway.

She jerked away from him.

He blew out an audible breath and turned away. "I screwed up. I know I did. If I could go back and fix it, say all the right words at the right time, I'd do it. But it isn't possible, and I don't know how else to get you to forgive me."

She looked at him, aghast. Was he really this clueless? "You haven't told me the one thing I need to hear."

He frowned, then his expression cleared. "That I love you?" His lips curled into a confused smile. "How can you not know that I love you?"

Her heart finally figured out a way to start beating again and was making up for lost time. He'd told her exactly what she needed to hear, but he still didn't get it. "I'm not an operative, Patrick. I'm not spending the rest of my days guessing your secrets. You have to talk to me. You have to communicate."

She drew in a deep rattling breath. Then he did something that confounded her. He got down on his knees.

"Audrey Lockhart. This is me begging you on my knees to give me another chance. I love you." He pointed his hands at himself almost angrily. "If this isn't obvious enough, how about the fact that one day I'd like to get down on my knees and ask you to marry me." She couldn't breathe. "One day, I'd like to think about settling in a home someplace where we can both go to work in the morning and both come home at night, and sleep in each other's arms. I'm hoping I'll get lucky and you'll want kids. Otherwise we can get a dog."

She opened her mouth to say something, but he shut her down.

"I'm hoping you'll forgive me, but I'm not expecting it. I nearly got you killed on a gazillion different occasions."

"Gazillion isn't a real number," she got out finally.

He narrowed his eyes and then climbed to his feet. "I love you. I fell in love the moment you started lecturing me about frogs while wearing those sexy specs. I did not expect you to tear down my world so that I had to rebuild it from scratch, but that's what you did."

He went to say more but she stopped him with a raised hand. "Okay."

He tilted his head to one side. "Okay? That's all you got?"

She smiled, and he must have seen the truth in her eyes. "You already have everything I have to give. You've had it since you rescued me in Colombia even if you were too blind to see it."

His nostrils flared. He took a step toward her, then he changed his mind and walked down to the bike and picked up both helmets. "So you wanna go on a road trip with me?"

She walked toward him and took the helmet from his hand. "Where are we going?"

"Figured we'd start in Arizona." He climbed onto the bike. "Hop on." His eyes crinkled with humor as he started the engine.

She shook her hair back and pulled on the helmet. More frog jokes. Something told her he'd never get tired of frog jokes. She slid her leg over the saddle and found her balance.

"You ready?" His voice came through a headset inside the helmet.

Wrapping her arms around his middle, she pressed her chest against his back and held on tight. She was giving herself to this man, and even though it was scary, it was a lot less scary than never seeing him again. "I'm ready."

She took a final look at her parents who were staring at them from the living room window. She waved as he peeled gently away from the curb. "So, what's in Arizona?"

"My gene pool." Amusement laced his tone, but something else too. Something richer, warmer. "Figured you guys might want to get acquainted."

USEFUL ACRONYM DEFINITIONS FOR TONI'S BOOKS

ADA: Assistant District Attorney
AG: Attorney General
ASAC: Assistant Special Agent in Charge
ASC: Assistant Section Chief
ATF: Alcohol, Tobacco, and Firearms
BAU: Behavioral Analysis Unit
BOLO: Be on the Lookout
BORTAC: US Border Patrol Tactical Unit
BUCAR: Bureau Car
CBP: US Customs and Border Patrol
CBT: Cognitive Behavioral Therapy
CIRG: Critical Incident Response Group
CMU: Crisis Management Unit
CN: Crisis Negotiator
CNU: Crisis Negotiation Unit
CO: Commanding Officer
CODIS: Combined DNA Index System
CP: Command Post
CQB: Close-Quarters Battle
DA: District Attorney
DEA: Drug Enforcement Administration
DEVGRU: Naval Special Warfare Development Group
DIA: Defense Intelligence Agency

DHS: Department of Homeland Security
DOB: Date of Birth
DOD: Department of Defense
DOJ: Department of Justice
DS: Diplomatic Security
DSS: US Diplomatic Security Service
DVI: Disaster Victim Identification
EMDR: Eye Movement Desensitization & Reprocessing
EMT: Emergency Medical Technician
ERT: Evidence Response Team
FOA: First-Office Assignment
FBI: Federal Bureau of Investigation
FNG: Fucking New Guy
FO: Field Office
FWO: Federal Wildlife Officer
IC: Incident Commander
IC: Intelligence Community
ICE: US Immigration and Customs Enforcement
HAHO: High Altitude High Opening (parachute jump)
HRT: Hostage Rescue Team
HT: Hostage-Taker
JEH: J. Edgar Hoover Building (FBI Headquarters)
K&R: Kidnap and Ransom
LAPD: Los Angeles Police Department
LEO: Law Enforcement Officer
LZ: Landing Zone
ME: Medical Examiner
MO: Modus Operandi
NAT: New Agent Trainee
NCAVC: National Center for Analysis of Violent Crime
NCIC: National Crime Information Center
NFT: Non-Fungible Token
NOTS: New Operator Training School

NPS: National Park Service
NYFO: New York Field Office
OC: Organized Crime
OCU: Organized Crime Unit
OPR: Office of Professional Responsibility
POTUS: President of the United States
PT: Physiology Technician
PTSD: Post-Traumatic Stress Disorder
RA: Resident Agency
RCMP: Royal Canadian Mounted Police
RSO: Senior Regional Security Officer from the US
    Diplomatic Service
SA: Special Agent
SAC: Special Agent-in-Charge
SANE: Sexual Assault Nurse Examiners
SAS: Special Air Squadron (British Special Forces unit)
SD: Secure Digital
SIOC: Strategic Information & Operations
SF: Special Forces
SSA: Supervisory Special Agent
SWAT: Special Weapons and Tactics
TC: Tactical Commander
TDY: Temporary Duty Yonder
TEDAC: Terrorist Explosive Device Analytical Center
TOD: Time of Death
UAF: University of Alaska, Fairbanks
UBC: Undocumented Border Crosser
UNSUB: Unknown Subject
USSS: United States Secret Service
ViCAP: Violent Criminal Apprehension Program
VIN: Vehicle Identification Number
WFO: Washington Field Office

COLD JUSTICE WORLD OVERVIEW
All books can be read as standalones

COLD JUSTICE® SERIES
A Cold Dark Place (Book #1)
Cold Pursuit (Book #2)
Cold Light of Day (Book #3)
Cold Fear (Book #4)
Cold in The Shadows (Book #5)
Cold Hearted (Book #6)
Cold Secrets (Book #7)
Cold Malice (Book #8)
A Cold Dark Promise (Book #9~A Wedding Novella)
Cold Blooded (Book #10)

COLD JUSTICE® – THE NEGOTIATORS
Cold & Deadly (Book #1)
Colder Than Sin (Book #2)
Cold Wicked Lies (Book #3)
Cold Cruel Kiss (Book #4)
Cold as Ice (Book #5)

COLD JUSTICE® – MOST WANTED
Cold Silence (Book #1)
Cold Deceit (Book #2)
Cold Snap (Book #3) – Coming soon
Cold Fury (Book #4) – Coming soon

The Cold Justice® series books are also available as **audiobooks** narrated by Eric Dove, and in various box set compilations.

Check out all Toni's books on her website
(www.toniandersonauthor.com/books-2)

ACKNOWLEDGMENTS

Thanks to Marcela Gergin who gave me some much needed help in regards to Colombian Spanish, which I'm assured is unlike any other kind of Spanish. I appreciate the insider tips, Marcela. Also thanks to my good friend Fred Pennell for putting me in touch with Vonnette Monteith. Vonnette provided me with some useful nuggets about locations in and around Louisville, Kentucky. Needless to say, I used artistic license with all information gleaned, and any errors in this story are mine.

Huge, enormous thanks go to my amazing critique partner Kathy Altman—I really don't know what I'd do without her. Also my editors, Alicia Dean, and Joan Turner at JRT Editing, who helped get this manuscript into shape in record time. Syd Gill—a woman on a mission and so very talented when it comes to creating the beautiful covers of the *Cold Justice Series*. Paul Salvette (BB eBooks) finally gets a mention for the professional formatting he does for me. He saves me from repetitive stress issues and helps me keep my sanity when stuff happens. And stuff *always* happens. Thanks to all the other people working behind the scenes to get these books on the digital shelves. I appreciate your help and support.

Thanks to Eric Dove for his brilliant narration of the CJS books. It takes a special kind of talent to do what he does, and even more to do it calmly and with a sense of humor.

I want to thank my family, for loving me, and understanding the weird schedule, scribbled notes on every available surface, and the thousand-yard stare at dinner. We're all busy and life never seems to slow down, but I hope we're never too busy for one another. I love you guys.

ABOUT THE AUTHOR

Toni Anderson writes gritty, sexy, FBI Romantic Thrillers, and is a *New York Times* and a *USA Today* bestselling author. Her books have won the Daphne du Maurier Award for Excellence in Mystery and Suspense, Readers' Choice, Aspen Gold, Book Buyers' Best, Golden Quill, National Excellence in Story Telling Contest, and National Excellence in Romance Fiction awards. She's been a finalist in both the Vivian Contest and the RITA Award from the Romance Writers of America. Toni's books have been translated into five different languages and over three million copies of her books have been downloaded.

Best known for her Cold Justice® books perhaps it's not surprising to discover Toni lives in one of the most extreme climates on earth—Manitoba, Canada. Formerly a Marine Biologist, Toni still misses the ocean, but is lucky enough to travel for research purposes. In late 2015, she visited FBI Headquarters in Washington DC, including a tour of the Strategic Information and Operations Center. She hopes not to get arrested for her Google searches.

Sign up for Toni Anderson's newsletter:
www.toniandersonauthor.com/newsletter-signup

Like Toni Anderson on Facebook:
facebook.com/toniandersonauthor

Follow on Instagram:
instagram.com/toni_anderson_author

Printed in Great Britain
by Amazon

29591917R00202